"*Closer Home* is a story as memorable and meaningful as your favorite song, with a cast of characters so true to life you'll be sorry to let them go."
—Sonja Yoerg, author of *House Broken* and *Middle of Somewhere*

"Kerry Anne King's tale of regret, loss, and love pulled me in, from its intriguing beginning to its oh-so-satisfying conclusion."
—Jackie Bouchard, *USA Today* bestselling author of *House Trained* and *Rescue Me, Maybe*

"King's prose is filled with vitality."
—Ella Carey, author of *Paris Time Capsule* and *The House by the Lake*

EVERY THING YOU ARE

ALSO BY KERRY ANNE KING

Closer Home: A Novel

I Wish You Happy: A Novel

Whisper Me This: A Novel

EVERY THING YOU ARE

a novel

KERRY ANNE KING

LAKE UNION
PUBLISHING

Text copyright © 2019 by Kerry Anne King
All rights reserved.

Published by Lake Union Publishing, Seattle

www.apub.com

Amazon, the Amazon logo, and Lake Union Publishing are trademarks of Amazon.com, Inc., or its affiliates.

ISBN-13: 9781542041966
ISBN-10: 1542041961

Cover design by Faceout Studio, Lindy Martin

Printed in the United States of America

Kevin, this one is for you

Without music, life would be a mistake.

—*Friedrich Nietzsche*

Chapter One

PHEE

1998, Seattle

Ophelia MacPhee, newly eighteen years old and full of life and curiosity, takes the stairs to the apartment above MacPhee's Fine Instruments two at a time. Granddad missed her birthday dinner, claiming old bones and exhaustion, but had called to say, "You'll come by afterward, Phee. I have a gift for you."

She can't wait to see what he has for her. Grandmother's emerald ring, perhaps. Or maybe something related to the MacPhee luthier business. She's become proficient enough at repairs that he trusts her with most of the instruments that come into the shop, and they've been making plans for her to build her first violin.

Maybe he'll give her a set of tools of her own, or a piece of wood that she will shape into an Ophelia MacPhee original.

"I'm here," she sings out as she hits the top of the stairs, and then she skids to a halt, staring.

A small, precise woman with a shiny black briefcase sits at the table. A stranger.

"You made it," Granddad says. He hugs Phee, kisses both of her cheeks. "Happy birthday. Have a seat, my girl. This is my attorney, Angela Toth."

The woman nods at Phee, managing to convey disapproval without a word.

Granddad pours three glasses from a bottle on the table.

"She's underage," the attorney objects as Phee picks up the glass and sniffs at the contents.

"Only in America. And the whiskey came with me all the way from the old country. Tonight, we celebrate."

It's far from Phee's first drink, but it is the first one countenanced by adults. The glass, the woman with the shiny briefcase, and her grandfather's unusual mood all create a mysterious solemnity, like high mass, only different.

"A toast," her grandfather says. "To Ophelia MacPhee!" He raises his glass, and Phee and the attorney follow suit. The whiskey is smooth and potent, and Phee can feel it warming her blood after the first swallow.

"You'll be wondering why Angela is here, of course," her grandfather says, draining half of his glass.

"I am," Phee admits.

He spreads his arms wide in a grand gesture. "I am giving you the business."

She stares at him in shocked silence, and he laughs.

"Don't look like that, child. I'd always planned to give it to you sooner or later. It's become sooner. A perfect birthday gift, don't you think?"

"I don't think I understand." She takes another cautious sip of her own whiskey, elation growing in her breast. She'll follow in his footsteps, maybe even surpass him. She'll be a brilliant luthier; maybe she'll create an instrument that people will still be talking about hundreds of years from now.

"It's all yours," Granddad says. But he looks tired and frail, smaller, not happy and excited about this unexpected gift. "Explain," he orders the attorney.

Angela lays her briefcase in the middle of the table and makes a production out of unsnapping the locks, opening it, and drawing out a set of papers.

"These are the legal documents. Read carefully, then sign here, initial here."

"Oh, explain it to her, Angela. It will take her hours to read all that."

The woman fixes him with a severe gaze. "She should read every word, Adrian."

He makes a rude noise with his lips. "She can read it later. You're turning my party into a boring legal event." He splashes more whiskey into his glass.

"You are in too much of a hurry," the attorney says. "This *is* a boring legal event. In general, Ophelia, these papers lay out the terms of your grandfather's bequest. Your signature indicates that you accept his gift of the building, the business, and everything within these walls, along with an account into which he has deposited a sum of money for your use."

"You accept all of my obligations," the old man interrupts, with emphasis. "It's part of the language."

"You should read it," Angela says. "We can wait."

"You can wait. I'm paying for every minute you are here. Once she's signed, Ophelia will be paying."

"We could have done this in my office."

"That's ridiculous. It needs to happen here. Tonight."

Phee takes the papers and tries to read, but the arguing is distracting. The whiskey has set up a quiet buzz in her head, and worry over her grandfather's atypical behavior aggravates everything. She scans through it, five pages of densely written legalese that twists on itself and makes her go back and reread, over and over. Still, she only grasps the high-lights, the terms already pointed out.

At the bottom, above the space for her signature, it reads:

I, Ophelia Florence MacPhee, being of sound mind and purpose, do hereby swear a sacred oath to accept and discharge all obligations, tangible and intangible, related to the post of luthier.

An unusual phrasing. Something in her belly objects. The walls seem to be closing in, and she pushes the paper away. "Why now? If you want me to have it, can't you just leave it to me in a will?"

"Wills take forever to execute. Besides, why wait? After I die, you'll feel like you should be grieving. Now you can sign the papers with joyful enthusiasm."

"And Dad?"

"What about him?"

"This would be a bit of a shocker for him, don't you think?" Phee's father is tone deaf and not musically inclined, but she knows full well that as the only son he expects to inherit the full estate.

"Your father will receive a financial bequest. But he would just sell the business to some stranger. I can't have that. I need you to carry on the MacPhee name."

Everything Granddad says sounds logical enough, but her father isn't going to see it that way. Besides the money aspect, he's dead set on Phee going to college and getting some kind of useful degree. What that would be, since she has no interest in anything other than music and instruments, is a frequent dinnertime debate. But he won't be at all happy about her taking over the luthier business.

"Would I move in with you, then?" she asks, half dizzy with possibilities. "Live here? And what's the 'intangible' part all about? I don't understand."

Her grandfather rolls his eyes. "What is it with young people today? My generation didn't think so much."

Phee glares at him, and his face sobers.

"I'm dying, Phee."

"Not now. Not yet." She shoves the papers away. "Not for a long time."

"Cancer." He lays the single word out on the table with the papers, and all three of them stare at its ugliness. Granddad with a resigned twist of humor. The lawyer as if she's seen it so many times it doesn't shock her. Phee with the terror of the untried young.

"Oh my God! Do Dad and Mom know?"

"Nobody knows. This is between me, you, and the doctors. Well, and Angela, of course."

"But, Granddad! You'll need help. We can—"

"The only help I need, Ophelia MacPhee, is for you to sign these papers and promise that you will accept the responsibility for all of my obligations."

Phee can't breathe. The pen seems exaggerated in size, a weight her slight fingers will never be able to manage. The old man lays a hand over hers. So thin, the skin so transparent she can see the tracery of blue veins beneath. How did she not notice? How did none of them notice he'd been ill?

"Who is to do this thing, if not you?" he asks her.

"You could try a different doctor. Radiation, chemo. There has to be something."

He shakes his head, more in impatience than sadness. "It's in my liver. In my bones. I'm an old man, on borrowed time already. There can be no waiting. Sign it, Phee. Say that you will be responsible for everything when I am no longer here."

"I go on record as saying I recommend you wait," the attorney says. But she makes no move to intervene.

Phee looks up at her grandfather. "You'll be here, to help?"

"Always. Dead or alive."

She doesn't understand her own resistance. He will die, whether she signs or not. He wants her to have the shop, and she wants to own it, wants to be a luthier.

Still, her fingers tremble as she signs.

It's on the last stroke of the pen, the upsweep at the end of the final *e* in MacPhee, that she first hears the music. A deep, sonorous tone, long held. It startles her so that she drops the pen. Her eyes meet her grandfather's, and she reads sorrowful awareness there. The attorney, not missing a beat, signs her own name on the document below the spidery signature that is her grandfather's trademark.

"I'll be going, then." The attorney lifts her barely touched glass and drains the whiskey like a gunslinger in a Western. She slams the glass down on the table and glares at her client.

"I should hate you for making me do this."

"But you don't. Goodbye, Angela." He reaches for her hand and kisses it.

"Go well, old man."

It's an odd way to say goodbye, but Phee lets it pass, not glancing away from her grandfather as the woman leaves.

"Why is she mad?"

"Because of what you signed."

"Why would that make her mad?"

"She thinks I have deceived and tricked you."

"And have you?"

He sighs. "Drink your whiskey, Phee. It was a good year."

Chapter Two

PHEE

2018, Seattle

Later, Phee will remember the shooting star framed perfectly in her bedroom window last night, the salt she'd spilled at dinner, the full moon that woke her at the witching hour. But in this moment, she has forgotten all about them. Superstitions are not permitted in her mother's comfortable kitchen, especially with cookies in the oven and a glass of milk in front of her on the table.

"Not oatmeal for the fund-raiser," Phee says, even as she lifts another cookie from the plate, warm and buttery, and stuffs half of it into her mouth. Crumbs tumble into her lap, and her huge black dog, Celestine, licks them up at once, leaving a pool of slobber soaking into her jeans. "Bake-sale people never buy oatmeal."

"You seem to have no problem with them," her mother says. "And have you still not learned manners?"

"Incorrigible, that's me." Phee grins, talking around a mouthful of cookie. "Born in a barn and all that." Nearly forty years of lecturing, and you'd think her mother would get the message by now that it's pointless, but Bridgette is not the sort of woman to be easily deterred.

"Make chocolate chip for the sale," Phee advises. "And those meringue things. Nobody really wants to eat raisins."

"Raisins are healthy." Bridgette slaps Phee's hand as she reaches for another cookie. "In moderation. I have no idea how you stay so thin."

"Hard work." Phee stretches, indolent as a cat, then tucks both legs up in the chair beneath her. "Physical labor."

Her mother makes a hmph sound under her breath, and Phee takes the hint. Push too far, and she'll end up doing dishes and scrubbing floors for the rest of the afternoon. She did work hard last week. Her eyes are tired. The muscles in her neck and shoulders are tight and her feet ache. The last thing in the world she wants to do is spend her remaining free hours suffering retribution from a fiery Irish temper pushed too far.

Her phone chirps and she ignores it. Probably a text message complaining about one of the recently repaired instruments. If she doesn't know, if she doesn't look, then she can't be responsible. She's been known to fix things at one in the morning for an overwrought violinist whose instrument is suffering. Obsessive beings, musicians, the whole lot of them.

Phee doesn't hold this against them. She is every bit as bad when it comes to the instruments in her care.

Her phone chirps again.

"Can you hush that thing?"

Bridgette disapproves of cell phones in general and Phee's in particular. "When I was young," she says, "we had freedom. Not at everybody's beck and call every minute of every day."

"When you were young, unicorns still walked the earth."

"Respect, young lady." Bridgette raps Phee's knuckles with the wooden spoon, bits of dough spattering onto the countertop, and both of them break into laughter.

"Why, thank you very much," Phee says, licking the buttery, sugary sweetness off her fingers before Celestine can beat her to it.

"You'll get salmonella. For the love of God, Phee, please stop that noise."

Phee rubs her hands on her jeans and picks up the offending phone. Not a text message at all. An alert blinks, baleful and ominous.

She remembers, then, the way the shooting star fell across her line of vision, right to left. The moon. The salt. What's waiting for her is infinitely worse than an unhappy musician.

"Oh, damn it all to hell and back again."

"What is it?"

"Heredity."

Bridgette's sigh could blow out a candle from fifty feet away. "Still that load of blarney from your grandfather? He was a crazy old man, Phee. Let it go."

Maybe not so crazy as all that, Phee thinks but doesn't say. She's had this argument with both of her parents so many times she knows the script by heart, forward and backward and upside down.

"I promised him."

"And he's dead. I'm certain sure he doesn't care about those old instruments anymore."

Phee makes a noncommittal sound, and Bridgette flings up her hands. "There is no *curse,* Ophelia MacPhee."

When Phee doesn't answer, her mother sighs again, then asks in a world-weary tone, "Which one is it?"

"The cello."

Phee scans the news article that triggered her app. A chill crawls up her spine, out of place in the heat of the kitchen.

"Don't tell me. A dark robed figure carrying a scythe was seen walking down the street where the cello resides."

"Mom, don't," Phee says. "It's truly horrible."

"I'm listening."

Underneath her bluster, Bridgette is the most kindhearted of women, and Phee needs a little bit of kindness right now.

"The girl who plays the cello—Allie—her mother and brother were both killed in a car crash."

Bridgette freezes in the act of dropping cookie dough onto a baking sheet. "Oh, the poor child. Has she a father?"

Oh, indeed she has a father, Phee thinks, *or had one, anyway.* Braden Healey, once a brilliant cellist, abandoned both his cello and his daughter and vanished off Phee's radar almost eleven years ago. She dreams about him at night and runs internet searches for him by day. Always, at the back of her consciousness, a nagging little worry eats away at her.

Something bad is going to happen.

Has happened.

She shivers. The brightly lit kitchen darkens, and she glances up to the window, expecting storm clouds, surprised by a serene blue sky.

"Phee," her mother says, calling her back to the present. "Tragic and terrible, but an accident has nothing to do with you and certainly nothing to do with the cello."

"I have to go." Phee clambers to her feet, stretching out the kinks in her back, waiting for sensation to return to her right foot, which is all pins and needles from being sat on. Celestine licks her hand, and she steadies herself against his solid bulk.

"Tell me you're not going to dash over to the house of the bereaved and check on an instrument," Bridgette demands.

"Of course I'm not."

It's a shading of the truth, not an outright lie. Phee learned as a very small child that her mother can smell lies, literally, with a little wrinkle of her freckled nose, a flaring of her nostrils. Bridgette has the second sight, although she'll deny it until the cows come home.

Phee won't go to the house now; she'll go Sunday, after the funeral. Take some flowers for Allie, offer condolences, use the opportunity to check in on the cello in person and ask about Braden. She's done repairs on the cello a time or two, so she can make a case for her appearance.

For now, she has other things she needs to do.

"Bye, Mom." She drops a kiss on Bridgette's cheek and grabs up a handful of cookies. "Remember what I said about the oatmeal and raisin."

"Because you want them for yourself, greedy girl."

Phee laughs. Under the influence of Bridgette and oatmeal cookies, it's nearly impossible to feel tragic or believe in mysterious forces at work.

Back at her little apartment above the luthier shop she inherited from her grandfather, it's a different story. Sometimes, Phee wonders if his ghost is haunting her. Little noises at night, bangs, and clatters. The random sound of strings from the shop below. On bright, sunshiny days, or even at night when the lights are on, she doesn't believe in hauntings or curses. But in the midnight dark, or when something horrible has happened to the people connected to one of her instruments, she finds herself sucked into her grandfather's mystique.

Celestine pokes her with a cold, wet nose, insisting that he is very much real and would like to be fed, thank you very much, so she gets him his dinner and pulls out celery and carrot sticks for herself as a compensation for too many cookies but also because crunching carrots is a fantastic deterrent to believing in the old stories.

She was eighteen the night Granddad laid the obligation on her to guard a group of instruments. "The specials," he called them. She keeps the book he gave her that night under lock and key, as she swore to do. His version of that was an antique safe. Hers is a beautiful cedar chest that also holds her mother's wedding dress; her grandmother's china; the first violin built by her own clumsy, inexperienced hands; and other treasures she has packed away over the years.

She retrieves the key from an old cookie tin full of salt that she stores on the top shelf of a kitchen cabinet, even though she sees no point in it. If some random thief were to break into the chest, pick the lock or splinter the wood with an axe, the old account book would hold no value for him.

Unwrapping the book from the towel in which she swathes it as one more level of concealment, she settles on the floor for what has become an evening ritual. Celestine, done with dinner, oomphs down beside her and rests his big head on her lap.

Thus fortified, Phee opens the first page, suppressing a sneeze as the familiar smell of dust and dry rot irritates her nostrils.

The first page looks as ordinary as her mother's kitchen, apart from its age. Spidery handwriting, the ink faded to brown, reads:

Client Pledges.

Some pledge. More like "Deals with the Devil," Phee thinks. The entries should be written in blood. The first is dated 1 June 1822, in the same handwriting as the header.

Thomas McCullough, violin, Derry, Ireland. A check mark after his name means that Mr. Thomas McCullough of Derry, Ireland, is dead, his contract with the violin ended.

She turns the brittle pages with care, feeling the weight of all of the lives marked by this book. The last seven names, on the very last page, are all in her grandfather's handwriting, but their names are as familiar to her as her own. She tracks their lives on a daily basis, watching for signs of trouble on Google and even the dark web. She's set up an app to trawl the internet and give her early-warning alerts, the same app that notified her of the upcoming funeral.

There is a check mark next to one of these names, the only one Phee has added so far. She's made it red and flamboyant to mark that account as done.

Marilyn Browning, violin, Kansas City, 3 May 1963.

"May you rest in peace," Phee whispers, tracing lightly over the name. The violin sits on a stand here in her apartment, and Phee plays it herself, these days. She's not prepared to sell it to somebody else.

Of the remaining names, five are violinists. The sixth is, or was, a cellist. The entry might as well be permanently burned into her retinas.

Braden Healey, cello, Seattle, 5 January 1990.

This man-and-cello pairing, the very last of the accounts in this book, has caused her more trouble than any of the others. Braden broke the terms of his contract and went AWOL about eleven years ago, leaving the cello behind.

In the wake of the tragedy that has befallen his family, though, she asks herself if she has really done everything she could.

She could have searched harder. Pressured Braden's wife. Hired a private investigator. When the first accident happened, the one that destroyed the sensation in his hands, she grieved over him, went soft. Who was she to insist that he continue to play when clearly that ability had been stolen from him?

The cello was in good hands. His daughter made a fine surrogate. Phee persuaded herself that the circumstances were exceptional and it was best to leave everything alone. For almost eleven years nothing has gone wrong, and she'd almost stopped worrying about the curse.

Now another tragedy has fallen, and even though so much time has passed without event, she has to admit that both she and Braden are in violation of sworn oaths to the same old man. According to that old man, when oaths are broken, the curse rolls in.

Phee is a product of twentieth-century America, raised on practicality, responsibility, and hard work. She's far removed from her Irish-born grandfather and the mythology and magic that he cloaked himself in. And yet, most of the time, she believes.

Musicians, and those who make instruments, are a superstitious lot. The tale of blues musician Robert Johnson and his meeting with the devil at the crossroads is a classic, but he's not the only one. Similar stories are told about legends of rock and roll like Ozzy Osbourne and Keith Richards. Much farther back in history, violinists Tartini and Paganini were both rumored to have received their unbelievable dexterity from a deal with the devil.

Even musicians who would be appalled at the idea of selling their souls have odd little rituals they perform before every concert, ceremonies of candles and foods and music that closely resemble incantations.

When Phee was eighteen, brand new to her inherited position as luthier, she'd scoffed at the idea of a curse. It was only the oath she'd sworn to her grandfather that held her to the duties, and she bore them relatively lightly.

Until an incident that turned her blood to ice. Coincidence, Bridgette still insists, when she'll discuss it at all. Phee is not so sure. And now, a new tragedy is connected to Braden and the cello, and Phee isn't taking further chances. One way or another, she has to get him playing again.

She wraps the ledger book back up in the towel and returns it to its place. In her desk drawer are six hanging file folders, one for each of her musicians, full of news stories and clippings. Braden's is anemic, full of a whole lot of nothing, but still she reviews what little she has, just in case she has somehow missed something.

The announcement of his engagement to Lilian Hayes. A wedding photo. Last known address. And a *Seattle Times* story with the headline "Seattle Symphony Loses First Chair Cellist." There is a grainy photo of Braden, younger, clear eyed, unscarred, and smiling. One hand rests on the cello, the other holds a bow. Phee knows the story by heart.

Braden Healey, first-chair cellist for the Seattle Symphony Orchestra, announced his resignation this week following a tragedy that left his hands severely frostbitten and his brother-in-law dead.

Law enforcement reported that Mitchell Conroy, thirty-four, of Colville, Washington, died of a massive heart attack after falling through rotten lake ice at a remote hunting lodge near Colville. The damage to Healey's hands occurred while attempting to rescue Conroy and administer CPR during subzero conditions.

"We are deeply saddened both for Mr. Healey and for this blow to the music world," said Yolanda Blaisey, spokesperson for the Seattle Symphony

Orchestra. "*Braden was a stellar talent and is loved by all of us. We will miss him deeply.*"

After that, there is nothing. Braden falls into complete internet oblivion. The orchestra hires a new cellist. There are no more recordings. No more stories. All she'd been able to elicit from his wife, Lilian, was a terse "He doesn't live here anymore."

Phee has in her possession CDs of all five of Braden's recorded albums. She likes CDs better than online music, even though logic tells her it all sounds the same. Choosing the Bach Suites for Unaccompanied Cello, she presses play and moves to the bed, where she can lie down and stare at the ceiling while listening to the soul of a man who was unable to die at the same time as his music.

She finds herself weeping for him, for Allie, and for the abandoned cello with an intensity of grief that has hitherto passed her over, even at the time of her grandfather's death.

Chapter Three

BRADEN

Braden Healey, unusually sober on a Thursday afternoon, looks around and wonders, not for the first time, how he managed to wash up here. The pile of dishes in the sink, the unmade bed, this dismal bachelor's apartment shared with another washed-up loser, where the only thing to look forward to is a brand-new bottle of Jack and the delivery of yet another pizza.

He's just hung up from the pizza order when the phone rings, loud and startling in the silence. Some question about the order, he thinks, and then he sees the caller ID.

Lilian.

Once his wife, still the mother of his children, Lilian hasn't talked to him in years. She might as well be living in an alternate reality, even though he lives in a neighboring suburb.

His first, his very first, reaction is hope, because secretly he's always waiting for the curse to be broken. Lilian will call, and all of the darkness of the last eleven years will be swept away. He'll wake up to find himself home, with Lili and their kids and the cello, and she'll have come to understand what music means and . . .

Reality reasserts its heavy-handed point of view.

Lilian is not going to forgive him. Ever. She already had religion in plenty, so it's not that she's suddenly found Jesus and is calling to share the love. Something must be wrong. One of the kids is sick, or she's short on money.

God. Has he forgotten the child support? It's the one element of human decency he still clings to. If he's descended to the ranks of dead-beat dad, then it's time to end his sorry life once and for all. He very nearly doesn't answer the phone but picks up at the very last second before the call goes to voice mail.

"Lil? What's wrong?"

The voice on the other end confuses him, pure brass where Lilian's is reedy and low.

"Braden? Hello? Can you hear me?"

"Ten-four. Loud and clear." He chases memories into shadowy corners looking for a name and a face to connect with the voice and finally finds it. The face is tight lipped, hard eyed, clearly disapproving of anything and everything Braden. Even back then, when he was the golden boy, beloved of the gods, and not a down-and-out bum trying to drink himself to death in a shit-hole apartment.

Lilian's sister, Alexandra. Allie's godmother. He'd argued against naming his daughter after her. Even Lilian wasn't overly fond of the name, but he couldn't argue with her reasons. "Alexandra is family, Braden. The only sister I have." And that ended his resistance because he knew, all too well, that family is a fact that refuses alteration.

"We have a situation," Alexandra says now. "Please tell me you're sober."

"I am never sober, thank God. Where is Lilian and why on earth are you calling me?"

A lie. He is momentarily and temporarily sober, the one problem for which he has a solution. But he doesn't reach to fill his empty glass. Not just yet.

Alexandra makes a strangled gasping sound that from any other human might be a sob. He's still trying to picture that emotion on her when she finally says the thing she's called him to say.

"Lilian has gone to be with Jesus."

Braden waits for these words to arrange themselves into a meaningful sequence. Clearly, Alexandra doesn't mean to use the euphemism for death. Lilian has never been marked for death, she is beyond and above it. So "gone to be with Jesus" must mean she's becoming a nun, or going on a religious retreat, maybe attending an intensive Pentecostal camp meeting.

"Braden?"

"I don't think I heard you."

"Lilian has passed on to the other side. She's singing with the angels now."

Braden fills his glass, watching his hand lift the bottle and pour as if it doesn't belong to him, as if he is a bystander whose heart will not be shattered by the next thing Alexandra is going to say.

"There was a car accident. A crash. They think she fell asleep."

He notices, from a vantage point up near the ceiling, that he can't breathe, that his heart is running off with a rhythm of its own. Watches himself slide down the cabinets to the tacky, unwashed kitchenette floor. Words are expected, and he utters the first ones that come into his head.

"When? How are the kids?"

"Monday."

Braden does the math, the number of days from Monday to Thursday divided by the distance between him and the drink he just poured, multiplied by the enormity of his failure and loss. All the calculations come out to the same answer: he is a miserable excuse for a human being.

Monday.

The day he started drinking again after nearly six months of sobriety.

Monday.

The day he was supposed to meet his daughter face-to-face after eleven years of absence.

If Lilian had to leave this world and abandon the kids, why did it have to be on that particular Monday, of all the days in the year?

"Braden! Are you listening?"

"I hear you."

"I need you to sign some papers. I just flew in this morning and—"

"Three days?" He's still stuck on the time frame. If Lilian dead is incomprehensible, the idea of time, of the kids alone for not only hours but days, is a concept beyond his grasp. Just one more minute, and he thinks he's going to be angry about that. Someone, namely Alexandra, could have tried harder to reach him.

"Allie stayed with a friend, but she can't stay there forever. You need to sign papers so she can come home with me."

Braden closes his eyes, listens to the sound of his own breathing, the music swirling in the room. Not the first time he's heard the cello in a quiet room, as clearly as if someone is playing right next to him. The Bach in C Minor this time, only it's discordant and wrong, tuned flat so it grates on his eardrums. His throat contracts around the words stuck sideways in his throat. It takes three tries before he can spit them out.

"Where is Trey?"

Silence.

"You keep saying Allie. What about Trey?"

"Trey was in the car."

"Is he hurt? How badly? Which hospital?"

If Lilian is dead—still an if, a big one—*if* Lilian is dead, the embargo is over. He can go home. He will go to Allie, and to Trey, he will—

"Trey didn't make it. He's gone."

Braden can't feel his body anymore, at all, not the restricted breathing or the erratic heart rate or the sinking in his belly; the whole thing has gone as numb as his goddamn hands. He bangs the back of his head against the cabinet, seeking sensation.

Thud.

A starburst of pain behind his eyes. Better.

Thud.

The pain clears him, puts his soul back in his body. Sensation comes flooding back, and with it come words and the anger that has been waiting for the cue to come onstage.

"Allie has been alone with this? For three fucking days? Jesus Christ, Alexandra. You should have called me!"

"Do me a favor and keep your profanity to yourself. I didn't have your number, and Allie wouldn't give it to me or to the social worker. She was very clear. She doesn't want you."

Of course she doesn't want him. He left her, and then he stood her up, and then her mother and her brother died. The only surprise in all of this is the amount of pain carried by those precise words, "she doesn't want you."

Braden is familiar with pain. He welcomes it in, cherishes it as penance.

"As soon as the funeral is over, I'll be taking Allie with me to Toronto," Alexandra says. "She has a passport. We can get her visa taken care of later. I just need you to sign to let me take her across the border for now."

"Is that what Allie wants? To go to Canada?"

"She can't possibly know what she wants, she's just lost her entire family. I will do what is best for her, even if it is difficult."

"Not her entire family," Braden whispers.

"I'm sorry? I didn't catch that."

"She's not orphaned quite yet," Braden says more loudly. "Where is she, Alexandra? At the house? I want to see her."

"I've just told you, she doesn't want—"

"You also just said she doesn't know what she wants. I need to see my daughter."

"Oh please. What use could you be to her? You'll just muddy the waters. It's best she doesn't see you. I'm only contacting you to sign the consent—"

"No." The word feels round and solid and right. Perfectly tuned.

"Braden. I know it's too much to expect you to be fully rational, but—"

"I'm coming home. Tell Allie that."

Braden hangs up before Alexandra can argue. Three incompatible thoughts keep playing on an endless loop in his head.

Lilian and Trey are dead.

Allie doesn't want to talk to him.

Allie needs him.

It's the last one that gets him up off the floor, that empowers him to pour the brand-new bottle of Jack down the drain, the contents of the glass behind it, without taking a single taste.

Allie needs me.

He repeats this like an incantation while he uses his phone to search for the time and place of the funeral. Three days away—just enough time to get sober.

One visit to the doctor. One trip to the pharmacy. Three days of Librium. Half a bottle of vitamin B. Another mathematical equation that should add up to Braden sober in time for a Sunday-afternoon funeral.

He tells himself he won't make a scene. He'll show up, find an opportunity to talk to Allie. Explain why he didn't meet her and how it has everything to do with how much he loves her, rather than how little. And then . . .

It depends. If she needs him, then nothing will ever drag him away again. If she doesn't? He doesn't dare focus on that. Get sober. Go to the funeral. One day, one breath at a time.

Chapter Four

ALLIE

Allie stares, unblinking, at the two coffins on the platform, stares until her vision blurs and doubles, until her eyes burn and water. And when her eyelids close against her will, she focuses in again, over and over.

I did this. I will not look away.

On her right, Aunt Alexandra sits upright and stiff, as if rigor mortis has reached out tendrils from the coffins to their front-row viewing seat and frozen her still-living muscles. Her brand-new black dress is as stiff as she is and gives off a queasy chemical smell that makes Allie breathe through her mouth and hope to God she doesn't puke. On the other side, blessedly warm and human and normal, sits Steph, her best friend since forever.

"Death sucks so hard," Steph murmurs.

Allie doesn't look away from the coffins. The words make a lump in her throat. Her eyes blur with tears, but she manages to blink them back. She hasn't cried yet. Not when she first heard the news, not when she watched her brother die, not even when they wouldn't let her go home. When she starts, which she knows she will eventually, she thinks it might kill her. She's got no huge objection to dying, she just doesn't want to explode right here, in front of all of these people.

If she could die quietly, just close her story as if it's a book she started reading and decided she didn't like, she would welcome that. But she has to keep turning the pages; she's not allowed to quit, because this is her fault and it's the punishment she deserves.

The funeral passes in a blur. Thank God the organist plays Muzak, nothing profound enough to break through the coating of ice and get to her heart. She feels flat and detached, as if the coffins are two big black boxes with nothing inside them. A theatrical staging. A play she's watching.

Until.

Until it's all over and they are filing out of the church. Everybody is staring at her, she knows it, even though she keeps her eyes down. One foot in an unfamiliar shiny black shoe setting itself down on carpet, another foot in an unfamiliar shiny black shoe repeating the movement. It's an ugly carpet. Mustardy, with flecks of blue and green and brown.

At the back of the church, the gauntlet very nearly run, an impulse draws her eyes upward. A gaze meets hers. Eyes like her own, a face both familiar and strange. She feels a jolt of connection and recognition that very nearly trips her. Steph's hand steadies her, nudges her forward, and she keeps walking, but only as far as the foyer, where she plants her feet and waits.

She watches him walk down the aisle. He's taller than most of the crowd, so she can study his face. He doesn't look like the picture she's kept hidden under her mattress all these years, the way other kids hide contraband magazines or cigarettes or pot. His hair is graying at the temples. His right cheek is marred by a long white scar.

It turns out her heart isn't completely frozen after all. Emotions surge through her, threaten to swamp her. Anger. Loss. Love. All in equal measure. She blocks his path, and he comes to a halt about a foot in front of her. The people behind him stop, confused, and then create an alternate course, flowing around the two of them as if they are an island in the middle of a river.

"So you *are* still alive," she says.

"I'm sorry."

She's not sure if he means he's sorry he's still alive, or what all he's sorry for. His eyes look anguished. His hands tremble visibly. It's this, the weakness on his part, that sets flame to her anger.

"Where the hell have you *been*?"

Aunt Alexandra pivots away from an embrace with a weeping woman and puts a restraining hand on Allie's arm.

"Language," she whispers. *Don't make a scene,* her expression says. Allie's own hands are clenched into fists. Maybe she'll hit him, beat her fury out on his chest. Scream at the top of her lungs.

Her aunt steps between them, giving her father a stiff-armed hug. "Braden. I'm so glad you were able to make it." Allie can hear the insincerity like a badly tuned instrument.

Her father's gaze doesn't break from Allie's. They might as well be alone rather than in the middle of a crowd, both of them oblivious to Alexandra, to the press of other bodies.

"I didn't know," he says. "Until Thursday."

It's a lame excuse, and only answers part of her question.

Where have you been all of my fucking life? Why didn't you meet me like you said you would? Where were you when I got the call about the accident, when I watched my brother die? That's what she really wants to know.

She feels the tears encroaching, and with them helplessness and abandonment and futility. She squeezes her hands into tighter fists, clenches her teeth, focuses all of her willpower on holding them back, but they get past her, anyway.

Damn it. Damn you.

Aunt Alex clamps a hand around her wrist and tugs. "Come, dear. We must go to the graveside. They are waiting."

Allie doesn't budge. "Dad comes, too."

"Allie—"

"We need to talk, and he has a way of vanishing."

"He can meet us at the cemetery. The car is waiting."

Allie feels her spine stiffen, and she turns on her aunt. "I'm not going without him. He can ride with us."

People are staring, whispering.

"Is that the father?"

"Pretty sure. He's been gone so long . . ."

"Ran off and left poor Lilian with two kids to raise . . ."

Allie doesn't care, but her aunt shoots a venomous glare at her father, then yanks harder on her arm.

"Come. Now."

Allie's hand clenches around her father's. "You are coming, too."

His body is as taut as hers. She can feel it in his hand. For a moment, she thinks he'll refuse, that she'll be towed away and lose him again forever, but as she begins to move and the tension increases on their linked hands, he takes a step to follow her, and then another, all the way out to the car.

A moment of hesitation at the open door, where it all hangs in the balance. He sucks in a huge breath and slides into the seat beside her. Round one. She still has a battle to fight, because as much as she hates her father at this moment, she is not going to Canada with Aunt Alexandra, and he is the only one who can save her from that.

Chapter Five

BRADEN

Braden is in desperate need of a drink.

The church was bad, worse than he'd anticipated. There had been a photographic memorial to endure, for one thing. Lilian, still beautiful but aged by life and responsibility. Trey, young and vibrant and golden. In every picture, he was surrounded by friends, always laughing, eyes looking directly out at Braden.

Where were you? Why did you miss this?

Impossible to imagine that face, that energy, confined to a casket. As for Lilian . . .

God. He and Lilian were married in that church. Every time he closed his eyes to blot out the stark reality of those two coffins, he saw her in her wedding dress with pearls starring her dark hair and her sweet lips murmuring "I do," in response to the minister's question. She'd looked like a goddess to him, so far above him he'd nearly knelt before her, worshipping her more than the God who presided over the union.

Well, he's been punished for that, and now he's being punished again.

Which is only fair. Of course he can't expect to just walk back into Allie's life as if he never left her. He deserves all of the rage his daughter can aim in his direction. The only thing that matters is whether or not he can be of any help or comfort to her.

For all she'd said she wants to talk to him, she utters not a word all the way to the cemetery, keeping her face turned toward the window. Alexandra, on the other hand, holds nothing back.

"You have plenty of nerve showing up here today, Braden Healey. All of these years you've left Lilian alone to do everything. Raise two kids on her own, work, manage the house. And now here you are, waltzing into the funeral as if you own the church. You have absolutely no right to be here. No right to grieve."

The venom finds its mark, dropping him into a flashback as dramatically as if he's just stepped into a sinkhole.

The car vanishes and he sits in a different church, staring dry eyed at a different coffin. His hands are swathed in bandages. His face feels stiff and lopsided, still swollen from a laceration on his cheek, the stitches pulling tight with any change in his expression. Beside him, his sister weeps for her dead husband, her shoulders shaking, but Braden has no tears.

I've got no right to grieve.

Mitch lies in a coffin because of him. There's a gap in his memory you could drive a tractor through, but he knows it's his fault.

"Are you even listening?" Alexandra pokes him with a sharp elbow.

"Sorry," he says, shaken, trying to surface. His entire body feels cold. His cheek throbs, as if the injury is still fresh. His hands are shaking.

The limo turns into the cemetery. Crown Heights. He's relieved to see that there are trees, that Lilian and Trey will be resting in a beautiful place.

A teenage girl is waiting when the car draws up. Black hoops in her nose and eyebrows, black eyeliner, stark black hair. Braden remembers her from the church; she was standing at his daughter's shoulder. Now she flings both arms around Allie's neck in a tempestuous hug.

"You okay?"

"Ish."

The girl stares unabashedly at Braden. "He doesn't look like the pictures. I mean, he does, but he doesn't. You know?"

"Steph!"

"Right. Just saying—"

"Perhaps we can chat later," Alexandra suggests. "We need to move to the graveside."

She leads the way. Allie and Steph follow, and Braden trails behind, wishing he could blend into the anonymous crowd rather than stand with the family. He catches a glimpse of a woman who jars his memory. Unusually tall; thick waves of auburn hair. She turns her face away before he can place how he knows her, and then he sees the burial site and that consumes all of his attention.

The two coffins, suspended by a series of straps and pulleys over the waiting holes in the raw earth, are brutal. In an agony of helplessness, he sees the blood drain from Allie's face, watches her begin to shiver.

The sermon is mercifully brief, and he thinks maybe it's over, maybe they can go somewhere, anywhere, away from here, but then four solemn young people file up to the graveside, all carrying instruments. Two violins. A viola.

And a cello.

"Oh no," Steph breathes. "I told them not to."

Two men place folding chairs, and the kids sit and begin to play.

Braden braces himself, but it's no good. The music insinuates its way past all of his defenses, goes straight to his heart. He's not the only one. He sees Allie's face go even whiter, sees her knees begin to buckle. He's at her side before he knows what he's doing. His arm goes around her waist, supporting her.

He bends and whispers in her ear, "Just breathe, little bird. I've got you."

She softens into him, letting him take her weight, and the moment of trust is a thread of light in all of the grief and darkness and guilt. Even when the music mercifully ends, Allie doesn't pull away. He holds her while friends and acquaintances come by to offer condolences, letting Alexandra revel in the pressing hands, the hugs, the lugubrious sighs and sobs.

"Yes, I agree, she is irreplaceable . . . So sad, so tragic . . . Yes, his life was cut off so short, but God knows best . . ."

"Whoa," Steph says. "What is *he* doing here?"

Braden follows her gaze and sees a tall boy walking toward them. Glossy black hair, black jeans, black motorcycle jacket, black helmet dangling from one hand. His eyes are the luminous amber of a panther, and that's what he reminds Braden of. A hunter on the prowl. His arm tightens, reflexively, around his daughter.

Allie pulls away.

"Ethan. Hi."

"Hey," he says, standing so close that Braden can smell leather and cologne. All of the hackles rise on the back of his neck.

"Not much to say, I know. Hang in there." The boy nods, as if he's said something deep, and then he makes his way through the thinning group of people toward the parking lot.

Both girls watch his retreating back.

"Whoa," Steph says again, a little breathlessly.

Allie says nothing.

"You want me to come over?" Steph asks. "Or you can come back to my house. Whatever you want."

"Not tonight. I'll text you."

"Come, Allie," Alexandra says. "You're as pale as a ghost. Let's get you home."

When Allie doesn't answer, her aunt clamps a capable hand around her wrist and tows her toward the car. Allie doesn't resist, doesn't look back.

Braden, uninvited, unsure of his place in any of this, stays where he is. His arm still feels warm from sheltering his daughter. As she moves away from him, loss fills him, is going to choke him. He can't let her go again. Whether she wants him or not, whether he deserves it or not, he needs her.

At the same moment as he takes a step to follow, Allie stops short and wrenches her arm from Alexandra's grasp.

"Wait. Dad's coming, too."

"Let's discuss that later," Alexandra says, impatient. "You can call him."

"No. He's coming now."

"Allie." He breathes her name, takes another step toward her.

"You are coming with us."

"I guess we could give you a ride to . . . wherever you're crashing these days," Alexandra concedes. "Is it far?"

"No," Allie says. "He's coming to the house. With me. To stay."

"Allie, I don't think—"

"You owe me," she insists. "I won't go with Aunt Alexandra. I won't go into foster care. Clearly, I need a parent, and guess what? I have one."

"Allie, honey, listen to reason," Alexandra says. She glances around, judging how many people are listening, how much of a scene is being made.

"No, you listen," Allie says. "Both of you. This is how it's going to be. In six months, I'll be eighteen, and then I can do whatever I want. So I need a father for six fucking months, and then we're all free of each other. Surely you can give me six months of your life?"

Her eyes, so very like Braden's own, lock on to his.

"You can't be serious!" Alexandra looks from one to the other, finally forgetting about bystanders in her clear outrage. "The social services people—"

"The social services people will be happy to have an easy solution. They don't like the Canada thing. It's a legal hassle for them. There's not really room at Steph's. And they don't have enough foster homes. And even if they did, I am not going to be in one."

"We'll figure out Canada."

"I still have rights," Braden says. "Lil and I filed a parenting plan, but my rights were never terminated. So, legally, I'd think—"

"Oh, that's just ridiculous, Braden. You haven't been around since Allie was six."

"Paid my child support."

"There hasn't even been visitation—"

"Lil asked that I not visit anymore. I gave her what she wanted."

"Mom did what?" Allie stares as if he's just said something incomprehensible.

The memory jolts him as if the wound is fresh. The empty, gaping hole in the fabric of his life when the Sunday-afternoon visits stopped. His own pain, and worse, the thought of Allie and Trey crying over his absence.

"Your mother thought—"

Allie cuts him off and turns away. "Whatever. We tell social services that Dad's been estranged, but he's here now. Going to stay with me. Case closed. When I turn eighteen, you're done. I go to college. Everything is fucking awesome."

"Do you even have a job? How are you going to support her?" Alexandra fumes.

"Insurance money."

Alexandra snorts. "Should have known you'd be in it for the money. I don't even know if Lilian had insurance. And if she did, I'll see to it that you don't get your hands on a solitary penny."

"My insurance money," Braden says, keeping his voice as level as he can. He will not get into a shouting match with Alexandra. Not here in public, not anywhere. "From the policy we had on my hands."

"Mom did have life insurance," Allie chimes in. "I'm the beneficiary. So there's also that."

Alexandra softens her tone, puts a gentling hand on Allie's arm. "Honey, you're not thinking clearly. How about we give it some time? I'll take you home, and we'll drop your dad off—"

Allie shakes her off. "We stop by Dad's place on the way home so he can pack a bag, and he comes with us. Now. Today."

Her gaze sweeps over her aunt, over Braden. "Are we clear? Good. Let's get out of here."

She turns her back and stalks away from them toward the waiting limo. Braden and Alexandra follow in silence, although it's clear from her tight lips and defiant chin that she's not done yet. He could make a run for it. Call a cab. Go home and drown this whole impossible situation in a sea of alcohol.

One thought holds him steady, keeps him moving toward the car. *Allie needs me.*

And that's the only thing that matters.

Chapter Six

PHEE

Phee slips into the back row one moment before the funeral begins. She feels like a ghoul, a death raven, turning up here, but if Braden is alive and going to surface, she needs to get a lock on him.

Not that Phee isn't sad; the two coffins up on the platform stab her through the heart.

She's never met Trey or Allie and has spoken about a dozen words with Lilian on the occasions when she brought the cello into the shop for maintenance. Dark eyes, a face that might have been beautiful had it been warmed by a smile. She'd carried the cello like an odious duty, unconsciously wiping her palms on her slacks after turning it over to Phee.

When musicians bring their instruments in for repairs they hover, make worried noises, spout all sorts of self-reproachful guilt over an accidental scratch or ding. Phee is used to soothing them, and they know they can trust her.

Lilian, bringing in the cello, would share only the briefest of facts.

"Allie says it's not holding a tuning properly," or "It needs to be restrung." This followed by: "How much?" And: "How long?"

When Allie was young, Phee felt guilty sending the cello back into that environment, as if it were a child in an unloving home. But Allie, she knows, has always loved the cello and is growing into a brilliant cellist.

Phee has cyberstalked her for so long the girl feels like family. They are friends on Instagram and Facebook, where Phee's handle is "Lucia Luthier." She posts music pics and memes and never anything personal. She knows that the girl with the harshly dyed black hair sitting on Allie's left is her best friend since grade school, Steph, who plays the flute in the orchestra and isn't as tough as she looks.

The woman on the right, as proprietary and possessive of Allie as Phee is of the violins and cellos entrusted to her care, is an unknown. She must be a relative and is therefore a problem. Because Allie is Phee's only remaining link to the cello—she thinks of it as "THE CELLO," all caps, sometimes followed by exclamation marks—and if Allie is whisked away to an unknown location, then this necessary surveillance becomes almost impossible.

Phee also feels guilt.

She hopes, and mostly believes, that her parents are right and her grandfather was crazy. Curses don't exist. Allie has lost her mother and her brother because of an accident. Just another tragic, random event. A car in the wrong place at the wrong time. Nobody's fault, certainly not Phee's.

It's been years since Braden stopped playing. Surely, if there were such a thing as a curse, it would have fallen long ago.

But Phee can't quite believe this comforting theory. Can't help thinking that if her grandfather *was* sane, and if the stories he told her were true, then these two lives cut short may be a direct result of the fact that she has not followed through on the oath she swore on the night the old man died. Her fault. Her responsibility to put things right before something else happens.

A movement in the aisle catches her attention, a tall man walking in late, just as Phee had done. His hair is dark and unruly, touched with gray at the temples. She catches only a glimpse of his profile as he passes her and slips into a pew two rows up. A face more dramatic than handsome, too thin, disfigured by a scar that bisects it from cheek to jaw.

And her heart surges.

Older than the last time she saw him, battered and scarred like a rental violin, but definitely Braden Healey, here and in the flesh. Phee's pulse accelerates, and not just because she'll have a chance to talk to him about the cello. She's been in love with the man and his music for almost as long as she can remember.

Phee stares at the back of his head as if her life depends on keeping it in sight, tuning out the funeral, the sounds of sobbing, the photographs of Trey and Lilian flashing across the screen. Eleven years she's been hunting for him. Now that she's found him, she doesn't know what to do with him, other than be damn sure she doesn't lose him again.

As soon as the service is over, she gets up and moves to the back. Braden is on the center aisle, he'll have to come out this door. A lot of people seem to have the same idea, not to catch up with Braden but rather waiting to offer condolences to Allie. Phee is jostled on all sides, hemmed in, edged away from where she wants to be.

She's tall, five ten without heels, can see over or around enough people to watch Allie walk down the aisle, then stop, turn, and plant her heels. Sees Braden come to a halt in front of her. Resorting to rudeness, Phee works her way closer where she can eavesdrop on the whole interaction. Talking to him here and now is an impossibility, too many people, too much going on.

Phee tails the little group out of the church, Allie, Braden, and the unpleasant relative. She watches Allie drag Braden into the limo, then follows the funeral traffic to the cemetery. She would have attended the funeral in any case. She forces herself to imprint all of it on her mind and heart. The two caskets. Allie's stricken face, and Braden's. All of this is a reminder of the dire necessity of what she is about to do.

After the funeral, though, when the car pulls away from the curb with Allie, Braden, and the relative in it, she draws a breath of relief and allows her intense focus to relax a little. If Allie is taking him home, then that's the perfect place for the conversation they need to have. No crowds, nowhere for him to go, plenty of time for Phee to make her case.

Chapter Seven

BRADEN

The bones of the house are the same, but it looks older. Weary. A little unkempt.

The paint is faded. The shingles are weathered. The yard needs to be mowed.

Braden's feet remember the sidewalk and the steps of the front porch, they remember to clean themselves on the doormat, and for a few seconds of free fall, he looks for Lilian in the entryway, hands on hips, pretending to scold while really waiting for a kiss.

How she'd loved playing house in those early days when they first moved in. She'd arranged and rearranged the furniture, had practically danced with the vacuum cleaner and the duster.

"You don't need to do all that, Lil," he would say, kissing her. "Let me help you."

"I love to do it," she'd protested. "I've always wanted my very own house."

He stops there on the front porch, remembering them happy, clutching the same suitcase that left the house with him eleven years ago. Now here he is, the prodigal returned, but there's no welcoming feast and nobody here who wants him.

Alexandra blows through the house like a storm wind, flipping on lights, breathing disapproval on specks of dust and clutter, talking incessantly about the funeral. Who was there, how perfect the photo tribute, how beautiful the music.

Her voice, her presence, grates on Braden's nerves. He craves silence, a chance to get his bearings, but Alexandra is not the woman to give him that small grace, even if she were able to recognize his need for it.

Memories clamor for his attention.

They'd fallen in love with this house, he and Lilian both, when they were still in love with each other. Lilian, usually so self-contained, had lit up like a child the first time they saw it. He can almost feel her cool fingers laced with his, towing him from room to room with exclamations of delight.

"Look, Braden! The kitchen is perfect! See the pantry? And here's a perfect place for a high chair—the baby can sit here while I cook. Oh, and this will be the baby's room, and this can be a playroom . . ."

Reveling in her excitement, still amazed and slightly awed that she has married him, that they are building a life together, and buying a house, still he sees the glimmer of a problem.

"I was thinking this might be my music room, Lil. I'll need a place to practice."

Only the faintest hesitation, a cloud shadow on her happiness, before she concedes. "Of course, you'll need a place for that. It's not like the kids will need a playroom. I sure never had one. Did you?"

"The whole back forty," he says, laughing. "Jo and I pretty much lived outside in the summer. Wait, did you say kids? As in plural?"

"Of course." She kisses him. "Our very own family, Braden. At least three, don't you think? Maybe four?"

The dream of a family took a beating after Allie was born. Postpartum depression hit Lilian hard. For weeks, she'd done little but feed the baby and cry. She'd wanted Braden, constantly, needing him to hold and soothe her, to take the baby, to give her a break.

He'd loved her so much, had fallen instantly in love with baby Allie, had tried hard to take over the care of both the baby and the house.

But his music suffered.

Do you have to practice right now? I'm sleeping. The baby is sleeping. You never spend any time with me. You don't love me . . .

He'd been caught in the middle between her needs and the music, the cello calling him out of bed at night, no matter how exhausted and sleep deprived he might be. There hadn't been enough of him to go around. And now, all this time later, there's no Lilian, no music, and he's deathly afraid there's no Braden left, either.

He shakes his head to clear it, realizing he is still standing in the open doorway. Alexandra says something about changing clothes and vanishes down the hall, but before Braden has time to be properly grateful, Allie appears. She's changed into jeans and a soft sweatshirt, her hair loose on her shoulders.

"Are you coming in, or what?" She glares at him, hands on hips, and she looks so much like her mother that he struggles with his breath.

"I don't know," he says.

"Don't be stupid," Allie says. "You're here now. Aunt Alex has Mom's room. You can have the couch. Or Trey's room, if you want it."

"I don't think—"

"You're not here to think, *Braden*." She emphasizes his name, making it clear that he's gum on the bottom of her shoe, not deserving of her respect, certainly not "Dad."

"Oh good. Thinking make head hurt," he says in his best caveman speech, angling for humor and falling pancake flat.

As he takes the monumental step across the threshold, a strain of music sounds like an alarm.

It almost stops his heart. He takes the next step, tentatively, and then the air is full of music and he looks around for the source even as he realizes it must be in his own head.

Oh God. The cello.

She's here, in the house. He can feel her. He should have known, he should have been prepared for this.

Allie stiffens. Her eyes widen and meet his. For one insane moment, Braden thinks she hears the music, too, but then she turns her back on him and stalks into the kitchen.

Braden can hardly move. The music swirls all around him now, almost a physical sensation. Imagination. Hallucination. Maybe withdrawal DTs, but he's been taking his Librium, should be well out of the danger zone of withdrawal, anyway.

He sets the suitcase down by the doorway and moves into the living room, trying to ignore the music while taking in the new furniture, modern and functional. The paint scheme is different, earth tones instead of the blues they'd gone with initially. A white carpet. New artwork. Framed photographs of the kids.

The pictures catalogue his absence. One, he had taken himself. Allie, gap toothed and precocious, Trey just moving out of toddlerhood, standing together on the front porch heading out for their first days of kindergarten and preschool. A day he remembers, unlike all of the others in which those two faces alter and mature, Allie's into the young woman currently slamming cupboard doors in the kitchen.

"You want a drink?" she asks. The floor plan is open, one of the things Lilian loved about the house. Braden looks up to say yes, please, water would be welcome, only to see a bottle and three wineglasses set out on the counter.

"Allie—"

She doesn't look at him, busy with the corkscrew, which she clearly has operated before. The sound of the cork popping out of the bottle is directly attached to a sick sensation in his belly. She splashes wine into three glasses.

Alexandra's voice precedes her arrival from the hallway. "Shall we order in for dinner? Pizza maybe? Something simple. God knows I'm not up for cooking . . ."

She stops short at the edge of the living room, her gaze sweeping over the bottle, the glasses, and settling on Braden.

"My God, Braden, couldn't you wait one hour for a drink? Out of respect to Lilian, I'd think, if not concern for your daughter. This is exactly why you are not a fit parent. Put that glass down at once, Allie. You are too young to be drinking."

Allie, rigid with defiance, takes a long swallow, staring at Alexandra over the edge of the glass.

"Mom let me drink wine."

"Your mother isn't here . . ." Alexandra catches herself.

"No," Allie says. "No, she's not. But my father is. And he likes to drink, right, Braden?"

She crosses to him, a drink in each hand. He smells oak and tannin, his eyes drawn inexorably to the burgundy liquid in the glass. He says nothing but puts his hands behind his back, out of the way of temptation.

"What's the matter?" Allie challenges. "I thought drinking was your thing. More important than anything else in the world, right?"

She takes another long swallow.

Which is when it really and truly hits him that Lilian is dead, and he's the only living parent of a teenager who is all fangs and claws. Lil was a good mother. She would have handled this situation decisively and well. Braden doesn't have a clue what he's supposed to do. His parenting experience is limited to small children he could pick up and carry off to time-out or bed.

"This is not a good idea." It sounds lame even to him.

"Right. And you've had so many good ideas in your life." Allie's voice drips sarcasm. "Let's get something straight. The only reason you're here is because you're the best of a bunch of intolerable options. No offense, Aunt Alexandra, but I'm not moving to Canada."

Braden needs a wall to lean on. He needs to be nicely inebriated, lubricated, sloshed, to protect him from his daughter's venom and the overpowering presence of the cello. He needs it so bad he can taste the wine in his mouth, warming his throat, creating a shield between him and his emotions.

Doubt wells up in equal proportion to his need for a drink. Maybe Allie would be better off with her aunt after all. It's too late for him to become a parent. Allie doesn't want him here, not really, in a parental capacity or any other. She just needs a punching bag. Sobriety in the face of this onslaught of reality is a laughable idea.

"Here's how this will work," Allie goes on. "You don't get to tell me what to do or how to do it. You live here to make the authorities happy. I do whatever. And when I turn eighteen, you're out."

"Not acceptable," Alexandra objects. "Clearly. You are not in a state of mind to be making decisions, and you are still a minor. You are coming with me, Allie, and that's the end of it."

"I'll run away," Allie says, eyes still fixed on Braden. "You'll never find me. This is harm reduction. Braden knows what that is. They teach it in AA, right?"

Braden's heart twists and twists again at his daughter's words, at the sight of her drinking, at the thought that his faulty genetics and personal weaknesses have infected her despite his long absence. Or maybe because of it.

It's nearly impossible to think, to find any words at all, let alone good ones.

"AA is about total abstinence," he finally says. "They aren't much into harm reduction. Drinking is not a good idea for you, especially right now."

"Oh please. If ever there was a perfect time to drink, this is it." Allie lifts the glass again.

Before it reaches her lips, Braden's hand acts without any conscious direction from his brain. As surprised as everybody else in the room, he watches it lift in a smooth arc and strike the glass from her hand. Time stops for an instant, just enough for him to know that the intensity of her hate is about to ratchet up three notches. Her eyes widen, her mouth drops open. The glass catches a rainbow of light before gravity brings the inevitable.

Glass shatters on the floor. Wine sprays out over the carpet and onto the wall. A red stain on Allie's breast looks like blood.

Braden, observing his fingers carefully so he doesn't fumble, lifts the other glass from her unresisting hand and carries it to the sink, where he empties it, sets it next to the untouched glass on the counter, and dumps what remains in the bottle down the drain.

"What the hell?" Allie's voice is closer to tears than rage.

Alexandra's could cut diamond. "And this is how you plan to parent?"

Braden dredges up a rusty voice of authority. "If I'm going to live here, there will be no alcohol in this house. No alcohol, period, for either you or me. You're a smart girl, and I'm sure your mother has explained why you, in particular, are at risk."

Allie still stands, unmoving, in the middle of a dramatic stain that mars Lilian's once pristine white carpet.

"Mom's not here."

"I think we've established that."

Lilian's absence is loud. She's not scurrying around blotting up the spill and planning how to get the stain out. She's not berating or lecturing. She is, simply, not anything.

Alexandra, on the other hand, is overly present and keeping up a stream of unwelcome and unhelpful commentary. "How on earth are you going to get that out? That was new carpet, what, just a year ago, wasn't it, Allie? Lil was so excited about it, and now look!"

Braden is too exhausted to move away from the sink. The empty bottle is still in his hand, the intoxicating smell of alcohol filling his sinuses.

"I wish—" Allie begins, then breaks on a sob. Deliberately stepping on the broken glass so it crunches beneath her shoes, she stalks out of the room. He hears footsteps on the stairs, the slamming of a door.

Alexandra switches up her approach. "Look, Braden. I'm not saying you don't mean well. But surely you can see this isn't going to work. Walk away. I'll give you a ride back to your apartment. Allie will be much better off in a structured environment with two adults."

He weighs the logic of the words against all of his weaknesses.

"And if she runs away?"

"She won't. You know nothing about teenagers, Braden. She's just making threats. She has no idea what she wants and certainly doesn't know what she needs."

Alexandra is offering him an out. If he takes it, he can tell himself it was all for Allie's good, that he made a noble sacrifice of his own wants and desires for her best interests. But he's already told himself that lie once before.

He's endured half a year of visitation, once a week, on Sundays. Lilian would drop the kids off at McDonald's after church. Braden would feed them burgers and fries, watch them play in the ball pit, on the slides. And then he'd hug them, kiss them, watch them get into the car, and drive away.

Every time, it broke him. Once, he couldn't bring himself to do it and stayed home drunk. Twice. And then the phone call from Lilian.

"Let's just cancel visits, Braden. They'll be better with a clean break. It's hard on them, this weekly visit. Allie cries for hours afterward, asks about you all week. And when you missed? Both of them were devastated. Do the right thing. Break it off. If you ever get sober, call me, we'll rethink it . . ."

Of course, he'd never called. He'd told himself they were better off without him. Maybe that was true, but it wasn't the reason he'd stayed away. His own pain, the drinking, that's what stopped him.

Now, though, Allie has asked him to be here. He failed at the last thing she asked of him. Unforgivable. But she still needs him, and if that need makes him a punching bag, a living body on whom she can take out her grief and rage, then he'll be that for her to the best of his ability.

"I'm staying," he says.

Alexandra's face flushes. "You're a poor excuse for a human, Braden Healey. Always have been."

"Tell me a thing I don't already know."

"You'll be drunk by the end of the week and I'll have to come back for her."

"Possible. I'm still staying. I don't suppose you have any idea how to get that wine stain out of the carpet?"

"I would have thought you'd be an expert at that." Her voice drips venom.

"Where I've been living, stains didn't matter very much." He turns his back and imagines to himself that Alexandra doesn't exist. Broken glass he can manage. Big pieces first. The vacuum is still in the hall closet where Lil always kept it, though she's bought a brand-new model. He welcomes the noise, which blocks out both the cello music in his head and further possibility of conversation with Alexandra.

When he glances up, she is no longer standing there.

Once the glass is all vacuumed up, he keeps going, cleaning the rug from one side to the other, welcoming the opportunity to do something, anything, rather than think and feel. Over by the door, he runs up against a pair of sensible shoes.

Alexandra stands there, holding her suitcase in one hand, an oversize purse in the other. He raises his eyebrows in a question.

"Leaving already?"

She shouts to be heard over the humming of the vacuum cleaner. "My flight is in the morning. I've arranged a hotel for tonight. In case you change your mind. When everything falls apart, or social services refuses to allow you to stay with her, you can put her on a plane and send her to me."

"Fly safely," Braden says, and mostly means it. If there could be airplane fender benders, he might wish that inconvenience upon her, but he can't summon enough hate to wish her or anybody wiped off the face of the planet.

Her lips purse together, and she gives her head a little shake of disapproval. And then she's gone.

Braden stares at the closed front door with mingled relief and panic. It's not too late. He could still run after her. She'd love nothing more than to see him grovel and beg her to take Allie after all. Instead, he puts the vacuum away. Finds a washcloth in the bathroom and uses it to wipe wine splatters off the wall.

An amoeba-shaped blotch remains on the carpet. It looks like blood, and he feels guilty that he's the one who put it there. If there are ghosts, and if Lilian is one, she will haunt him for this, on top of all of his other sins against her.

His relief at Alexandra leaving dissipates almost immediately. He's alone with his memories. Alone with the cello. The music is louder now, and is taking on the shape of his name, first calling him, pleading, then summoning.

Braden.

In all of the years since he walked away from his music, his home, and his family, the cello has followed him into his dreams, inhabited all of his waking moments. A phrase of music here, a sensation of strings beneath his fingers there, a phantom bow in his hand when he's drowning his memories in a bar.

This is the first time it has called him by name.

Braden.

Feeling like he's dreaming, he steps over the stain, walks down the hallway, opens the door to his old music room.

Nothing has changed. The old desk where he once sat composing music still sits in the corner. His favorite chair is in place by the window, sheet music on the stand in front of it. The cello case, scuffed and scarred, stands beside it.

He glances at the music, and the room around him spins. Bach's Suite in C Minor. The same music he'd been practicing before music was torn out of his life. His own handwritten notations to himself are still there.

It makes no sense that the music would be sitting on the stand, less sense than the fact that the cello is still here.

He undoes the latches on the case, swings the cover open.

The cello steals his breath. Same burnished red gold. The perfect curves, the tiny chip on the scrollwork where he once caught it against a door. A new scratch on the body that he traces with an insensate finger, imagining that he can actually feel the smoothness of the wood beneath his touch.

He plucks a string, surprised that it is perfectly tuned.

"Hello, beautiful," he whispers.

The cello hums an invitation.

"I can't," he murmurs. "You know I can't. Hush now."

He lays his hand across the strings. The connection is immediate and fierce, the lock of a powerful magnet to a shard of iron. It was like this when he was twelve years old and met her for the very first time. It was like this every time he touched her.

The shock of loss hits him all over again, as fresh and overwhelming as it was that very first morning when he woke up in a hospital bed with bandaged hands. Every day for the last eleven years, he has wakened to the same shock and disbelief, the dark wonder that life can go on, day after day after endless day, when he is barred from the music that gave it all meaning.

Now, though, a faint joy threads through his grief. The cello has been cared for, played. The bow has recently been re-haired.

Allie. It would have to be Allie, just as he had always hoped. He set up music lessons for her when she was twelve, the same age he'd been when the cello came to him, but he communicated the plan through an attorney and never inquired about her progress. All he knew was that money transferred from his account into the cello teacher's every month.

He allows himself the small pleasure of lifting the cello out of the case and setting her on the stand, a fierce hope rising within him. Maybe he and Allie still have a chance. Maybe they can connect over the music. If he could teach her, it would be almost like playing himself.

His left hand circles the cello's neck, his fingers settling onto the strings. Such a familiar gesture, and yet so different and so wrong. If he focuses, he can vividly recall the sensation of finger pads on strings. It's the very last memory fragment he retains from the far side of a black chasm of nothing.

He inhabits that memory as fully as he can, hoping and fearing it will carry him on into the next one.

In the first memory, he's alone at his parents' cabin in the woods and he's deeply, devastatingly sad, faced with a decision that is going to break him, no matter what choice he makes. The cello rests warm against his knee and he's playing, not the C Minor that he's meant to be practicing but something different, Allie's song, a lullaby he created for her when she was just a baby.

That's one bookend.

In the next, he's in the hospital. His cheek is stitched back together after being flayed open somehow. His hands are bandaged from serious frostbite. And his sister is telling him that Mitch, his brother-in-law, is dead. People keep asking what happened. How did Mitch come to fall through the late ice on the lake? He's a big man, so how did Braden get him from the lake to the cabin?

Then, as now, he doesn't know the answers.

As always, when he tries to push his way into the blank space, panic hits him with hurricane force. He can't breathe, his chest hurts, his vision narrows down into a tunnel, and, oh God, what is he doing here? Everything he has been running from is in this house. Who does he think he is that he can face it all, especially sober?

For Allie, he reminds himself.

He staggers to his feet, away from the cello, slamming the door behind him. But this house is a minefield, trip wires of memory hidden everywhere he walks. He wants, needs, *requires* a drink.

Water. Librium.

He makes it to the kitchen, manages to fill a glass with water, although his hands are shaking so violently he spills half of it when he tries to drink. There's the bottle of Librium in his suitcase, meant for withdrawals, but he knows from experience that it's also good for anxiety. He'd packed in five minutes, stuffing clothes and toiletries into the bag without folding or sorting, and the whole thing is a twisted mess he can barely navigate.

By the time he locates the bottle, jeans and socks and underwear are strewn everywhere. The childproof cap nearly defeats him. Between his shaking and his numb fingers, it takes him three tries, and then as the cap opens, the whole damn thing slips from his grasp and lands on the floor, the contents spilling everywhere.

Which is when the doorbell rings.

He ignores it, chasing down one of the capsules and trying to pick it up. He hears himself laughing like a maniac.

The doorbell buzzes again, and then again, and relief floods through him.

Alexandra, surely, come back to press her point. Perfect timing. She was right, he was wrong. He's not up to this, can't do it, in fact it's going to kill him. He'll let her care for Allie and he will hit the closest store, buy a bottle, and drain it.

He dry swallows two of the capsules and then flings the door open without bothering to look through the peephole, words already spilling off his tongue. "Fine. You're right."

Chapter Eight

PHEE

"I am?"

Phee has a rudimentary plan. She's brought flowers. She'll offer condolences to Allie and Braden. But when Braden answers the door, uttering the last words she expects to come out of his mouth, shock steals all of her words and apparently also her brain cells.

"I mean, yes, of course I'm right," she says, pulling herself together.

She's disoriented by music, a haunting cello melody that twists her heart in her chest, weakens her knees.

Braden's hair, always unruly, is wild. His hands shake visibly. The years have etched themselves deeply into his face. A fallen angel, Phee thinks, beautiful and ruined and in need of saving.

"I am not in the business of saving people," she mutters under her breath. "Not even you."

"Pardon?" he asks. And then his eyes narrow with recognition, and he finally asks the question she's armored herself against. "What the hell are *you* doing here?"

Phee raises the flower arrangement she's carrying, as if that makes her presence self-evident. "Would you mind if I bring these in?"

Taking advantage of his inclination to be polite, she brushes past him, across the threshold and into the living room. A battered old suitcase spills jeans and underwear and socks out onto the floor. A pill bottle lies on its side on the coffee table, open. Green-and-black capsules are scattered on a white carpet marred by a crimson stain.

Librium and a wine stain. Phee is an expert on both. She ignores the evidence, traipsing through the house as if she is a frequent visitor. She finds the dining room, also carpeted in white and decorated with a stark minimalist elegance.

The shining black lacquered table is nearly obscured by floral arrangements, all funereal and formal, unlike the profusion of color Phee has selected. The sadder the occasion, the brighter the flowers should be, she always thinks, and she's brought a loose bouquet made up of sunflowers, dahlias in pinks and purples, blue cornflowers, and irises.

"Listen, this is a bad time," Braden begins as Phee turns again to face him.

Her eyebrows go up at that bit of obviousness, but he plows on.

"Not that there will ever be a good time. I can't believe you would come here now. Like this."

Phee can't quite believe it, either, and yet here she is. The contract—his contract, the one he is in violation of—is folded into her purse. That's why she's here, and he knows that's why she's here.

In her head, she hears her grandfather's voice.

"Get it over with, Ophelia MacPhee. Open your bag, show him what he signed, hold him to his oath. Your emotions have nothing to do with this."

But the truth is, her emotions have everything to do with it.

The moment that Phee fell in love with Braden Healey is lodged in her memory with the same pristine clarity as her first glass of Scotch. Both had a similar effect on her. The burn, the sense of melting away, the instant addiction. Both have been eradicated from her life, but she is now in the way of temptation. It's almost eleven years since their last disastrous conversation, and yet every nerve in her body is tuned to his voice, to the movement of his hands.

She wants to gentle those hands between her own, to run a finger over that scar on his face, to kiss him. Hell, she wants to clean his house and make him dinner, and Phee is not a domestic creature.

But none of this is why she is here.

"I came to check on her," she says.

"I assume by that you mean the cello and not my daughter." His tone and his eyes are dangerous. "You'll stay away from her, Phee. Oh hell. Too late."

His gaze shifts and Phee's follows.

Allie stands at the edge of the room, a personified question. "Who is staying away from whom?"

Even if Phee hadn't been cyberstalking Allie for years, hadn't seen her at the funeral, she'd have recognized the girl anywhere. Her face is modeled on the same plan as Braden's, same cheekbones, same strong jaw and cleft chin, only more rounded, the cleft more of a dimple. Her hair is darker, and straight where his is wavy, but the resemblance is obvious.

"Allie—" Braden begins, but she cuts him off.

"Who are you?" she demands.

"This is the luthier who maintains the cello," Braden cuts in before Phee can answer. "She brought flowers. She's leaving."

"I'm so terribly sorry about what happened." Phee knows the words are useless, that Allie has heard them uttered so many times already she's probably sick to death of them. She bites her tongue before she can add the usual "if there's anything I can do" claptrap, because clearly there is nothing.

Allie's gaze is unsettling, her eyes so like Braden's, but the soul looking through them is entirely different.

The girl says nothing more, just swivels and stalks away. There's the sound of footsteps running up the stairs, a distantly slammed door.

Braden follows her with his eyes. He looks stricken.

Phee's knees have begun to quiver. She still hears the cello music, louder and clearer, if anything, and it's not Allie playing. It has to be a recording, with a damned impressive sound system.

"I haven't a clue how to do this. Do you? Have kids, I mean?" Braden asks.

Phee shakes her head. "A dog. And a family of instruments."

"Easier to manage," he mutters, evidence that he has never met Celestine and doesn't understand the first thing about Phee's relationship to the instruments under her care.

"May I see her? The cello?"

Allie has taken the fight out of him. He shrugs. "If you must." He leads her down the hallway and stands aside to let her enter a large room that holds only a desk, a chair, and the cello. A window looks out onto a fenced backyard.

Whatever kind of speakers are wired into this house, Phee needs to get herself some. The music is as clear in this room as it was in the living room and in the dining room. An alarming suspicion grows inside her gut, the place where she sometimes knows unknowable things. *It's not a recording. It's the cello.*

Which is ridiculous, of course. The strings aren't vibrating. Nobody is playing. No instrument, even one of her grandfather's specials, can play itself. Whatever Phee is hearing is all in her own head, which is another problem to add to a rapidly growing list.

"How are your hands?" she blurts out, needing to say something, do something, and managing to get it exactly wrong.

"God. Not this again."

"It's been a long time. Healing happens."

"Not for me." He almost spits the words at her. "I can't believe you are still on about this. Now, of all times. Yes, I still have nerve damage. No, I can't play the cello. I can't feel the strings or the bow. Can we be done with this?"

His hands are shaking again. More than anger or nerves, she thinks. There's the wine stain on the living room carpet, still damp. The Librium. As usual, words pop out of her before she has the sense to keep them to herself.

"You look like a man who needs a drink."

Braden flinches as if she's struck him. His face goes dead white. "Now? I . . . can't . . . ," he stammers.

"Oh God. No. I wasn't offering one. Just observing."

"Good to know my sins are so clearly visible."

"Been there, done that. Look. I know you think I'm an opportunistic bitch or some such, but consider this, anyway." Phee scrabbles in her purse, not for the contract but for a scrap of paper and a pen. She scribbles an address and holds it out to him. "There's a meeting here, tomorrow afternoon at four."

"AA? I'll think about it."

"Oh, this is so not AA," Phee protests. "All that powerlessness shit gets depressing after a while, don't you think?"

His gaze scours her face. "What could you possibly know about AA?"

"Ten years in the trenches."

"I don't believe you. You don't look like a longtimer."

"I bounced in and out of AA like a rubber ball, always wondering what was wrong with me that it didn't seem to take. I was drinking the last time we, um, talked." It hadn't been much of a conversation. She's forgotten how much of a mess she was back then, and how horribly she'd bungled things after his accident.

"But you're sober now?" he asks, with a tone that says this visit would be so much more understandable if she were totally soused.

"'Sober' is such a bleak word. Makes me think of Quakers. Or nuns. Amazed and alive, that's what I am, five years now."

"So what is this meeting, then, if it's not AA?" He's still skeptical, but also still talking. Maybe she can help him. If he trusts her, even a little, she's likely to get further than she will beating him with the same old story she gave him the last time she saw him.

"Come and see."

He shakes his head, takes a step back.

"I've sampled the church recovery groups, too. Not for me."

Despite the sorrow in this house and the sad state her own heart is in, Phee laughs at the very idea.

"You thought I was about to turn evangelical on you? Sorry, but that's funny right there."

Her laughter sparks an answering emotion in Braden. A smile lights his eyes, activates an inner warmth that softens his face. "Enlighten me."

"I'm an Adventure Angel."

"A what?"

"An Adventure Angel."

"And that means what, exactly?"

"Tomorrow. Four p.m. Come and see for yourself."

He considers. "Tell you what. You stay away from Allie. No giving her any of the bullshit you laid on me about how this cello has a soul—"

Phee sighs. "It's not Allie's contract, Braden, it's yours."

"—and I'll come to your meetings."

This is easy to agree to, since Allie has only been the surrogate for her missing father, anyway. "Done." She holds out her hand and Braden shakes it. Even though his is trembling, it's warm and strong. The fingers curve as they are supposed to do.

Braden releases her and stuffs his hands in his pockets. "I see what you're thinking. They look fine. They do what I need them to, for the most part. I just have to operate them like they're . . . robotic. A handshake is a different skill set from, well, you know."

Phee feels the tears gathering in her eyes, blinks them back as best she can. "I'm sorry for your loss," she says. Impulsively, she hugs him. Before he has time to react, she turns and rushes down the hallway and out the door.

Braden doesn't follow.

Chapter Nine

ALLIE

Allie used to love Mondays.

Today, her steps slow as she approaches the high school and she begins considering the alternatives. She'd thought about driving, had actually slid behind the wheel of her car and put the key in the ignition before a mental image hit her of her mother's car, twisted and broken, and she'd bounced right back out again.

So she's on foot, which is not unusual. She's always liked the quiet time of walking to school, a chance to get her thoughts together and prepare for the day. Now her thoughts are to be avoided, and the whole idea of school, with its chaotic hallways and inquisitive teachers, is overwhelming.

But she can't stay home, can't be so close to her father all day. There's the library, but the last time she went there, a tent was pitched, right there on the sidewalk, and a woman with two dirty little kids sat in front of it asking for a handout.

It made her cry to think about people living like that. She'd given the woman all of her allowance money, despite Steph's vehement whispers that it was probably wasted and going to fund the drug trade. Allie didn't care. She doesn't think she can handle despairing faces today.

She could go to the zoo. Or the locks. Or Golden Gardens Park. Or she could just snag a table in a coffee shop and spend the day surfing the internet. But she seems to be utterly incapable of making a decision. When her phone chimes, she stops to look.

Steph: Are you coming to school? Please say yes. It's a wasteland without you.

Allie sighs, letting Steph make the decision for her. There in a minute.

She starts walking again, but the closer she gets, the more she dreads what awaits her. The questions. The murmurs. She reminds herself of who she is and what she has done. School is part of her penance.

Besides, she can't think of anywhere else to be. The house is a mausoleum. The cello mournfully calling her. Trey's room, exactly the way he left it, with dirty clothes all over the floor, a cereal bowl full of souring milk in the middle of the bed. Even the TV is still on, set to the channel where he left it before he went to school that morning. Aunt Alexandra was going to turn it off, that first day home, but Allie had fought her, consenting only to put the thing on mute.

Her mother's room is also unchanged. If Braden has slept there, there's no sign of it. The bed is neatly made, the pillows undisturbed. This morning, when she slipped out the back door, he was asleep on the couch. She's taken aback by a thrill of relief she feels at having him there, home, despite all of the reasons she has to hate him.

Now, as she enters the school and presses through the crush of bodies to get to her locker, she keeps her head down, avoiding the sympathy or pity or curiosity she's sure to see on the faces of her classmates. She doesn't want to answer questions or pretend to smile or have to talk to anybody.

Steph, waiting by her locker, is expected. Ethan, leaning against the locker next to hers, is not.

The old Allie wasn't interested in dangerous. Playing the cello when she was supposed to be studying was as close as she ever came to breaking rules. Ethan is everything she is not. He manages to pull off grades just above the failure line without ever seeming to attend class or study. He's heart-stoppingly gorgeous, with dreamy dark eyes and hair that falls in silky black curls onto his shoulders.

Allie has been aware of him in the same way she is aware of stars in the sky, beautiful but outside her reach. She hangs out with the music kids and takes AP classes. He dates the wild girls and is in the general track. Stars and boys like Ethan are great at a distance. Too close, and they'll burn your wings and dump you into the sea, a lesson she learned both from the story of Icarus and watching the drama of other girls who have dared to fly too close to the sun.

But now here is Ethan, inexplicably hanging out beside her locker.

Steph catches her eye and shrugs, indicating that she is also clueless about the reason for this sudden visitation.

"Hey," Ethan says.

"Hey." Allie busies herself with her combination lock, hiding her face behind her hair and then behind the open locker door.

"Thought maybe you'd like to get out of here today," Ethan says. "I could take you for a ride."

The bell rings for class. Lockers slam. Kids start moving down the hall. Allie needs to go to class. She's missed all last week. The teachers will cut her a little bit of slack, given the tragedy and the funeral, but they can't extend that forever.

Her hand rests on her biology book. She envisions herself in her preferred desk, front and center, book and binder open, ready to take notes. Mr. Gerard looking down at her, his prize pupil, but instead of pride and joy in her mastery of the material, there is pity in his eyes. She feels sick thinking about it.

They are studying bones, and if she looks at the pictures, she knows she'll see her mother's body and all the ways it must have been broken. Trey's skull, with the fracture lines running through it.

Ethan is offering an escape. She looks up at him. "For real?"

He shrugs one shoulder. "Too nice of a day to be stuck in class. I'm thinking of a ride to Mukilteo. Take the ferry to Whidbey Island, go hang out on the beach."

"I'm in."

Steph's mouth drops open. "Can I talk to you for a minute?" She grabs Allie's arm and tugs her away down the hall. "What are you *thinking*?"

"That I don't want to stay cooped up in here all day."

"What about your perfect GPA? Your full ride? There's a concert next weekend and you haven't practiced . . ."

Allie doesn't plan on playing the cello ever again, so missing practice for the concert is a bonus, not the compelling clincher Steph thinks it is. As for school, what difference does one more day make in the grand scheme of things?

"I'm leaving," Ethan calls, raising his voice to be heard over the clamor of the hallway. "Coming or not?"

"Allie!" Steph's fingers dig into her arm.

Ethan saunters over. "Sorry there's not room for two," he says with a lazy grin at Steph, but he doesn't look sorry.

Allie feels a twinge of guilt. She and Steph do everything together, and it's weird to be going off on her own, especially with a boy like Ethan. But everything has changed, and she is not at all the same person she was last week. She gives Steph a quick hug.

"I'll call when I get back. Promise."

Ethan holds out his hand, and she takes it, his fingers warm around her cold ones. Walking with him in the hallway is different. Kids make room for them. The eyes on her are envious instead of pitying.

The bike is sleek and black, with dancing skeletons shadow-painted on the tank.

"Ever ride before?" Ethan asks, and she shakes her head.

"Here, I have an extra helmet. Climb on."

The helmet is a little looser than Allie thinks it should be, but she buckles it on tight. Ethan starts the engine, and she immediately loves the fact that it drowns out the cello music that has been playing in her head ever since the accident. The rush of wind on her face, the danger-ous free-fall sensation of riding in the middle of all of the cars, death never more than a couple of feet away, makes her feel alive again for the first time since the accident.

The I-5 is backed up like always, the 525 not so bad. Their timing for the ferry is perfect, with very little wait time before they drive on board and park the bike.

"Come on," Ethan says, "let's go up on deck and watch people."

It's only a short crossing, and the majority of the passengers stay in their cars. Allie is more interested in Ethan and the expanse of water than she is in the few people sharing the deck with them, but Ethan has different ideas.

"Let's play a game."

"Okay," she says, cautious.

"Pick a person, any person, and I'll make up a story about them. Who's first?"

Allie surveys the possibilities and nods toward an elderly couple holding hands at the railing. "Them."

"He's got cancer. They're taking this one last day together, and then he's going to swallow a bunch of pills and take himself out."

"Oh my God!" Allie stares at him. "That's awful."

"Is it? What's yours?"

"It's their anniversary. They love each other. They're going to Whidbey to visit the grandkids."

"Fairy tale," Ethan says. "Okay, now that little kid over there."

Allie watches the toddler running back and forth between two adults, laughing out loud as if this is the most amazing game in the world. He clutches a bear in one hand. The adults have dark hair, his is blond.

"He's being adopted," she says. "The bear is all he has left of his birth parents. But these people are so excited to have him and love him already."

"I'll give you that," Ethan says. "Only, about five minutes from now, they hug each other because they're so happy, and in the minute when they're not looking, the kid climbs up on the railing and falls into the water and drowns."

"Stop it!" Allie exclaims. "Let the kid be happy."

"We're born, we live, we die. Shit happens. It's an ugly world; you think there's some magic protection for kids?"

Allie wants there to be. But then, she wants some sort of magic protection for herself, some way to unravel heartbreak and tragedy. She wants to play the cello again, she wants to be right with her father.

She wants Trey and her mother back and alive.

"You of all people should be beyond rose-colored glasses, Allie."

"I just want it to be different, is all."

"It hurts less when you just accept that it sucks. Come on. We're almost there."

She follows him back down to the bike, and they don't talk while the ferry docks and unloads. Once they're away from the terminal, the traffic thins and they have the road almost to themselves. When the bike picks up speed, Allie immerses herself in the experience. It's like nothing else exists. The thundering bike beneath her, her arms tight around Ethan's waist, the wind on her face. Off and on, there are glimpses of the water.

But then, on a straightaway, Ethan veers over into the opposite lane.

Allie thinks maybe he hasn't noticed the oncoming car. Her arms tighten around his waist. He leans forward, revs the engine, and accelerates. Fear and wind steal her breath. She wants to beat on his shoulder but can't seem to move to release her hands. The car is hurtling toward them, and Allie braces herself, horribly aware of how exposed they are. No seat belts, no metal framework.

She can see the driver's face, a woman, sees her eyes widen, her mouth open in what looks like a scream as the car brakes and begins to skid. Allie hides her face against Ethan's shoulder. She doesn't want to see the moment of impact. The bike swerves sharply to the right. Her head comes up, eyes wide open. They are back in their own lane, traveling smoothly along as if they've always been here. She manages to gulp in air, one breath and then another. Her body is vibrating from head to toe.

Ethan pumps one fist up in the air. His shoulders are shaking, and she realizes he's laughing.

Allie isn't having fun anymore. When he finally turns off into a parking lot beside a beach, she's off the bike the instant it comes to a stop. Her quivering knees will hardly hold her. Helpless tears roll down her cheeks.

"What are you doing?" she screams at him, her voice breaking on the words.

The laughter fades from his face. "Hey," he says. "Hey. It's okay."

He takes a step toward her and she backs away, keeping distance between them.

"We're fine." He looks bewildered. "We were never in any real danger, Allie."

"You're sick! Death isn't some sort of stupid joke. It's not funny!" She's sobbing, knows her face is all screwed up and her makeup running, but she doesn't care anymore.

"Of course it's not funny."

Ethan puts his arms around her, tries to gather her to him. She presses the palms of her hands against his chest and holds him back.

"Don't you touch me."

"Allie. I wasn't laughing at you, or even trying to scare you. It's . . . exhilarating, playing with death. Don't you see?"

She doesn't see. Not in the slightest.

His face goes patient. He lets go of her and reaches for her helmet, unbuckling the chin strap, pulling it off her head.

Wind blows through her sweat-dampened hair, cool and wonderful, at the same time as the sun warms her. The sky is an incredible blue. She can hear the music in the car tires, the way every one is different, hears the wind playing a lament.

"You see it, don't you? Feel it, hear it? Don't answer. I can tell you do. A brush with death makes me feel alive for a minute. Come on."

She follows his lead down a trail that takes them to a beach. Ethan heads for a driftwood log, high up on the dry sand. Allie follows, still at a distance.

"Don't be mad," he says, patting the space beside him.

She finds herself yielding. He's right. She feels alive, wide awake. He didn't mean to hurt her, he was sharing something with her, something important to him.

When her phone chimes, she wants to ignore it, but she can't. The last time she ignored her phone, tragedy happened. She's compelled to look at every single text that comes in, to listen to every voice mail. She hasn't been answering them, but she looks.

While she was on the motorcycle, the text messages have escalated to mega drama.

Aunt Alex: Are you okay? Is your father drinking?

Aunt Alex: I worry. Let me know you're okay.

Aunt Alex: Do I need to call DSHS? Maybe the police to do a welfare check?

"My aunt has gone insane," Allie says. She texts back: I'm fine! Dad's sober. I'm in the middle of an exam! Call soon.

Honesty, apparently, is part of the Allie that was.

"I threw my phone away," Ethan says. "Into the ocean. The fucking thing was a time suck. Here we are in this beautiful place. Together. And your aunt is here with us."

"My dad would have a fit if I got rid of my phone." Allie has no way of knowing if this is true, but it works as an excuse.

"He's probably tracking you with it. Parents do that, you know."

"Pretty sure he's not."

"You never know. You won't believe how freeing it is to unplug. Want me to chuck it for you?"

Allie's fingers tighten around the phone. "I can't."

Ethan shrugs. "Whatev. You wanna be glued to that thing, feel free."

"I'm not glued to it. Just need to check some messages real quick, and then I'll put it away. Okay?"

In addition to Aunt Alex, there are about twenty texts from Steph, which is really about normal for the course of a day.

Steph: Chemistry. J just broke beakers & created fire. Thinks he's the fire god now.

Steph: Exam Friday. Study date?

Steph: Worried. You okay?

Steph: Dude. It's been, like, hours. Check in.

Allie answers with another lie: Ethan took me home, hanging with dad. take notes for me

Steph: k. will bring notes over after school

Allie: nah, still weird with me and dad. maybe weekend?

Steph: test Friday, remember?

Allie: fuck the test

A pause follows this response, and then:

Steph: you're being weird. are you, like, suicidal or some shit?

Allie: OMG no. study Wednesday then. promise

While Allie texts, she watches Ethan take off his shoes and socks and set them neatly side by side next to the driftwood log. He makes a disgusted noise.

"Seriously. Let me make a free woman out of you. Let's feed your phone to the fish."

Allie barely hears him. Trey's unanswered messages are staring up at her, accusing. Also the ones from her mother.

She's read them a hundred times, but it never gets easier than the first time. Her hand is locked around the phone. It's the only thing that exists in the world, the only thing that matters. No more Ethan. No more ocean. No sand. Just Mom dead and Trey dead and the knowledge that it's all her fault.

"Allie?" Ethan's voice breaks through the void. "Allie."

His hand is over hers, prying her fingers loose. Taking the phone. She hides her face in her hands, waiting for him to read the story of her guilt.

"Oh God, Allie."

His arms go around her, warm, but the heat can't touch her because she is made of glass. She can't move. Can't anything. The guilt feels like a boulder in her chest. Boulders and glass. Not a good combination. Any moment now she's going to break, going to shatter into a million pieces.

"God," Ethan says again. "That's some serious shit."

His voice sounds far away, like it belongs in another universe. Allie isn't breathing. Her heart isn't beating. Glass doesn't breathe, of course. Doesn't have a heartbeat, or blood.

She can see, now, as if she's behind a camera lens. The driftwood tangled together. The sky. The waves in their endless, repetitive rhythm, breaking on the shore. Seagulls.

A slant of light strikes blue highlights out of Ethan's hair as he gets up and walks toward the surf.

He's still got her phone in his hand.

His steps speed up, his stride lengthens into a run. She tries to scream after him, but the wind snatches away her voice.

It turns out she's not glass after all. She runs after him, but it's like running in a dream. The sand drags at her feet, slows her down. She's only halfway across the expanse of the beach when she sees him come to a standstill. His arm, the one attached to the hand that holds her phone, draws back and then snaps forward.

The phone catches the light as it arcs up and out and then down. The crest of a wave reaches up for it, engulfs it, pulls it under.

"No!" Allie's scream tears something loose inside of her. Her feet hit the icy water, but she keeps running, sending spray up all around her. She drops to her knees, feeling around frantically, stupidly, as if it's not lost forever, as if it would still work if she found it.

Ethan's arms clamp around her like a vise and he hauls her up onto her feet. She kicks and struggles, blind and crazed, fingernails raking over his face. Her knee connects with some part of his body that elicits an outrush of air and a grunt from him. Still he doesn't let her go, dragging her back up onto the sand.

Sobs crash through her, as relentless as the waves. They are going to tear her apart. She can't survive this. Her legs won't hold her, but Ethan keeps her upright. "It's okay," he tells her, over and over and over. "It will pass."

Miraculously, it does. The intensity eases. The tears slow. She feels hollowed out inside, which is better than the giant boulder. Sensation returns to her body, the cold wind whipping through her soaking clothes making her shiver at the same time as sunlight warms her. Ethan's body presses against hers. She lets her cheek settle against his chest, feeling it rise and fall with his breath.

"Better?" he asks.

Not better, exactly. Different. Lighter, as if the wind could lift her and carry her up to ride the sky with the seagulls. Free, even. There is nothing to hold her, nothing to tie her down. Nothing matters. Her own life doesn't matter. No ties, no consequences.

Suddenly she is laughing. Ethan laughs, too, and spins her around.

"You're shivering," he says then. "Let's get you warm."

He carries her, still laughing like a wild thing, up onto the dry sand to where the hill shelters them from the wind and the sun can warm her. He sits her down, as if she's a child, on the driftwood log, and then fetches his jacket and drapes it around her shoulders.

"What?" he asks, in answer to the look she gives him.

"You're different than I expected, is all."

"Don't you dare blow my reputation." He sits down beside her, digs in the pocket of the jacket, and comes up with a lighter, a pipe, and a little baggie of weed.

He fills the pipe, lights up. "Does this restore my street cred?"

"I dunno. Maybe?"

"Wanna try?"

Allie considers. Her life has been structured and controlled up until now. The one time she broke the rules, it ended in tragedy. But she's got nothing to lose. Her mother is beyond being hurt. Her past life seems to belong to somebody else. Now she's the girl who killed her family, who doesn't care about anything.

"Why not?"

She inhales deeply. The smoke burns her throat and sets her coughing.

"You'll get used to it," Ethan says. "Try again."

When she hesitates, he grins. "Gonna take more than that to get you high."

"Why?" she asks, taking another hit, shallower this time. It still burns, but not quite so much.

"Why what?"

Why anything, really, but what she wants to know is more specific. "Why me? Why now? You've never talked to me before the funeral."

"I like you."

"You could have liked me all year."

He takes the pipe out of her hands and inhales deeply, then forgets to give it back. His gaze is fixed out over the ocean.

"My dad killed himself. When I was fourteen."

"Oh my God. That's horrible. I'm sorry."

He shrugs. "Long time ago."

"Not that long." The words feel strange leaving her lips, slow and heavy. The whole world seems to have slowed down. The waves have a pattern she hadn't noticed before. Three smaller ones, followed by a bigger one, and the sunlight reflecting on the water is a wonder.

"I still don't get why you brought me here."

"It's a thing in common," he says. "I needed . . ." His voice drifts off.

"So this is what—a club? Grief 'R' Us?"

He laughs. "Survivors Anonymous? Guilty as Charged? The thing is, the other kids don't get it, right? They don't have a clue. And I do like you, so I hope you don't take that all wrong."

Allie considers. This girl Ethan wants to hang out with isn't the real Allie, it's Grief Allie, this stranger she has turned into. Nothing to lose, she reminds herself. She might as well go with it.

His arm still rests on her shoulders.

"Cool," she says. "Again, not what I was expecting."

"Which was what, exactly?"

She shrugs, feels heat rising to her cheeks, and says what she would never have said before. "Sex, I guess. I figured you'd worked your way through all the usual girls and were looking for innocent and unsuspecting."

He's looking at her, now. Directly into her eyes, and he's so close his breath whispers against her cheek.

"And are you? Innocent and unsuspecting?" His voice has changed, deepened, there's a bit of a growl in it.

"Try me."

And then one of his hands is tangled in her hair at the base of her skull, and his lips touch hers, gentle at first, a question.

Allie answers by deepening the kiss, letting go of memory and guilt in a rush of sensation that drowns, blessedly, everything else.

Chapter Ten

BRADEN

When the bus lurches to a stop on Mercer Street, Braden still hasn't made up his mind whether he's going to get off or not. Phee's scribbled scrap of paper is folded in his hand like a talisman. He doesn't need it; the address is engraved in his memory along with the color of her hair and the low, sonorous timbre of her voice.

She's crazy. Obviously. But she's managed to get under his skin like an itch he can't scratch.

In his *before* life—before the accident, before he lost his family, before the alcohol—he hadn't thought of her as crazy at all. At least once a year, more often if something seemed off, he would bring her the cello and she would croon over it as if it were a living creature. The two of them had been a team, united in the quest to bring out the most mellow, resonant tones possible.

In what he thinks of as the *after*—the long alcoholic haze in which he's been living—Phee showed up twice, once at the house, once at the hotel he'd moved into when he was still hoping the separation would be short and he'd soon be back home. On both of those occasions, she'd spouted insane nonsense about some contract between him and the cello, an idiot piece of paper he'd signed when he was still a child—rambling on about a curse that would befall him if he didn't play.

He remembers that last conversation vividly, one of few clear memories in the days and weeks after he'd lost his music. She'd stood with her foot in the door so he couldn't slam it in her face.

"You have to play."

"I can't."

"You don't understand. Granddad said there's a curse if you don't."

His laughter in response to those words had hurt more than the tears he'd been unable to shed.

"I'm already cursed. How much worse could it get?"

Plenty worse, as it turns out. Not that the cello or any mysterious curse is to blame. Braden is his own curse. Everything that has happened is his fault. All of it.

As for Phee, he doesn't hold her behavior against her. He's done plenty of crazy shit when he was drunk.

He's so lost in thought, he's surprised to see that he's gotten out of his seat and begun following an elderly woman up the aisle. She moves at a snail's pace, letting out a little puffing breath of pain with every step. When they reach the door, she pauses, preparing herself.

"Can I help you?" he asks, offering a hand.

She elbows him in the ribs and hobbles down alone, one painful step at a time.

There's a bar right across the street, its neon light flashing: *You Are Here.* Laughing people sit in chairs out on the sidewalk, an advertisement better than anything television could come up with. *See? Drinks are harmless. Fun. Come on in and join us. It's even happy hour.*

He crushes the folded paper in his hand and stuffs it into his pocket as he walks into the bar, breathing in the familiar smell of beer and sweat. He slides onto a stool and smiles at the young girl who appears as if summoned by magic, ready to take his order.

"What will it be?"

"Whiskey. Neat. Make it a double."

The words have been spoken so many times they are automatic.

"You got it."

She's young enough that he wonders, idly, if she's really old enough to be serving drinks. Not much older than Allie. He watches her open a bottle, pour the amber liquid into a glass. His brain puts Allie's face in place of hers, the expression on Allie's face when she offered him a drink.

God. Allie. What the hell am I doing?

Before he can do any more thinking, he's off the stool and out on the street, physically shaking with the craving. He staggers as if already drunk, desperately scanning storefronts for the one labeled *Fins and Feathers*.

There it is, a mirage in a desert.

A soft chime signals his entrance. He pauses, one hand still on the door, sure that either Phee played a joke on him or he's managed to find the wrong place. Birdcages hang from the ceiling, containing a living kaleidoscope of color. A chorus of trills and chirps and warbles overlays the sound of bubbling water. Directly in front of him, artfully illuminated, is a fish tank holding, unexpectedly, seahorses. The air feels tropical.

Before his doubts take him right back out the door again, Phee emerges from a back room, her face lit up with a smile of welcome that must surely be meant for a more deserving man.

"Braden! You made it."

"Barely."

"That bad?"

He can only nod.

"Well, come on, then," she says, and he follows her.

A circle of people sit around a folding table set up in the stockroom behind the storefront. Shelves all around them hold birdseed, fish food, water treatment products, and an array of empty fish tanks and birdcages.

"Hey, everybody, this is Braden," Phee says.

Five faces turn toward him: two women and three men. The youngest must still be in her teens, the oldest close to eighty. The only thing they have in common is that their expressions are engaged and interested and alive. Braden feels like a zombie in comparison, dull and slow.

"Hey, Braden, I'm Len," the oldest man says. "We don't bite. And the piranhas are all contained for the moment. Let me guess, Phee conspired to get you here without telling you a single thing about this clandestine meeting."

Good-natured laughter follows from the rest of the group. Phee sticks out her tongue at the speaker.

"True," Braden manages. "She has magical powers of persuasion." He hesitates, unsure how to proceed. He knows how to do AA, but "Hi—I'm Braden Healey and I'm an alcoholic, now and forever, amen" is probably not the right opening for this group.

"Have a seat," Phee says.

Braden lowers himself into the empty chair across from her.

"Welcome!" A youngish man unfolds himself to standing and holds out his hand for a shake. "I'm Oscar. Glad you're here." Black hair, a serious face, an accent that is faintly Latino.

"Oscar owns Fins and Feathers," Phee informs him. "If you ever need fish or birds, he's your guy. You want coffee?" She's already pouring two cups out of a stainless-steel carafe. It smells fantastic, nothing like the church-basement brew served up at AA meetings.

"Katie is our barista. She always brings the coffee. She's opposed to what Oscar brews. Or even what the rest of us sometimes import from Starbucks."

"Life's too short to drink shit. That's my motto." The young girl doesn't look like a Katie. Her face is more metal than skin. Nose rings, eyebrow hoops, lip rings. Full-color serpent tattoos coil around both of her forearms. But her smile is sweet, her eyes bright with enthusiasm. "I hope you don't require cream, because I didn't bring any. We are all black-coffee people, except for Dennis. Dennis doesn't drink coffee *at all*."

Dennis shrugs and toasts Braden with a half-empty bottle of water. "Burned beans. Not my mojo. Welcome to the party, Braden."

"Nothing burned about Katie's coffee," Oscar says.

The other woman at the table says nothing, watching the proceedings with eyes that look a little wild. She's thin to the point of skeletal, arms wrapped around her rib cage, hands disappeared inside too-long sweater sleeves. A knitted hat is pulled down low over her forehead. Her body is shaking visibly.

Phee lays a hand over her arm. "Breathe. It will pass."

The woman nods, her lips twitching into what is almost a smile.

"Time to get this meeting underway," Oscar says. "Phee, you want to start?"

Phee tilts back in her chair and savors a mouthful of coffee as if it's a French wine at a five-star restaurant. "It was sort of a boring week, I'm sorry to report. My saving grace is that I enticed a stranger to the meeting. Does that count?"

Everybody laughs, with the exception of the thin woman, who remains huddled inside herself.

"Nice save," Oscar says. "Thank you for that. Rather an adventure for Braden, too, I'd guess, to be dragged into our weirdness. So yes. Points for you." Beside Phee's name on a whiteboard propped up beside the table, he writes a *10*.

"Anybody else? Jean?"

To Braden's surprise, the woman beside Phee lets go of her death grip on her own body and holds up two fingers. Oscar smiles at her. "When you're ready, love."

She nods. Takes a breath. Her voice begins tight and small. "There's this girl in my building, crazy about horses. Has read every book in the library that features something with four hooves. Hadn't ever even seen a real horse, though, you know? So I made some calls, and this weekend I took her and her mom to a riding stable. All I'd asked of the owner was could this kid come down and look at the horses, maybe pat one on the nose or something."

Jean leans forward, her voice warming, her body loosening. "But the owner was amazing. She saddled up this gentle old nag and actually let the kid ride. You should have seen her face. As if that wasn't enough, she's now got an open invite to come down and help out after school."

"Awesome, well done, that's fantastic!"

Jean's cheeks flush red under all of the attention, and she retreats back into herself, but not quite so far this time.

Oscar writes a *20* beside her name.

Phee bestows a glowing smile on her.

"The points are just for fun," she explains to Braden. "We add them up at the end of the month and take the person with the highest score out for dinner or something." She turns to Katie. "And you, my dear?"

"Spirited this old dude out of the nursing home and took him to the tattoo parlor. We did it like a jailbreak—didn't tell anybody we were leaving. That was his idea, so don't look at me like that. And, before you say anything, so was the tattoo. Brin gave him a small one for free. I also scored him a cigarette. Hey, it was his adventure. Who am I to object?"

The circle is quiet, tension in the air for the first time since Braden's arrival.

"Were any laws broken?" Oscar asks.

"No! My God, what do you take me for? Rules, yes. I didn't sign him out of the fucking old-people jail. We begged the smoke off somebody, and besides, I'm eighteen. I can buy cigarettes if I want to!" Katie's face darkens, her body stiff with rebellion and outrage.

Braden's heart clenches. Her anger reminds him too much of Allie.

"Easy, Rocky," Phee says. "We've got to keep each other honest. Nobody means offense."

Len breaks the tension with laughter. "If ever I'm stuck in one of those places, I'll be counting on you to come and rescue me. Bless you, Katie, you are a breath of fresh air."

Katie softens. Her hands loosen, her jaw eases, a hint of a smile comes back onto her face. "He asked for a hooker. I didn't get him one. But I thought about it."

Everybody laughs now. Oscar writes another *20* on the board.

"What about you, Len?" Katie asks. "You always do fun stuff."

"This was a planning week, but I think I have the details worked out." He grins like the Cheshire cat, leaning back in his chair, playing the crowd.

"What?" Oscar finally demands.

"Skydiving."

"You sure this is altruistic?" Dennis has been quiet until now, observing the others. There's a tightness around his eyes, an uneasiness that rings a warning bell for Braden.

"Got me!" Len isn't fazed in the slightest. "Yes, it's a thing I've always wanted to do. But I'm taking this guy I know. He's a man in a hard place. Used to travel all over the globe but is currently stuck taking care both of his father, who has dementia, and his sister, who has cancer. He's feeling trapped and depressed and needs a rush of endorphins."

"Fair enough," Dennis says. "Can I come with you?"

"Only if you bring somebody."

"I have a candidate in mind. I'll look into it."

"What did you do, Dennis?" Jean asks. "You've been awfully quiet."

Braden knows the look Dennis wears; he's seen it before, has worn it on his own face. He holds his breath, dreading what's coming next. Silence grows and stretches, punctuated by the bubbling of fish tanks, the chirp and flutter of birds, one long, melodic warble.

"Mine was a solo adventure," Dennis says, finally. "Down the forbidden aisle of the Safeway. Explored the merchandise. Bought a bottle. Took it home and drank the whole thing."

Braden is not the only one who has been holding his breath. A collective sigh runs around the circle, dissolving the illusion he's allowed himself to entertain. This is nothing but a card table in the back room of a pet store surrounded by a group of crazy people. For a few minutes, he'd forgotten all about the drink waiting for him in a bar just down the block, but now it calls with a whole new intensity.

He very nearly shoves back his chair, gets up, and walks away. He's been party to enough interventions in his life. He doesn't think he can handle one today. Katie's face holds him. She looks as if all of the lights have gone out in the middle of a party. Once again, she reminds him of Allie. There's nothing he can do to help her, but at the very least he can stay.

Phee's expressive features show only compassion. No pity, no disappointment. She leans forward slightly in her chair and asks the question. "And when the bottle was done?"

Dennis sighs. "Threw it in the trash. Considered putting a gun to my head, but didn't. Sobered up. That was Tuesday. So far, I've stayed sober, but the shit is talking to me."

"What's your decision?"

"I'm still in, if you'll have me."

"You know the penalty." Oscar's voice is dire. Everybody in the group looks grim, dialed in like a cat on a mouse.

Dennis swallows, the muscles in his throat contracting visibly. "God help me, yes. I'm at your mercy."

"Step outside, please. Wait by the door. And don't even think about running off, we know where to find you."

Dennis wipes his forehead and paces out of the room.

Braden watches him go, confused by the proceedings. Uneasy. He'd expected an intervention. Maybe a question chain, dragging the man through his relapse, through the hours before the drink. Not this, whatever this is.

Everybody holds a tense silence until Dennis is out of the room.

"All right, then, what will it be?" Oscar asks conspiratorially sotto voce.

"A party." Jean drags her chair closer to the table. There's a small spot of color in each cheek. "A surprise party."

"At the zoo," Katie says.

"How about a boat? We rent a sailboat, spend a day out on the water. Dennis used to own one, right? He'd love it."

"He said sailing was kind of stressful," Len objects. "Loved the water, but the sails and all require a lot of attention and he wasn't into that."

"What about one of those party barges?" Oscar suggests. "Easy. Fun. Repurposed from what we're not doing to what we are."

"I love it!" Phee glows as if there is a light inside her. "Can we afford it, though? Gonna be pricey."

"I've got this one." Len grins at them all. "My projected life span is much shorter than my projected cash flow. And I like boats."

"Agreed?"

A chorus of ayes goes around the table and stops at Braden. All of the gazes follow, waiting for some sort of reaction.

"Braden?" Phee prompts. "Are you in?"

"I'm just visiting," he says, carefully. *Appease the lunatics. Tell them it's a great idea, sounds like fun. Evade. Avoid. Get out of here and go have a drink.*

But there is Phee. As infuriating and crazy as he knows her to be, his eyes are drawn back to her over and over again. The light on her hair, the way her smile makes her glow as if there's a hidden light source inside her. She reminds him of his cello—resonant, deep.

Dangerous, he tells himself.

Katie draws him back to the moment. "Everybody gets a voice. Don't tell me you don't have an opinion."

"I have one. I don't think you want to hear it."

"There are no bad opinions," Len says. Braden disagrees. Opinions cause a lot of trouble in the world, but in this case, expressing his will piss these people off and free him from the spell he's under.

"Since you asked for it," he says, "I think you're all way off the rails here. Somebody relapses and they get a party? You're completely rewarding the addictive behavior. Addiction is deceptive and sly and needs to be—"

"Punished?" Phee snorts. "We are reinforcing life enjoyment. We've all got enough guilt without other people piling it on. Does it help you when people beat you up about drinking?"

He has to admit she's right. All of Lilian's haranguing, the guilt that sinks him every time he tries to work through the twelve steps, all of it just makes him want another drink.

"Which would be the greater incentive?" Oscar asks. "A shaming session from your support group, or the promise of a superfun day on the water celebrating your choice to come back to sobriety?"

"The party, of course, but—"

"So are you coming?" Phee asks. "Will you be there?"

He stares at her, at all of them, everything he thought he knew about life and alcohol and sobriety jumbled into unfamiliar shapes.

"I'll be there." The words come out of his mouth before he knows he's going to say them.

"Excellent. Give him the contract. I'll go let Dennis in." Oscar shoves his chair back from the table and heads for the door.

"You have to sign in blood," Katie purrs in a low, theatrical voice.

Len shoves a sheet of paper and a ballpoint pen across the table to him. "Nothing quite so dramatic."

Braden reads:

Adventure Angels Manifesto

I hereby commit to falling in love with life in all of its manifestations of trouble and triumph, joy and grief, boredom and excitement.

I will treat each day as an adventure, full of possibility, and I will seek to be present for every moment, whether pleasant or unpleasant.

I will resist the lure of alcohol, always vigilant against its many deceptions.

I commit to the pursuit of honesty regarding my relationship with alcohol. If I should be overcome by temptation, I promise to share my struggle with the Adventure Angels group and allow them to support me back into life.

I commit to becoming an ambassador for adventure, bringing new experiences into the lives of others while engaging in them myself.

And I solemnly promise to hold sacred the confidences and stories shared in this group, along with the identities of individuals who attend.

If I should fail, I commit to picking myself up and trying again.

On this day, I do so solemnly swear.

Braden's pen hovers over the signature line.

So many promises in his life made and broken. The only elements that make sense to him in this weird little contract are confidentiality and the commitment to stay sober. If he signs, he will surely fail, and it seems to him that if he breaks one more promise, that will be the end of any hope for him. The very last clause, though, gives him permission for the inevitable failure.

If I should fail, I commit to picking myself up and trying again.

He has to try something.

Allie needs him.

He signs. As the pen makes the last upsweep of his signature, he hears the sound of a plucked string, so loud and clear he startles. Except for Phee, the others at the table don't even blink, talking quietly among themselves. But her eyes widen as if she hears it too; her gaze holds his.

A half memory surfaces, or maybe it's a fragment of a dream. Another pen, another signature, that same sound of a plucked open C string. It's not mortgage papers, or his marriage license or the insurance contract, or even the divorce papers. He's younger, the writing is less automatic, he has to think about the formation of the letters in his signature.

Damn it. This is Phee's fault for bringing up the bizarre contract the luthier made him sign when he'd bought the cello. He doesn't want to think about that, about how he'd felt on that day and how he feels now.

Oscar and Dennis come in and resume their places at the table.

"We have plotted the terms of your intervention," Oscar intones in an official voice. "You will be informed of time and place when we have the details confirmed. Bring a friend. And maybe a potato salad."

"Thank God. I thought you were going to make me go scuba diving with a bunch of sharks."

"What makes you think we're not?"

"Potato salad."

"Fish. Seagulls. Both love potato salad." Oscar grins at him. "You'll be here next week?"

"I'll be here."

"Braden?"

He looks around the circle of faces, eyes lingering on Phee. She gives him that half smile, and his heart surprises him by skipping a beat.

"I'll be here."

"Awesome!" Katie exclaims. "Make sure you take somebody on an adventure!"

Chapter Eleven

BRADEN

Braden stands in the kitchen, summoning up the willpower to make yet another doomed breakfast. It's both pointless and hopeless, and yet he persists. He's always believed that good parents make sure their kids are fed, sheltered, educated, and loved. It had never occurred to him that all or any of these offerings could be refused.

Allie has yet to eat a bite of anything in his presence. She must be eating somewhere, because she's not wasting away, but for seven days now, he has been preparing breakfasts and she has yet to touch one of them. There's evidence that she's raiding the refrigerator at night after he goes to bed, heating up leftovers in the microwave and eating them in her room.

Maybe Allie isn't a breakfast girl, and logic tells him he should abandon his efforts, but he can't seem to stop. He's tried scrambled eggs. Omelets. French toast. Pancakes. Cereal. Even chicken-fried steak. Every weekday morning, she stalks into the kitchen, fully dressed, her backpack hanging over one shoulder, as pale and dire and quiet as a vengeful ghost. Every morning, she glances disdainfully at the breakfast, pointedly ignores his "good morning, how did you sleep?" and pours herself a to-go mug of coffee.

Then she slams out of the house, returning late, long after dinner has cooled and been put back in the refrigerator. Her vehement, steadfast rejection is wearing him down, day after day. He reminds himself that he's here for her, that his own heartbreak is irrelevant, but his resolve is crumbling. He's so damned thirsty, and not for water. His brain and body hurt in a physical way.

Phee is wrong about sobriety. It sucks.

This morning, he is seriously debating giving up on breakfast. Repeating the same act over and over and expecting a different result is said to be the definition of insanity. Maybe he'll skip it. Go back to bed. She'll be relieved not to see him in the kitchen.

A memory hits him.

Allie, tiny, her hair in pigtails so short they stuck straight out of her head, humming happily over a bowl of oatmeal.

"Daddy's oatmeal is the bestest," she'd proclaimed.

Braden hunts through the cupboards and finds a carton of oatmeal and prepares it the way she used to like it, with cinnamon and bits of chopped apple. He dishes it up when he hears her bedroom door open. Pours cream over it and sprinkles brown sugar on top. When she appears in the kitchen, he's standing there holding the bowl in both hands, a supplicant to an exacting goddess.

Allie's eyes go wide. One hand covers her mouth. She makes a choking noise, like she can't breathe properly. And then she swivels around and literally runs out of the house, as if the gates of hell have opened and a thousand demons have been unleashed.

"Well, that went well," he mutters, sinking down onto one of the stools at the counter.

He desperately needs advice but has no idea where to get it. Maybe he should call Alexandra. Maybe he should call social services. Maybe the mysterious Phee knows something about teenagers. Probably he should take Allie to a grief counselor.

Maybe he should call his sister. Jo always knows what to do.

Impossible. He brushes the idea aside, but it refuses to go away. Jo. Practical, capable.

But he can't, won't, call his sister for help. He burned that bridge for a very good reason. You don't call somebody you haven't spoken to in years at seven o'clock in the morning and ask for help with your teenage daughter. Especially when . . .

Well. You just don't.

Unless you have hit the absolute end of your rope and have no other options. If helping Allie means calling Jo, then that's what he's going to have to do. He stares at the pot of congealing oatmeal on the stove. At the untouched bowl abandoned on the counter.

Braden picks up the house phone. Despite the intervening years, his fingers dial automatically, the number practically part of his DNA. Maybe she won't answer, it's early yet. He'll leave a message. Or he won't. Even if she answers, he can just—

And then her voice is on the line, clear and vigorous and thoroughly Jo. "Hello? Hello? Listen, Lilian, I don't know what game—"

"Jo. Hey." He closes his eyes, resisting the urge to smack himself in the head with the receiver. Of course Jo has caller ID. Of course that's what she'd think.

"Braden?"

He grips the receiver a little tighter, plastic digging into bone. Waits.

"What the hell are you doing? If you've moved back in with that woman—"

"Jo."

"Six fucking years, Braden. What the hell?"

"She's dead, Jo. Lilian's dead, and so is Trey."

Nice work, he mocks himself. *Way to break the news gently.*

He hears the little gasp on the other end of the line, the silence that says more than words.

"Braden? Are you there?"

His blood surges loud in his ears; music plays in his head like a movie soundtrack that refuses to be put on mute.

"Here."

"And Allie?"

"Alive. Unhurt. But she's . . ." He doesn't know how to explain Allie.

"I can come, if it would help."

"I don't think . . . it's not like she knows you. Although anybody is probably better than me."

"Nonsense. You're her father."

Laughter is bitter in his mouth. "She hates me. She won't talk to me, won't look at me. She explained, very clearly, that I am here as a figurehead adult until her eighteenth birthday, and then I'm out of the picture."

Jo is so much better at being a human being than he is. She skips the recriminations, the questions, and gets straight to the point.

"She's an angry, grieving teenager and you're the perfect target. That's expected."

"I don't know if she's sleeping, or eating. I don't know anything. A counselor, maybe?"

"Give her some time."

"I don't have much of that."

"How long do you have?"

He does the math. Allie has an August birthday. Six months. He has half a year to repair a breach that took eleven years to create.

"Just be there," Jo says. "Don't let her push you away. My God, Braden, what happened?"

"There was an accident. Lilian was taking Trey to a doctor's appointment, is what I understand. Police are still investigating, but she might have fallen asleep at the wheel."

"God."

"I was supposed to meet Allie that day, but I . . . didn't. Now she won't let me near her. Has completely cut me off."

"Well, that sounds familiar, anyway. She always was like you, I thought."

This is as close as Jo is going to get to laying on the guilt about the way he's cut himself off from his own family. "It's not the same," he wants to tell her. "It's not the same at all."

A silence falls between them, full of years of important things that have never been said.

"How's Dad?" he finally asks, because it's the one question he can handle.

"Declining. I've moved him in with me." Jo lets him shift the subject without pushing the issue. For all of her forthrightness, she has always had an incredible awareness of her brother's more sensitive nature, has sheltered him from their father, who does not.

"Come home, Braden," she says. "Bring her here. It's beautiful in the spring."

He closes his eyes, remembering. Spring in Colville is a slow emergence of leaves and flowers that spans a month or more. The quality of the light, the freshness of the air. It's winter there yet, but in another month . . .

"I can't." His words are strangled in his throat, so quiet he wonders if she can even hear him.

"It wasn't your fault," she says. "Nobody blames you."

"*I* blame me."

"Well, then." She sighs. "When you think you've punished yourself enough for what you haven't done, come home. And bring your daughter. She needs her family."

Mitch's dead face stares up at him, eyes blank and open. "Dare you," the blue lips say.

Dare me to what? Go home? Remember?

Mitch doesn't answer.

"Listen, Jo, I have to go—"

"Don't you vanish on me again, Braden, you hear? Call me."

He ends the call so she won't hear him falling apart as memory flashes come at him like a strobe light.

Mitch's dead face. Snow. Darkness.

A blast of pain as his fist connects with Mitch's jaw . . .

That staggers him.

In all of his known life, Braden has never engaged in a fistfight. His hands were too important to risk the injury. Besides, he's always hated violence. This can't be right, must be a product of a nightmare, not a memory. He feels himself poised on the edge of a dark chasm, about to free fall.

Lilian's voice, accusing. Jo's face, stricken.

The doctor, his own hands protected by gloves, gently turns Braden's this way and that, inspecting the palms, the fingertips.

"They'll heal, I believe. You're losing a little skin from the frostbite, but the deeper tissues seem fine. Except for the right—you've bruised the knuckles. Some sort of a blow?"

"No," he says aloud. "No, no, no, no, no."

He can't stay here, alone in the house. He has to get out, away. But there's nowhere to go, nothing to do. There's a meeting of the Angels today, but not until four. He paces through the house, rebounding off memories whichever way he turns. Something needs to be done about Trey's room, but he can't bring himself to touch it.

The cello is a constant demand that he can't answer, haunting every waking minute and then showing up in his dreams.

He cleans up the kitchen, disposes of the oatmeal, stands with the refrigerator open contemplating options for dinner. The fridge is empty, with the exception of a half bottle of ketchup, a quarter of a jug of milk, four eggs, and the bacon he found in the freezer and set out to defrost. They've worked through all of the funeral casseroles dropped off by church members, all of the food that was in the fridge.

His phone pings and he checks the message.

You still living here, or what?

God. His roommate, Charlie. Braden has avoided making any decisions about his living arrangements, just as he avoids so many other things, because he can't see far enough into the future to know what he's going to do. He'd left a hastily scribbled note when he packed his suitcase on the day of the funeral.

Rent is paid, right? he texts back, realizing even as he hits send that the calendar has shifted to March and he hasn't yet paid up.

Super late with that. Got a chick wants to move in.

Shit. Braden's living situation is based on an informal agreement, nothing in writing. Charlie holds the lease, can evict Braden anytime he wants because he doesn't officially live there. He pictures his few belongings tumbled out into the street, or just reabsorbed into the life of a new occupant.

Braden: I'll get you money today. Can you hold it for me?

Charlie: No offense, she's hot. You're not.

Braden: Asshole. Come on.

Charlie: Ah, man. Don't be like that. Chicks first, right?

Charlie: You coming to get your shit?

Braden considers, running through the cramped apartment in his mind. Most of the disability insurance he collects for his hands has gone to Lilian and the kids; he's held back only enough to secure some sort of shelter and plenty of booze, so his belongings are few. He brought all of his clothes and a toothbrush with him. What's left? A pillow and bedding. His winter coat and boots. Pots and pans and a set of dishes scored for next to nothing at the Goodwill.

The security bottle of Jack tucked into the closet, just in case. The one on the top shelf of the pantry, behind the cereal, although Charlie has likely discovered and drained that one by now. None of it is worth the hassle of finding transportation.

He texts back: Keep it.

Charlie: You mad?

Braden contemplates the question. No emotion surfaces. He doesn't care, one way or the other. If he can't fix things with Allie, nothing will matter. He deletes Charlie from his contacts. Blocks his number, mentally erases him.

The bottle of booze in the closet in his old bedroom is more persistent. He can see it. Feel the weight and heft of it in his hands, the smell of the whiskey as he opens the bottle and . . .

He has got to do something useful. What do normal people do with their time? Cleaning. Cooking.

Groceries.

He latches on to the thought like a life ring tossed to a drowning man. They need groceries. It will give him something to do. Vegetables. Bread. Milk and cereal. Maybe some chicken. Allie used to love a chicken-and-rice casserole when she was little. Just because she's developed a hatred for oatmeal doesn't mean she doesn't still like chicken.

While he's at it, he'll buy comfort foods to tempt her out of her shell. Potato chips. Chocolate. Ice cream. Peanut butter. Maybe he'll make Rice Krispie treats.

Shopping will get him out of the house, away from the cello and his memories.

Maybe you could buy yourself a little something to take the edge off. You deserve it.

He tells himself he's not listening to that temptation, but it takes up a cadence with his footsteps all the way to the store.

Chapter Twelve

ALLIE

Allie begins the day with good intentions. Monday again. A whole new week. Perfect time to make a new beginning. She'll go to school, she'll talk to Steph, she'll buy a phone so she can stay connected. Maybe she'll even say good morning to her father and eat some breakfast. After all, she did invite him into the house, and the snacks she's been eating to keep her going while she punishes him by refusing meals are not really sustaining.

Her stomach growls in harmony with her thoughts, and she thinks of yesterday's uneaten bacon and eggs with regret, her mouth watering in anticipation. But when she walks into the kitchen, instead of bacon and eggs and perfectly toasted sourdough, she's assailed by the smell of oatmeal. A memory weakens her knees.

Mom standing at the counter, making sandwiches for school lunches. It's supposed to be Daddy's job. Mom sleeps days after working nights at the hospital. The last couple of weeks Allie has made the sandwiches, because Daddy's hands hurt him. Sometimes he's still asleep when Allie and Trey leave for school. On those mornings, there is an empty bottle on the table.

This morning, there's no bottle, and Mom is making sandwiches, and Allie feels in the pit of her stomach that something even more horrible than the accident to Daddy's hands has happened. Mom's back looks strange, her whole body stiff and un-bendy, and she doesn't turn around when she says, "Good morning. How did you sleep?"

"Fine," Allie says, but it's a lie. What Daddy calls her spidey senses are all quivering. Her body feels hot. Something is wrong, but she's learned that asking Mom questions when something is wrong is not a good idea. Trey, shoving past her into the kitchen, has yet to learn this truth. He bounces across the floor, Tigger style, and clatters into a chair.

"Is Daddy sick again? Why aren't you sleeping? Can I have Frosted Flakes?"

Allie holds her breath, waiting.

Mom doesn't turn around, nor does she answer the important question.

"No to the Frosted Flakes. I've made oatmeal. Allie, would you dish some up for your brother, please?"

Allie stretches up on her tiptoes to reach bowls from the cupboard. Gets a big spoon from the drawer. Mom clatters knives around way too loudly for the requirements of sandwich making. The cheese falls onto the floor—smoosh.

But she doesn't pick it up, just braces both hands on the countertop, head bent, and stands there. A choking sound comes out of her, and she turns and fast walks out of the kitchen. She keeps her head down, but Allie sees the tears, anyway.

"Is Mom okay?" Trey asks. "Where's Daddy?"

Allie doesn't answer. She carefully spoons the oatmeal into his bowl, and then her own, even though the smell of it makes her throat do little warning spasms. She turns off the stove, something she's learned to watch for when Daddy is cooking because he forgets, and then carries Trey's bowl to the table.

He looks down at the thick goop in his bowl, pokes at it with a spoon. "Yuck," he says.

"Eat it."

"You eat it."

"I have to finish our lunches."

"Can I put sugar on it?"

"I don't care." Allie isn't sure if Mom will care or not, but she thinks it's more important to keep Trey from throwing a fit. She picks up the cheese and wipes off the bits of dirt and fuzz stuck to it, then slices it and lays it on the bread. *The hot, prickly feeling spreads from her belly into the rest of her body.*

Mom still hasn't come back when the sandwiches are done.

The bedroom door is closed. Allie knows not to bother Mom when she's sleeping. Everything is okay, she tells herself. Mom's just tired. Maybe Daddy went on a trip. He used to travel lots with the symphony. Maybe this is a good thing. Maybe his hands are better and he's playing the cello and that will make him happy again . . .

But he wasn't happy and he wasn't traveling. He was just . . . gone. Without a word of explanation or a goodbye, and now he's standing in the kitchen with a bowl of oatmeal. She turns and bolts for the door, away from him, away from the oatmeal, away from her mother's absence and Trey's museum of a room and the freaking cello music that haunts her whenever she's in the house.

She takes her car, driving just below the speed limit, over checking the mirrors, her foot riding the brakes. When she parks outside the coffee shop, she takes a deep breath of relief, waits for her heart rate to settle before going inside. Ethan is there, waiting to meet her, same as he has every day since their trip to Whidbey Island.

"Thought you weren't coming," he says with a smile that spins her heart in her chest.

She shrugs, then gets in line and orders a latte with double shots of caramel. Her mother's voice pops into her head, unwelcome and uninvited.

"That's not breakfast, Allie."

"Well, you're not here to care, are you? So shut up already."

"What are we doing today?" she asks to silence the clamoring of the guilt.

He leans across the table and kisses her. "I have an idea," he says, holding her gaze.

"Tell me."

"It's a surprise. Let's go."

Excitement and expectation rise unexpectedly to the top of her grief, and she catches herself looking forward to whatever he's got planned.

Today's ride is short, though, and ends in the parking lot of a run-down motel. When Ethan kills the engine, her heart sinks and she doesn't get off the bike.

This is what she wants, she reminds herself. When Ethan saved her from school the very first time, she'd been ready to have sex. Now, she's in love with him. Over the last week, he's been her everything. But this motel, the pavement full of cracks and potholes and trash, the faded sign, feel like discordant music.

Ethan takes off his helmet. Gets off the bike. Allie sits still, swallowing down something that tastes like disappointment.

"Here?"

"Does where matter?" He bends down and kisses her. His lips warm hers, ignite a heat low in her belly that spreads out into the rest of her body until all of her skin is awakened and her brain shuts off its arguing.

"I want you," he whispers, his lips tracing a line of pleasure from her ear to her collarbone. Allie lets him take her hand and lead her into the office. It smells of old cigarettes and body odor and dry rot. The clerk's eyes take liberties with Allie's face and body, making her uneasy, but Ethan puts an arm around her waist and pulls her close against him. He pays cash. The man gives them a key.

Immediately inside the room, before she can get too good of a look at the shabby walls and the dirty carpet, Ethan's lips are on hers again, urgent, his hands warm under her shirt. Allie lets herself go. Closes her eyes to the dismal room. Breathes in the scent of Ethan. Tunes out the stink of mildew and despair. This moment, she tells herself, this is the only moment she has and the only one that matters.

There is an unexpected awkwardness about clothes, but once that's over, she immerses herself in the pleasure of full-body skin contact, the way her senses light up and block out memories and grief and even the dull meaninglessness she's come to accept as comfort. When he rolls on top of her, she wants to tell him to wait, but words seem far away and she says nothing.

She doesn't know what to expect, is surprised by the pain when he enters her, the deep ache where she had expected only deeper pleasure.

And then, with a few thrusts of his hips, and a hoarse "Oh God," he collapses on top of her, breathing hard, his face buried in her shoulder. Allie waits for something else to happen, her body still all lit up in expectation and need, but he rolls off her and she realizes it's done. Over.

This big event, the act her friends whisper and giggle over, the thing all of the boys have been angling for, is a meaningless nothing. Tears well up behind her eyes, and she blinks them back, embarrassed suddenly by the wetness between her legs, shivering in the cold where Ethan's body had warmed her. She reaches for the sheet and pulls it up to cover her nakedness.

Ethan rolls on his side and strokes the side of her face, tucks her hair behind her ear. "You're beautiful," he whispers. "That was amazing."

Allie smiles, because that seems expected, but says nothing.

Ethan rolls onto his back, stares up at the ceiling. *"La petite mort."*

"What?"

"La petite mort. The little death. That's what the French call an orgasm."

There's nothing to say to this, so Allie says nothing. She has never felt so empty, so lost. If she still had her phone, she might slip into the bathroom right now and text Steph, but she has no phone, and Ethan doesn't have one to borrow.

She wants the cello more than anything.

Always, she has made sense of her world through music. When she was a little girl, it was the notes her father played that sorted her emotions. When she was five, she could see colors in the music, could watch it carry away the black and the harsh red, bring out her favorite hues—the vibrant blues and purples and greens—sometimes a pure, bright yellow, the color of happiness.

Ever since she learned to play her first song, the cello has been her refuge. And now she doesn't deserve that comfort ever again.

"Do you ever think about it?" Ethan asks, propping his head up on one elbow so he can gaze down into her eyes.

"About what?" She's lost the track of his words, distracted by the memory of music.

"Death. Dying."

She searches his face, trying to find the meaning she's missed without admitting she hasn't been listening, but he doesn't seem to require an answer.

"You and I both know that life is pretty meaningless, right? There are a few moments—like this one, being here with you, riding the motorcycle—that are worth being alive for. But most of it is pointless. So I wonder, sometimes, if the French were on to something."

"French fries?" Allie asks, trying to shift this mood away from a precipice she sees coming and isn't ready for. Her body is trembling with reaction. She needs to pee, but she doesn't want to be naked in front of him anymore. She feels—that's the problem. She feels everything and nothing.

Her old life, her old self, seem like tangible objects she should be able to reach out and touch. That self, the old Allie, would not be having this conversation. Wouldn't be here, in this room, in this bed, having regrets about unprotected sex and wondering when was the last time these sheets were washed. Her old self would be disgusted and frightened and revolted, and crazy in love with Ethan all at the same time.

She can't feel any of these things. It's like they're behind glass in a museum. What she does feel is something different. Recklessness. Anger. Resentment. And a loss so overarching that she only touches a single point of it. Like she's a tiny speck trying to encompass the vastness of the entire universe.

Ethan rolls away from her onto his back again. "If the little death is so amazing and transcendent, then maybe we're completely wrong about the real death. Maybe it's not something to fear and hate, but the ultimate experience."

Or, Allie thinks, *if death is anything like what just didn't happen here, maybe it's not even an event. More like an afterthought. Life is like the buildup, all of the expectations and sensations and anticipation, and then all of the juice goes out of everything, and pfffft. You're flat.*

"Too bad nobody ever comes back to tell us," she says.

"Oh, I think they try. My dad's ghost hangs around the house. But he can't speak. I tried the Ouija board once, but all that came through was garbled nonsense."

"Maybe because he shot himself in the head," Allie says. She meant to think it, but the words come out of her mouth somehow.

To her surprise, Ethan laughs. "Brain scrambled in life stays scrambled in death? That's a good one. This is what I love about you, Allie. Nobody else would say a thing like that. But you get it."

Allie notes that he doesn't say he loves her, not quite. But still the words warm her, just a little, enough to ease her shaking.

Ethan rolls over and kneels, straddling her hips. She doesn't want to do it again. Not now. Not here.

"Die with me," he says.

Allie stares up at him, mesmerized by his dark eyes. She's not sure what she means. Probably the whole *petite mort* thing, because without any warning, he thrusts into her again. This time it really hurts, she isn't ready, she should have told him to wear a condom and, oh God, she really, deeply, wants her mother.

This time, when he rolls off, she gets out of bed, gathers up her clothes, and scuttles into the bathroom. It hurts to pee and there's some blood. Normal, she tells herself. Normal for the first time, but she's worried about staining her underwear. How much blood is normal? If there's more, what if it soaks through her jeans?

The bathroom is definitely not clean. Bits of fuzz and hair are visible in the corners. Allie closes her eyes against tears, but they leak out, anyway, and she covers her mouth with her hands to silence her sobs. She stays there until Ethan calls after her.

"Allie?"

"Out in a minute." She washes between her legs with a washcloth that seems to be clean enough. Splashes cold water over her face. Puts on her clothes.

When she walks out of the bathroom, Ethan is dressed.

He meets her in the middle of the room, puts his arms around her, and pulls her close, just holding her, smoothing her hair.

"We—this—was meant to be. Think about what I asked, Allie. We could die together. There's nobody I'd rather take with me on that adventure."

"What exactly are you thinking?"

"Romeo and Juliet."

Allie hears Steph's voice in her head. *That is, like, the stupidest play ever written. I don't believe Shakespeare had anything to do with it. Killing yourself over a boy. Seriously?*

"I don't . . . ," Allie starts, but doesn't finish. Because the idea of death is growing on her. Not because of Ethan, but because she can't get her mind around the world she is living in now. The one where she might as well be a murderer. The one without music in it. The one where she doesn't have a kick-ass GPA and isn't going to college and can't connect with her best friend. The one where the father she once adored is a slacker who didn't love her enough to be there when she needed him.

"Pills," Ethan is saying. "I don't see why it needs to be painful or messy. I'm thinking we take the pills, and then we make love. Or we make love, and then take the pills. And then we drift into the next great adventure together."

"What if it's not an awesome adventure?" Allie asks. "What if there's really a hell and we go there?"

What if my mother and my brother are waiting to get revenge on me? She doesn't say this, but the very idea starts her shaking again. What if her mother were to start haunting her, the way Ethan says his father does? What words would show up then on the Ouija board? Allie doesn't want to know.

"Can't be much worse than what we're leaving here, I figure. You don't have to decide now, this minute." He kisses her, his lips so much gentler now. "Shall I take you back?"

Allie shakes her head. She feels like where she has been and what she has been doing is written all over her, and she doesn't want her father to see.

"Let's do something fun."

"This was fun," he teases.

"Some other fun thing. There's a party tonight at Paige's house. Take me there."

Ethan tilts her chin up so she has to look him in the eyes. "You know her parents will be out? What kind of party it's going to be?"

"That's why I want to go."

"You don't strike me like a party girl."

"I've never been to a party. Never even been invited. That's why I want to go. What if I love parties so much I don't want to die? It's research."

He laughs. "Everybody should get thoroughly blitzed at least once in a lifetime. All right. But that's hours away. What now?"

Allie shrugs. "The mall? I don't care."

She feels like she's been given a reprieve. She can't come to the conclusion until all of the facts are in.

But when she's settled on the motorcycle, her arms around Ethan's waist, he turns to look at her before starting the engine.

"Don't wait too long, okay? I'm going, one day soon. With or without you."

Even once they are moving, weaving in and out of traffic at a pace that tempts death to take them now, the words ring in her ears.

With or without you.

Without Ethan, what does she have left?

Chapter Thirteen

BRADEN

Braden walks a mile to the QFC, reciting the list in his head, over and over like a mantra to block out the call of the one thing capable of drowning the clamoring memories. The store isn't crowded, and he moves easily down the aisles, marking items off his mental list. Gets through the checkout line without incident.

All the while, he's exquisitely aware of the liquor section in the same way he always knows the location of the cello at the house. He refuses to look, to even glance in that direction, but he knows the booze is up front. It has its own section, its own cash register. Much less risky than the Safeway, where he'd be likely to run into a bottle of whiskey on his way to the peanut butter.

The checker scans his purchases like an automaton. She looks weary, dark circles under her eyes, and Braden wonders what her story is. He dredges up a smile for her, tells her thank you. She glances up at that, briefly, and he wishes he'd left well enough alone. There's a deadness to her, a hopelessness, that makes him wonder how many bottles she's got stashed away.

Maybe she needs an adventure.

The thought comes with a flash of Phee's face, the light in her eyes, her smile. Right. The Angels meeting is this afternoon, and he has not even thought about an adventure. Well, no doubt this woman needs something good in her life, but he's not the guy who can give it to her.

He picks up his grocery bags, distributing the weight for the long walk home. *Almost done. Almost there.* His eyes betray him, straying from the straight and narrow, skimming over the bottles of Washington wines and seeking the whiskey.

Keep on moving, Braden. There's nothing to see here.

His feet slow, then detour. A man can look, as long as he doesn't touch. He's just browsing. But he can taste it now, can almost feel the reprieve it offers. A smoothing of his rough edges, a numbing of his raw nerves, a space to forget his memories and his guilt.

Again, he thinks of Phee, remembers the Adventure Angels contract, but it all seems distant now, a small blip on his consciousness compared to the whiskey that has always been there for him. It won't hurt to pick up a bottle, just to hold it.

It doesn't hurt at all.

When he walks out of the store five minutes later, his bags are heavier by the weight of one bottle of whiskey. It's just a security bottle, in case the pain gets overwhelming. He'll put it away somewhere and not touch it until Allie turns eighteen. He doesn't have to drink it.

What's six months?

All the way home, he tells himself this fairy tale, almost laughing at the way he believes his own bullshit. Denial is his superpower. He should wear a cape with a giant *D* on it, standing for Denial Man, or maybe just Dumb Fuck.

His denial dissolves before he's halfway home. Who is he kidding? Of course he's going to drink. What Allie doesn't know won't hurt her. He'll ration it out, make it last. This time will be different. Other people can drink and be functional, why can't he? His steps quicken in anticipation of that first swallow, always so much more amazing after a period of dryness.

But when he reaches the house, there's a teenager sitting on the porch.

She could be pretty, if it weren't for the distraction of the nose ring, the eyebrow rings, the harshness of the black eyeliner that fades the impact of her brown eyes. She was at the funeral, glued to Allie's side.

They stare at each other in silence, and he's aware she's making judgments about his appearance just as surely as he is about hers.

"I don't think we've met," he says.

"I'm Allie's friend. Steph. Her *best* friend."

"And what can I do for you, Allie's best friend Steph?"

He wonders, if she's Allie's best friend, why isn't she with Allie? He doesn't ask. He wants her to go away, let him escape into the house and settle in with his own best friend.

Steph levels an accusing glare at him. "Where is she? Allie?" The subtext is clear. *What have you done with her?*

"Excuse me," Braden says, making a detour around her and putting his key in the lock, his actions belying the politeness of the words. He hopes she'll take the hint and leave him alone.

But Steph gets up, stretches like a cat, and follows him into the house.

"She's at school. Where I'm guessing you should be," he says.

"School's out. And she wasn't there." Steph stops dead at the edge of the amoeba-shaped red stain on the carpet. "Oh my God! Did you kill her?"

She edges backward toward the door, her fingers fumbling with her phone, her eyes wide and alarmed.

"Hey, hold up. It's a wine stain. Cabernet. Turning Leaf, I believe. You can ask Allie."

He sets the grocery bags on the counter. The whiskey makes a satisfying little thump. He gets out a glass. He'll drink like a human being instead of a bum. One glass. That's all. He'll savor it. Slowly.

"I can't ask her when I can't find her." Steph isn't entirely convinced, but at least she hasn't called 911 yet. "I can't ask her anything. She won't answer my texts."

"Have you tried actually calling her? Like, using the phone to talk on?" He pulls the chicken out of the bag, starts to put it in the fridge, but hesitates. Maybe he should start dinner first, before he opens the bottle. That way he can relax, enjoy the drink, feel virtuous over completing his parental duties.

Also, if he's honest, so he doesn't forget about dinner if he should decide to have more than one glass.

Steph interrupts his musing. "Yes, I've tried calling her. I've called. I've texted. I've Facebooked and Snapchatted. I even e-mailed. This isn't normal!"

Braden takes a breath, flattens his hands on the counter, thinks longingly of the bottle still in the bag. Alarms are going off all over inside his head. If Allie is shutting out her best friend, too, the problem is bigger than he'd thought.

"I don't imagine things are normal for her right now," he says carefully.

"Last text I heard from her, she said she was with you. That was, like, a whole week ago! Allie doesn't lie. So what have you done with her?"

Braden thinks back. Monday. The first full day here in the house. "She went to school last Monday. She's gone to school on all the school days."

"She didn't stay there. She left with Ethan before classes started, and then she texted she was here. With you. Getting acquainted, she said."

"Ethan? You think she's with him now?" Braden sounds unusually threatening, even to himself. A mistake. Steph's gaze goes back to the wine stain. Her hand reaches into her backpack and emerges with a can of pepper spray.

Braden raises both of his hands, palms up. "Whoa! Easy there. I swear I don't know where she is. She comes home in the evening and goes straight to her room. She gets up in the morning and leaves. If you feel the need to search the house for body parts, you go right ahead. The freezer is in the basement."

Her hand tightens on the pepper spray. "You think I'm stupid? I'm not going into the basement. I've got nine-one-one all lined up, too," she says. "No sudden moves."

"You've been watching too many cop shows."

"Maybe. Maybe not. You stay right there." She backs out of the kitchen and into the hallway, pepper spray at the ready.

Braden follows at a distance as Steph opens doors and looks into rooms. Pepper spray is not a life experience he feels the need to undergo.

"Allie?" Steph calls. "Are you here?"

"I was joking about the body parts," Braden objects. "Do you really think I'm holding her captive?"

"If you didn't already kill her. We don't exactly know anything about you, do we? Gone all these years. You show up and Allie goes missing. What am I supposed to think?"

He follows her up the stairs. She yanks open the door to Trey's room, then freezes. "Oh. Oh no."

Even beneath the thick coat of makeup, he can see she's gone white. She sways a little, her breath coming in shallow gasps. Braden pries her fingers off the doorknob.

"Come away," he says, very gently, his annoyance melting into sympathy. He has got to do something about that room; the shock of it is overwhelming.

Tears well up and spill down Steph's cheeks, making black tracks of mascara and eyeliner. One hand comes up over her mouth to suppress a choking sound. Pressure grows behind Braden's own eyes.

He closes the door. "Come away," he repeats. She doesn't recoil from his hand on her shoulder, and he steers her back down the stairs to the living room and into a chair. Gets her a glass of water. She lets him put it in her hand, but doesn't drink, just sits there with silent tears making those black rivers down her cheeks.

"It's horrible." Steph's voice is softened and subdued. "I mean, I knew, but I didn't *know*. You know?"

Braden presses the heels of his hands into his eyeballs until white lights explode into his skull. "I know. You really haven't seen Allie, at all?"

"Once. On Monday. I already *told* you. She came to school in the morning, but then she left with Ethan and she hasn't been back."

So many questions.

"What do you know about Ethan?" He tries to keep his voice casual, turning his back to look out the window.

"Not Allie's type at all. Skips school. Parties a lot. She took off with him on the motorcycle that morning. She texted me in the afternoon, and I haven't heard from her since."

The fierce rush of protectiveness that floods through him is new to Braden. His fist clenches, and again he flashes to that instant of impact with a jaw.

His knuckles aching. Darkness, snow, a freezing wind cutting through his clothing. He's not wearing a jacket.

Why on earth was he not wearing a jacket? Or gloves? He was raised inland, he knows about winter, isn't stupid enough to wander around in the snow without the appropriate protection.

In the present, he takes a breath. Tries to corral his thoughts. Okay. Allie went off with Ethan a week ago today. She came home that night. She's been home every night, so she hasn't been raped and murdered.

"She said she was going to school. Every morning when she left," he says, back to repeating the obvious.

"Didn't you get a robocall?"

"A what?"

"A robocall. What kind of parent doesn't know about that?"

Steph is starting to recover, which he should probably consider a good thing, but he has his doubts. She crosses the kitchen to the landline phone. Sure enough, a light is blinking. It was blinking this morning when he'd called Jo, but it hadn't occurred to him to check the messages. None of them would possibly be for him. He doesn't live here.

Without asking permission, Steph punches the button.

Alexandra's voice comes on. "Allie? Call me. I've been trying to reach you. Braden, if you're still there, and you'd better be, pick up the phone. Before I call the cops to do a welfare check."

"You might want to call the lady," Steph says, skipping ahead. The next message is also from Alexandra. But the one before that is, sure enough, a robocall, informing him that Allie is absent from school. Steph moves relentlessly through the missed messages. Two more from Alexandra, four from the school, and one from Lilian's attorney, asking Braden to call to go over the will.

Steph starts to bite her lip, encounters a silver ring and starts worrying it with her tongue.

Braden looks at the clock. Just now three p.m. No reason to expect Allie early today. No reason to believe something horrible has happened, at least nothing more horrible than Ethan, who is most probably not a serial killer.

Steph slides onto one of the stools at the kitchen coffee bar. "It's possible she's with Ethan."

He dials Allie's number and it goes directly to voice mail. He sends her a text, but it just sits there, inert. No delivered or received notification.

"I told you, she's gone incommunicado. You should put your produce away. It's getting wilty." Steph peers into the grocery bag and starts unpacking it. Celery. A bag of salad. The bottle of whiskey.

Her eyes meet his, assessing. Judging.

"Allie said you're a drunk."

"As you said, Allie doesn't lie."

"Except about school attendance. Apparently. Are you going to drink that?"

104

"I was planning on it."

Steph shoves the bottle toward him, with enough force that he has to grab it before it slides right over the edge of the island and onto the floor. "My mom drinks. It sucks. But whatever. Your life, I guess."

The familiar shape of the bottle in his hand promises comfort. Oblivion. Ease.

All of it a lie.

He fills his glass with water to allay temptation. "I don't suppose you have contact info for this Ethan person."

"He's on Facebook, sort of." Steph concentrates on her phone, thumbs moving at speed. "He has an account but hasn't been on it in, like, ever."

Braden distracts himself both from his thirst and his new worry about his daughter by putting groceries away. Steph is right about the celery, which was already limp when he bought it. The inside of the refrigerator still looks too empty when he's done, but at least his thoughts are clearer.

"Listen, Steph. Allie's got some major shit going on. It's maybe not so surprising for a kid to skip school, given the circumstances."

Steph snorts. "Were you listening to anything I've told you?"

"I was listening. I just think—"

"Let me tell you some things about Allie. The two most important things to her, that she would never, ever mess with, are her GPA and her music. She missed a concert. Didn't show up. When she had the flu last year, she tried to play with a fever of one hundred and two and was pissed when they made her go home. She had a solo and everything. Mal tried to play it, but nobody plays like Allie and it sucked."

"She hasn't touched the cello since I've been here."

"Weirder and weirder. Maybe this is one of those Mandela Effect things," Steph says after a minute. "Has to be. Doesn't make any sense. Like at all."

"I'm sorry?"

"The Mandela Effect. It's this weird reality thing. Like—some people swear it's Beren*stain* Bears and some say Beren*stein*. And some people believe for sure that Mandela died in prison, only others believe equally for sure that he didn't. You see?"

All of this is too much for a reluctantly sober Braden to process. "I'm afraid I don't."

"Google it," she says.

"Steph. Grief is a powerful force. It changes people. I suspect that's more probable than some alternate reality theory."

"Whatever. Allie packed that cello everywhere. There were places she wouldn't go because it wouldn't fit in somebody's car. They were inseparable."

Steph slides off the stool and onto her feet. "Give me your cell number."

She doesn't wait for his permission. Before he can decide whether giving her that information is going to be a good idea, she's already tapping something into his phone, and then her own.

"There. We're connected. Text me when she shows up. Somebody needs to worry. I guess that somebody will be me."

Without another word, she walks out of the house, slamming the door behind her.

Braden stands there in a daze. Half an hour ago, his path was clear and simple. Open the bottle. Have a drink. Rinse. Repeat. Make dinner.

Now there's Alexandra to call. An appointment to make with Lilian's attorney. Worry about Allie on a whole new level.

He sends her another text message: Should I be worried? Contact me please.

And then, after pacing the length of the kitchen and living room once, twice, three times, he picks up the phone again and dials not Alexandra or the attorney or his sister but another number altogether.

Chapter Fourteen

PHEE

"Hold still!" Phee orders, meaning it.

Celestine's tail droops at the tone of her voice and he obeys, unhappy about the water pouring over him from the handheld shower wand.

Phee turns off the water and starts lathering on the dog shampoo.

Amazing how one dead rabbit can turn an afternoon upside down. One minute, the two of them are having a lovely walk in the park, and the next, she's face to nose with a giant and malodorous dog who could not resist rolling in the carcass.

It's a cold, rainy day, not conducive to outdoor dog baths, and the two of them now stand in the shower: Phee naked and shivering, Celestine bedraggled, both of them unhappy.

"Next time ask me first," Phee admonishes. "*Is it okay if I roll in this putrid mess, mistress?* I will tell you no and save you all of this suffering."

She turns the water back on and begins rinsing, aware from past experience that at any moment Celestine might decide he's had enough and make a run for it.

She's about half done with the rinse job when the phone rings. Not just any ring, either, but the ringtone she's assigned to Braden in the unlikely event he should ever decide to contact her. Not a call she wants to leave to the mercy of voice mail.

In an attempt to speed up the rinse cycle, she gets the wand at just the right angle so that water spurts backward and into her face, blinding her. Celestine takes advantage and bolts, taking the shower curtain with him.

Phee slams off the water, fumbles her way to a towel with one hand and the phone with the other.

"Hey, it's Phee."

A brief pause, and then Braden's voice says, "I need an intervention."

Celestine, blocked from further rampages by a closed bathroom door, shakes himself, spraying now-cold water all over Phee's still-naked body.

"Shit!" she says.

Another pause. "I'm sorry. I shouldn't have bothered you."

She mops her face with the towel again, tries to dry her body one-handed. "Oh, you totally should have. Bothered me. I mean, you're not bothering me. Sorry. That was meant for my dog, not for you. Are you drinking?"

"Three minutes from it. Maybe two. Depends how long it takes to get the bottle open."

"Where are you?"

"At the house. In the kitchen. Bottle in my hand."

"Is it open?"

"Not yet."

"Set it down. Walk out the door," Phee says.

"Phee . . ."

"I mean it. Walk out the door. Do you have your keys?"

"Yes."

"Set them down. Leave them there. Lock the door behind you."

She hears him breathing. A door slams shut.

"Are you outside?"

"I'm thinking I should have maybe brought my jacket."

"Oh my God. Why didn't you?"

"Well, you didn't say. I was following your directions."

Phee starts laughing. She can't help herself. This whole situation has reached the level of absurd.

"I'm not sure this is funny," Braden says, but there's just the barest hint of what might be laughter in his voice for all that.

"Do jumping jacks or something. Run in circles. I'm on my way."

"You're coming here?"

"Be there in twenty unless the canal bridge is up or the traffic is bad. Wait for me."

"Where else would I go? It's cold out here. The neighbors are staring."

"Do a dance or something. They'll think it's performance art."

She clicks off the phone and whirls into action. Celestine is just going to have to be rinsed enough. She towels him down as best she can and opens the bathroom door. He barrels out into the apartment, crashes into the couch, rolls on the floor. She leaves him to it. There's nothing precious or breakable to worry about.

Her own bedraggled and besmudged appearance is more of a concern. She finishes drying herself. Runs a comb through her hair, wishes she had time for makeup, but she can't waste time getting beautified when Braden has actually asked for her help. All the way to his house, she keeps reminding herself to breathe.

The traffic is on her side. It moves easily, no clogs. All of her lights are green. The bridge is down. Still, it seems like a lifetime before she pulls into his driveway.

He's huddled on the porch, shivering, arms wrapped around himself for warmth. The mist has settled into his hair, his eyebrows. He unravels himself when she stops the car. Phee leans across and opens the passenger door. He sticks his head in and encounters Celestine, who has shoved his head through the opening between the seats and is growling, skeptical of this stranger.

Braden recoils.

"What on earth is that?"

"Celestine."

"And what is a Celestine, exactly?"

Celestine's tail is now at work, whacking against both seat and door. He snuffles at Braden, curious, no longer on alert.

Phee laughs. "Equal parts Newfoundland and random stray. He won't hurt you. He growls when he's happy."

"Right. Of course. Could you have found a bigger dog, do you think? Or perhaps a bigger car?"

"Get in," Phee says.

Braden's eyebrows go up as he examines the interior. He's a tall man. The seat is as far forward as it will go to make room for Celestine. It takes him a minute to fold himself into the available space. His hair brushes the ceiling liner; his knees press against the dash.

Celestine sniffs him eagerly the whole time, finishing his inspection with an approving swipe of the tongue. Braden wipes his sleeve across his face, mopping up slobber.

"Congratulations, you passed the canine test," Phee says, shifting into reverse. "How's the craving?"

"Ever present. If I drink, does your dog eat my heart and liver? Is that how this works?"

"You're not going to drink."

"Good to know." He leans his head back and closes his eyes. His damp hair curls around his face, softening him. Phee wants to put her hand against his cheek and counts her lucky stars that Celestine has thrust his head forward between them, blocking the impulse.

"What set you off?" she asks. She can think of about a million things, starting with the death of his wife and his son, and ending with his hands and the unplayed cello.

"It's a long story."

"Give me the short version. By the way, you might want to move before you are awash in dog saliva."

He leans toward the window just in time to save his face and hair, the worst of the cascade landing on his shoulder.

"It's Allie, mostly."

"Not going well?"

"She hates me. For good reason. And she's skipping school and is currently AWOL, probably with a boy."

"Was she a sheltered type? I mean, helicopter mother and all that?"

"I wasn't around to know, but even when she was five, she was . . . God. That kid . . ."

"What?"

"After my hands . . . before Lil kicked me out, I caught her making sandwiches for Trey because I was hungover and had slept in. She had to stand on a stool to reach the counter." He pauses, then asks, "What kind of man lets his five-year-old cover for him?"

Phee aches for him, for Allie, with a physical bone-deep pain that feels like it will turn her inside out.

"Don't ask me about the shit I neglected while I was drinking," she says. "Here's the thing, though. No more drinking *now*."

He's quiet for a long moment. Then: "What about you?"

Phee tenses, sensing dangerous questions ahead. "What about me?"

"What made you drink?"

It's the opening she's been waiting for, one of the things she needs to tell him, but she doesn't take it. "Stupidity?"

As if the event that landed her in the ER with alcohol poisoning isn't the reason why she is here with him, right now, trying to find a way to explain. Her grandfather, gone but never forgotten, has something to say about that.

"Ophelia Florence MacPhee, what the hell do you think you're doing?"

"Saving an alcoholic from himself. He can't play if he's sloshed all the time."

"You have to talk to him."

"Get out of my head. Go away."

"You swore to me, Ophelia. An oath."

"I was eighteen. What did I know?"

"An oath is an oath. You were of age."

"You tricked me. And was Braden of age when he swore his?"

"He knew his own mind."

"Are you okay?" Braden's voice startles her back into the car, out of the nonexistent conversation with someone long deceased.

"Fine," she says, but she hasn't been less fine in years.

Braden's expression says he knows full well she's holding back. She waits for him to push her, to call her on her shit, remind her that "fine" stands for "fucked up, insecure, neurotic, and emotional."

But he doesn't. "Fair enough," he says. "Since you're the fearless leader of this band of adventuring angels, tell me, what do I do next?"

"I think the answer to that question is Chinese."

"I . . . you . . . what, exactly?"

"Food. Do you like Chinese food?"

He shifts in his seat, whether to read her better or be ready to leap out the door as soon as she stops at a light, she can't tell.

"Yes, I like Chinese food," he admits, as if it's a trick question.

Right answer. Phee has already called in an order to her favorite place. Whatever the fallout of this day, there will always be the consolation of egg rolls and crab angels.

"Awesome," she says. "You asked what next, and Chinese food is the answer. Part of the old 'don't get too hungry, too lonely, too tired, blah, blah, blah' from the original AA. Or in today's lingo, don't get hangry."

"I am all of those things. Definitely hangry."

He speaks lightly, but the shaking in his hands has spread to his whole body. There's a glazed look on his face. Jean looks like that when she's having panic attacks.

"Flashback?" she asks, taking a guess.

"Not quite."

Silence, broken only by his breathing, rapid and shallow, Celestine's panting, the traffic noise. And music. The same, haunting cello melody she'd heard the day of the funeral, only barely audible, a soundtrack for her thoughts.

"It's not a proper flashback," Braden says, as if he's discovering words for the first time and is not sure how to piece them together. "There are memories, and there's this . . . nothing . . . at the middle of them. Like, a black hole at the center of me that sucks in bits of information and won't let them out again. When I bump up against that? Yeah. Panic. Plus, I'm worried about Allie. Her friend stopped by to tell me that, basically, I'm doing a shit job as a father and that my grieving daughter is out running around with a bad boy."

"No wonder you want a drink," Phee says. "I'd want a drink. If it's any consolation, very probably the worst thing that's happening to Allie right this minute is sex."

"That's not a consolation!"

"Better than being kidnapped by some serial killer."

"Am I allowed to strangle a boy who has sex with my daughter? I'm new to this father-of-a-teenager thing."

"I think the law frowns on it."

"You know I can't get into the house as long as she's gone."

"She'll come back."

"Where are you taking me? Should I be worried?"

"I already told you. Chinese."

To Phee's relief, he settles back into the seat, releasing a long, shaky sigh. She can feel the tension dissipating as he retreats from the dark chasm. Her whole being, it seems, is tuned to the key of Braden Healey. She wants to touch him, his hand, his knee, his shoulder. She wants to soothe his hands, trace the line of the scar on his cheek, help his lips remember the shape of a smile. The last thing in the world she wants to do is cause him further pain.

Bits of teaching from the AA big book flash into her head. Codependency, they'd call this. They are probably right. Her heart is definitely getting in the way of a very clear MacPhee directive.

Chapter Fifteen

PHEE

"Here we are." Phee wedges her car between an oversize SUV and a smart car.

"This may not be a parking space," Braden says, and Phee can't help laughing at the expression on his face.

"Bonus of a tiny car. If it fits, it sits."

She loves the flicker of mischief in his eyes, is sad when it goes out.

"Wait here. I'll be right back."

"You promised me, Ophelia."

Her grandfather's voice is so clear, she catches herself scanning the restaurant for a glimpse of him, as if he's going to be sitting in a booth eating moo goo gai pan with a pair of chopsticks.

"Hold on to your old bones, I'm just feeding him first."

She pays for the food and hurries back to the car, relieved to see that Braden hasn't fled during her absence.

"That smells amazing," he says when she opens the door and hands him the bags.

"Best food in town."

"Are we eating in the car, then?"

"We have choices. The Angels are meeting . . . now. We'd already be late."

"Or?"

"I could surprise you."

"I'm not so good with surprises."

He shoves at Celestine's head as he strains to get at the bags of food. "Is dog slobber of any value? Because if it is, you're sitting on a fortune here."

"Tourists would probably buy it. What would the marketing slogan be?"

"Hmm. Man's Best Friend in a Bottle?" He laughs as he says it but then goes serious. A silence grows, awkward and unwieldy.

Phee shifts into gear and eases out into the street. "How about Discovery Park?"

"Lovely day for a picnic."

Phee stares out at the heavy sky, the rain, remembers that Braden doesn't have a jacket.

"Sunny days are hugely overrated," he says. "Far too cheerful. All of that bright light in your eyes, not to mention the heat."

"I do have an extra coat."

"It's a date." The word hangs between them. *Just an expression,* Phee admonishes her accelerating heart. *He doesn't mean it like a* date *date.*

"You know everything about me," he says after a silence, "and all I know about you is that you repair instruments and are possibly crazy."

"Is there a problem with any of that?"

"There's an imbalance, I feel. Are you from Seattle? Married? Kids? Did you always plan to be a luthier?"

"Ask me something easy. Like how gravity works or the theory behind jet propulsion."

"Seriously. Not every girl dreams of repairing instruments when she grows up."

"Any conversation that begins there ends with me showing up at your door and demanding that you play the cello before your hands have even healed. Ask something else."

Coward.

Blurt it all out, get it over with. It's not like he doesn't know.

"About that," Braden says, and Phee feels the car grow smaller around her under the weight of promises that won't allow themselves to be broken. "Is that why you've really interrupted me from my drinking? To give me a pep talk on getting back to playing the cello?"

"I thought we'd eat dinner first. Take a walk. See a movie."

"But all roads lead there in the end? You're like Coleridge's ancient mariner, you know that? Minus the beard and the albatross, but equally obsessed."

"Oh, the albatross is there, all right, you just can't see it."

The fragrance wafting out of the take-out boxes, once mouthwatering, now makes her feel ill. The conversation on the horizon is about as appetizing as a bowl full of maggots.

Braden is the one who finally breaks an increasingly uncomfortable silence. "You showed up at my door like a visitation from fate or the furies. There was even this wild red sunset behind you, storm clouds piled up over the houses across the street."

"I remember."

"You stood there in the doorway with the sky burning behind you, cold wind flowing in, and asked, 'Are you playing? You need to be playing.'"

"You slammed the door in my face." The moment is etched in Phee's memory. The ominous red shift to the light, dry leaves scuttling in the wind, the fresh scar on Braden's face and the despair in his eyes.

"It was the day the bandages came off for the last time. As long as my fingers were all wrapped up, out of sight, I'd told myself my hands would be fine; all of the weird sensation was from too-tight dressings. And then the bandages were off, and the skin was all healed, and still . . . Lilian always said the music was a curse. That was the day I knew she was right."

His ragged breathing tears at Phee's heart.

"It's not the music that's a curse, it's the absence thereof," she says. "Listen, I don't blame you for thinking I'm evil—"

"Not evil per se—"

"Or insane. But we have this good food and we're here at the park. Let's call a truce. Let's take a walk and eat Chinese food and pretend that we've never met and have no history."

"That is probably the craziest thing you have said yet."

"Humor me."

"Is this your idea of an adventure?"

"Oh no. I wouldn't take a total stranger on an adventure. And if I did, there would be a scavenger hunt or a murder mystery party or some such. Nothing so boring as a picnic in the rain."

"No plans to throw me into the bay or kill me with pneumonia?"

"Are you prone to pneumonia?" Phee snaps the leash on the dog and digs out the spare windbreaker she keeps under the seat in case of emergency.

It covers most of what it's supposed to when Braden puts it on. His wrists stick out beyond the sleeves, and it's a little narrow in the shoulders, but otherwise it works okay.

They set off, side by side, Phee keeping Celestine between them as a physical barrier. The parking lot, crowded in the summer, is almost deserted now. They pass an elderly couple walking a small, nondescript dog. A couple of teenagers stare at them defiantly.

Braden returns their stare, and Phee knows he's thinking about his daughter.

"Talk to me," he says, after a moment. "Something, anything. How about the Adventure Angels. Are they your brain wave?"

"Mine. And Oscar's. I suck at following rules. AA just depressed me. Same old people doing the same old thing for the rest of their same old lives. Like driving through Kansas, only all of the fields are dust and you're stuck in some sort of purgatory where that's it and all it's going to be. That's how it felt. I kept going back to it, because it seems to work for everybody else. And I'd always get tripped up on the making-amends step, because I couldn't really make amends, and I'd go back to drinking. It felt like playing a video game, only I could never level up."

"And then?"

"And then I met Oscar. We met in a bar, actually. Both of us already wasted. We started talking about what sobriety should look like. I blacked out and didn't even remember most of the conversation, except that I'd scrawled things on a napkin. So I woke up the next morning, took a morning drink to get me balanced, and there was this message to myself on the kitchen table. A list: *make life fun; account-ability; meaning; give back somehow.* And then in handwriting I didn't recognize—*adventure's the word.* Beneath that a phone number.

"I called the number, and this guy named Oscar answered. He only vaguely remembered the bar or me, and didn't remember the napkin or giving me his number, but when I read the list to him, he was all excited. We made a pact to try an experiment of each taking somebody on an adventure and then meeting somewhere to talk about it. And that, as they say, is how it all began."

"And the others?"

"We took them on an adventure. They wanted in."

The food is cold by the time they reach the water's edge, and although the rain has stopped, it's even colder with wind coming in over the water. Braden makes no complaint, just starts setting out the food while Phee ties Celestine to a convenient log and gives him his scraps.

She watches Braden's hands and realizes he is watching them, too, forehead creased in concentration as if he's driving a robotic arm with a remote control.

"I'm messy," he warns as he fumbles a plastic fork.

"Celestine likes messy people."

They each grab a carton and dig in.

Braden makes an appreciative sound. "Mmmmm. This is good."

"The best."

But try as she may, Phee is not enjoying herself. Celestine's eager sniffing, the rush of wind, the sound of waves on the shore—all fail to drown out the phantom music and her granddad's voice.

"Nothing good can come of this, Phee."

"Not hungry?" Braden's voice brings her back.

"I was thinking about my granddad."

"The man responsible for the deadlock you and I are pretending not to be in right now?"

"He died twenty years ago."

"Funny how grief hits you out of the blue."

"Or outrage," Phee counters. She sighs and munches her last egg roll. It's cold, grease congealed in the wrapper.

Braden checks his phone.

"Anything?"

"Just another message from my informant. She's heard nothing." He shivers.

As an adventure, this one has fallen flat. They round up the cartons and set off back up the trail, damp and demoralized. Even Celestine is subdued. The walk seems to take forever, and by the time they get back to the car, Phee is cold to the very marrow of her bones.

"Thank you." Braden offers her a twisted smile. "You definitely got my mind off things for a while."

"Don't thank me," Phee says, grimly. "This adventure isn't over yet."

Chapter Sixteen

BRADEN

The mood between them has shifted, darkened. Phee has gone remote, withdrawn. Braden is physically weary, unaccustomed to this level of activity. A blister throbs on his left heel.

Phee drives with a doomsday intensity. There's no joy in her now, no laughter. Her lips are tightly pressed together, hands locked to the steering wheel. A pervasive wet-dog smell mingles with the lingering odor of fried rice and egg rolls.

He checks his phone again for word from Allie. Nothing. Steph also has heard nothing. Celestine's head rests on his thigh, rainwater and drool further soaking his jeans. Another glance at Phee's grim face, and the question about where they're headed now dies on his lips. He guesses he'll find out when they get there.

If this were a fairy tale, this is the part where he'd get kidnapped by a blackhearted crone disguised as a beautiful woman, dragged away into the deep, dark forest as a sacrifice to some bloodthirsty being. The dog would transform into a preternatural beast with bloody teeth and slavering jaws.

But it's not a fairy tale. When Phee drives down a familiar street and pulls into a tiny private parking area back behind a storefront he knows well, he sighs his resignation.

"Back to the scene of the crime, is it?"

Her gaze meets his, and he reads equal parts grief and determination. The intensity of the phantom music he's been hearing kicks up a notch. He can feel the vibrations, a ghostly sensation of strings beneath his fingers.

If Phee is crazy, then so is he.

He doesn't move when she gets out of the car. Neither does Celestine, whose damp, heavy head still rests on his thigh. Braden strokes the soft ears and the dog sighs contentedly.

"Celestine, come," Phee commands.

Thumps of the tail, eyes looking up at her pleadingly.

"Celestine!"

The dog yawns and stirs, drawing away from Braden, leaving him cold and unexpectedly vulnerable.

A déjà vu feeling matches the volume of the music and a sense of inevitability. Might as well get this over with. He gets out of the car and follows Phee through a door into the back room of the shop.

A violin lies on a workbench, naked without strings or a soundboard. There's a lathe, a row of tools laid out neatly, the smell of wood and varnish and rosin. The air feels warm and alive. He's been here before, when he brought the cello in for small adjustments and repairs.

"Come on." Phee leads the way into the showroom. "Remember the first time you came here?"

"A lifetime ago."

He feels dizzy, disoriented, caught between two realities. The room is dark, shadowy, mysterious. The instruments take on nearly human shapes, and he can hear their voices, a faraway music that would have words if he knew how to listen properly.

When Phee takes his hand, he doesn't resist, lets her lead him through the shop to the front door and turn him around to face the display as if he'd just walked in.

"You came in here, with your mother. My grandfather was there . . ."

Braden drops directly into the memory.

An old man stands behind the counter, thin and bald, a long white beard growing down over his chest. A young girl sits on a high stool behind the counter, re-hairing a bow. She looks up from her work, staring at him with curious eyes.

He fills himself with air that smells like music, his eyes caressing a row of violins hanging on display. He's only played a few different violins in his life, but he knows that each of them has a different soul, a different voice.

Once his teacher put her instrument in his hands. The violin, aged and beautiful, belonged to her and didn't want him, and it was his teacher's music that he played, not his own.

Maybe one of these violins could be his, would play his music if he asks, but he knows he won't get to choose. Mama will pick one for him. It will be about price, because money is tight, and although she thinks she knows all about Braden and his music, she really doesn't understand at all.

She bustles over to the counter where the old man seems to see everything with his dark, watchful eyes and begins chattering to him about violins, pointing at the one on the far right.

Braden prays, Please, let it be a violin I can love.

And it's then, at that moment, that it happens.

A phrase of music vibrates through his entire body, not high and bright like a violin but deep and sonorous. His mother doesn't notice, but the old man does, and so does the girl. Braden sees their focus shift, away from his mother and the violins, away from Braden, to the far side of the store. And then he sees the cello, and understands that even though nobody is playing and the strings are not moving, the cello is the source of the music.

His feet carry him closer.

The cello is beautiful. Her wood is luminous. His hand reaches out to touch, but then he snatches it back. An instrument like this must be expensive, is certainly not for the likes of him.

But when he glances up, the old man, still watching, nods permission. His expression is intent, almost hungry. Braden lays one hand tentatively on the cello's burnished shoulder.

Feels her shudder beneath his touch, sigh. "At last," she sings to him. "All this time I have waited for you."

"Braden!" His mother's voice is sharp, and he knows the words she's not saying by heart. Are you five? Can't you keep your hands to yourself?

The heat of shame rises through his body.

"No harm." The luthier shuffles over to him. Up close, the old man's eyes are almost black, glittering. "You like this instrument?"

Braden lets his hand stroke up the cello's neck, just skimming the strings. A whisper of music floats into the room. Mama shuffles her feet and clears her throat, impatient, but she seems far away. The cello is immediate, already becoming his own personal universe.

"She likes you. She has invited you to play," the luthier says.

"We're here to talk about violins." Mama has her no-nonsense voice on.

"Yes, yes. The violins. But first, five minutes to play the cello. She wants to be played, and we always must do what she wants. She is the boss of us, yes? Not the other way. Here. Sit." The old man motions Braden toward a chair.

Mama tsks disapprovingly but doesn't interfere.

If Braden looks at her, she'll shake her head and pinch her lips to signal no. He sits.

The old man lifts the cello with a little grunt. "She's full size. Not a child's instrument, but you are not a child. How tall are you, boy?"

"Five six."

"And growing yet. Fourteen, are you?"

"Twelve."

"Young, but the cello has spoken. Now, sit with your knees apart. Yes, like so." He sets the cello down and rests it at an angle against Braden's left knee. Braden's hand settles on the curve of her shoulder, and it feels solid,

familiar, right. A violin has always felt fragile, a thing to be shielded and protected. The cello whispers of strength.

"Ophelia, bring the bow."

The girl slides down off the stool and pads over, soundless, and puts a bow in Braden's waiting hand. Her eyes are wide with wonder, her hair the same warm gleaming red brown as the wood of the cello.

"You will find the action different than a violin—"

Braden sweeps the bow across the strings, not waiting for the old man to finish. Yes, he feels the difference. The curve of the bridge, the way the bow shapes his arm so that each note sings true. He moves his fingers over the fingerboard, experimenting with the pressure required to depress the strings.

The cello is generous in her response, gifting him with rich, mellow tones that resonate even after his bow hand drops away. His entire body is trembling, as if he's been too long out in the cold.

The cello whispers, "I will always play for you. Don't be afraid."

He wants to whisper back, to say that all he fears is loss, but he dare not break the spell with words.

"You will be buying the cello, of course," the luthier says, as if there truly is no question. "This boy is not a player of violins."

Mama bristles. "He excels. He went to state last year, with a cheap rented violin—"

"And he will do more with the cello. With this cello."

"Nonsense," Mama says. "We came for a violin. We will be buying a violin. Get up, Braden. Put that instrument away before you break it."

Braden's hand closes around the neck of the cello, possessive. She is his, or he is hers, one way or the other or both.

"I could play the cello," he tells his mother. "This cello. It won't take me long to learn."

"I will give you a good price," the old man says. "No more than the violin. I am old. I have seen many matches made. This boy and this cello belong together."

"He is already very skillful on the violin. We are not starting over again." Mama's voice sharpens. "Put the cello away. Talk to me about this violin." She points at an instrument that looks to Braden now like a child's toy.

"Trust an old music seller." The old man's hand rests on Braden's shoulder, lightly. "I know these things."

"I don't need you to know things." Mama has reached the end of her patience. "Braden, come and try this one. See how pretty." She lifts an instrument that glows warm in the light.

Obedient, understanding it is pointless to beg, Braden gets up, feeling like the boy who walked into the store has vanished. His body feels big and clumsy, the violin too small. His hands won't stop shaking, and the bow doesn't glide true across the strings. It doesn't love him, this violin. It will take time and effort to make it his.

"Not this one." He puts it back in its place and tries another. And another.

"Enough!" Mama snaps. "Stop sulking over the cello. You are not giving any of these a chance."

"I'm not sulking. I just . . ." He has no words to explain. Mama reads something in his face that softens hers. She touches his cheek. "We will rent one from the school. How about that? We will buy you your own violin and rent a cello. If it turns out that you are a cellist after all, then we will try to find money to buy you one. All right?"

Braden can't answer her, his whole being submerged in unfathomable longing. Even when he doesn't look at the cello, he can feel her, as if she's a part of him now. What will be left of him if he is forced to walk out of this store without her?

"Try another violin, now," Mama urges. "Give it a chance."

"There is no point," the luthier says. "I will not sell you a violin. Only the cello."

Mama is speechless, but only for an instant.

"I don't understand. You sell violins—"

"To people who wish to play them, yes. This boy is a cellist."

"That is ridiculous."

He shrugs a bony shoulder. "Many people come in to look at instruments. Some are not music people at all, and I send them away. The boy and the cello are a matched set. They belong together."

The old man's eyes look deep into Braden's, right into the depths of his soul.

"A forever home, you understand. A marriage. This cello is not a thing to be acquired and cast aside. And when you die and the bond is broken, your next of kin will bring the cello back to me. Here."

Phee's voice pulls him back. "Do you remember?"

Braden nods, a long way from words. "You were there," he manages, lips stiff. "I'd forgotten that part."

The memory of that first meeting is so vivid he can still feel the warmth of the cello between his knees, the easy sweep of his bow arm, the tiny adjustments made so automatically by his hands. It's as if he's lost her all over again. His grief over Lilian and Trey, compounded by this fresh loss of the cello, threatens to break something loose at the core of him.

"Come upstairs." Phee walks away from him, the dog at her heels.

He hesitates, every nerve in his body signaling warning. The hair on the back of his neck prickles, his belly feels full of wet cement. All the same, this moment is predestined, like he's dreamed it, maybe even lived it before.

He follows Phee back into the workroom, and from there up a flight of narrow stairs.

"Music is a curse," he hears as he sets his right foot on the first step.

Lilian said that, not long after they met.

The words were said so lightly, with an upward sweep of her black lashes and the slightest tilt of her rounded chin, that he'd missed the conviction that marked them. He'd kissed away the tang of bitterness the words left on her lips, kissed her eyelids, her cheek, her hands.

"Music is magic," he hears as he sets his left foot on the second step. He'd said that, had believed it. *"Music is a gift from the gods."*

And when he played for her, just for her, coaxing songs out of the cello that were new in the world, born of his love and the wonder he felt that Lilian allowed the liberty of his kisses, he'd felt like a god himself. Anything was possible.

Braden stands still on the stairs. Phee and Celestine have both vanished out of sight. He can go up, or down. He chooses up, finds himself in a light-filled, high-ceilinged space with floor-to-ceiling windows and skylights above. Outside, the city is moving into evening. Fog creates ghostly haloes around the streetlights, half obscuring the bumper-to-bumper traffic down below.

"Sit," Phee says.

Braden sinks into a comfortably worn armchair. Celestine flops down at his feet.

"Why did it have to be you?" Phee asks.

Braden, not understanding the question, doesn't try to answer.

She bends over an antique cedar chest, inserting a heavy, old-fashioned key into the lock. A fragrance of old linen and lavender wafts upward when she lifts the lid.

"My grandfather left the shop to me, along with all of the instruments he built, and all of his clients. There are certain strings attached. When I came to talk to you, after your accident, I told you that you have to play. I didn't tell you why."

Braden's throat is dry. A sense of something heavy compresses the air.

Phee kneels in front of his chair, a book in her hands. It is clearly old, the binding a faded green. Drawn by curiosity and dread, Braden watches her turn the pages, catching glimpses of handwritten transactions.

Thomas McCullough, violin, Derry, Ireland, 1 June 1822.
Daniel Marcus, violin, London, 1 November 1884.
Julia Weisel, viola, Berlin, 15 August 1901.

Some of the names he recognizes, well-known violinists and cellists. Others he has never heard of. As the pages turn, the handwriting changes, once, twice. Phee stops on the last page. He sees his own name, the last written, blank spaces below it.

Braden Healey, cello, Seattle, 5 January 1990.

Only a transaction record. Nothing unusual or terrifying about that, and yet he feels the jaws of a trap closing around him.

"This book was my grandfather's. It was his father's before him, and his father's before that. A long, unbroken line of luthiers passing lore down from father to son. My father has no interest in music or instruments, and so it fell to me."

"Did you want to be a luthier?"

"I wanted to build and repair instruments."

"Isn't that what a luthier does?"

"Ordinary luthiers, yes. My family line has other . . . responsibilities. This book was used to keep records only of certain—special—instruments. Not all were entered here."

Braden registers this. "My cello. The maker's mark, the color of the varnish, all indicate Stradivarius. You're telling me it's not?"

"It is, and it isn't."

Another cryptic comment that answers nothing. Phee wraps the book in a towel and locks it back in the trunk. She rifles through folders in a desk drawer, draws out a single sheet of paper, and holds it out to him. Braden stares at it, his hands locked together in his lap.

"No point in resisting. Fate has caught us up." She tries to laugh, but he reads only regret and sadness in her eyes.

Braden takes the paper.

The first thing he sees is his own name scrawled at the bottom. It barely looks like his signature, his twelve-year-old self still laborious at a task that has since become as automatic as breathing. Even with his numb fingers, his signature always comes out the same.

He reads:

I, Braden Healey, being of sound mind and purpose, do solemnly swear to enter into a forever bond with this Cello. I understand that the consequences of breaking my oath are unpredictable, and possibly dire. I will keep her, care for her, and play her, until such time as death parts us.

Braden Healey

"Your grandfather was a great luthier," Braden says, "but a crazy one."

"That's the easy answer." Phee walks away to look out a window.

"Surely you don't believe this shit?" When she doesn't answer, he presses on, stumbling over his own words. "Things happen. Musicians sell their instruments, acquire new ones."

"Not this musician, not this instrument. Not any of the musicians on that list or their instruments, all the way back to 1822 and probably before that."

The weight of what she's saying crushes the air out of his lungs, raises a cold sweat on the back of his neck. "If there's any truth to what you're saying, then Lilian and Trey are dead, not because I was absent and drinking but because I wasn't playing the cello."

He waits for her to deny this, to admit that the whole idea is out of the question. Instead, she makes a strangled sound, half sob, and says nothing. She's a strong woman, not given to dramatics, and her emotion shakes him more than anything she's said so far.

"Oh, come on, Phee. There's no logic to any of this! I blame myself for their deaths because I should have been there. Not because some magical curse befell them. You don't really believe that. You can't."

Allie, he thinks. *If a curse exists, then Allie is in danger.*

Phee turns to face him, her back pressed against the window, a creature at bay. Tears track down her cheeks, and she lets them flow with no attempt to wipe them away.

"You stopped playing. I tried to warn you."

Braden laughs, a wild, twisted sound. He holds up his hands. "The curse came before the not playing. What do you want from me? My fingers feel like there's cotton between them and anything they touch. I can't play."

"Even so," she whispers. "Even so."

He tries to steady his heartbeat, his breathing.

"This is crazy! All that shit about Paganini selling his soul to the devil? The idea that Stradivari soaked his woods in blood or in a waterfall before crafting his instruments, all of it is bullshit! Science says the mystical Stradivari secret was probably all about the varnish made by a local chemist. There's no curse, Phee."

Her back stiffens, she moves away from the window. "We're not talking about Paganini or Stradivari. We are talking about the MacPhee luthiers and you and the contract you signed for your cello."

"And that your grandfather laid some sort of curse on me."

"He never laid a curse on you. You broke the contract."

"That's ridiculous."

"Is it?" She flings the words at him, a challenge.

He throws up both hands to deflect them.

Celestine rumbles a protest and goes to Phee's side, protective now, the fur along his spine raised.

Grief and rage heat Braden's skin. "Music was everything to me, do you hear? Everything I had, everything I was! I'm nothing without it. Nothing! And you have the nerve to stand there and tell me that I'm cursed *because* I don't play?"

The room is too small. Braden stumbles toward the door, but Celestine intercepts him, a growl rumbling in his chest.

"Celestine," Phee commands. "Come here."

Celestine doesn't come. He bares his teeth, still growling. Braden steps back, cautious. When the dog doesn't move, he retreats another step, and then another.

Phee is weeping, and Braden feels like a brute. He can't take back anything he's said. There's nothing he can do to fix any of this. "Listen. I know you're just relaying some message from your grandfather—"

She shakes her head, denying, takes a steadying breath.

"I used to be like you. I loved the old man, but I thought it was all superstitious insanity. What difference did it make to an instrument who played it? As long as it was well cared for, how could it possibly matter?"

She stops. Takes a breath.

"And?"

"I was wrong. There was this other guy on my list who sold his violin—"

"People sell their instruments, Phee. Every day, for God's sake. No great tragedy befalls them."

"Out of all of the instruments he made and sold, my grandfather left me six to take care of. Your cello, and five violins. And the guy who sold his violin—"

"I don't want to hear it."

"You asked why I started drinking. I'm trying to tell you."

Braden presses his hands to his temples. His head is going to explode. Memories creep and crawl in and out of the dark space inside him like flies, like maggots. The more Phee talks, the more likely it is they'll get out. He can't have that.

"Don't!" he shouts. "Don't tell me some coincidental horror story and try to connect it to mine."

Her tears, he sees, are not weakness but strength. She feels what she feels, and does what she needs to do, anyway. "I need to tell you a story about your cello, about why she needs to be protected."

"Oh my God. She is protected. She's safe and warm and cared for. Allie's been playing her. I know everything I need to know—"

"You don't, actually. He said, if you should ever put aside the cello, I should tell you this. I'm not going to leave you alone until you hear it, so you might as well sit."

Braden hesitates, but the dog decides for him. He's not going anywhere without permission.

"My grandfather fought in World War Two," Phee begins. "He called it the Great Evil. He was a musician. A craftsman. How must that violence and destruction have marked him? He wouldn't talk about the war itself, only of the aftermath.

"He told me about bones and gas chambers and tattoos and mass graves. And he told me about Hitler's instrument collection. He targeted fine violins—Stradivari, Amati, Guarneri . . . the Nazis stole and collected them, the same way they collected art.

"Some of the soldiers took pleasure in torture, and how easy is it to torture a musician? To destroy her instrument in front of her eyes, to mutilate his hands. Musicians in the concentration camps were forced to play while others were marched into the gas chambers, or to provide weekly concerts for their captors.

"My grandfather said there was nothing he could do about the dead, but the instruments and the surviving musicians, that was different.

"After the war, before he and my grandmother immigrated here, he set up a repair shop in London. Many came to his shop asking him to help them. Most had lost everything—homes, money, family. There was no replacing an instrument that had been in the family for generations, one built by the masters. Some brought instruments to be repaired. Violins, violas, cellos, guitars—instruments that had survived concentration camps and bombings.

"He did much of this work for free. To restore what was lost, to help them heal.

"Some—some brought him fragments. 'This is what is left of my Guarneri,' they would say. 'Can you help me?' And he would build a thing that was both new and old, marked by the scars of the war but made beautiful again. He did this work at low cost, his repayment, he said, for Ireland's staying out of the war."

Phee pauses. Her face has a faraway look, as if remembering, and her voice fades.

"And my cello is one of these?" Braden asks.

"Yes . . . and no. The cello is made of fragments. Stradivarius, yes, and Amati and Guarneri. He said she had a soul. Here are the words he made me memorize:

"'This cello carries the soul of a woman murdered in the gas chamber, the soul of a gypsy shot like a dog in the street. She has been beloved, she has been abused, she has suffered the touch of evil. I promised her, when I coaxed the pieces into one, that she would be ever loved, that if she would give of her music, she would not be passed from hand to hand but cherished by one musician and one only. And so I made the boy swear an oath to me when he bought her.'"

Braden stares at Phee. He wants to deny this, all of this. A cello cannot have a soul, and yet he has always felt that his does. He tries to shake off the mood Phee has created with questions and logic.

"Wait. You said the MacPhee luthiers have been creating these . . . contracts . . . between musicians and instruments for generations, long before the war. So this is just a bullshit story, meant to make me feel guilty."

"I'm telling you what he told me," she says. "Some of the MacPhee specials were built from scratch. Some were pieced together as was your cello. All of them, he said, carried a soul. Whenever he spoke of the cello, he became more . . . intense . . . than when he spoke of the others. You remember your oath?"

"I remember."

He stands, one hand on the warm wood of the cello, feeling that she is already a part of him and he a part of her, and it is easy to lift the other hand and repeat after the strange old man, "I swear to love and cherish this cello as a part of my own soul. I swear to play her until the day of my death. If I should break my oath, the consequences be on me and my children."

Braden, in the first heady rush of falling in love, had barely registered the solemnity of the oath. Of course he would love the cello and play her as long as they both should live.

His mother, practical and disapproving, had rolled her eyes, tolerating this foolishness as the eccentricity of a master maker, even as she must have dimly understood that she herself was under some kind of spell or she would never have consented to the shift from violin to cello in the first place.

"I know how it sounds," Phee says. "When he first told me this tale, I asked so many questions, but he would tell me no more. He wouldn't tell me by what craft or magic he believed he had put the cello together. He never told me what dark magic he believed he had invoked that any of the instruments should carry a soul. But he made me promise I would hold you to your oath. You, and the others on my list. So here I am, and here you are, and the only question is, What do we do now?"

"We do nothing," Braden says. "Because there's nothing to be done. Even if this wild fairy tale were true, which it can't possibly be, my hands don't work and I can't play. Lilian and Trey are still dead. I don't suppose the old man suggested a remedy for any of this?"

"He would say that you must play again."

"Which I can't."

"Are you certain? There's nothing that can be done?" She crosses the room, takes his right hand in both of hers.

Braden looks at her hands, strong for a woman. Calluses on the fingertips, the nails short. He can feel her touch on the back of his hand, on the part of his palm that adjoins his wrist, but on his upper palm, and where her fingers touch his, he feels only pressure.

"I went to physical therapy for a while. Then occupational therapy. I even saw a shrink. Somebody, somewhere, thought that might be helpful."

"Was it?"

"I learned how to make my hands work for basic tasks. It didn't bring me back my music."

"Nerves regenerate slowly. There have been cases—"

The hope in her voice hurts more than his familiar relationship with despair. He jerks his hand away. "It's been eleven years, it's not coming back. And I know what you're going to say next. I could still play. I tried that. It sounded like a five-year-old child. And that's what really set me to drinking, if you want to know. That horrible noise, where the music used to live. I can't—I just can't."

He gets to his feet. "I have to get out of here. Please move. Let me go."

"I'll give you a ride."

"No. Please." He needs his feet on the sidewalk with the stink and blare of the busy city around him. Anywhere away from Phee's mesmerizing eyes and the timbre of her voice and the creepy sensation that the old luthier is looking over his shoulder.

"I'll find my own way. I'm sorry," Braden says, to Phee or the dog or the ghost of the luthier, or maybe all of them. "I'm sorry."

Chapter Seventeen

BRADEN

Braden takes a bus, gets off and transfers to another, letting the familiar reality of bodies and noise jolt him back to what is real. This. The hard, cramped seat. The dirty windows. His neighbor with the sharp elbow and the earbuds, exuding an aroma of pot into his environment like a skunky atomizer.

By the time he walks home from the last bus stop through darkness, a cold drizzle soaking through his clothing, he's back to familiar, sharp-edged facts.

The cello is a thing of wood and strings with no emotions to be wounded. She does not carry the souls of musicians broken and murdered during the war.

His hands will not be magically healed. The disaster and tragedy in his life has not been caused by a curse. The disembodied music he keeps hearing must be stress-induced psychosis or some weird form of alcohol withdrawal.

Allie is his whole focus now. Maybe she'll never love him, never forgive him, but that is not the point. He needs to see that her life doesn't get sucked into the ruin that has claimed the rest of her family.

Tomorrow he'll get her set up for survivor benefits and counseling. He'll tackle Trey's room. He'll call Lil's attorney and go over the will.

If he can get inside the house. If he can find Allie.

Hoping against hope that maybe she's made it home, he knocks. Rings the doorbell. Wonders if the neighbors are watching him, locked out of his own house. If they remember the last time he stood there, a supplicant at his own door, begging. The memory is vivid in his own mind.

His key won't go into the lock. Because he's drunk, maybe, so he tries again. And still it doesn't fit. He sees the sawdust then, telltale on the porch, and knows what she's done. Changed the locks. Not given him a key.

"Lili! Open up!"

He rings the doorbell. Knocks. Then rings again.

He fumbles with his cell phone, calling hers, and then the house phone, listening to it ring and hearing his own voice through the door as he leaves a message.

"For the love of God, Lilian, let me in. We need to talk."

The killing silence continues, retribution. Braden stumbles around the back of the house, tosses a pebble at the bedroom window, calls her name softly, not so drunk that he can't be humiliated by the thought of the neighbors knowing what she's done.

Still no answer.

And then the back door swings open, and Allie stands there, eyes wide with sleep and confusion.

"Daddy? Did you lose your key?"

"That's exactly it, little bird."

He hugs her, tight, and picks her up to carry her to bed.

And the next morning . . .

The next morning he'd left without saying goodbye to either of the kids. He couldn't face them, couldn't bear to tell them he was leaving.

This time there's no Allie inside to rescue him and let him in. Maybe there's a hidden key. He looks under the doormat, the flowerpot, and

Kerry Anne King

when he doesn't find one, he is half grateful that Lil was smart enough not to stash a key in the obvious places. She would have left a spare key somewhere, though, in case one of the kids got locked out.

Which leaves the neighbors. Damn it. He knows which one of them it will be. Steeling himself for the encounter, he knocks on Mrs. Jorgenson's door.

She jerks it open midknock, covered from neck to ankles in a bathrobe, fuzzy slippers on her feet.

"Well, well. Come to borrow a cup of sugar, then?" Her gaze rakes over him, top to bottom.

He knows full well how he looks. Damp, disheveled, and drunken. It makes no difference that he's actually sober.

"Mrs. J., I've lost my house key. Any chance you could help me out?"

She stares at him, reprovingly, through her half glasses, lips pressed in a tight line.

"Are you drunk?"

"Not yet."

She sighs, as if he's asked her to drive him to Canada or help him bury a body. "How is that poor child doing?"

"She's managing."

"I told them they could leave her here, after the accident. Until her aunt could show up. I told the social worker straight up, I said, 'Are you going to let bureaucracy win over the needs of that poor child?' They said she was staying with a friend, but surely—"

"Do you have a key?" Braden asks, trying to cut this conversation short.

Mrs. Jorgenson makes a tsking sound with her teeth. "Poor thing. Life is a vale of tears, for certain. One thing after another." She turns away and leaves him shivering on the porch, but since she doesn't slam the door in his face, he's hopeful that she's gone to get a key.

A moment later she's back.

138

"Those kids missed you," she says. "I never agreed with Lilian kicking you out like that. How are the hands? Did they heal?"

A lump gathers in his throat at this completely unexpected kindness. He shakes his head, not trusting his voice, and accepts the key she drops into his palm.

"You need anything else? Because I'm heading off to bed."

"This is great. Thank you." He means for more than the key but doesn't know how to tell her, hoping she'll hear it in his voice.

The door closes between them with a small and final click, and he returns to a dark and empty house.

Nothing has changed. The bottle still sits on the counter where he left it. Music plays in his head. He's wet and shivering and miserable.

Phee is a brightness in his mind—an oasis—and that is yet another loss. He can't see her again, not after this. Can't go back to the Angels. He'll need to find a real AA group tomorrow. His list of things to do feels weighty and overwhelming.

Now, tonight, he needs to get rid of the bottle on the counter, pour it down the sink. Before Allie comes home. Before he succumbs to the comfort it offers. But when he picks it up, he hesitates. It won't hurt to smell it. A small allowance for everything he's been through today.

His hands are only too ready to open the bottle. He lifts it to his nose and breathes in, deep, the rich, seductive smell of it flooding his senses.

Maybe just one swallow before he sends it down the drain.

Such a shame to waste it.

It's been a hard day, he needs something to settle his nerves.

Basically medicinal.

The first swallow warms his throat, his belly. The second eases the knot of fear in his chest. By the third, he's no longer shivering, but the music is louder, more tormenting.

Bottle in hand, he walks into the music room and opens the case that imprisons the cello. Light gleams on burnished wood. With his eyes, he caresses the curves of her, the beautifully carved scrollwork, the silvery line of the strings.

"You."

The music in his head goes quiet, but he feels the presence, as if the cello is breathing.

"It's not my fault," he says, lifting the bottle to his lips and sucking in a long draught. "You know that, right?"

Silence.

His face is wet before he realizes he is weeping. "Damn you," he says. "Let me go."

The cello says nothing. What did he expect? He laughs, wildly, and leaves her there, settling down at the table with his bottle.

When his phone rings, he fumbles the answer button with an upsurge of relief, not checking the caller ID.

"Allie?"

"What is going on, Braden?" Alexandra's voice, not Allie's.

"I don't—"

"I just had a call from an officer. A police officer, Braden."

His heart stops. He feels like he's falling, can't find any words to ask the question that looms in his mind.

"Are you not watching her at all? My God. Arrested at a house party. My heart about stopped when they called me—"

"She's at a party?"

Braden starts laughing. It's totally the wrong response, but he has absolutely no control over the sounds coming out of his body. A heady relief floods him, from his toes to the top of his head. Not dead. Not murdered. Not in a ditch somewhere, just a teenage girl caught out at a party.

Such a normal, wonderful thing.

"This is not funny, Braden Healey! Are you drunk?"

She's right. It's not funny at all, but still he can't stop laughing.

"I am. Gloriously drunk. Yes."

"I see that nothing has changed. Put that poor girl on a plane and send her to me before she has a chance to ruin herself completely."

"Where is she?"

"That's the sort of thing you're supposed to know."

"But I don't. And they called you. So if you would kindly relay the information, since you are thousands of miles away and not available to rescue her, I will take care of it."

"You are not going to drive—"

"Hell no. Not driving. I'll call an Uber."

"Can you even write down the address?"

"Just a minute. Yes." He gets to his feet. The room tilts a little but then rights itself. Good. Not too drunk to manage.

He makes his way to the kitchen and opens what in any other house would be a junk drawer. In Lilian's kitchen, it's efficient organization, stamps, pens, a letter opener, notepaper, and other list management materials all neatly separated into compartments. There's even a to-do list, written in Lilian's precise hand.

Call yard care
Pick up dry cleaning
Schedule Trey's sports physical

He closes his eyes. Not enough alcohol on board to protect him from the blow.

"Braden?"

"Yeah. Here." He scribbles down the address while Alexandra continues with a tirade of bitter I-told-you-sos and then hangs up on her in midsentence. He checks for Allie's car, still missing from the garage. Just as well, he's got no business driving.

He books an Uber, makes himself coffee, and swallows it black and scalding.

By the time a car pulls into his driveway, he's able to walk in a straight line. He's had plenty of practice functioning under the influence and hopes for a quiet ride in the back seat, but his driver is nosy and eager. She leans across and opens the front passenger door. "You can ride up front! It's so much easier to have a conversation that way, don't you think?"

Braden considers closing the door and climbing into the back, but he can't bring himself to this level of rudeness. He hasn't been in the car for more than thirty seconds before he regrets his choice.

"I'm Val, and I just love doing this Ubering thing, you know? I get to meet such interesting people and go such interesting places! You, for example. I'd think you'd have your own car."

"I do," Braden lies, to hush her.

"Good for you, being responsible about drinking and driving. Going to a party, then? That's a beautiful neighborhood. I've been there."

Braden maintains his silence, but she doesn't seem to have heard that it takes two to have a conversation. A glance in his direction and she shakes her head.

"You're not *dressed* for a party."

Which reminds him that he's rain soaked and muddy, covered in dog hair, and probably encrusted in drool. Nope. Not dressed for a party. He checks through the emotional bandwidth available to him and discovers that he really doesn't care. He's exhausted. The warm haze of alcohol has turned into an irritant now that he's required to think and feel and act. Val's chatter is a discordant screeching.

"I'm a writer," she volunteers. "It's why I drive for Uber. I don't really need the money, you know. But I meet people and I see all of these different parts of the city, and I hear such fascinating stories!"

She waits expectantly, but Braden remains steadfastly silent.

Val is not a woman to take a hint.

"You, now, for instance." She glances over at him. "You don't look like somebody who would go to this neighborhood. You're a mystery. You could be an investigator, or a red herring, or even the bad guy . . ."

She sobers at her own words and glances at him again. "You're not, though, right? The bad guy?"

"I just need a ride, is all," Braden says.

The woman's jaw hardens, her body language shifting to what might be wariness or just a fit of the sulks because he won't play her game.

"Well, if you don't want to talk, let's have some music," she says after a drawn-out silence long enough for Braden to fervently wish himself into the back of an anonymous yellow cab and not about to be gossip or the villain of some mystery novel. His relief at the idea of music is short lived, as what fills the car is, of course, the last thing in the world he wants to listen to.

"I just love orchestra music, don't you?" Val asks. "So soulful. This is Beethoven, I think."

"Bach," Braden mutters under his breath.

"Pardon?"

"It's one of Bach's cello suites. Beethoven didn't write for cello."

"Really?" She sounds skeptical, and Braden lets it go. Let her believe what she wants. "Well, it's beautiful, whatever it's called."

Beautiful, yes. Tormentingly, hauntingly beautiful. Braden closes his eyes against it, which doesn't help, at all, just puts him on stage with the cello, the two of them creating this music in their own way, her soul and his, entwined . . .

"Here we are!" Val chirps.

Braden's eyes open on a towering, ugly brick house whose whole purpose is to shout that money lives inside. The wrought-iron gates are open, and two cop cars are parked in the cul-de-sac. Parents escort subdued kids out to an assortment of sleek and expensive vehicles.

He's been in houses like this, has rubbed elbows with the people who live in them. He didn't like them then, and he's pretty sure he's not going to like them now.

The idea of subjecting Allie to Val's curiosity makes him cringe, but he needs to get her home. Even if her car is here somewhere, neither of them is fit to drive. The irony of that strikes him. Like father, like daughter.

God. He can't let her turn out like him.

"Can you wait?" he asks as he gets out of the car.

"Happy to!" Val is in her element, probably, watching all of this human drama.

The woman haranguing one of the cops on the front porch would make a perfect stereotypical character for Val's book. Little black dress with artificially enhanced cleavage. Botox. Lips chemically plumped. Salon hair.

"What about the cars?" the woman is asking. "They are all leaving their cars here."

"They can't drive; they are intoxicated. I'm sure the parents will be back for the cars in the morning."

"I want them towed. Every single one of them. Trespassing."

"Ma'am, the cars are parked on the street. They are allowed to be there."

"This is outrageous."

"What is outrageous," the cop retorts, "is that you have fifty-two intoxicated minors in your house tonight."

Braden stands just below the steps, waiting for an opening. The woman turns to him, trying to raise her perfectly arched brows, her skin so taut they barely move.

"Yes? Can I help you?"

"I'm looking for my daughter."

The woman presses her lips together disapprovingly. "Maybe next time you could keep track of her so you don't have to come looking."

Braden opens his mouth, but thinks better of it and stands quietly waiting while the cop flips through pages of notes.

"Name?"

"Alexandra Healey."

"She's inside. She'll be charged with Minor in Possession."

"What does that mean, generally?" Braden asks.

"Drug and alcohol classes, community service. If she has no priors, it won't go to court." The cop frowns, taps his pencil on the page. "She doesn't have any priors, right? The name sounds familiar."

"Not that I know of." Braden wants only to go in and find Allie, picturing her drunk and frightened.

"Come with me," the cop says, and leads the way past the woman into the house.

Three girls huddle together on a sofa, arms around each other, tearstained and bleary eyed. A group of boys, all bravado, gather in the corner of the room, laughing as if it's all a big joke, but Braden can hear the undertones of anger and fear. And then his eyes find Allie, lying flat on her back on the floor. Ethan sits cross-legged beside her, his eyelids heavy.

Braden drops to his knees beside his daughter, cursing the whiskey. He needs a clear head for this. Allie is flushed, her forehead damp. Alcohol poisoning, or maybe she's overdosed on something, is unconscious, dying, dead. He checks her pulse. Steady. Her breathing is even.

"She's okay," Ethan says. "I'm looking out for her."

"This is looking out for her?" Braden snarls.

"Hey, man. Nobody's touched her."

"How many drinks has she had? What other drugs?"

"Just a couple drinks. She was tired. Just lay down right there and fell asleep."

"Did you bring her here? What were you thinking?" Braden feels his hands curl into fists. Protective fire burns in his chest.

"Hey, I didn't make her drink anything."

"You brought her here."

"Her idea." Ethan shrugs.

It would feel so amazingly good to wipe the smirk off that face with a fist. Braden feels the crunch, sees the entitled attitude give way to pain, *sees Mitch collapse backward into the snow . . .*

God. Not here, not now. He focuses on breathing, makes himself register details all around him. Shoes. A small stain on an otherwise pristine carpet. Allie's face, childlike and innocent despite the flush of alcohol on her cheeks.

He shakes her shoulder gently.

"Allie. Allie? Wake up, little bird."

Her eyes open, half-mast and clouded. "Daddy?"

His heart turns over in his chest. "I'm here, Allie."

"I want to go home." Her words are slurred.

She pushes herself up to sitting, closes her eyes. "Make it stop."

Braden puts a hand on her shoulder to steady her. She opens her eyes again, peers up at the officer. "I know you," she says.

"Thought your name was familiar," he replies. "I'm sorry to see you here."

Allie draws her knees up to her chin and hides her face.

"You know each other?" Braden looks from his daughter to the cop.

"I picked her up and took her to the hospital after the accident. Stayed with her until social services could get there." His tone sharpens. "Asked if I could call her dad, and she said he wouldn't answer. She'd already called, she said."

Braden has no answer to this, or to the wash of shame and guilt that threatens to swamp him.

He should have been there. He should have been with her.

The cop gets down on the floor by Allie, puts a hand on her shoulder. "So did you hear back from UW? Will you get in?"

"Doesn't matter," she slurs, still hiding her face.

"Of course it matters."

Her only response is a small sound of misery that tears what little of Braden's heart is still intact into confetti.

"I'm not going to charge you," the cop says. "This time. Because of what you've been through." His gaze drills into Braden. "The least you could do is be sober."

There's no response for that.

"Are you driving?"

Braden shakes his head. "Got an Uber. It's waiting."

The cop grunts. "Well, at least there's that. Kid deserves better, you ask me."

Braden agrees. Wants to thank him, but his throat has constricted into a knot.

"C'mon, little bird," he manages. "Let's get you up."

In slow motion, every movement exaggerated, Ethan gets on the other side of Allie, and the two of them haul her up onto her feet. She sways a little, but she's able to stand, to walk, with support.

"You," the cop says to Ethan. "Sit down. You're not going anywhere."

"I'm just helping her out to the—"

"You are going to sit right back down, and then I'm taking you in."

"I'll call you, Allie," Ethan says. "As soon as I make bail."

Braden keeps moving, an arm around Allie's waist, holding her up, guiding her toward the door. She doesn't resist. The Uber is still there, waiting, for which he supposes he's grateful.

"Oh dear, oh dear, oh dear," Val clucks, getting out and opening the door to the back seat. "Can I help?"

"We're fine." Braden buckles Allie's seat belt, assailed by memories of settling her into a car seat, of her first time in a lap belt. He climbs into the back beside her.

"Is she going to puke, do you think?" Val hovers beside the still open door. "I'd have to charge you the cleaning fee . . . Here. I have a grocery sack somewhere . . ." She disappears for a moment. The trunk opens, closes, and she comes back with a plastic bag. "Just in case."

"I'm fine," Allie says, but she takes the bag, anyway, clutching it in both hands when the car starts to move.

"Teenagers, right?" Val chatters. "Went through this with all three of my boys. Don't worry about the MIP, it's not a big thing. Won't go on her record. More of a hassle than anything, but she has you to help her through it. Scary, though, isn't it, when they get old enough to just go off and do things on their own?"

He lets Val drone on, her voice almost a comforting backdrop to the tangled weave of his thoughts and emotions. Allie dozes, her head on his shoulder, and he lets himself pretend, just for the moment, that she's happy to have him here, that she takes some comfort in his presence. When the car finally pulls up in front of the house, he wants to pick her up and carry her like a child, her head resting against his chest. He wants to ease her misery.

But he's had enough time to think on the way home to know that this is not the time for comforting.

"We're home, Allie. Time to wake up."

She stirs, blinks at him, bleary eyed and disoriented.

He walks around to her door. "Come on. Out you get."

"S'all spinny."

"That's what happens when you're drunk. Come on."

"Well, goodbye, then," Val calls after them. "Good luck!"

Braden waves but doesn't answer, keeping pace with Allie as she staggers up the sidewalk. She's shivering. Braden is shivering. A cold wind is blowing, and neither of them is wearing a jacket. Braden turns Mrs. J.'s key in the lock.

Lilian and the cello are waiting when the door opens.

"Really, Braden? I've been dead what, three weeks, and already you've let this happen?"

The cello underscores her words with a melancholy tune, not Bach anymore but an unknown melody in a minor key.

Allie's wavering feet stop, right at the edge of the stained white carpet.

"Make it stop."

"Best way to stop the room from spinning is to lie down and sleep it off," he says.

She shakes her head. "Not that. The music."

She makes a choking noise, presses both hands over her ears, and lurches up the stairs toward her room. Braden follows. Helps her off with her shoes, covers her with the blankets. He'd tucked her in this way as a child, only that was so very different. Her arms around his neck, the kiss on his cheek.

"I love you, Daddy."

She'd smelled then of soap and clean pajamas, not beer and smoke and sweat. Braden longs to smooth her forehead, to tuck her hair behind her ears, but she pulls the covers over her head and rolls onto her side, away from him.

Her breathing is fine, he reassures himself. She isn't unconscious. This isn't alcohol poisoning. Tomorrow he will talk to her about alcohol and genetics and why she must not go further down this path. For now, there's nothing he can do but keep an eye on her, let her sleep it off.

But worry trails after him as he moves like a sleepwalker through the house that is his, but not his, cello music swirling around him, heavy with memories.

The bottle waits on the kitchen counter where he left it, half empty, after Alexandra's call.

You might as well finish it. Your daughter hates you and you've already ruined her. What hope is there for either of you?

His hand closes around the bottle.

Just enough to get warm again. Just enough to take the edge off the guilt, off the tormenting sliver of the memory of violence.

He slams the bottle down onto the counter. Thud. And then slams it again. He hates the booze, loves it and hates it and is sick to death of it.

Allie needs him sober.

Holding his breath, he pours the rest of it down the sink and runs water to rinse it.

A hot shower, to warm him and stop this shaking. Sleep. He needs sleep. Things will be clearer in the morning.

The cello tries to draw him in as he passes the music room. "Leave me alone," he mutters. "This is your fault."

A hot shower warms his skin but not his insides and does nothing to stop either the music or his memories. He's still half intoxicated, although he can feel the hard edges of sobriety. Bed. The bed he used to share with Lilian. In the dark, he's not entirely sure she's not lying there, pretending she's asleep. He slides under the covers and into a memory.

A glance at the clock. God, it's two a.m. He's been playing the cello for hours.

Beside him, Lil's breathing is quiet and even, but something about the quality of her stillness warns him that she's awake.

She's curled in on herself, faced away from him. Not that this is new. She's been shutting him out this way for years now, waking or sleeping.

Braden goes along with her pretense. He's too full of music to talk now. He'll sleep. In the morning, he'll make it up to her, somehow.

But then the stillness of her shifts into slow shudders, and he realizes she is weeping silently, right there beside him in the bed but so very much alone. The sound of it tears his heart open, and he lays a hand on her shoulder, whispers, "What is it, Lili? Talk to me."

"You love her more," she whispers brokenly. "No matter what I do, you will always love her more."

"Who?" He runs through the faces of women he knows, searching for her meaning. Has he looked too long into someone's eyes, hugged someone too sincerely, lingered over a hand offered him on introduction?

"It's like you have a mistress. Only worse. She has no other commitments, no other life. Only you. Always there. Always wanting. How am I supposed to compete with that?"

Oh God. She means the cello.

A paralyzing bolt of fear hits him in the belly, and he says the first words that come to him. "You're not meant to compete with the cello. You can't."

A harsh sob is her response, and he understands, too late, too late, how she will take what he has just said.

"Lil, listen." He strokes her hair, tries to gather her into his arms, but she stiffens and pulls away from him.

"Don't take it that way," he pleads. "I meant it's not a competition. I love you. But music is what I am, Lili. You know that. You knew it when you met me."

"How could I know what that meant? I didn't know you'd always put her first. Over me. Over your children, Braden. Over all of us. The cello gets the best of you, and there's nothing left over for us."

He rolls over onto his back and stares up at the ceiling, which is dimly visible in the dark room, beginning to panic. He doesn't know how to explain, to make her see. "I love all of you. You can't compare—it's like apples and oranges."

"And which am I, then, Braden? An apple or an orange?"

"Lil—"

"I'm not a thing. I'm a human being. The cello is a thing. You spend more time with it—it, Braden, not her—than you do with me or the kids."

A defensive anger flares. "Music is my job, too, don't forget. It helps pay for your house and your clothes and the visits to your sister—"

"So get a different job."

The words have the effect of a bucket of ice water. He sits up, gasping, all of the oxygen in the room in sudden short supply. "You can't mean that. What else would I possibly do?"

"I don't care. Something that doesn't steal your soul away from me. Because I can't go on like this."

"What is that supposed to mean?"

"It's not secret code."

"I'll do better. I'll play less. I'll—"

151

"You've tried that. It takes all of you. Even when you're with me, you're really with the cello. I can't deal with that anymore. I want you to give it up."

"That's insane! I'm a musician."

"Fine. Be a musician, just be one elsewhere."

"You can't mean that. It's late. Things will look different in the morning." He sits up, stares at the defensive line of her back, wants to shake her.

"I'm done," she says. *"I've put up with this since we got married. You have a week to think about it."*

"Lil!"

"You heard me."

"Please," Braden says now, aloud into the darkness. It's a prayer, a plea, to God, to his dead wife, to his memories, to the cello, to Allie. He doesn't expect an answer. He's trapped now, just as he was trapped then.

This bed, Lilian's bed, feels hostile. Exhausted as he is, he'll never be able to sleep here. Scooping up a pillow and a blanket, he heads for the less comfortable anonymity of the couch. On the way, he pauses in Allie's doorway. She lies on her belly, arms and legs flung wide, snoring softly, and he passes her by. Passes the call of the cello.

He settles himself on the couch and finally, finally, feels sleep coming to meet him.

He's backstage in a concert hall, waiting for a solo performance. The familiar nerves of anticipation thrum through him, but the cello answers with a deep and grounding note.

"The two of us, together," she reminds him. *"You and me, forever."*

And then it's time, and as he carries her on stage, he pauses, aware that this is a dream. He can wake now, if he chooses. But the lure of music, the sensation of his fingers flexible and completely sensate, the desire of the cello, the rustling expectation of the crowd, are too powerful.

And so he sits at center stage in a soft circle of light, and begins to play. The cello responds as she always does, and the two of them become one, a new thing that is more than either man or cello, channeling music into the range of hearing of the listening crowd he can sense in the darkness but never see.

At the center of the music, he is whole. All of his confusion—his anger, his grief, his guilt—turns to gold, a process of alchemy. He hears the audience sigh and weep as the music washes over them, feels their hearts lighten through the release, knows that this is what he was called into the world to do.

Chapter Eighteen

ALLIE

Allie wakes to music, Bach's cello Suite in C Minor, the Braden Healey version. No two cellists play it alike, no two cellos sound alike, and she knows the voice of this cello under the touch of her father's hands.

Her head throbs, dully, as she pushes herself up to sitting.

She's still fully dressed. For a moment she's disoriented, and then the memories come back in bits and pieces. The party. The cops. Her father and the Uber and Ethan.

Ethan. Where is Ethan? Did he get arrested? Did she?

The music is an affront to her aching head and to her heart. What the hell, anyway? Braden must be playing the recording to punish her for getting drunk. Or maybe he's drunk himself. Either way, she needs to make it stop.

Shivering with the transition from warm bed to the nighttime chill, she pads out of her room and follows the music. The door to the music room is open.

Light from a streetlamp spills in through open blinds, pooling on the floor, illuminating her father and the cello. His eyes are closed. His face looks otherworldly and ethereal in the dim light, his lips parted. His body is fluid, graceful, he and the cello one soul, the music swirling around them, around Allie, real and true and not the product of a fevered imagination.

Time ceases to exist as the music draws her in. She stands there long enough for him to reach the third movement. Long enough for her bare feet to grow icy on the hardwood floor. Long enough for guilt and grief to escape from the spell that holds her entranced. She remembers what she has done and what he has done and why the music has to stop.

"Braden." She whispers his name first. Then, louder: "Braden!"

His body jerks. His eyes fly open. The bow clatters to the floor.

He stares at her, at the cello, as if he's never seen either of them before.

The music lingers, just for an instant, and then it slips off into the corners of the room and disappears into the shadows.

The loss of it stuns her. It's hard to breathe. She's aware of tears on her face, of the pain building in her chest, powerless to stop any of it.

"What are you *doing*?" Her rising voice breaks on a sob.

"I was dreaming," her father says, as if he's having to invent each word as he says it. "I was dreaming I could play, that my hands were healed, that—"

A choking sound in his throat. A great, shuddering breath, a single sob, torn up from the depths of him. His skin is ashen.

"You were playing like you used to." Allie's voice is accusing, sharp. "Flawless. I thought it was the recording."

He shakes his head. His lips shape the word "no," but no sound comes out.

"You lied!" All of the years of hurt and rage come tearing out of her at once. "Your hands are fine. You just needed an excuse so you could go be an alcoholic."

An excuse to leave me, her heart cries.

"No," he says. "My hands—"

"There's nothing wrong with your hands."

"They're numb. I can't—"

"Bullshit. Mom told me. It's all in your head. The doctors said."

"That's not true!"

"Play," she orders harshly. "Play it again."

He shakes his head. "I can't."

"You can. You just did. Do it!" She picks up the bow and shoves it at him.

"Allie. Stop it!"

His hands are shaking. She can see the torment written on his face as clearly as if he stood in a ring of hellfire, but she stares him down, rage filling the emptiness in her belly.

She thrusts the bow at him again. "Play!"

He accepts the bow, draws it across the strings, tentative. Plays the first few notes of the Bach, and they are discordant and wrong.

"Stop it! Play it right!" She hurls the words at him, weapons, but his hands fall to his sides, useless.

"Maybe you could play something, Allie. I saw the music on the stand. I've always hoped—"

"No! I learned to play because of you. I wanted to be like you. I thought maybe you'd come home and be proud of me."

"I *am* proud of you."

"Right. You don't even know me. You didn't show up to meet me."

A wracking sob doubles her over, nearly drops her to her knees. Her father doesn't move. Just sits there, frozen.

When she can catch her breath, get control of her voice, Allie straightens and delivers her condemnation. "I hate the cello, and I hate Bach, and I hate you. I want the cello out of the house. Get rid of it."

Her father looks like she's stabbed a knife into his chest and twisted it.

"I can't. You don't understand." His lips are white.

"No, you don't understand. I need it gone. Craigslist. Goodwill. Whatever. Just get it out of this house."

There's an empty, dead look in his eyes, and she has the horrible thought that she's killed him, too, along with the rest of the family, but still the ugliness pours out of her.

"Mom was right about you all along. You're a terrible father, a horrible, selfish human being. Are you done? Can we sleep now?"

"Are you sure?" he asks, very quietly. "That you want the cello gone?"

"Oh my God! Yes. I'm sure."

Allie turns away from the expression on his face, from the reproach of the cello, but music follows her to bed and into restless dreams of destruction. In her dreams, she wears a military uniform and stomps on the cello with her boots, splintering the wood beneath her feet. Strings snap and break. A wailing of agony fills her ears. This is not enough, and she drenches it with gasoline, lights it with a match. And still the perfect tones of the C Minor sarabande drift upward with the smoke of its burning.

Chapter Nineteen

BRADEN

Braden is afraid to sleep.

He craves the oblivion but is too shaken to risk another episode of sleep playing, or whatever the hell just happened. He feels shattered and shell shocked, the walls of the forbidden dark territory in his mind breached, memories scurrying like roaches, in and out of consciousness.

He paces the living room, unable to sit for more than a minute before grief and restlessness drive him back to his feet.

Phee's words and Allie's run counterpoint in his head, twining around each other, all wrapped in the song of the cello that will not stop.

You have to play.

There's nothing wrong with your hands.

Get rid of the cello. I want it out of this house.

You swore an oath.

In the wakeful dark, the oath and the curse take on weight and substance. As dawn breaks, at last, and light seeps into the room, Braden swallows scalding black coffee and anchors himself back into logic.

Allie is right. The cello has to go. He should have sold her years ago. One thing he knows for certain—he can't handle another midnight concert, and the only hope of repairing his relationship with Allie follows this path.

Allie is everything. All that is left of his life, and the only thing that matters. He wants to soften life for her this morning, but that's not the answer. If there's one thing he's an expert on, it's drinking, and what he does today in response to her drinking last night will have a lasting impact.

When he looks into her room, she's lying on her side, still asleep, and he steels himself for what he is about to do.

"Morning, sunshine."

She moans and pulls the pillow over her head.

He lifts the pillow away from her. Opens the blinds to let light pour in.

"Go away," Allie croaks, retreating under the covers.

"It's time to get up. School today."

She doesn't answer. Doesn't move. God, if she hates him already, she's really going to hate him now.

"Come on, Allie." He strips the blankets off her and dumps them at the foot of the bed.

"Seriously?" Her eyes open and try to focus. She covers them with her hands. Swallows hard.

"Trash can's by the bed if you need to puke."

"Sleep."

"No, you need to get up and go to school. Sit up."

She struggles upright, squinting against the light. Her little moan as she puts her head in her hands goes straight to his heart, but he holds the line.

"No school. I'm sick."

"No, you're hungover. Which is not an excuse for missing school. Now—do you need the bucket or can you walk to the bathroom?"

"Give me the blankets." She reaches for them again.

Braden bundles them up and dumps them in the far corner of the room.

"Get up, Allie."

"I hate you."

"All the more reason to go to school. It's a beautiful day." He opens the window. Fresh air flows in, smelling of rain and wet grass.

Allie shivers, presses her palms over her eyes. "Oh my God! What are you *doing*?"

But she swings her legs over the side of the bed.

"There's ibuprofen in the bathroom. Take two and drink some water. Have a shower. If you're going to drink, you need to face up to the hangover."

She mutters something he doesn't understand and runs for the bathroom. He's won round one, but this fight is far from over. Despite the fan, he can hear her heaving, and his own stomach rolls in sympathy.

Even so, he moves on to round two.

When he hears the shower shut off, he stands outside the door and calls, "Breakfast is ready. Come get it while it's hot."

"Are you fucking kidding me?"

"Breakfast. Then school."

He walks back to the kitchen, holding his breath. This is the tricky part. He doesn't know what he'll do if she retreats to her room and barricades herself behind a locked door. She's too big for him to drag her anywhere, and he's not prepared to kick in a door.

But she walks into the kitchen looking pale and fragile. Slumps into a chair. Braden sets a plate in front of her.

"Eat."

"I hate you."

"Best thing for a hangover. This is the one thing I'm an expert on. Trust me."

She picks up a piece of toast and nibbles at the corner. Small victory, but he'll take it.

He sits down across from her, takes a bite of his own eggs and toast, even though he's far from hungry.

"Now, do you want to tell me where you've been all week?"

"School."

"No. You haven't."

Allie's eyes meet his, then drop away. She pokes at the eggs with her fork. "I thought we agreed that you weren't going to do this parental bullshit."

"Because you were going to be responsible and not need a parent."

"Fine. I'll go to school."

"Breakfast first."

"Whatever!"

She swallows coffee. Breaks off a piece of bacon. Progresses to eggs. When she's cleared about half her plate, she pushes it away and looks at him again. Her eyes are clearer, her color better. There's also more fight in her.

"Can I go now?"

"Sure. Get dressed. Then school."

Braden cleans up the kitchen while she changes, dreading the next phase of his plan. Maybe he should stop here. Count this as progress and let her off the hook.

But that's the cowardly thing. When the cry of outrage comes, he's ready.

Allie stalks into the kitchen, fully dressed, still a little pale and puffy but with makeup on and her hair combed.

"Where are my *car keys*?"

"Better question. Where is the car?"

He meets her glare with one of his own.

"None of your business where it is. It's my car!"

"And if the cop last night hadn't been so sympathetic, you'd be without your license for a year."

"You can't—"

"I can. We could get you a bicycle, if that would make you feel better."

The exaggerated shock and horror that meets this statement would be funny if it wasn't pounding the nails into the coffin of their relationship.

"Now, since the car isn't here, if we're going to make it to school on time, we need to get going."

"What do you mean, we?"

"I'm walking you to school."

"How about you walk me to my car—"

"I'll be walking you to school for a while, I think. Your driving privileges have been revoked."

"I don't believe this!"

"Which part?"

"Any of it! I bought the car with my own money! I've been driving to school for over a year!"

"Yes? And how much school did you skip? How many parties did you get arrested at?"

"That's not fair! None of this is fair!"

"Let's go." Braden walks into the living room, jingling the keys in his hand. He hears her footsteps behind him, hears her stop short when she sees the cello case waiting by the door.

"Maybe you can drag me to school, but you can't make me go to orchestra. I'll—"

"You want me to get rid of it, right? You need to go to school, I need the car. I'll walk you to school and then go get the car. I will also pick you up after school. You're officially grounded."

She stands there, like he's hit her with some sort of stun gun. All of the breath whooshes out of her in one long sigh.

Her eyes meet his for a heartbreaking moment before she turns away.

"Fine."

Watching her walk out the door, Braden thinks she looks smaller, defeated, even though she just got what she said she wanted. Doubt hits him. The cello weighs a ton.

Dead weight, he thinks. It's a long walk to the school, and he's feeling less than marvelous himself.

"You could text me the address. Of the car," he says, after he locks the door and takes a few running steps to catch up with his daughter.

"Parked on Ballard, outside Caffe Umbria."

"Unless it's been towed," Braden says. "By the way, any particular reason why you don't return any of my texts?"

"I lost my phone."

"I'll get you a new one."

"No, thanks."

"You're kidding, right? How does a kid navigate without a phone?"

His question is met by silence.

"I would like you to have a phone so we can communicate. I need to know where you are and when you're going to be late."

She glances at him out of the corner of her eye. "Are you going to track me, then?"

"I was thinking you could text me."

"Oh please. Ethan says all cell phones are just tracking devices."

Braden bites off a retort, shifts the weight of the cello case to his other hand. *Choose your battles, Healey.* School today. With any luck, Ethan didn't get bailed out last night. Ordering Allie to stay away from him will push her into mutiny.

"Look. I don't want to track you. I want you to let me know when you're going to be home late. I'd like to trust you. I worry."

"You are so full of shit!"

"Elaborate."

Allie stops walking and turns to face him. "What's so different now? I mean, you're fine going for, what, eleven years at a time without knowing where I am, and now you want to know every single minute?"

"I always wanted to know where you were, Allie. I just—"

She starts walking. "Right. I know. You were drunk. Forget it."

There's an opportunity here, of some sort, to teach her about addiction, but he doesn't have the heart for it, and they walk in silence until they're a block from the school. Allie stops walking.

"You can leave me here."

Braden keeps right on moving. After a minute, she runs to catch up with him, stage-whispering furiously. "You are not walking me in the door like I'm in kindergarten!"

"I am walking you in the door."

"I said I'd go! You don't trust me."

"Should I?"

"All right. You've made your point."

"What's your first class?" he asks.

"You are fucking kidding me."

"Not remotely. First class."

"It's English. And you are not walking me to my classroom. You're not even allowed in the school without a pass. I'll go to English if you just leave me the hell alone. And get rid of the cello."

Braden can feel the waves of fury wafting off her. God, he's bad at this. Doing everything wrong.

"I take your word as a contract," he says. "Have a good day, Allie. I'll pick you up after school."

Curious stares and whispers follow them to the front door, and when he opens it for her, Allie stalks away from him without a backward glance.

Braden wants to stand on guard at the door, but he knows he can't push it that far. Also, there's no point. There are other doors. Not a thing prevents her from walking through the school and out the back. He has no power, no leverage. He's barely her father, certainly not her jailer, and the time for enforcing parental control is long past.

The cello by now weighs a ton, and the music in Braden's head has switched from Bach to dirges. By the time he makes his way to Ballard Avenue, his arms are aching and the blister that started on his heel yesterday has worked its way into a full-on throbbing pain. He deserves it, of course, every bit as much as he deserves his headache and the way the light spikes into his skull.

When he sees Allie's car, still parked in front of the coffee shop, relief and resolve join forces. He loads the cello into the hatch, wishing it was an honest-to-God old-fashioned trunk he could lock her into, like a mobster hiding a body. What he's about to do is going to be hard enough without listening to her pleading.

He slides in behind the wheel, adjusts the seat. It's been years since he actually drove. Hasn't owned a car since he moved out of Lilian's house. It's been buses and taxis and the occasional Uber.

Like riding a bicycle, he tells himself as he shifts into reverse and eases out of the parking space. You never forget.

From the back, the cello ratchets the music up a notch, a funeral dirge.

There is no curse, he chants to himself. *The cello is inanimate. Allie comes first.* He switches on the radio and scans through the channels for classic rock, turning up the volume until it thumps in his ears.

Morning rush-hour traffic occupies his full attention. He wants to put distance between home and the scene of his upcoming crime. It takes him over an hour to get to Everett, and longer to find the Amtrak station. He pays for parking. The cello case feels like it's been loaded with rocks when he goes to lift it out of the hatch, but the music has gone silent.

Braden lugs the case into the station, then stands there for a few minutes, long enough for any bystanders to have moved on. Then he steps back outside and sets the cello down next to the front doors. He fakes a call on his phone, wandering away from the cello as if deep in conversation, then quickens his steps and almost runs back to the parking lot.

It feels like abandoning a baby outside a church. Surely somebody will find her and sell her. She'll be played. If he sells her himself, he'll always know where she is, be tempted to go back for her. This is the only way he can think of, short of destroying her, to remove her from his life forever.

Music swells in his head.

Allie's song, this time. The one he wrote when she was a baby and played for her every night after he'd tucked her into bed and given her a kiss. The song that started every practice session for him, the one that steadied his nerves and transitioned him into his best mind-set for practice. He needs to make it stop, but it follows him all the way home, and after he parks the car, it drives him back out onto the street, onto a bus, and into the nearest bar.

Chapter Twenty

ALLIE

School is a nightmare, as Allie knew it would be.

She can't think, can barely manage to hold herself together. She wants to go back to bed, to bury herself under the covers and seek oblivion. Waking to find her father playing the cello last night, playing like he'd never damaged his hands, like he'd never left her, was worse in a way than the phone call about Mom and Trey.

For just a moment, she'd believed that music had come home with her father, and that the accident was all a dream.

Instead, she now knows once and for all that he never loved her, that he's a hypocrite and a monster, and that everything her mother ever said about him was true.

How she used to love him, adore and idolize him. She never believed what her mother had said, that he was faking about his hands. Why would he do that? But now there's proof.

An uneasy twist in her belly reminds her of the expression on his face, of the sound he made after he woke, but she dismisses it. She saw the bottle in the kitchen trash. He was drinking again last night and has no right to get on her case for doing what he does all the time.

Forcing her to go to school today was just cruel. Her head hurts, the nausea is creeping back in. Curious gazes and whispers follow her. People will be talking about last night. They'll be talking about her father walking her to school.

She searches the crowded hallway for a glimpse of Ethan with equal parts hope that he'll be here and that he won't. He was meant to be an escape, and now he's another complication. There's no sign of him, and the press of kids propels her forward.

The buzzer rings for class just as she walks through the door into English. Steph, always the optimist, has saved her a desk. When she sees Allie, her face lights up in a smile and then goes straight to a frown.

"I thought maybe you were dead," she whispers when Allie slides into the seat and starts digging in her backpack for her books.

"I lost my phone," Allie says. "Don't be mad."

"It's been over a week! How hard would it have been to let me know? I worried."

"I'm sorry. It's just—"

"Girls, if I could have your attention," Mrs. Gardner cuts in. "Nice that you could join us, Allie," she adds, without even a hint of irony, as if it's normal for a kid with perfect attendance to skip a ton of school. Maybe it *is* normal, given the circumstances.

Mrs. G. doesn't create a scene, doesn't offer sympathy or give the others time to stare at her with pity. She just starts right in, asking questions about *Hamlet*, and it turns out Allie is up to speed after all, because she read the play the first week it was assigned, all in one sitting.

Her relief freezes in her chest when the discussion ends and the class begins taking turns reading lines out loud:

Gertrude: *Good Hamlet, cast thy nighted colour off,*
And let thine eye look like a friend on Denmark.
Do not for ever with thy vailed lids
Seek for thy noble father in the dust.
Thou know'st 'tis common. All that lives must die,

Passing through nature to eternity.
Hamlet: *Ay, madam, it is common.*
Gertrude: *If it be,*
Why seems it so particular with thee?

The next line is Allie's, and she can barely find her voice to read, "'Seems? I know not seems . . .'"

Heat rises in her cheeks, the walls start closing in. Her heart rattles against her ribs. She's going to choke.

"Sorry," she mumbles, grabbing up her backpack and her book. "I'm sorry." She flees the classroom, tripping over somebody's foot and almost falling. Once in the hall, she puts her back against a wall and bends over, trying to catch her breath.

A hand on her shoulder. A familiar voice. "Allie? Are you okay?"

Mr. Collins, her orchestra teacher. Three weeks ago, she would have welcomed him. Would have been in his office telling him all about everything. Now he is the last person at school she wants to see.

"I'm okay," she manages. "Just had a moment."

"Not surprising. I'm glad to see you. We've missed you at orchestra."

"Sorry."

She straightens up, drags her sleeve across her watering eyes. Takes a breath and then another.

"Nothing to be sorry about. We managed. Are you ready to come back?"

"I'm not coming back." She glances up at his face, expecting disappointment, surprised to see understanding.

"I get it."

"You do?"

"Sure. Music makes us vulnerable. You're not ready for that in a group setting right now."

He has the vulnerability part right, the rest all wrong.

"I'm not playing at all," she confesses, and he nods, as if he understands this, too.

"You will. It will come back."

His words catch her off guard. Not the lecture she was expecting. Not a grilling. It's like he's looked right into her soul and sees everything except the guilt.

She shakes her head, denying. "No. I won't. Not now, not ever."

"Oh, Allie. I can't imagine how hard this is for you. But music . . ." His face is so full of sympathy and kindness, it's going to make her cry in a minute, and that would suck. "It will make you feel, yes, but it also heals."

The way he says it, she thinks maybe he does know something about what she's going through. Like maybe he's had his own grief and lived to tell about it. But her problem is more than grief.

"Grief is a strange place, Allie. Everything is upside down. Don't make any permanent decisions now."

The hallway is empty. He's so understanding, the closest adult to her, really, outside of her mother. Maybe she'll tell him. Maybe it would help if somebody knew.

"How did the audition go?" he asks, as if reading her mind. "You'll need to stay in practice to be at your best when university starts in the fall. If it would help, we could set up some structured time to play together to help you ease back in." He notices, three steps too late, that she's stopped walking and comes back to her.

"What is it? Did the audition go badly? Nerves?"

She opens her mouth to tell him, all of it, but then the buzzer signals the end of class. She jumps half out of her skin. Doors slam open, and kids fill up the hall as if summoned by magic.

"Come by my office." Mr. Collins raises his voice above the chaos. "We'll talk. We can get you another audition. Or I'll help you apply somewhere else, if you'd rather."

"Later," Allie lies, taking cover in the crowd.

Promise or no promise, she is not going to calculus or any other classes. She won't go and talk to Mr. Collins, either, or set up an audition anywhere else. Nobody tries to stop her as she walks out the front doors and keeps going until she is down the street and well away. Dazed, disoriented, she tries to remember where she parked the car, before memory comes rushing in.

Her father. Making her come to school, taking her keys, and leaving her blowing in the wind again, just like when she was a kid, just like the morning of the audition.

That was supposed to be the best day ever, the one that set her free from her mother's insistence on med school. The one where she embarked on a life of music.

The one that reconnected her with her father.

She'd schemed for years to get that audition at the University of Washington while keeping her intentions to herself. Mom's plan was for Allie to be a doctor, and she'd gone along with the admission process to premed, keeping her dreams secret.

Mom would have listened if she'd had some valid alternative to medical school—teaching, accounting, science, whatever, but Mom had a block about music. She tolerated Allie's playing in the orchestra, but no way was she going to countenance a waste of time and brainpower on a music degree.

Once Allie had her acceptance to UW, though, it was easy to request an audition into the music school and to keep it a secret from her mother. When and if she was accepted, then she'd have ammunition for that battle. Easier to ask for forgiveness than permission.

Mr. Collins and Mr. Blair, the private teacher she'd worked with since sixth grade, had both helped her prepare for the audition. Why she'd ever been allowed to work with Mr. Blair in the first place was always a bit of a mystery, because Mom hated music, always had as far back as Allie could remember, unless it was hymns in church.

This is lesson day, she realizes with a keening note of loss that takes her back to that very first lesson on that very first day.

A terrible day. For some reason Allie can't understand, the girls in her class at school have turned on her. There have been snide comments and cold shoulders, rolled eyes and colder laughter all day long.

And when Mom shows up to pick them up after school, both Allie and Trey can tell at once that something is wrong.

"Uh-oh," Trey says before the car rolls to a stop. "It's one of those days."

First sign, Mom's got her hair twisted up into a bun. Her lipstick is red. She sits staring straight ahead, hands on the steering wheel at precisely ten and two.

"You get shotgun," Allie shouts, racing for the car. The last thing she needs is to be stuck in the front seat with Mom when she's in a mood.

She skids to a halt when she reaches the car, staring through the window in confusion.

The back seat is full of cello.

Dad's cello. Or, at least, Dad's cello case. When he left, it vanished with him and she hasn't seen it since. Her heart gets stuck in her throat, and the rest of her body goes numb. A thread of Bach finds its way through the closed window and onto the sidewalk, wraps around her heart, and tugs.

Trey is already in place in the front seat, smart enough to keep his mouth shut.

"Get in, already," her mom says. "Some people might have all day, I do not."

Allie squeezes into the back seat beside the cello case. She can't draw a proper breath, maybe because the cello is crowding her, but mostly because she's caught between hope and fear.

She hasn't seen the cello since Dad left, has always thought he took it with him. Did he come home? Or has the cello been at the house all along? But if that's true, then why is it in the car now? Maybe Mom is going to sell it.

Allie remembers being so small she could stand tucked between Dad's legs and the cello, dwarfed by its magnificence. Remembers the hum running through the wood and continuing on into her body.

"Feel that, little bird?" he'd asked. "That's as close to magic as we get in this lifetime."

Allie touches the case. Lightly, questing, feeling the impossible vibrations. Nobody is playing. The cello is in its case, and still the music circles up and around her.

Her mother slams on the brakes hard enough to jolt Allie into her seat belt.

She doesn't recognize this place where they've stopped, on a quiet, tree-lined street.

"What are we doing?" Trey demands. "Why are we stopping here? I'm hungry."

"Allie is going to have a music lesson." Mom's voice is cold and sharp. It cuts.

"I'm what?"

"Don't be difficult, Allie," her mother says, as if she's thrown a tantrum instead of asking a reasonable question. "Your father wants you to have cello lessons; therefore, you are going to have cello lessons."

Tears fill Allie's eyes, spill down over her cheeks. She can't suppress a little sob. She doesn't know why she's crying, only that she can't seem to stop.

Her mother sits stiff and unbending, staring straight ahead. "Take the cello. Go into the house. Your teacher is a Mr. Blair, and he is waiting for you. You'll be coming here once a week for lessons."

Trey swivels to look at Allie, his eyes big.

She shrugs her shoulders at him, wipes her nose on her sleeve, and wrestles the cello case out of the car. It's as big as she is, and it's hard work lugging it up the sidewalk. Mr. Blair meets her at the door with a smile.

He doesn't look like a musician, is her first thought. All musicians in her mind look like her father, tall and thin and dark. Mr. Blair is old and tiny, and flits about with quick, unexpected movements that make her jumpy.

He insists on taking the cello out of the case and setting it up for her, muttering all the while.

"Stradivarius, my foot," he says, peering through the sound hole at the label. "Fakes everywhere these days. Ah well, what does it matter for a girl so young? Good enough, good enough."

When the bow is rosined to his satisfaction, he gestures her into a chair. "Let me introduce you," he begins, and Allie can't help laughing.

Her father made the only introduction that matters years ago. The cello is already an old friend.

Was. Was an old friend. Because she won't be playing anymore, and if her father keeps his promise, the cello will be gone when she gets home.

Chapter Twenty-One

PHEE

Phee visits her grandfather's grave every year on his death day to bring him a progress report and a shot of whiskey. Once, back in her drinking days, she brought herself a bottle and a violin and sat here playing jigs with some idea that he needed cheering up. A family of mourners had threatened to call the cops, and that was the end of dance tunes in the cemetery.

Today, as she settles cross-legged beside the green mound that marks his spot, the only music she's brought with her is the phantom cello that plays in her head these days, waking or sleeping.

"We have a problem," she says. "In case you didn't notice."

He doesn't answer, not that she expects him to. All he ever does is hang out in her head telling her what to do. He never tells her how she's supposed to do it, and Phee is out of ideas.

She unzips the gym bag she's carrying with her and draws out a paper grocery sack, shoving away Celestine's nose as she does so.

"Sit. This is not for you."

The dog whines and drops onto his haunches, his nostrils twitching. Phee unwraps the bone she's brought for him and tosses it a few feet away, and Celestine pursues it with glee. With the dog occupied, her next order of business is the customary libation.

Quickly, before she can be tempted to drink it herself, she opens a pint-size mason jar and pours whiskey into the grass. The smell of it makes her mouth water, and she inhales with as much enthusiasm as the dog did over his bone. Temptation out of the way, she screws the lid back on and tucks the jar back into the bag. Celestine's big head comes up as Phee pulls out the ham-and-cheese sandwich.

"You've got yours," she admonishes.

Celestine whines, but only half-heartedly, and goes back to his bone.

Phee sets half the sandwich on the headstone, in lieu of flowers, then takes a big bite of the other half.

The food she brings always disappears, and she knows the birds will get it, most likely the raven that is already observing her from a nearby tree, but it seems rude not to bring Granddad something. She also feels the need to appease him. Not that she's ever seen his ghost. Not that he's spoken to her outright, or slammed doors in the apartment or set anything on fire. And when she thinks she hears him talking in her head, it's just her own thoughts.

Probably.

But maybe she'll hear him more clearly from here, and God knows she needs all of the clarity she can garner.

"About the cello," she says, tossing a piece of crust in the raven's direction. "Braden really can't play. So the whole thing is remarkably unfair. Isn't there a release clause, somewhere? Because there ought to be, for special circumstances."

The raven tilts his head and makes a noise halfway between croak and knock, but he stays where he is.

"I'm not talking to you," Phee admonishes him. "Unless you're a message bearer. Let me rephrase, Granddad. I'm not just venting. I'm asking." She sets down the remains of her sandwich, clasps her hands, and intones, formally, "Please release Braden Healey from his contract with the cello due to extraordinary circumstances."

Silence. The raven flies down from the tree and settles into the grass no more than ten feet away, his black eyes fixed on the crust. Phee ignores him and keeps talking to her grandfather.

"Yes, I know he could still technically play. 'Three Blind Mice' or something horrible. Broken notes and bad bowing. Asking him to do that, though—that's cruel and unusual punishment."

More silence. Phee reaches into her paper sack and pulls out one of the cookies she lifted from her mother's kitchen. "No, you don't get this, stubborn old man that you are." She takes a bite of buttery, chewy sweetness.

Clouds obscure the sun, the graveyard darkens.

"Nice try, but I'm not buying it," she says, taking another bite. This time of the year, the weather is mostly rain, rain, drizzle, fog, mist, and more rain, so the sunshine of the morning was a blessing and the rain clouds rolling in have nothing to do with supernatural displeasure. They've been hanging on the horizon for hours.

"And don't tell me I've gone soft," she says. "I've never agreed with these deals you've made with musicians, like you're some sort of Dr. Faust broker for the devil. And I still haven't forgiven you for tricking me into agreeing to this. Just so you know."

The raven stretches his wings. Ruffles his feathers. Hops closer.

"Fine. All right," Phee grumbles. "Yes, I love Braden. I hardly know him, it makes no sense, and it's a very bad idea. And yet, there it is. So you see my quandary. If there's any mercy to be had for either Braden or for me, now would be good. If you can hear me at all. Which, of course, is doubtful."

The first raindrops splatter cold on her head. The wind picks up. As usual, she's forgotten her umbrella. Phee tosses the last bite of cookie to the raven. "It's yours. Eat up.

"Really, though," she says to her grandfather as she stands and brushes grass off her jeans. "Give it some thought. If you have any ideas about how he's supposed to play, or how I'm supposed to make him do it, that would be fantastic. Enjoy your whiskey. Come on, Celestine."

The dog follows, bringing his bone, as Phee stalks off to visit the other graves on her radar. Truth is, she feels worse rather than better, a small but insistent clamor inside her wishing she'd poured the whiskey down her throat rather than into the grass. Probably she should stop bringing it to him. It's a dangerous game that one of these days is going to lead her right into a relapse. Especially now.

Her next stop is a plain marker for Evan George, beloved husband and father, 1927 to 1999.

Evan is collateral damage, a man the curse should never have touched. Phee's guilt over his death feels woven into her soul.

"Hey," Phee says, standing respectfully at the foot of his grave. "I just needed to say, again, that I'm sorry. I didn't understand. There was no reason at all for you to get sucked into this, and I formally apologize on behalf of my grandfather and myself. And the violin. It didn't have any volition in this matter, and I sincerely hope you know it meant no harm."

She draws a simple bouquet of daisies and ferns out of her bag and sets them on his tombstone. Rain pelts down on the flowers, flattening the petals.

"All right. I'm not going to linger. May the music be always with you." She bends at the waist in a little half bow, and moves on. One more stop, one more apology.

Through the gray curtain of rain, she sees from a distance that there is already a visitor at the place where Braden's wife and son are buried. A visitor or a victim.

A human form lies facedown on one of the graves, head pillowed on folded arms. Long dark hair. No jacket. Just a cotton hoodie and jeans, soaked and clinging to a slender female form. Motionless, despite the pouring rain.

Phee's heart jolts in her chest and she starts to run.

Celestine beats her to it, poking at the obscured cheek with his wet nose.

The prone figure screams and explodes into action, sitting up and scuttling backward in one wild leap. Celestine, undeterred, follows, trying to lick her face.

"Hey," Phee says gently. "Allie, right?"

The girl crouches in the wet grass beside the grave, dark eyes wide, every muscle taut and ready to flee or fight.

"The dog just wants to lick you. We didn't mean to scare you. I'm Phee, remember? The luthier who cares for your cello."

"It's not *my* cello." Allie spits the words at her, vehement.

Fight, then, Phee thinks. *Not flight or paralysis. Good to know.* Her own heart is pounding like a sledgehammer. "All right," she agrees. "That's the truth of it."

"We're getting rid of the cello, anyway," the girl says, wrapping her arms around Celestine's neck to avoid being bowled over as a big, wet tongue swipes her cheek.

Phee says nothing, feeling her way into this scenario, her mind rabbiting for the best thing to say, the best action to take, even as her heart breaks and breaks again. Allie is shivering. Her eyes are swollen and red, her clothing mud stained from the fresh graves, not yet softened by grass.

"What are you doing here?" Allie challenges, as if the graves are her territory and Phee an intruder.

"I was visiting my grandfather. And I stopped here to pay my respects."

"Are you done?"

"I am. Why don't we walk out together?"

"I'm staying."

"Honey, you're soaking wet."

"I'm fine."

"You're not. You're shivering. Listen, your mother would want you to be warm and dry and safe. And Celestine is never going to let me leave you here. Let me walk you to your car, okay?"

Somewhere in these words is the magic key Phee's been looking for. Allie's defiance melts. Her shoulders soften, her back curves, and a sob escapes her and settles directly into Phee's already wide-open heart.

Allie nods acquiescence, though she says nothing, and Phee nods back.

"One sec, I need to leave my flowers."

Phee opens the gym bag and pulls out two last bouquets. One for Trey. One for Lilian. *I'm so sorry,* she whispers, so Allie won't hear. Just before she straightens, she catches a glimpse of white under the edge of a sheaf of lilies on Lilian's grave. Glancing over her shoulder, she sees that Allie's back is turned, and she nudges the flowers aside to find an envelope, the ink of a single word rapidly blurring from the rain.

Mom.

Not your business, Phee tells herself, even as she gently folds the envelope into her pocket.

"Where's your car, then?" she asks, stuffing down her guilty conscience over the pilfered letter.

"Sorry?"

"Your car. Where are you parked? We'll walk you there." She starts to walk, relieved when Allie falls into step beside her, one hand resting on the big dog's back.

"I don't . . . My father confiscated it. I took a bus."

"I'll give you a ride. Don't worry, I'm safe. The worst thing you have to worry about is dog slobber, and you're already awash in that."

"I don't want to bother you."

"No bother. Besides, Celestine likes you. Here we are. Right over there."

"Does Celestine even fit in there?" Allie asks when she sees the VW Bug. "If you don't have room, I can take a bus."

"Don't be ridiculous. Celestine can ride in the back."

"I can't go home," Allie says. "He thinks I'm at school. Can you drop me somewhere else?"

"Like where?" Phee asks, buying time to think. She does not want to get between Allie and Braden, but she feels the precariousness of this girl's trust, and she owes her, besides.

"I dunno. The mall, I guess."

"Um." Phee gives her an exaggerated once-over. "You look like a zombie. And your clothes are soaking."

"There's nowhere else."

"In fact, there is. I have the perfect place."

Fifteen minutes later, the three of them stand dripping inside the door of Phee's parents' house. At least, Phee and Allie stand there. Celestine dashes into the center of the room and promptly shakes himself, sending a spray of water over everything.

"You!" Bridgette orders. "Into the laundry room at once. You'll stay there until you're good and dry."

Celestine gives Phee one rueful, pleading look, but she just shakes her head at him. "I'd obey forthwith if I were you."

"As for the two of you, take off your shoes and socks and stay right there," Bridgette orders, vanishing down the hallway with Celestine.

Allie doesn't question the directive, and when Bridgette returns with two large bath towels, they are both barefoot.

Phee wills her mother to get this right, and Bridgette doesn't disappoint. Tossing her daughter a towel, Bridgette takes it upon herself to dry Allie's face and blot the water from her hair. "I have some dry clothes I think might fit you. Come with me." She wraps both the towel and her arm around Allie's shoulders, and leads her down the hallway without asking a single question.

Phee betakes herself downstairs to her old bedroom, where she finds a faded pair of jeans and a sweatshirt neatly folded in the bureau as if her mother knew she'd be needing them. Which, given Bridgette's uncanny ability to prepare for every eventuality, maybe she did. She carefully extracts the envelope from the pocket of her soaking jeans and peels out the damp but still legible paper.

Dear Mom,

You were right. About Dad and the music and every-thing. I need to tell you what happened and that I'm sorry and that I wish I could go back and change everything, but I can't.

I've been lying to you for a year. Maybe you know that, already. Maybe you see everything and understand, in which case, I wish you could talk to me because I don't understand anything. Anyway, here's the truth.

I never meant to go to medical school. I know you wanted it for me, but all I ever wanted was to be a musician like Dad. So I let you think I was going into pre-med so you'd help me with my application and stuff. And then I applied on my own to the music school and got an audition. That's where I was when you died. That's why I didn't pick up Trey and why I ignored you when you tried to reach me.

So you were right about the music, that it's a curse. And you were right about Dad, like I said. I wanted him to be there, at my audition. I thought he'd be proud of me. So I found him last year, on Facebook. And we messaged and stuff, and he agreed to meet me that morning, only he didn't show up.

I'd even learned the C Minor, pretty much the way he played it. Mr. Blair helped me. He said I was an extraordinary talent, truly my father's daughter. I wanted to believe him, but I blew the audition, I think, so even that wasn't true.

I'm so sorry I lied to you. I'm sorry I didn't pick up Trey.

If it helps, I persuaded Dad to get rid of the cello, so neither one of us will be playing anymore.

I love you,

Allie

Phee drops onto the bed with this missive in her hand.

"Oh, Allie," she whispers. Tears well up and spill down her cheeks, and she wipes them away. This whole situation is even more of a mess than she'd thought, and apparently Braden hasn't listened to word one of what she's tried to tell him.

By the time she returns upstairs with her soaking castoffs wrapped in the towel, Allie is ensconced at the kitchen counter with a mug of hot chocolate. Her face has been washed, her hair has been combed. She looks small and waiflike in an overlarge flannel shirt and sweatpants.

"Hey, don't I get hot chocolate?" Phee asks.

"Soon as you put those wet clothes in the dryer and mop up the floor. A dog that size needs to go to obedience school, Ophelia. I keep telling you."

"This is delicious," Allie says. "Mrs. . . . I'm sorry, what do I call you?"

"Mom, this is Allie. Allie, this is my mother, and you might as well just call her Bridgette."

"Sure enough. Mrs. MacPhee, that was my mother-in-law, and one of her in the world is enough for anybody."

"Mom . . ."

"You know it's true, Phee. Now, I was in the middle of making cookies. And since the two of you are here, you can help me."

Phee groans to herself. She had forgotten about the infernal bake sale. She hates baking. But before she can think of an excuse, Allie says, "My mother never made cookies. My dad used to, when we were little, but then . . ." Her voice trails off.

"Perfect," Bridgette says. "I need help and you can learn. The batter is already made for the first batch, all you have to do is drop them on the sheets, like this. And then we'll do the roll-out ones, those are the most fun."

"Fun" isn't the word Phee would use for any of it. "Tedious" and "monotonous," more like it, although there are compensations. All broken or deformed cookies are for the bakers, for one thing. And the reward of hearing Allie actually laugh when Phee deliberately cracks a sugar cookie down the middle and says, "Damn it. Gonna have to eat another one" is even better.

But the whole time she's itching to get to Braden. To remind him that he cannot, must not, sell the cello. She's going to have to tell him the full story about what got her started drinking, a story she's never told anybody, ever, in all the years that have fallen between then and now. And if that doesn't convince him, then she's out of ammunition and has no idea what she's going to do.

Chapter Twenty-Two

PHEE

The door of the house opens before Phee's car even comes to a stop. She can see Braden standing there, backlit from the lights inside, and guilt smacks her upside the face. She should have called him and let him know she had Allie. He'll be worried sick. She'd meant to be here sooner, but the cookies had led to a Netflix movie and dinner.

It's dark already, the streetlights creating little halos in the mist.

"Where the hell have you been?" Braden demands.

Allie shoves past him without answering, and his gaze shifts to Phee.

"I found her in the graveyard." She tries to signal a warning with her eyes. *Go gently. She's so incredibly fragile.* She wants to stomp her foot in frustration when he completely misses the message.

"In this weather?" He turns away from Phee and directs a parental tirade at his daughter, oblivious to the subliminal messages Phee continues to transmit at his back. "Were you thinking at all? You don't even have a jacket. You could have caught your death of cold!"

Allie turns to face him, a wild creature at bay. "Big loss that would be."

Phee tries again to intervene, brushing past him into the house without waiting for an invitation. Something is wrong about the house, nagging at her. "I'm sorry, I should have called sooner. I took her to my mother's and got her warm and dry—"

"It's eight o'clock! You couldn't have brought her sooner? You couldn't have called? For God's sake, Phee, you're as bad as she is!"

"I already said I was sorry! She didn't want to come home." Phee says this slowly, with emphasis, trying to herd him back from the edge, but he's already back on Allie's case.

"I thought you promised you'd go to school."

"I thought you promised to stop drinking." Allie's chin lifts in defiance.

That volley silences him. All three of them stand like chess pieces at an impasse. Allie glaring defiance. Phee with her warning undelivered. Braden still holding the door open as if it takes too much energy to close it.

"This isn't about me," Braden finally says. "Just because I fucked up doesn't mean you have to."

"I'll probably fail the semester now, anyway," Allie says. "What difference does it make if I go to school?"

No music. That's what's wrong about the house. The pervasive music from the cello is missing. *Oh please. Don't let that mean what I think it means.*

Before Phee has time to ask any questions, to crystalize the fear, Celestine barrels up the steps and barges past her, flinging his wet, muddy body at Braden's legs, tail wagging up a windstorm. Braden staggers backward, catches his balance, steadies himself with a hand on the shaggy head. That shakes him out of himself, and he turns to Phee, his tone a little stretched and desperate.

"Thanks for bringing her home. I'm sure you'd like to—"

"Allie was telling me you're planning to get rid of the cello." Phee stands unmovable, her eyes boring holes into him. *Too late,* the silence whispers, and Braden's clear motivation to get her out of the house confirms her fear.

"Look, can we talk about this later? I really think that what's going on with Allie is more important than—"

"What's going on with Allie is part of why I'm here."

Allie slams the door closed. "Part of what?"

"Nothing," Braden says. "Go to your room, Allie. This doesn't concern you."

"It concerns her more than you think." Phee can't contain her dread any longer. "Where is the cello?"

"You should leave."

Phee pushes past him and heads for the music room.

She hears his footsteps behind her as if from a distance. "Phee—"

But she's already standing at the open door. The chair still sits by the music stand, but the room is empty of the only thing that matters. Phee's knees go weak. She supports herself against the doorjamb, tries to breathe in a world where somebody has cut off all of the oxygen.

"Braden Healey, what have you done?"

"I tried to tell you, Phee. It had to go. I asked you, begged you—"

"So we're saying 'it' now? No more 'she'? After everything I showed you—"

"I told him to get rid of it," Allie breaks in. "It's, like, the one thing he's done right since he moved back in."

"Oh, honey," Phee says. "He can't—"

"Don't you dare tell her." Braden's voice is fierce. "You need to leave this house, now."

"She has to know. She's part of this."

"Do not drag my daughter into your delusions!"

"What are you even talking about?" Allie demands, looking from one to the other.

"There's nothing to tell."

"Oh puh-leese. I *hate* being lied to, and I am not a child."

"Braden. You have to listen to me. I know you think I'm crazy. But you have to get the cello back. You have to do it now!"

"Not possible."

"Fine, tell me what you've done, who you sold her to, and I'll go get her back myself."

"I didn't sell her."

Phee's hand goes to her heart, her vision darkening around the edges. "Tell me you didn't—"

"Break her and burn her?"

Celestine's barking resonates through the house, followed by the doorbell. All of them ignore it.

"I don't know where she is," Braden says.

"You don't know what you're saying! You don't know what you've done!"

The doorbell chimes again. The barking intensifies. "Are we expecting company?" Braden levels the question at Allie, a challenge. "Because if that Ethan character dares to show his face . . ." He hears his own words and strides back toward the door, Allie at his heels.

"Dad! It wasn't his fault about the party. It was my idea."

Braden yanks the door open.

The young man standing on the porch is a stranger; the cello case he carries is not. All three of them stand frozen, staring.

"So sorry," the man says. "I couldn't find time to bring it to you before now. I know you must have been crazy with worry."

Before Braden can say something stupid, Phee claims the cello. "Thank you so much. You're right. We were desperate. I don't know what we would have done if we'd lost it."

"Saw the address label on the case and looked you up. Glad I grabbed it when I did; there were a couple sketchy-looking dudes eyeing it. Well, I guess I'll be going, then."

"For your trouble," Phee says, producing a wad of bills from her pocket, but he holds up his hand.

"No, please. I play guitar. Can't imagine how I'd feel if I left it somewhere and lost it. And a cello? Wow. Have a good night."

Phee closes the door and carries the case to the middle of the room. Opens it and strokes the cello soothingly. "It's okay, beautiful. You're home now."

She's rewarded by a melancholy strain of music. A surge of protective anger wells up. "What did you do? Abandon her at a bus stop?"

"This isn't happening," Allie says. "I mean, this is all so totally weird, I can't even."

"What happened," Phee says, "is that your father swore an oath that he would love and play the cello for always. Only now that he can't play—"

"Oh, he can play all right." Allie's outrage is equivalent to Phee's.

"Allie. Phee." Braden sputters, caught between the two accusations. "Does one of you want to explain?"

"I can't—" Braden starts, but Allie cuts him off.

"He says he can't play. Just like he says he's not drinking anymore. But he played the C Minor last night."

Phee just looks at Braden.

"I was dreaming," he protests. "I can't explain what happened. My fingers are numb, I can't feel the strings, the pressure on the bow, any of it."

"Mom said it was all in your head. She said a doctor even told you that."

"Doctors said all kinds of things. They aren't the ones who are living with this!"

"I have to tell you something," Phee says. "Something I should have told you before."

"I don't want to hear it."

"I do," Allie says.

"Does the name Alfred Garner mean anything to you?" Phee asks.

Braden's body jerks with the shock of the name, his eyes widen.

"You knew him," Phee says. "You would have played with him. You saw what happened."

"I . . . played with him. But what happened to him was an accident." There is horror written plain as print on his face, though, and he adds as an afterthought, "Surely."

"What are you talking about?" Allie looks from Phee to her father and back again.

"Nothing!" Braden actually shouts it this time. "Our charming and oh-so-helpful friend Phee is a lunatic. She believes that your mother's car crashed because I stopped playing the cello—eleven fucking years ago, Phee! And if I read it right, she believes further disaster will strike if I don't start playing again. And if I sell or give the cello away, then God will strike us down dead where we stand. Is that about right?"

"Not God, exactly," Phee murmurs.

Allie's face has gone so white that Phee takes a small step forward, tensed to catch her in case she falls. But the girl seems to be operating on a formidable reserve of willpower and defiance. "You can both go to the loony bin for all I care," she hurls at them. "Take the cello with you."

She stalks out of the room, head high. Celestine whines, then follows her. A few seconds later, there is a small thunder of feet on the stairs, dog and human.

Phee sucks in a breath and fortifies her own resolve. She needs every bit of it.

"A week before Alfred was horribly burned—except for his hands and arms, so miraculously spared—he sold his violin to a very sweet old man. You know what Alfred said? He said he was tired of the violin, he was bored and wanted variety. He'd bought some new thing with an electric pickup. Sold her for less than she was worth."

"It's not like he traded in his wife and children."

"That's what I said. I was nineteen and stupid and felt trapped by an oath I swore to my grandfather—oh yes, Braden, I'm every bit as bound as you are! I'd been doing a half-assed job of monitoring the MacPhee instruments. I only heard about the transaction from a friend of a friend. And I did nothing! I didn't go talk to Alfred. Never tried to warn him. Never tracked down the old man and told him what he'd gotten caught up in. His name was Evan George. He had five grand-children and three shelter dogs. He helped out at soup kitchens three days a week." She feels the familiar thickness in her throat, grief and guilt and responsibility, waits for it to settle before she goes on speaking.

"Oh dear God." Braden's voice is softer now, a conflicted sympathy on his face. "You can't think what happened to Alfred was your fault! The gas exploded on his stove. He was drunk."

"And somehow, miraculously, his hands are fine."

"He was wearing oven mitts. For the love of God, Phee. This can't be because of a curse! We are not living in the Middle Ages. Curses don't exist, not real curses."

"I said that, too," Phee goes on. "Recited it to myself like a mantra all day long. Denial is an interesting thing."

"It's not denial!" Braden interjects. "It's logic. Reality."

"The day after Alfred's injury, that sweet old Evan George dropped dead from a heart attack. They found him with the violin still in his hands."

"Coincidence." But Braden's voice sounds increasingly desperate. "You said he was old. He could have had a heart attack at any time."

"Could have," Phee agrees. "But that's a lot of coincidence, don't you think? He was healthy. Active. His death made Alfred a believer. I took the violin to him as soon as he was able to have visitors. He didn't argue. He's still playing it."

"But that's horrible," Braden says. "Coercion. He's not allowed to play anything else? Like, ever?"

"Of course he can. He can play whatever he wants, as long as he plays the violin occasionally . . . Oh hell," she says. "I agree. It is hor-rible. Do you think I like this, walking into your house like some cursed old witch? I have to, don't you see? Because what if it is all true? I can't take that chance. You have to play her, Braden. And for the love of all things holy, please promise me you won't try to give her away to some innocent bystander again."

Braden sinks down onto the sofa and buries his head in his hands. A harsh laugh emerges from between his fingers. "And yet, I can't play. What do you want me to do?"

Phee kneels in front of him, draws his hands away from his face and holds them in hers. His head comes up and he looks into her eyes, so close she can see the mosaic of green and brown in his irises.

"Did you really play the C Minor?"

"Allie says I did."

"Do you believe her?"

"I want to believe we were both dreaming."

"But?"

"The cello was tuned to scordatura. So somebody tuned it for the C Minor. It could have been Allie—the music is out on the stand—but she swears she didn't touch it."

"What if you could play again?" she asks him, holding him with her eyes and her hands. "If you played last night, then maybe—"

"I was dreaming. Somehow—I don't know—it's like, people can do things under hypnosis that they couldn't normally do, right? The subconscious taking over. So it must have been like that."

"So maybe a hypnotherapist, then—"

Braden wrenches his hands away from her. "Let me show you. I have sensation here." He runs fingers across the backs of both hands.

"And here, from the crease of the wrist to where the thumb joins my palm. The rest feels like—you know that thing where you sleep on your hand and when you wake up it feels like it's not yours? Dead and heavy and useless. Sometimes—on a good day, I get pins and needles. I did months of occupational therapy to learn to do basic things like hold a mug, zip and unzip my fucking pants so I didn't have to live in sweats. Every action requires that I watch what my hands are doing, navigate like I'm operating a remote control. And you think that some-how, magically, I'm going to be able to play!"

"You played the C Minor. With your eyes closed."

"Oh my God. You are incorrigible!"

"So I've been told. What happened? The night of the . . . accident."
Her eyes search his, begging him to answer.

"I don't remember."

She can hear his breathing, rapid and shallow. The room is cool,
but there's a sheen of sweat on his forehead.

Phee goes to the kitchen and brings him a glass of water.

"Drink."

He doesn't answer, staring off into the corner.

"Braden." She touches his face. He startles, recoiling from her
touch, his eyes wild.

"Are you all right?"

He licks his lips. Swallows. "Flashback," he croaks. "Just a small
one. Night. Snow. Cold. That's it. All I ever get."

He takes the water and drains the glass. When he's done, his face is
a better color. His breathing has eased.

"Do you really think I haven't tried, Phee? Music was everything!
Without it, I'm nothing. Have nothing."

A rhythmic thudding draws Phee's gaze. Celestine sits at the edge
of the room, his tail thumping on the floor. Allie stands beside him,
looking heartbreakingly young in a pair of fuzzy pajamas.

Braden stretches a hand out toward her. "I didn't mean that how it
sounded, Allie. You know that. That's why I—"

"Spare me," Allie says.

Celestine starts to follow, but Allie stops him. "Stay here." The dog
whines but obeys, fixing Braden with a look of pure reproach.

He groans. "Take the cello, Phee. Take it back."

"You know I can't do that."

"Even for Allie?"

"Because of Allie. Can't you see how much she needs the music, too?" She should tell him about the note Allie left on her mother's grave, but reading it herself was already such a huge breach of Allie's privacy that she can't bring herself to do it. Somehow she'll just have to make him see.

The silence that falls between them is difficult and heavy. "I should go," she says. She allows her hand to settle on Braden's head and rest there. She doesn't stroke his hair, as she wants to do. Doesn't run her fingers through the loose curls.

"If I call an emergency meeting of the Angels, will you come?"

She's not sure if the look he gives her is a promise or an acknowledgment of her words. "Somebody will pick you up," she says, not taking chances. "I don't suppose you're going to want it to be me, so I'll send one of the others."

"Not somebody else. You." He gives her a half smile. "We're in this together, apparently. Whatever this is."

"Tomorrow, then. Three thirty. Don't make me hunt you down."

"That," he says, "is a terrifying thought. Good night, Phee."

Chapter Twenty-Three

BRADEN

Braden, left alone with the cello, feels a pervasive sense of dread creeping up on him, as if he's wandered into a horror movie and is about to be devoured alive by a seemingly inanimate object. Maybe the cello will strangle him, or bludgeon him to death. Allie will find him in the morning, bloody and lifeless, wrapped in strings and wood fragments.

Get a grip, he mutters to himself. *Phee is a crazy woman. There's no such thing as a curse.*

The problem is, he's known crazy people. He shared lodgings with a schizophrenic for a while, and is familiar with the lapses of attention, latencies of responses, the emotional flatness. Phee is not like that at all. Her clear and cogent presentation of what she believes will befall him and Allie has unsettled him deeply. He has his own experiences to consider, his sense that the cello didn't want to be given away. The music that will not stop playing in his head.

The cello's presence fills the room, a jarring counterpoint to Lilian, who is also very much present here. Probably he's the one who is crazy, because he can hear Lil's voice: *"Would you take that thing back to the music room, Bray? Bad enough the way it devours your life, I don't need a reminder in the middle of the living room."*

Most couples fight over finances, religion, and kids. That's what the marriage counselor said the day they went in for a consult. Affairs are a symptom, not the cause, and there are all different kinds of affairs.

"Infidelity doesn't have to involve sex," he said, tenting his fingers together, elbows resting on a massive wooden desk that clearly separated him from the couple facing him. "If an individual is more invested in a relationship with another person than they are with their spouse, that's an affair. In this case—"

"It's the cello," Lilian finished for him. "This is how I feel. This is how it is. Even when he's with me, his heart is with her."

"Lil," Braden protested. "I love you with all my heart. I don't understand—"

"Yesterday, when you hugged me, your fingers were moving on my back, like you were practicing chord progressions."

"Lil—"

"You never come to bed at the same time I do. Every night, I fall asleep to the sound of you playing."

She began to weep. The counselor fixed him with a professional gaze that still managed to say, *You're an asshole, Braden Healey. Now look what you've done.*

So he tried to do better. Lilian switched to working nights and slept during the day. He took over responsibility for the kids, for the housework and the meals and the grocery shopping. Evenings were his only time to practice, and they always seemed too short, but still he tried to cut back.

For a few months, he made a point of stopping his practice at precisely eight p.m., spending the two hours before Lilian left for work discussing the kids, listening to her stories about patients she'd cared for at the hospital. All the while, the cello called him, and he often played music in his head, careful to keep his hands still so Lil wouldn't see.

But then the recording contract came in, an opportunity for Braden to perform the Bach suites live at a Bach festival in Germany. This was a career marker, and he was both heady with the opportunity and terrified by the prospect of failure. He'd recorded the suites on CD, but playing live required a new level of mastery. He began practicing longer and longer hours.

And Lilian, at last, gave him an ultimatum.

"Choose me, or the cello."

And now he has neither, and he can't imagine how the words Allie heard him say have made her feel.

His feet as heavy as his heart, he makes his way up the stairs, past Trey's room, to stand in front of Allie's closed door.

He knocks softly, calling her name. "Allie?"

"Go away."

"Allie, please. Can I come in? I just want to talk to you."

"So talk."

He leans his forehead against the door, draws a steadying breath. "What you heard me say, downstairs. It's true, but not the whole truth. You . . . and Trey . . . I loved you both so much. It's not that I loved the music more. What I meant is that music was a part of me in a way that I can't ever explain. Without it, I'm just . . . empty, I guess."

Silence from her fortress. He's making a mess of this, as he makes a mess of everything. He can't seem to say it any more clearly.

"Do you hear me, little bird? I love you. I've always loved you."

"Please just go away."

For a long moment, he stands there, then with a sigh he makes his way back downstairs, where the cello still waits for him.

"I don't know what you want from me," he says out loud.

He remembers Alfred, and the shocking scars on his face. The stiff way he walked. His hands the only part of him unscathed, smooth and supple and able to coax music from his violin like always.

"Oh hell," he says, thinking of Allie upstairs in her room, of Trey and Lilian in their graves. If there's any truth to this curse business, even the tiniest little bit, he can't risk something happening to Allie.

"Come on, then," he says to the cello. He picks her up and carries her into the music room. Settles her against his knee, positions his hands over the strings, visually checking that they are in the right position. Bracing himself for what he knows will follow, he picks up the bow and draws it across the strings.

He played better than this when he was a child.

"Is this what you want?" he demands of the cello. "Really? Isn't this torture for you, too?"

She doesn't answer, and he works a C major scale for fifteen minutes by the clock, one excruciating note after another. The longer he plays, the more his nerves crawl, the more he feels something trying to break loose from the dark, forbidden space at the center of him.

Anxiety escalates. His hands are shaking, slippery with sweat. His awkward fingers slip off the strings. Beaten, he leaves the cello on her stand and flees the room and the house, walking the streets for hours before finally returning home and falling into a sleep of pure exhaustion.

Chapter Twenty-Four

ALLIE

"The cello was everything. Without it, I'm nothing. Have nothing."

Familiar words. Allie can't really hold them against her father, because they were already waiting in her own heart, unspoken.

The truth is, she's exactly like him.

When the man brought the cello back, she'd wanted to hug him. Had very nearly dropped to her knees and rocked it like a baby, crooning, seeking forgiveness. All she wants to do right now, this very minute, is to lose herself in the music. But she can't, she won't. Not now and not ever.

The fumbling, broken notes of a scale drift up to her. Her father had played like that after the accident, before he went away. She'd been too little to understand, but now the knowing comes with a fresh burst of heartbreak.

He'd lost his music. That's what made him drink, what drove him away. It occurs to her, for the very first time, that the two of them have suffered the same losses. That they might take comfort in shared grieving. Maybe she'll go down to him. Maybe she'll forgive him.

But then she hears the front door slam and knows he's gone out. *Hypocrite*, she thinks, *he's off to get drunk again.* Torn between relief and disappointment, love and anger, she wanders around her room, picking up things and putting them down, then sifts carelessly through the stack of mail her father has left on her desk.

None of it has been opened. Today's offerings are the usual: postcards from universities inviting her to apply, a clothing catalogue, a music catalogue. And one official-looking white envelope from the University of Washington.

She sits in her chair with the envelope in her hands. She should throw it away unopened. She's got no business yearning for what she is never going to have, but she's weak and spineless.

Tearing the envelope open, she unfolds the letter, the holy grail she'd worked toward since her freshman year.

> *Dear Ms. Healey,*
> *Thank you for your audition on February 12.*
> *We were surprised by your decision to perform Variations on a Lullaby in place of your original proposal, the Bach Suite No. 5 in C Minor for Unaccompanied Cello. Perhaps you were not aware that we do require a performance of a piece from the traditional repertoire for cello?*
> *However, we were sufficiently impressed by your obvious talent and skill to invite you to submit a video audition. May we recommend something less demanding than the C Minor? Perhaps Elgar or a Bach prelude.*
> *Please submit prior to March 30 to be considered for fall semester of 2018.*

Damaged pride claws at her insides. They don't think she's capable of the C Minor, that she changed her mind at the last minute out of nerves. Oh, she could show them. She knows the C Minor inside and out, has listened to her father's recording of the suites every night since he left. Since her very first cello lesson, she has been working on them, one bar at a time. It would be so easy to record the demo and send it in.

Maybe just to get the acceptance letter, to prove to the world what she can do. Or, maybe she could pull this last semester of high school out of the toilet if she works her ass off and asks her teachers for extra credit. The life she always wanted is still within her reach.

She shreds both letter and envelope into pieces and throws them in the trash. Exhausted, restless, wanting nothing more than sleep, but afraid of that place between dreaming and waking where the real realities lurk, she opens her laptop.

Almost immediately, Ethan sends her a message, then opens a video chat.

He smiles as if she is the single most important being in the universe, his voice tuned perfectly to her ears, and her heart turns over in her chest.

"I was waiting for you." Ethan's voice is a caress.

"When did you get out?"

"This afternoon. Had to go to court. My bitch of a mother couldn't be bothered to bail me out."

"I was so worried. Are you okay? Was it horrible?"

"Could have been worse."

"I'm so sorry, Ethan. The party was all my idea."

"When can I see you? I missed you."

Ethan wants her, wants to be with her. To him, she's important, even now, as she is.

"Tomorrow?" she asks. "Might as well keep my no-school streak going."

He laughs. "Impressive! How's your old man handling that?"

"He doesn't matter," Allie says, trying to mean it. "Hey, how about tonight? He's not even here right now."

She loves the way Ethan's expression shifts to eagerness and maybe even admiration. "You sure? We could meet at the motel. Spend the night together."

"Problem. He's got my car keys."

"And I no longer have a license."

"Well, there goes that, then," Allie says. She feels both deflated and relieved, a nagging rational part of herself pointing out how much she hated that motel, that the experience was less than amazing.

"Are you kidding? I need to see you. I'll pick you up. In an hour?"

"In an hour."

It gives her time to put on makeup. She's forgotten to do laundry, and most of her favorite clothes are dirty, but she finds a pair of jeans that are clean enough and a dressy shirt to go with them. Tired of being cold, she grabs her warmest jacket, sexy or not.

She stands at the top of the stairs, listening, making sure the house is still empty. The downstairs and stairwell are dark and quiet. She hears cello music, even though she knows damn well nobody is home and nobody is playing, and she shivers a little, remembering Phee.

Haunted, she thinks, and then brushes that thought aside.

Still, she finds herself creeping down the stairs, skipping over the creaky fourth step, as if the cello will hear her. There's nothing to prevent her from walking out the front door, but instead she slips out the back, opening it slowly and closing it as gently as she can. It always sticks a little, and she has to give a firm tug, but she's outside now. The air is cold but not quite freezing. A full moon lights the sky, creating shadows on the lawn. Allie sneaks around the side of the house, breath held, with only a minute to spare.

Ethan is right on time. She hears the motorcycle coming and runs out to the curb. Without taking time to put on a helmet, she swings up behind him.

"Quick!" she says, a rush of unreasonable fear sending a burst of adrenaline through her body.

She turns her cheek into the shelter of his shoulder and closes her eyes, arms tight around his waist, and stays that way. When he stops the bike and kills the engine, she looks up, expecting the dark, grungy parking lot of the motel. Instead, she sees neon lights and smells French fries and something savory. Her mouth waters in response. She's hungry, even after the dinner and cookies Phee's mother fed her earlier.

"I've never taken you on a real date," Ethan says. "Dinner? Yes?"

"Yes."

Her heart swells and she feels the smile blossoming. A real smile, not a made-up one. *He really does understand,* she thinks. *He knows what I need without me even telling him.*

"How did you know I was hungry?"

"I know everything about you, Allie. You're the girl I want to spend forever with."

His hand wraps around hers, warm and strong. Admiring eyes follow them as they walk in and sit down, and she feels lucky to be chosen by him. Half an hour later, with a hamburger and fries warming her empty belly, rock music drowning out the ever-present cello, and Ethan's eyes gazing into hers across the table, soul to soul, she feels better than she has any right to feel.

Ethan leans forward so he can be heard over the music.

"So. Was the party worth staying alive for?"

Allie's heart stops. Her hand freezes halfway to her mouth, the French fry dripping ketchup onto the table.

"No," she whispers.

"Neither was jail."

"Ethan, I'm sorry—"

He waves off the words. "I'm done, Allie. With this world. There's nothing in it to hold me. Except you."

"Well, good?" she says, having no idea what to say, really. "I'm glad you're in it, too, Ethan."

"I don't want to stay in it." His eyes are so compelling, his voice speaking to her own desire to just let everything go. "So if you came with me . . ."

Allie drops the fry, her appetite gone. Wipes up the ketchup smear with a napkin, giving herself a minute, just one, to get her brain working again.

Ethan reaches for her hands. "Look at me, Allie."

She does, losing herself in the darkness of his gaze.

"Give me one reason why we shouldn't do this."

"What if it's worse? The other side, I mean."

He smiles, dark and dazzling. "And what if it's beautiful? I think it will be. You know? To make up for how fucked up everything is here."

"I don't know," she says. Hope or no hope, her soul recoils from the idea of death.

Ethan's smile fades. He drops her hands, leans back in his chair. "I want you to come with me, so much. I don't want to go alone. But I will. You have two days to think about it."

"That's all? Come on, Ethan. This is huge. A week, at least."

He shakes his head. "Two days. I'll be at the motel, same room as before. If you want to come with me, be there."

"And if I don't?"

"Then this is goodbye."

Allie shivers, all of the warmth of the burger joint unable to touch her. The smell of fries and burgers turns her stomach.

Ethan leans forward again, taking both of her hands in his warm ones. His eyes gaze into hers with mesmerizing intensity. He lowers his voice, making his words a secret just between the two of them.

"Come on, Allie. Please. Die with me. Say yes."

"Yes."

She's surprised by the relief that washes over her. Yes. She can let go of everything. The cello and the broken relationship with her father. Her guilt. The wasteland of a life stretching ahead of her.

"That's my girl. I knew you'd be the one."

"Why wait?" she asks. "If we're going to do it, why not just—do it?"

"No way! People spend a year planning for a wedding, you know? This is the most important day of our lives. It needs to be a ceremony."

"What do I need to do?"

"Leave it all to me, Allie. Just leave it all to me."

Chapter Twenty-Five

PHEE

Phee has a name and a town, and it turns out that's all she needs. Josephine Conroy is the only woman of that name in Colville, Washington. Her number is in the directory, and she answers on the second ring. A TV is loud in the background and the music is loud in Phee's head and she's already on edge. She consciously wills her fingers to relax their grip on the phone, tries to slow her breathing.

"Is this Josephine Conroy?"

A brief pause, canned TV laughter in the background. Then: "Sorry, I don't want any."

"Wait!" Phee blurts. "Please. I'm a friend of Braden's and I need to talk to you."

"Who is this?" The voice is sharp, but Phee hears the sound of a door closing, and the TV noise mercifully fades.

She'd meant to lie, but in response to this woman's directness, the only real approach is honesty. "My name is Ophelia MacPhee. Your brother isn't doing so well and—"

"That's the understatement of the century."

"I'm trying to help him, but I need to know—"

"How do you know him? Because if you're some reporter snooping around for what you lowlifes call backstory so you can dredge up the old tragedy and hook it to the new one, you can just go directly to hell."

Phee reminds herself to breathe. "I'm not a reporter, Josephine. I—"

"See, that's the thing. Nobody calls me that except telemarketers. So if you're really a friend of his, then you'd know better."

"He doesn't exactly talk about his family a lot," Phee shoots back, her voice sharpening.

To her great surprise, the woman on the other end laughs. "Point for you, Ophelia."

"Nobody calls me that. It's Phee."

"Jo."

"All right, Jo. I'm the luthier in charge of the cello. So you're right, it's not like Braden and I are close. But I'm worried. He's not playing. Now Allie's not playing."

"Maybe in light of the recent tragedy, that's expected. For the girl. Braden hasn't been able to play in years. Ever since . . ." A short silence. A breath. "Ever since what happened. But I'd guess you know about that or we wouldn't be having this conversation."

"I only know what was in the papers. He won't talk about it. I feel like I could help him more if I knew what happened to him."

"Nobody knows. That's the thing. Mitch is the only one, and he . . . Look. Maybe you mean well, but after all these years, I don't see how any of this could be helpful. I really do need to go now."

"If he could play again, though. He says he's nothing without the music. It's what started him drinking, he says."

A long silence stretches out, and Phee bites her tongue to keep from filling it.

"I always blamed Lilian for that," Jo finally says. "A real princess, she was. Wanted to be up on a pedestal with him kneeling at her feet. I always thought what broke him was her kicking him to the curb, but maybe you're right about the music. Are you sure you're not a reporter? I've talked too much already. I'll need to clear you with my brother before I say any more—"

"Jo, wait! He doesn't know—"

Phee is talking to herself. Damn it. She should have lied about her name. Now Braden will know she's digging. She tosses the phone onto her mother's kitchen table in disgust and looks up to see Bridgette, hands on hips, glaring at her.

"What are you up to, Ophelia MacPhee?"

"Nothing."

"Try again."

"Making a phone call."

Bridgette pulls out a chair and sits, waving the phone at Phee. "Is this about that poor girl's father?"

Phee gives in. Her mother will win sooner or later; it's a waste of energy trying to hold out.

"Yes. About him, and about Allie, too."

"And one of your grandfather's instruments, is it?" Bridgette's voice is unexpectedly gentle, and Phee's resistance melts.

"It's all such a mess," she says. "Braden's supposed to be playing the cello, but he has this injury to his hands and can't play. So, he drinks. And then Allie . . . well, before I brought Allie over here the other day, she left this on her mother's grave." She smooths Allie's letter out on the table, watches the sadness transfer from the paper to Bridgette's face as she reads.

"Poor lass. Does he know this? Her father?"

Phee shakes her head. "I doubt it. She's not talking to him."

"Will you tell him?"

"She needs to tell him herself. And she needs to play again."

Bridgette folds the letter up and pushes it away from her before leaning forward and making eye contact with her daughter. "Phee. Listen to me, and listen to me closely. These people's lives are not your responsibility. I know you learned something about codependency in those AA meetings."

"This isn't codependency. Probably." She laughs at the familiar expression on her mother's face, but it's a half-hearted laugh and she's quickly serious. "I know, I know. But I can't take the chance that Granddad was right. I have to—"

"You have to do nothing. I'll never forgive the old man for laying this on you. I know you adored him, Phee, and he was a wonderful person, but he was half crazy."

"So you keep telling me."

"Here's what I didn't tell you. He came home from the war seriously ill, your grandmother said. He couldn't eat, couldn't sleep, raving about hearing music when there clearly was none to hear. His family admitted him to a psych unit. He was medicated and sedated. When they let him out, he seemed fine on the surface, but he was obsessed with his instruments."

Phee thinks about a certain envelope in her cedar chest, the one she has never yet opened. The one her grandfather told her contains the secret rite that finishes a MacPhee creation off properly. "Only open it if you wish to create a binding oath," he said. She's considered burning it, unopened, about a million times, but it's still there, lurking at the bottom of the trunk.

"What about his father?" Phee asks. "And grandfather? Were they all crazy, too? What about Dad? Because he said this shit has been handed down for generations."

"Insanity can be generational. It's possible. Your father wasn't touched by it. But he takes after his mother's side of the family more than the MacPhees. Maybe only some of them were crazy and just sold the story to the next of kin. The point is, curses aren't real. This oath he bound you to isn't real. You don't have to do any of this."

"I do, though." Phee thinks uneasily about the music she hears all the time now, and wonders if her turn in the psych unit is coming. "I would, anyway, whether I'd ever sworn an oath or not. This is beyond Granddad's stuff, Mom. Not playing is tearing the both of them apart."

Bridgette's sharp eyes scan her face. "You're in love with him, aren't you? The cellist."

"Why would you say that?"

"It's written all over you. All these years I've been waiting for you to fall in love. Sooner or later, I tell myself. One of these days, the right man will walk into her life and she'll be unable to resist. She'll forget all about this insanity of her grandfather's and make a family. And now some broken-down alcoholic cellist walks on stage and he's the one?"

Phee laughs out loud, in spite of everything. "That life you keep trying to plan for me is more a fantasy than the curse. What man would ever tolerate my obsession?"

"I was wishing that the man would become your obsession, child."

"Be careful what you wish for," Phee whispers.

"Oh, Phee." Bridgette reaches across the table and covers her daughter's hand with her own. "You never could do anything by halves."

~

When Phee arrives on Braden's doorstep on Wednesday afternoon at 3:29 and rings the bell, she gives herself a serious pep talk. She'll be friendly but keep good boundaries. She's not taking him on a date. The way her blood surges at the smallest thought of him, the way her heart beats faster and her breath seems to live in her throat at the sound of his voice, all of this is irrelevant. She's here as a sponsor and a . . . coach. That's it. A person with a job to do. Keep him sober. Get him playing the cello.

She has a rudimentary plan forming in her head, only she needs help to make it happen.

"Look what you've gotten me into," she mutters to her grandfather as she punches the bell again. Music swirls between her ears, this time nothing classical, a mournful lament.

The door swings open, and her heart does a series of rolling somersaults, despite all of her best intentions.

"No Celestine?" Braden asks, looking behind her.

"He's not exactly well behaved at the pet store. I half expected that you wouldn't be here," she adds, getting back in the car.

"I almost wasn't." He busies himself buckling his seat belt, avoiding her gaze. "I confess that I actually fled the premises, but then I came back."

"Why?"

"Which thing?"

"Both. Why leave. Why come back?"

"Afraid to face the group. Afraid I'll drink if I don't go. Afraid of you, frankly. Did you tell them about my relapse?"

"Hey, my interference and enabling goes only so far. Tell or don't tell, that's your decision to make."

"But you called a special meeting."

"I told them I was thinking about drinking. They were all having fits because I missed on Monday. I never miss."

"Are you? Thinking about drinking?"

"Crossed my mind."

It's not a lie. The aroma of the Scotch she poured on her grandfather's grave is still making her mouth water. But that's not why she's called this meeting, which is all about Braden. As much as she's struggling with her boundaries, though, she knows it won't do him any good to talk about his relapses unless he brings it up himself.

They drive the rest of the way in an uneasy silence, Phee alternating between her own thoughts and trying to read his. When she parks the car, he makes no move to get out.

"You coming?"

"I tried to play last night. Just so you know."

"Oh, Braden."

"It was absolutely horrifying. Spent the rest of the night walking around and trying not to think. Or drink."

"Did you pop into a bar? Buy a bottle?"

"I did not, oddly enough."

"Come on," she says. "Come inside. We're late."

The whole group cheers when they walk in.

"Hey, glad you made it," Oscar says. "We were starting to worry. Phee is never late."

"And she never misses meetings." Katie glares at Braden, as if sensing that he is responsible for Phee's absence.

"I'm only here because she dragged me," Braden says, pulling up a chair.

"You wouldn't be here if you really didn't want to come," Jean says. She's wearing a long sweater, her hands completely disappeared inside the sleeves, but she holds eye contact with Braden for a long moment, reading him. Jean always can see things that everybody else misses.

"Let's talk adventures. Braden, as our newest member, you are on the hot seat." Len uncaps his marker, ready to write down adventure points.

"I didn't take anybody on an adventure. I thought about it, for about half a second. The checker at the grocery store looked like she needed one. Are there points for good intentions?"

"Yep. A zero," Len says good-naturedly.

"Technically, we took each other on an adventure," Phee interjects, trying to lighten his mood, ease his way. "Just a picnic in the rain. So split it up, half for each of us."

Braden meets her eyes across the table. "I won't let you do it, Phee."

"It's true! Technically."

"It's not true," he says, carefully and deliberately. "I was on the edge of drinking. Phee advised that I lock myself out of the house, which I did. And then she took me to the park."

"Sounds like an adventure to me," Dennis says. "Letting Phee whisk you off is bound to be unpredictable. Was Celestine involved?"

Braden takes a breath. "He was. And despite an enormous amount of dog slobber and getting drenched in the rain, I returned home and drank half a bottle."

Phee realizes she's been holding her breath. He's fessed up to his relapse, that's the important thing. He's also completely left out the bits that helped drive him to drink, namely Phee badgering him about curses and oaths and playing the cello.

"You were able to stop at half? That's pretty impressive control," Dennis says. "I sure didn't manage that."

"Only because I got a call to come pick up my drunk and underage daughter from a party." He's tight as an over-tuned string, ready to snap, waiting for judgment from the group.

Katie pours a mug of coffee and sets it in front of Braden. "Black, right?" is all she says, but her fingers graze the back of his hand.

Jean smiles at him. Not pity, not judgment, just pure understanding.

"Sorry to hear it, man. What set you off?" Oscar asks.

Braden grimaces, an attempt at a smile that doesn't make it past good intentions.

"Guilt. Grief. I abandoned my kids when they were little. My ex and my son were killed a few weeks ago, and now my surviving daughter hates me. It all got too big."

"How's she coping?" Jean asks.

"She's not. Former 4.0 GPA apparently, and she hasn't been to school since the accident. Skated away from an MIP at the party. Hanging out with a boy who is . . . I don't like him. And then Phee found her in the graveyard the other day, in the rain. Grass stained and soaked, and I just—" His voice breaks.

Tears gather behind Phee's eyes and a lump grows in her throat. She wants to comfort him but doesn't have any comfort to offer. She won't spout lies, won't tell him it will be all right when there's no reason to believe it to be true.

All of them are silent for a little too long.

"Wow. That's fucked up." Trust Katie to find the perfect words.

"I've tried to make things right with her, but I'm getting nowhere. She knows I've been drinking, which doesn't help at all."

"Look, man." Dennis leans forward. "You're in a touchy situation. Maybe a counselor. I mean, that's a lot of shit for a kid to manage."

The cello, Phee thinks at him. *The cello is at the center of this. Allie needs her music. And she needs your music.*

"You're not expected to be a superhero," Len says.

"But you're a good man," Jean whispers.

Braden laughs, short and sharp. "I left my family for booze. I hardly think that counts as good."

"You're here, right?" Oscar says. "Here and sober."

"More or less. I've been drinking."

"Are you sober now?" Jean asks.

"All you have to do is stay," Katie says. "She's pissed right now. And horribly wounded. But she wants you to stay, so the most important thing is that you can't run off."

A missing word hangs in the air. Braden says it.

"Again, Katie. Can't run off *again.* I'm not sure she can forgive me for the last time."

"If my dad ever came back? Like, even now? I'd treat him like shit. But I'd hope that he'd stick around and prove me wrong." Katie's voice cracks. She sniffles, hides her face in her hands. "Oh fuck. Now look what you made me do."

Phee feels the tears on her own cheeks. Len's eyes are wet. All of them know better than to offer Katie sympathy. They all just sit with the emotion, trusting that she's strong enough to handle it, that they all are.

Katie drags her sleeve across her eyes and sits up straight, a fierce expression on her face. "Braden relapsed. He needs consequences."

"You're kidding," Braden says. "I mean, I get the adventure thing, but—"

"She's right. Come on, man. Out in the hall with you." Oscar pushes back his chair.

Braden glances around the table, fixes a pleading gaze on Phee. "Don't you dare run off," she admonishes.

"Wouldn't dream of it."

"Promise?"

He sighs. "Cross my heart and hope to die."

From his lips, the old words are not exactly comforting, but it will do for now.

"There's always skydiving," Len says as soon as Oscar closes the door behind Braden. "Or maybe even just a ride in a small plane. I know a guy who does flight lessons. Maybe he could take a turn at flying."

"Wait," Phee says. "This is a special situation. Whatever we plan, it needs to include both of them. Something they do together, to help repair what's broken between them."

"How about something fun," Katie suggests. "Like a rock concert."

"I think it should be something that lasts awhile and pushes the two of them together," Phee argues, nudging them in the direction of her plan. "I mean, we can all go, but then leave them alone together." *With the cello,* she adds silently.

"Camping," Dennis says.

"It's way too cold for that."

"African safari?"

"Smart-ass."

"Tough time of year for outdoor shit. Snowmobile trip in the mountains? Dogsledding in Alaska?"

"How about a week in a cabin somewhere?" Phee says casually. "We drive up in a couple of cars, stay for the weekend, then leave them there to work things out."

"Hate to be the spoilsport," Len says, "but isn't Allie supposed to be in school?"

"Supposed to be, yes. But she's not."

"School is way overrated," Katie says. "Can we make it in the mountains? A ski cabin maybe? I've never actually been snow skiing!"

"How about tropical?" Dennis asks, laughing. "Can we rent an island?"

"My old bones vote for a place with hot springs." Len speaks lightly, but his shrewd eyes narrow as he scrutinizes Phee.

She puts on her most innocent face and claps her hands. "We're agreed on a cabin getaway, yes? I'll do the research and find a place. When?"

"Well, Dennis's consequences adventure is this Saturday."

"We can always change that," Dennis says. "Allie's need seems more pressing."

"It's going to take some time to set things up," Phee says. "Maybe the weekend after, if I can pull it off?"

Assent follows from around the table, and Oscar goes to the door and ushers Braden back to his seat.

"What is my fate? Will I be licked to death by kittens?" he asks, looking at the circle of faces with that twisted half smile that hints at the humor that once was part of him.

Katie giggles. "It would be a long, slow death. Mark off a whole week, not this one but next."

He sobers. "I can't leave Allie."

"She comes, too," Phee says. "Two adventures for the price of one."

"You can't argue with an all-expenses paid vacation with all of us," Len says. "Got anywhere else to be?"

"Can't say as I do."

"Then consider it done. All right. Who had an adventure this week? Jean?"

Phee spends the rest of the meeting paying surface attention while spinning a complex plot in her head. For the first time since the inception of the Angels, she can't wait for the meeting to be over so she can get to work.

Finally, the last adventure is celebrated, the numbers are tallied. Katie draws Braden off to show him the arrival of a new bird, a parrot that can whistle "Row, Row, Row Your Boat" with surprising accuracy.

Len takes the opportunity to have a private word with Phee.

"What are you up to?"

"Me?"

"Don't even. You're scheming."

Len's ability to read people is almost as alarming as Jean's, and definitely more problematic. Jean gets psychic hits but hardly ever dares to say anything about them. Len, on the other hand, honed his skill during a forty-year career as a clinical psychologist, and has absolutely no problem calling people on their shit.

Phee gives him her widest, most innocent smile, the one that Bridgette has always said makes her look guilty as sin. "I need to ask you a hypothetical question."

"On a personal or professional level?"

"Professional."

"Hmmm. Why do I feel like the wrong answer will induct me into a secret society without my knowledge or consent?"

"Hush. It's about somebody I'm taking on an adventure, and I need some help. If an individual has a bad case of, say, PTSD, so severe that they've blocked out a whole set of memories, is it possible they'd also have a physical component?"

She holds her breath, hoping his suspicions will be overridden by professional enthusiasm. When his eyes light up with interest and he looks through her without seeing her, she knows she's scored a hit.

"PTSD is such a fascinating combination of chemicals and psychological blocks, Phee. Very complex. Many sufferers do have a host of physical ailments. They are much more likely to suffer from inflammatory diseases and immune disorders. Chronic fatigue, fibromyalgia, rheumatoid arthritis. Not to mention higher incidence of blood pressure and even diabetes due to the continual presence of stress hormones—"

"How about something more specific?" Now that Phee has got him talking, the trick is to head him off before he gives her a one-hour lecture on the role of stress in immune disorders. "How about loss of function in a part of the body?"

Len's gaze sharpens, and she keeps her face open and noncommittal, eyes wide, channeling all of the genuine curiosity she can summon up.

"What I think you're asking isn't necessarily connected to PTSD, although there is usually trauma involved. There is a fascinating condition we call conversion disorder. A person is faced with a set of circumstances so impossible to reconcile with their belief system, or a trauma so intense, that an elaborate defense mechanism emerges. I know of a four-year-old child who saw her father commit a murder. For months, she exhibited total blindness. Didn't even blink if we shone a flashlight in her eyes. But there was absolutely nothing wrong with the eye or the optic nerve . . ."

Len stops himself, and Phee realizes she's forgotten to manage her expression.

"What are you up to, Ophelia MacPhee?"

"Research. Like I said—"

"No, you're plotting. I know that gleam in your eye. This is dangerous territory. Not some sort of game. If you are thinking for one minute about creating an adventure that's going to make someone with PTSD confront their trauma—"

"I'm not an idiot," she says stiffly, as if he's hurt her feelings. "I'm just trying to understand."

"I mean it, Phee. Even trained professionals mess this stuff up. It's like dynamite, and you never know which way it's going to blow.

Dealing with it requires all kinds of safety structures in place. Are you listening to me?"

She pats his arm reassuringly. "I understand. Dynamite. Only for professionals. Thanks, Len."

He doesn't quite believe her, smart man that he is. She can feel his eyes boring holes into her back as she hugs Jean and Katie good night, thanks Oscar for running the extra meeting, exchanges jokes with Dennis about his upcoming consequences party. All the while she's watching Braden and thinking about explosions.

Chapter Twenty-Six

ALLIE

Allie parks the car but just sits there, hands at ten and two, leaving the motor running. The headlights illuminate a yellow grocery bag caught up on the branch of a sickly shrub. She wishes it were daylight. She'd like to see the sun once more, or even the moon, but today was dim and gray even before the sun went down.

For the very last time, she asks herself if she has other options.

But just thinking about the year ahead shrivels her up inside. If she fails this semester, she'll have to face the humiliation of going back to school in the fall, or settle for a GED. Even if she does pass, her grades are gonna suck. And then what? Even if she can get another scholarship to UW, she'd feel obligated to do premed, follow her mother's wishes.

Her life was always music. That's all she wants to do, all she is, but she can't do that, either. She makes herself face the memory of the tragedy, the day that tore her life apart forever. If she's going to chicken out of living, the least she can do for her mother and brother is face up to the memory, and she lets herself sink into it, one last time.

The sun is shining, the day full of promise.

She's going to meet her father. She's going to nail this audition and show him what she can do.

It all starts to go wrong when she swings by the kitchen for a glass of orange juice and a muffin. Her mom is usually sleeping, but instead she's in the kitchen with a cup of coffee.

"I need you to pick up Trey after school."

Allie whirls around in dismay, spilling orange juice all over her dress. "I have plans."

"Well, your plans will have to be changed. I have appointments this morning. I need to sleep before I go in to work."

Damn it. There's a stain right between her boobs. Allie's mind skims over the other things she could wear today. "He can take a bus. Or walk—"

"There's not time. He's seeing a specialist about his knee."

Allie, desperate, goes for a half truth. "Mom. I have a commitment. It's an orchestra thing—"

"They can do without you for one day."

"I have a solo!" This part, at least, is true.

"And your brother needs his knee fixed so he can keep doing track. Which is just as important as your music."

"Like he's going to spend the rest of his life running," Allie retorts.

"Alexandra Marie Healey. Do you hear yourself?"

Allie takes a breath. "Music is—"

"A waste of your time. You're going to be a doctor, not squander your life on music."

"Can't he Uber or something? I'll pay for it. Out of my own money—"

"He's fourteen! He can't go alone, and I need to sleep. I need you to do this."

"But—"

"Enough! You're just like your father. Music was his god and nobody else mattered. Do you really want to be that person?"

"But—"

"Pick your brother up after school. Here's the address and a note giving him permission to be seen."

Allie stops arguing. Feeling hopeless and defeated she changes into her usual jeans and shirt. But when she picks up the cello case to put it back in the music room, the cello whispers a caress and rebellion kicks in.

Her whole life depends on this audition. This one time, she'll do what she wants. She just won't show up. Trey's appointment can be rescheduled.

Allie kills the engine and leans her forehead on the steering wheel. God, she'd been so selfish, defiant, rebellious, and that had killed Mom and Trey. Ethan is the only spot of color in a world gone gray, and he's about to leave her. If she doesn't go through with this, she'll be betraying *his* trust, breaking her word again.

She breathes in the car smell for the last time, catching a faint whiff of Trey, sweat and feet and enthusiasm.

"You've got the whole world still, Allie," his voice says, as clearly as if it comes through the speakers.

"I don't want it," she whispers, and that gets her out of the car and into the room where Ethan is lying on the bed, waiting.

He'd said he'd make preparations, that this would be a celebration, and he'd meant it. The cheap, scarred table is transformed by a white tablecloth. Laid out, as if on an altar, are two crystal glasses, a bottle of whiskey, and two small crystal bowls. A candle burns at the center.

He doesn't move when she walks in, his dark gaze burning all of her doubts away.

"I was afraid you wouldn't come."

"I wasn't sure."

"Are you sure now?"

Allie floats to the bed. Her body has no weight. Now that she's decided, everything is easy. Nothing holds her anymore. She's free.

This time, the lovemaking feels natural, inevitable. She loses herself in the pleasure of Ethan's hands and lips, the way her body rises to meet his when he enters her. After it's over, she lies quiet against him, both emptied and filled with a sense of wonder.

He strokes her hair, and she drifts on the edges of sleep.

"Ready?"

Her heart contracts out of rhythm, a hard squeeze in her chest, sending a burst of heat out to her skin. Cold follows.

Her certainty has vanished again. The pleasure of sex has wakened the possibility that there might be other pleasures in the world. What might she be missing if she leaves her life behind now?

Ethan is certain enough for both of them.

"Here, I brought you something."

He rummages in a backpack beside the bed. Allie watches the muscles in his back ripple under his skin. She's awed by the miracle of muscle, how the cells form together to create bands that contract and release together on command to make the body move. What a wonder the human organism is. How did she live all of her life and never notice?

A wave of sadness washes over her, grief that this beautiful boy will no longer be in the world, that those muscles will be cold and stiff tomorrow. Her own life is a small, dark thing, but his seems beautiful to her, glorious even.

Ethan turns to her with something white and floaty in his hands. "Put this on."

She takes it from him, a flimsy bit of silk and lace. Heat rises to her face.

"Please," he says, and she sees in her imagination the tableau he's creating. The table, with its candles and roses. Allie dressed in white.

"Here, I'll help you."

She raises her arms as if she's a child, and he pulls the nightgown down over her head, smooths it over her breasts and hips and thighs. He runs his hands through her hair, arranging it on her shoulders.

"There. You're perfect. Shall we?"

His hand closes around hers, warm and steady where hers is cold and trembling. She lets him lead her to the table. Sits when he pulls the chair out for her.

He lowers himself into the chair across from her. She watches him pour amber liquid into their glasses. His eyes glow with anticipation as he raises his glass for a toast.

"To what comes after."

Allie lifts her own glass and touches it to his. "To what comes after."

Ethan drinks effortlessly and smoothly. Allie lifts her own glass to her lips and swallows. The whiskey burns, and she chokes, coughs. It's a full-size tumbler, and she's not even halfway through when Ethan pours himself a second glass.

He smiles at her. "You're smaller, so it will hit you harder. Take your time. No rush."

While she sips, he brings out three pill bottles and divides the contents into the crystal bowls. One for him, one for her.

"What are we taking?"

"Just trust me."

She thinks about stories she's heard. Failed attempts. Ruined livers and kidneys. Brain damage.

"I want to know."

"Don't ruin it. Okay? I planned everything. One of these first."

He hands her a small tablet, and she turns it over and over in her fingers, looking at the markings etched into it and wondering what they mean.

"So we don't puke. Melt it under your tongue."

They dissolve the pills together, and Allie takes another drink to wash the taste away.

"I'm glad you're with me," Ethan says. He picks up his dish of pills and dumps half of them into his mouth, washing them down with the whiskey.

Allie picks her pills up one at a time, filling her palm. Twelve oblong tablets. Ten small round ones. They feel cold and alien, an overwhelming amount, and it's not even half of what's in the dish. If she doesn't consume them all, it won't be enough. She'll still be here, left behind, while Ethan is gone.

She glances behind her at the door. She could run out, only she's wearing the nightgown and where would she go? There's nothing out there for her.

"You can do it," Ethan encourages, and she shoves the whole handful into her mouth. Her throat fights her, closing against the chalky ovals. She swallows whiskey, but that chokes her too, and she gags on the whole mess, eyes watering. By the time she fights off the spasm of nausea and manages to swallow, Ethan has emptied both his glass and his entire dish of pills.

He leans back in his chair, watching her. Already there is a distance in his eyes, his face. He's moving away from her.

Allie still has half of her pills to go. Her stomach is churning. Her throat burns with whiskey and a bitter chemical aftertaste. She can't do this.

Panic hits.

Ethan is going to die and leave her behind. She's going to sit here and watch him stop breathing, stop being Ethan. She'll be left in this wretched place alone, alive, have to call her father and ask him to come and get her.

This is not an option.

Maybe she can take the pills with water. Maybe she can swallow them one at a time. Maybe she can still . . .

I don't want to die.

The thought begins as a slow vibration at her core. It spreads up through her spinal column and into her skull, down through the bones of her legs, into her arms, her hands.

I don't want to die.

It resonates outward, through her muscles and into her skin, every delicate nerve, every blood vessel and capillary. Into the room, which is spinning now, gently.

Allie hears music. Not the cello this time but a song with words, her father singing to her as he tucks her into bed. She feels safe, drifting off to sleep, knowing he will be watching out for her.

She doesn't understand the words, something French, but she knows they mean he loves her. All of the music he shared with her is still with her.

A realization comes to her, now, when it's too late.

Her father does love her, always loved her. The hours spent listening to him practice, the times he put the bow in her hand and guided it to make music. The cello lessons he insisted on, even after he was gone, that was love. And the breakfasts she's despised, the oatmeal, that also was love.

Ethan is slumped in his chair. His pupils are dilated, his lids half closed. He looks younger without the tension in his jaw, almost child-like, and Allie wants to stop him from dying, only the room keeps spinning and her limbs are swaddled in cotton.

"Almos' forgot." He fumbles with something in his pocket and brings out a phone. It's an old phone, worn. The screen is cracked. This means something, but before she can grasp it, the strains of the Bach suite in G drift into the room. Not just any version, not Casals's or Yo-Yo Ma's, but the Braden Healey version.

At first she thinks it's the music she's been hearing in her head, and then she understands. She wants to tell Ethan no, but her lips won't work and the word sticks in her throat.

"'Cause you loved the cello," Ethan says. "Downloaded the album just for you."

Loved. Past tense.

Only it isn't past, not at all. *Loves.* She loves the cello. More than anything else in the world. As the music washes over her, she understands her father's words to Phee. He does love her, just as she loved her mother and Trey. It's just that the cello is a part of him, a part of her.

Cut that away, and what's left is something undead, like a zombie. A tortured thing without a soul.

"Beautiful music to die to," Ethan says.

Allie shakes her head, which is a mistake. The room spins faster, and she closes her eyes. It takes two attempts, but she finally coordinates her mouth and tongue to shape words.

"Have you ever seen anybody die?"

Ethan doesn't answer. His eyes have drifted closed, his head nodding forward.

"Ethan. Have you?"

"What?"

"Have you seen anybody die?"

Still he doesn't answer.

Allie watches Trey die all over again, as if her closed eyelids are a movie screen. His body twitching, convulsing. The desperate, ragged breaths. It wasn't beautiful, at all. It was horrible and wrong.

Is this different?

She tries to force her eyes back open, but they are too heavy. Her limbs are weighted. She fights it.

The phone. There's something about the phone.

A dim memory, her own phone hurtling into the ocean. Ethan's lecture about phones and tracking devices.

"Whose phone?"

Ethan blinks slowly. He's sliding out of his chair, leaning sideways. "Mine."

No. You don't have a phone. You said.

She's waiting for the answer that never comes before she realizes she hasn't spoken, that the words are only in her head. It's so hard to think, the music making it even harder. She can't give in, not now, something is wrong.

Allie wrestles with her body, trying to make it sit up straight, to make it arms and hands work. Little by little, she manages to fumble one of the pill bottles into her hand. This seems like the most important thing, a reason not to die. Her vision keeps going in and out, but she can just read the name on the prescription.

Ethan Bannister.

Not right. A doctor wouldn't prescribe all these for him.

And then she sees the letters following the name. *Sr.*

But Ethan's dad is dead. He said so. Died from suicide years ago. These pills can't be his, unless that was a lie, just like the phone.

Her tongue is made of cotton, and her lips are disconnected from her brain. She manages to get her eyes half open.

Ethan's breath snores in and out of his throat. Drool trails down over his chin. He's not beautiful anymore.

Her brain is a small spark of consciousness, but it flickers like a candle in the wind.

Ethan lied. About the phone. About his father.

She doesn't want to die as part of a lie.

Call for help.

She reaches for his phone, but her fingers won't work right, and it slips away, out of reach. She tries to stand, but her legs seem to belong to some other girl and drop her onto the floor. The carpet stinks of mold and old tobacco. Her eyelids are heavy while the rest of her body is floating. Moving is hard, too hard. She'd like to say goodbye to her father, to tell him that she loves him. But even that seems too far away. Maybe it's too late for it to matter.

Chapter Twenty-Seven
PHEE

Phee lays a clean white cover over the instruments she's working on and puts her tools away. Everything as usual, everything in its place, except for her thoughts. She's thoroughly at war with herself, not that this is anything new.

"Obsessed," "incorrigible," "obstinate"—these are words that have woven themselves into her being from the time she was a very small child. Every lecture that came her way from her parents or her teachers involved the word "too." Too loud, too excited, too bossy, too opinionated, too much.

Somewhere along the line, she's made peace with that, has turned the words into an inside joke for her own private amusement. Her business cards read:

Ophelia MacPhee, Luthier
Your instrument is my obsession

She has to make a decision and make it soon. A vacation rental cabin somewhere in the woods or the cabin she has in mind. Just because Braden's sister didn't want to talk to her doesn't mean she can't figure out where it is. Does she proceed? Or take a step back. Let Braden and Allie find their footing with each other. At least the cello is in a place where she can keep an eye on it.

She's just getting ready to climb into bed and let go of the day when her phone rings.

Braden.

Her hand moves toward the phone in slow motion, and her voice sounds dry and tight when she answers.

"Phee. Thank God you picked up. It's Allie. She's tried to kill herself and she's taken the car and—"

"Oh God. Oh, Braden. Keep talking. I'm already moving."

Adrenaline floods her as she squeezes the phone between her shoulder and her ear and puts on her shoes and jacket.

"She's at the Sunset Motel. The cops are on their way. I've booked an Uber, but it's going to be a bit and you're closer than I am. I can't bear the waiting. Go there, Phee, don't come here."

"All right." She can hear his panicked breathing, the sound of him pacing. "Easy, Braden. Maybe she's okay. How do you know—"

"I was worried. Had a bad feeling. I looked at her laptop. She always takes it with her, she never leaves it here. There was an IM conversation between her and Ethan . . ." His voice breaks on a wrenching sob that threatens to turn her inside out.

She grabs her keys and runs to her car.

Braden manages a quavering breath, and goes on. "They made a pact, Phee. And they were meeting hours ago. If she's . . ." He breaks off again, unable to say the words.

"I'm on my way. Give me an address."

He rattles off the number and street, and she enters it into her phone. "That's not far from here. Stay with me, Braden. I'm in the car. Moving."

"Oh God. I should have done something, Phee. Taken her to a counselor. Sent her off with Alexandra. All of this is my fault."

"Sounds like Ethan has some blame in this."

"Lilian would never have let her date that boy."

"Did you?"

"No, but—"

"She's a seventeen-year-old girl. You can't just stop a kid that age from doing shit unless you physically lock her in a room. Maybe not even then. I speak from the voice of experience."

She sees flashing lights ahead. Dread writhes in her belly. The seedy motel is garishly lit, on again, off again, by the red and blue lights. Two cop cars. An ambulance. A group of people huddles beside the ambulance watching the show.

"Phee?" Braden's voice asks. "Where are you? What do you see?"

"I'm here. There are cop cars. An ambulance."

"Oh God." It's a groan, a prayer.

"I'm going to see what I can find out. I'll call you back." Phee disconnects. If it's bad news, she doesn't want him to hear it live.

The motel has two floors, all of the doors opening out toward the parking lot. Up the stairs, to the right, one of the doors is open. A uniformed officer stands outside.

"Hey," she says, approaching the bystanders. "What's going on?"

"Suicide. That's what the cop told the EMT," a girl says. She can't be much older than Allie, but the high boots, short skirt, and amount of makeup hint that her presence in the motel is more professional than recreational.

"Asshole kids creating trouble," a man says. He's skeletal thin, twitchy, his right front incisor missing. "Should never have rented them a room."

The girl surprises Allie with a swift response. "You're right, Finn, you shouldn't have."

"And you'd better make your pretty ass scarce before the cops come out here and get interested in you," he retorts with venom.

Phee walks away from both of them, starts climbing the stairs.

The cop swivels toward her, one hand automatically resting on his service weapon.

"Ma'am, go back to the parking lot."

"I'm family. Of the girl, Allie. Please."

His voice softens, but he moves to block the top of the stairs. "You'll help her best right now by letting the medical team work. Please go back down."

"But can you tell me anything? Anything at all. Please." She presses her palms together like a prayer.

"They're alive, that's all I know and all I can tell you. Now, please."

"What hospital will they take her to? At least tell me that."

The cop's face registers sympathy. He hesitates a moment. "I'll ask if you wait right here."

"Promise. Not budging." She grips the railing with both hands to signal her intent, and he turns and walks to the open door. She can't hear what's said, no matter how she strains her ears, and it seems an eternity before he returns.

"Swedish. Ballard Campus."

"Bless you." Phee retreats but doesn't rejoin the others. The girl, she sees, has vanished, but her place has been taken by a middle-aged woman who is filming the open doorway and the cop outside it with her phone.

Phee calls Braden back. "Alive," she says.

"What happened? What did they . . ." She hears the words stick in his throat, knows he's envisioning blood and ropes, guns and pills, the same images that are filling her own brain with graphic intensity.

"They wouldn't tell me."

"Is she . . . will she be okay?"

"They'll be taking her to Swedish. What do you want me to do?"

"I'll cancel the Uber. Come get me."

"On my way. She's in good hands, Braden."

~

He's waiting in the driveway, shaking so badly he can't get the door open. Phee leans over and opens it from the inside. As soon as he's in, she throws her arms around him, and he grabs on to her as if she's a life preserver, his cheek pressed against her hair. He begins to weep, and Phee feels her own grief and guilt and fear cresting along with his.

He needs her, though, and she forces herself to breathe. A long inhale, a controlled exhale. Slow and easy. Gradually, his trembling eases, his breathing slows and steadies to match hers.

"Thank you," he sighs, releasing her, blotting at his eyes.

Phee blinks hard to clear her vision, then puts the car in reverse. They are silent all the way to the hospital.

"What if . . . ," he begins as she pulls into the parking lot.

"Shhh," she answers. "She'll be here. Don't even think it."

She reaches for his hand, and his fingers clamp around hers so hard it hurts.

ER reception is small and crowded. Two women sit in chairs side by side. A man talks to the receptionist, a bloody towel wrapped around his arm. A set of official-looking double doors are posted with a sign: *Staff Only*. Another door is marked *Family Room*.

When the locked doors open and a woman in scrubs helps the guy with the bleeding arm into a wheelchair and then back into the ER, Phee holds Braden back, feeling his muscles tense as if he's going to make a break for it.

"How can I help you?" the woman behind the desk finally asks, her eyes weary but kind.

"We're looking for our daughter," Phee says, low and steady. "We understand an ambulance may have brought her in."

"Name?"

"Allie Healey."

The woman frowns, taps a few keys.

Braden fidgets while the woman consults her computer. Phee squeezes his hand, her own heart accelerating in an agony of impatience.

"Oh, here we are. You can wait in the family room. I'll buzz you in."

"How is she?" Braden asks. "Can you tell me anything?"

"Please wait in the family room. A doctor will be in to talk to you shortly."

A buzzer sounds, and Phee opens the door and pulls Braden through behind her. The family room is mercifully empty, with the exception of a young woman trying to soothe a crying baby. There are comfortable chairs, magazines, coffee, and Styrofoam cups.

"God, Phee. I can't."

"She's here, they're taking care of her," Phee says. "Try to believe in the best."

If only she could follow her own advice.

Braden paces, staring at the door on the other side of the room, as if willing it to open. Phee sits in a chair, focuses on her hands in her lap, her feet on the floor.

Was the receptionist trying to keep something to herself or just being professional? If Allie was okay, maybe she'd have said something. Maybe waiting in the family room like this means the worst has happened.

Braden comes to sit beside her. He's barely holding it together, she can tell.

"Hey," she says, a hand on his forearm. "Hey. Stay with me."

"Panic attack," he says through stiff lips. "I don't have time for this shit. I need to be here for her."

"Breathe, Braden. Slow it down."

She puts a hand on his chest and wills calm into him. Little by little, his breathing eases.

"What if she dies, Phee? I don't think I can—"

"She's not going to die."

Please make it true, she thinks. *Please.*

The door opens, revealing a woman in surgical scrubs, blonde hair escaping from a clip that tries to hold it back. Both of them get to their feet, linked together by their hands and a single indrawn breath.

"Mr. and Mrs. Healey?"

Braden nods. Clears his throat but doesn't speak.

"I'm Dr. Javitz."

"How is Allie?"

"She overdosed, Mr. Healey. She's responded to the naloxone—that's something that counteracts an opiate overdose, so that's encouraging. We've pumped her stomach and she's breathing on her own. We're running a tox screen, but it would be helpful to know what all she took."

"I—I have no idea. She's going to be okay, right? Please tell me the truth."

"Do you have any prescriptions she might have taken?"

"None. I . . . had some Librium, but it was gone. My wife might have had something . . ."

The doctor looks at Phee.

"No, no, my wife's dead."

"Your daughter has been drinking, in addition to the pills. She's got a blood alcohol of 1.2."

"No alcohol in the house as far as I know."

"The police did recover prescription bottles from the motel room. They belonged to the boy's father, apparently. Oxycodone and Xanax."

"God," Braden says, and Phee isn't sure if it's a prayer or an epithet or both combined.

The doctor's expression shifts to sympathy again. "I'm sure this is very hard to hear, Mr. Healey. There were two small bowls on the table. His was empty. Your daughter's still contained pills, so she didn't swallow all of hers."

Phee should have said something. Should have told Braden about what really happened in the graveyard. The signs were all there. The girl lying on the grave in the rain, the note she'd written. God, she's screwed this whole thing up so badly.

"We've had to put the boy on a ventilator, but I think your daughter will pull through without any extraordinary measures. Lucky it wasn't hydrocodone—the acetaminophen in that is so hard on livers."

"Can I see her?" Braden asks in a strangled voice.

"Yes, of course. If she remains stable over the next few hours, as I think she will, we'll be moving her up to the general unit. Come with me."

Allie looks very small and young lying on the stretcher in a room filled with machines and medical equipment. Her eyes are closed; her mouth gapes just a little. An IV runs into one arm. A tube inserted into one nostril connects to a suction bottle on the wall. Oxygen hisses through nasal prongs. Leads on her chest connect to a machine. A steady beeping indicates her heart rate. The IV machine clicks and whirs as it pumps fluids into her body.

Braden bends over her, brushes a strand of hair out of her eyes, takes her hand in both of his. Her eyes flicker open and try to focus.

"You're here," she whispers.

"I'm here."

"Ethan?" she whispers.

"Alive."

She sighs, and her eyes drift closed again. Slow tears trickle from the corners of her eyes, streaking her temples, dampening her hair.

"It's all going to be okay, little bird," Braden says. "We'll figure it out."

Phee feels she is one person too many in the room, a voyeur. Dashing the tears off her cheeks, she retreats, wordless, leaving the two of them alone together.

Chapter Twenty-Eight

BRADEN

Braden feels Phee's absence the minute she leaves the room. She reminds him, in some ways, of his sister, Jo. Strong. Somebody he can lean on. Lilian was never that. She could be strong enough for strangers—she had to be as a nurse—but when it came to her own family, she was brittle, unable to bend. Even with the kids, it was all rules and schedules, everything laid out, neat and orderly and controlled. Anything that fell outside of the lines she drew sent her into meltdown.

Phee will be back, Braden tells himself, shifting all of his attention to Allie.

"Lucky," the doctor said, and that word is a raft to cling to in a surging sea of shock and fear.

Lucky.

Not a word he has connected with himself in years, but Allie is still alive, and that's the luckiest thing in the world.

Memory fragments surface and sink, none of them connected by a thread of logic or order or time.

Allie, barely more than a toddler, tucked between his legs and the cello, absorbing the music.

Allie, singing to herself when he tucked her in at night. "Sing the lullaby with me, Daddy."

Her tiny, perfect face on the day she was born, and how he held her and marveled at the miracle of her existence, wondered who she would turn out to be.

An alarm goes off and a nurse bustles in, checks the IV, and adjusts something. "Nothing to worry about," she tells him, but the sound sends his memory down another track.

Waking in a hospital bed under a pile of blankets, his hands swathed in bandages, an IV dripping warmed fluids into his arm.

His sister's face, broken by grief.

He hears music, loud and insistent, the tones so clear and perfect he looks around for the cello and the player, but of course it's all in his head.

Hold it together, Braden, this is no time to lose your shit.

The nurses move in and out, checking vitals, reassuring him that Allie is fine, she'll make a full recovery.

Phee pops back in, squeezes his shoulder, tells him she'll be back in the morning and all he has to do is call if he needs her before then.

Every time he needs to step away from Allie, even for a minute—to go to the bathroom, or when the nurses come in to do procedures—it edges him toward panic, and when he's asked to return to the waiting room while they transfer her to a room upstairs, it's agony.

Lucky, he reminds himself.

Lucky she'd taken oxycodone rather than hydrocodone and been spared the liver damage. Lucky she didn't take all the pills. Lucky she didn't vomit and aspirate. Lucky they found her when they did.

The nurse who comes to tell him he can go into Allie's room now is very kind. "She's doing so well. Are you sure you don't want to go home and sleep?"

"I can't leave her," he protests. "Not now, not yet."

And the woman smiles and shows him into the new room. It's softer, not so clinical. Allie is still connected to monitors, but the tube has been removed from her nose and the oxygen discontinued. Her sleep looks more natural. There's a hint of color in her cheeks.

Braden pulls a chair to the bedside and wraps his hand around hers, wishing for full sensation but grateful for what he has. He needs the physical link between them to reassure himself that she's here, alive, not in a coffin, not dead in a tawdry motel room.

His hand, her hand, and then her words, echoing in his head.

There's nothing wrong with your hands.

It's not the first time he's heard these words, though he's worked hard to submerge them under gallons of alcohol.

"What if there's nothing wrong with your hands?"

The psychologist is short, thin, with a ratlike nose and wire-framed glasses, a know-it-all who dares to suggest the loss of sensation—paresthesia, he calls it, drawing out all of the syllables—is in Braden's head.

Braden laughs at the absurdity of the question. "I have no sensation in my fingers. Pretty sure that's not normal."

"Your medical reports say your hands are fine now. Fully recovered."

"The docs are welcome to borrow my hands and see for themselves. How do they know what I feel?"

"Can we talk about what happened?"

"I don't remember what happened."

"What do you remember?"

"Only what I've been told."

The psychologist tents his fingers. "Don't you want to remember?"

"Of course!" He says it vehemently, knows it's a lie. Dread coils in his gut whenever he dares to stare into the abyss of what he's forgotten.

"What if remembering could heal your hands?"

"Memories can heal frostbite now?" A deflection. A desperate one, but the psychologist is not to be deterred.

"There is a condition called conversion disorder, a psychological block that affects the body. It's caused by trauma and protects the sufferer from having to face a decision or action that is too horrific or terrifying for their consciousness to handle."

"The only thing I'm suffering from is nerve damage brought on by frostbite."

"Possible."

Braden bolts up out of his chair. Shouts: "I don't believe this. I came here so you could help me deal with this loss. And now you're trying to tell me it's not a loss at all. I don't need your psycho mumbo-jumbo quackery. Excuse me, but I'm out of here."

Out of the office, into a bar. Drowning the very possibility in an alcoholic haze.

Braden drifts in and out of memories and sleep, sometimes waking sharply with no idea where he is or what he is doing here, whether he's been remembering or dreaming. The nurses move in and out on quiet feet. Sometimes they work around him. Sometimes they rouse Allie to check her level of consciousness, to care for her personal needs, shooing him out to pace in the hallway. Always, when he returns, he takes the chair beside her bed and claims her hand again while the slow clock ticks away the hours of the night.

Chapter Twenty-Nine

PHEE

Phee also watches the clock, restless in her own bed, clear now on what she needs to do. Long before dawn, she gets up, showers, takes Celestine out for a walk.

Time crawls as she waits for a reasonable hour to start making phone calls. Nine o'clock, her mother always taught her. Phee lasts until seven. If she wakes people, so be it. Her first call is to Braden to check on Allie. Then to Oscar. Her last is to Braden's sister.

"Jo. It's Phee."

"Well, aren't you the early riser."

"Sorry if I woke you."

Scoffing laughter. "I get up at four. Have for years and can't break the habit. I haven't talked to Braden yet, so—"

"Something's happened, Jo. It's Allie."

The silence on the other end is deep and shocked, and Phee rushes ahead. "She's alive, she'll be fine, but—"

"You shouldn't do that to a woman. Near gave me a heart attack."

"Sorry. Didn't want you to hang up."

"My God. What happened?"

Phee tries to soften news that can't be softened. "She took a bunch of pills. She was with a boy."

"Braden must be wrecked. Where is he? Can I talk to him?"

"He's at the hospital with her."

"And you're calling because?"

"Because I want to help. Allie is a casualty of what's going on with Braden. If we help him, we help her."

"What do you want me to do?"

"I want to bring them both out to the place where your husband died."

Silence. "I don't think that's a good idea."

"He needs to remember what happened."

"And you think that's going to help him? Excuse me, but none of us wants to remember that night."

"If you don't remember it, you can't grieve it. Trust a former alcoholic on that one. Did he always drink?"

"No," Jo says. Phee can almost hear the wheels spinning in the other woman's brain. "Now that you mention it, he never did. He hated the way our father got when he was drinking."

"Abusive?"

"I don't know that I'd say that. Belligerent. Not physically, just—he would say things. He was hard on Braden at the best of times, worse when he was drunk. You know, add alcohol for instant asshole."

"Why was Braden out there in the first place? Do you know?"

"He and Lilian had some kind of fight. He said she was making him choose, either her and the kids or the cello. He'd come away to the hunting cabin to think about what he was going to do. Had the cello with him, of course. I can't imagine that sat well with her. He was obsessed with music, I'll grant that. Not an easy man to be married to, but she should have known that before she said yes. It's not like he ever tried to hide it."

Phee closes her eyes. An impossible choice for a musician like Braden. It wasn't like music was a thing he did, more of a thing he was.

"And your husband?" She gentles her voice to soften the bluntness of her question. "What was he doing out there?"

"Nobody knows," Jo says. "I mean, he spent lots of time at the cabin, but it wasn't hunting season. The ice was too rotten for ice fishing. He packed a cooler, mostly with beer, and said, 'I'm taking that poor bastard some liquid encouragement.' Only it's not like he and Braden were ever close, you know? And like I said, Braden didn't drink."

"And your husband?"

"Functional alcoholic. That's what they call it, right? Never missed a day of work. Good with our son. But he drank a lot in the evenings. Wasn't the nicest drunk, either. Not so mean as my dad, but he could be a dick. Didn't think my brother needed that, so I told Mitch to stay home, that Braden had gone out there to be alone. He was acting weird, anyway. Twitchy. Unsettled. Wouldn't listen, manlike. 'Later, Jo.' That's what he said when he got in his truck to drive off. The last words I had from him."

"I'm so sorry to drag this up for you," Phee says.

"You're not sorry. Dragging it up is exactly what you're trying to do."

"All right. I admit it. But I am sorry for causing hurt. Not my intention."

"I've told you all I know. Mitch went out there. Next thing I know, I get a phone call. My husband is dead, my brother's in the hospital, everybody's very sorry for my loss, yada yada yada. Are we done? I need to go make breakfast for Dad."

"So, can I? Bring Braden and Allie to the cabin?"

"And what if he doesn't remember? Or what if he does and it makes him worse?"

"I know it sounds crazy, but with all due respect, I don't think it can get much worse. Allie wants to die, and he's not far behind."

"When you put it that way, not so crazy as all that. Good luck getting him here. He hasn't been in town since the accident. Didn't even come for Mom's funeral."

Phee takes this as a yes. "How do I get to the cabin?"

"If you can get him out here, you bring him straight by my place first. Do you have a time frame?"

"As soon as they release Allie, so it depends on her recovery. How big is the cabin?"

"Why?"

"Well, if I could, I'd like to bring a few of his friends."

"There's a loft, two bedrooms, a pullout sofa. We've slept eight, but it's pretty cozy."

"Perfect," Phee says. "Do I need to bring sleeping bags?"

"I'll take care of the bedding if you take care of the food."

"Done. Please don't tell him I called. We're going to need the element of surprise."

"You're going to need the element of ambush," Jo says. "Good luck. I think you're going to need it."

Chapter Thirty

ALLIE

It's nearly nine o'clock before Allie's eyes flicker open, and she withdraws her hand from Braden's grasp.

Phee has called, twice, to check on her and see if Braden needs a ride home. The doctor has made rounds, assuring him that they'll keep her today for observation but that she's fine, really. No permanent damage. Also to warn him that a crisis worker will be stopping in to make sure there is a plan going forward.

"Have a good sleep?" Braden asks as his daughter's eyes focus in on him. She answers him with a question of her own.

"Why?"

This isn't going to be one of the innocent questions of her childhood. No "why is the sky blue?" or even the dreaded why of the birds and the bees. He braces himself to give her the truth about whatever she asks, keeping his tone as light as he can. "Why what? You'll need to be a little more specific."

"Why didn't you come and meet me that day? Where were you?"

That day. The day her mother and her brother were extinguished from her world.

It's an effort to breathe past the obstruction in his throat, the tightness in his chest that could be grief or the beginnings of a panic attack or an ill-timed heart attack. He can't lie to her. Not here. Not now.

"I was drunk." He wants to soften the harsh truth, to shield both of them, but he bites back the excuses.

"Too drunk to remember?"

Braden pokes at his memory of that day, taking his time. Sorting through the feelings, the thoughts and decisions. Allie makes a small sound like a wounded creature and rolls away from him.

"I didn't forget, Allie. It was the only thing on my mind for days. I'd stopped drinking the day you messaged me on Facebook. Had stayed sober for months. You, coming back into my life, was the first thing worth getting sober for in years. You have to believe that."

"Then *why?*"

All the pain of the weeping world in her voice. He wants to beat himself to a bloody pulp for having added to her suffering. But his penance is the slower and more exquisitely agonizing act of feeling her pain, and his own, and speaking truth when lies would be easier for both of them.

"I was afraid . . ."

And there it is, the panic. Waiting in ambush.

His vision darkens at the edges. His heartbeat thrums through his body, too fast, too loud. He's suffocating, can't get control of his breathing.

"Dad! *Dad!* Are you okay?"

He manages to nod, to get a good breath in, to gasp: "Panic attack. It'll pass."

Little by little, the flood of adrenaline fades, leaving him limp and exhausted. "I had a bad attack that morning," he says.

She doesn't voice the why this time, but he feels it, hears it in the tension of her body, in the way she breathes.

"I woke up excited. Finally, I was going to get to see you. And then the panic hit, and the next clear thought I had was three days later when Alexandra called to tell me—well, to tell me."

"I was scared, too," Allie says. "But I showed up, anyway."

"I've got no excuse. It was just . . . all of the lost years swamped me. The fear that you would be a stranger to me. The idea of being awkward with you, of not knowing what to say, of seeing judgment in your eyes and knowing how deeply I'd failed you."

"Why panic today, though? Why now? Is it still me?"

"Well, I *am* terrified by the thought of losing you, that you tried to kill yourself. But the panic . . ." Dark wings flutter at the edges of his vision. He takes a breath. "Something happened at the cabin, when I hurt my hands. Phee showing up and talking about that ridiculous curse, trying to make me remember, that's making the panic worse."

Both of them are quiet for a long moment.

"I was going to take you to my audition," Allie says in a small voice. "For the University of Washington School of Music."

Pride and shame and a sense of wonder fill his heart to overflowing.

"I'll never forgive myself for missing it. What did you play?"

"I was supposed to play the C Minor."

"That's incredibly impressive. Steph said you were brilliant, but I thought she might be a tiny bit biased."

"Steph is over the top about everything." She smiles as she says it, but then her eyes narrow. "When did you talk to Steph?"

"She was worried about you. Came over to the house a while back to check on you and threatened me with pepper spray."

Allie actually laughs at that, the most beautiful sound Braden thinks he's ever heard, but it ends far too quickly.

"I should let her know what happened." Silence for a moment, and then: "C Minor is the piece you were working on. Before. The last one I remembered."

"Oh, Allie." He lets this all sink in. "You said you *were* going to play the C Minor. What happened?"

"I played the lullaby," she says very softly. "The one you used to play for me. Do you remember?"

"Whatever possessed you to play that?"

"Because it was yours," she says simply, as if this is the sort of obvious thing he should have known. Grass is green, the sun provides light, and his daughter played a song at an audition that he wrote for her when she was a baby. Something classical would surely have been expected, and yet she had played something new, a song that linked her to her father.

The awesome audacity of her rocks him, shifts his internal architecture in a way he feels but could never find words for.

"I wish I'd been there" is all he can say. "Maybe you could still play it for me. When you're out of here. After we get home."

"It got them killed." Allie's voice, quiet before, is now barely more than a whisper. "Mom had to take Trey to an appointment because I snuck off to my audition instead."

Her words knock the breath out of him.

"Oh my God, Allie. You can't be thinking this is your fault! It was an accident. Accidents happen."

"There's no other way to think about it. If I hadn't gone, if I'd done what Mom asked, they'd both be alive. But I was playing the cello instead."

"What happened to your mom, to Trey, was a horrible, terrible, tragic thing, but it's not your fault! Do you have any idea how many other kids were playing hooky in Seattle that day? And none of them had their families wiped out like that."

"Maybe it's the curse, the one Phee was talking about. Because I was playing the cello. Mom always said music was a curse and—"

"No!" She startles at the vehemence in his voice, and he softens it. "If there were a curse, which there's not, it's from *not* playing. You did exactly right, Allie. It happened because your mother didn't see all that you are, and tried to make you somebody else."

Braden holds his breath. Allie might be listening. There's a quality to the silence that feels different. A slight easing of the tension in her jaw.

"Your mother wouldn't want you to ruin your life out of guilt."

"No. She'd expect me to make her sacrifice worthwhile. Go to medical school. Be a doctor."

"Is that what you want?"

"Does it matter what I want?"

"Of course it matters. It's your life. You get to live it however you want. But if you're a musician, Allie, then you have to play music. It's part of who you are."

"What about you? You're not playing."

"Don't model your life on mine, for the love of God," he says. "And I really can't use my hands. I'm not faking."

Before she can answer, the door opens and a man comes in. He has a nice face, a pleasant, open smile, but the name tag clipped to his shirt labels him a professional. "Mind if I come in?" he asks, but doesn't wait for permission before drawing up a chair on the other side of Allie's bed.

"How are you doing?" he asks.

She eyes him with mistrust and says nothing, using the remote on the bed to adjust herself to a sitting position while simultaneously drawing the blanket protectively up around her chin.

"Allie Healey, yes?" the man asks. "And are you her father?"

Allie nods. Braden reads the name tag. *Tom Michaels, Crisis and Commitment Services.* "You're the mental-health guy."

Tom hands Braden a business card, smiling and nodding as if he's admitting to being the tooth fairy, rather than the man who could lock Allie in a psych ward.

"Is this really necessary?" Braden asks, recoiling from the word "commitment" on the card. "I'll hook her up with a counselor. Keep a close eye on her."

"This is necessary," Tom replies, serious now. "You don't have to talk to me, but it's in your best interest. Allie, it's my job to decide whether it will be safe to let you go home, or whether we need to hold you somewhere safer as soon as you're medically clear."

Allie stares at him in shock. "What do you mean, safer?"

"There's a mental-health unit especially for juveniles—"

"A psych unit, you mean? Like, the loony bin? No. You can't send me there." She turns to Braden, her eyes wide with shock. "Dad. You're not going to let him do this!"

"I'm not going anywhere" is all Braden can think to say.

Tom hands over papers that explain the laws under which he operates. Anything Braden or Allie say can be used in the decision to hold her against her will for seventy-two hours.

"After the seventy-two hours, there would be a court hearing to decide whether to release you or keep you longer," he explains.

"Well, then, I'm not talking to you," Allie says, pale but defiant.

Tom smiles gently. "You can do that, of course. But the fact is that you tried to kill yourself. So, if you don't want to go to the psych unit, you'll need to convince me why it's safe to let you go home."

"This is bullshit!" she says. "Dad, tell him!"

There is nothing that Braden can say. He looks again at the very official paperwork in his hands and then at the man sitting beside Allie's bed. He thinks about how close she came to death and wonders if maybe Tom is right.

"I'd rather be safe than sorry," Tom says. "A life is a beautiful thing to waste."

"I'd watch her, of course," Braden says. "Around the clock."

"I'm sorry to say this," Tom says apologetically, "but my understanding is that you didn't know where she'd gone last night. So I'm not sure about your ability to keep her under observation."

"But I won't run off anymore," Allie pleads. "It was all Ethan's idea . . ." Her face goes slack and she lets out a little cry. "I'm a horrible person. I didn't even ask. Is he okay? Can I talk to him?"

"He's been transferred to Harborview," Tom says quietly. "He's on a breathing machine, and they don't know yet if he'll recover. But he's still alive, and that's good news."

Allie starts to cry.

Helpless anger simmers in Braden's belly. He wants to shield her from all of this. Carry her somewhere far away from the harsh realities she's facing. "This isn't exactly helpful," he says. "Could it maybe wait until she's stronger?"

"We're not discussing anything she's not going to be feeling within the next few days, Mr. Healey, and we're doing it here where she's safe. Avoiding talking about things is much more dangerous than having conversations." Tom levels an assessing gaze at Braden. "Are you an avoider, Mr. Healey?"

Braden takes a breath, struggles to keep his tone level. "This isn't about me—"

"I'm afraid it's very much about you, sir. Suicide always involves family dynamics. How could it not? Professionally, what I would suggest is that Allie be voluntarily admitted to the psych unit, rather than detained. That way you keep the legal system out of her treatment."

"I am not volunteering for that!" Allie declares.

"You're underage," Tom says gently. "In your case, your father would be the one to voluntarily sign you in."

"I'm seventeen years old! He doesn't get to decide anything for me!"

"Actually, he does. How about it, Mr. Healey? Get her urgent help, keep her safe, avoid the legal system getting involved in her treatment."

Braden feels the room closing in. This is how he felt the night Mitch died. Trapped. Horrified by a choice that is not a choice. Allie's safety is of the utmost importance. But the small, fragile trust that has just begun to grow between them with the conversation they've just had, this is also of the utmost importance, not just for him but for her. Maybe it, too, is connected to her safety.

"If you do this, I will never forgive you," Allie says. "Never."

"And if you don't?" Tom asks. "If you don't and she tries again, and succeeds, will you forgive yourself?"

Braden has never forgiven himself for anything. Not for the ruin of his marriage. Not for Mitch's death. Not for the alcohol, or leaving his kids, or the accident that killed Lilian and Trey. If something happens now, to Allie . . .

"Am I interrupting?"

In that moment, Phee looks to Braden like an angel in a flannel shirt and faded jeans, smelling of French fries and bacon, a bulging McDonald's bag in her hand.

"They're trying to put me in the insane asylum," Allie says.

Tom gets to his feet. "We are having an important meeting, if you would excuse us. We won't be much longer."

"Phee is family," Braden says. "She should be here." The words don't feel like a lie. Phee is the one person in the world who understands what is happening here. The only person he trusts to help him with this impossible choice.

"The more support Allie has, the better," Tom says. "Come on in, then. Maybe one of the nurses could find us another chair?"

"I'll stand." She crosses the room and stops behind Braden's chair, one hand coming to rest on his shoulder. He covers it with one of his own. "You look better," she says to Allie.

"Well, I'm not! This is so incredibly unfair!"

"What's unfair about it?" Tom asks. "Tell me. I want to hear it, Allie."

"I don't even want to die! I told you it was all Ethan's idea."

"But you went along with it."

"Everything was so utterly fucked up. I didn't see the point. And then, when it was too late . . ." The tears begin sliding down her cheeks again, and her sob destroys whatever is left of Braden's heart. "When it was too late, I realized what I was doing was all . . . He lied to me!"

"Who? Your father?" Tom asks.

"No! Ethan. He had this whole story about death that was all a lie. He lied to get me there, because he didn't want to die alone. He lied when he threw away my phone. He even lied about his dad killing himself. He spun this whole weird reality story that made death seem like the only option. And when I figured that out, I thought . . . I thought if I was going to die, I at least wanted my death to be true. I tried to call for help, only my fingers wouldn't work and I dropped the phone . . ." Her voice breaks, and she buries her face in her knees and sobs.

Braden feels the tears on his own face now. Phee's hand tightens on his shoulder. There are no words for the heartbreak and guilt and love he feels for this woman-child. She's been hurt so much already, but she's so incredibly strong.

"I don't think the psych unit is the right place for her," he says when he can get his voice under control. "Please. I'll schedule her with a counselor. I'll watch her."

"You have to sleep sometime," Tom says. "I know this is hard, but safety—"

"We'll all watch her," Phee says. "Her father. Me. Our friends. We'll take it in shifts."

Braden tips his head back to look at her. What friends? He wants to ask, but her face tells him not to ask questions, not now.

"Please," Allie begs. "Can we just do that? Steph would come, too, I know she would, whenever she doesn't have to be at school. I promise to stay at the house and never go anywhere ever again. Just don't make me go to that place."

Tom takes his time considering, his thoughtful gaze traveling from Allie's face, to Braden's, to Phee's. Finally, he nods.

"All right. I'm going to get all of you to sign a safety plan that lists the responsibilities you've each agreed to. Okay?"

"Of course," Phee says, her voice low and steady. "Whatever it takes."

A few minutes later, they are all signing a document. Allie agrees to go to counseling, to refrain from self-harm, to let her father know if she's having suicidal thoughts. For the next week, she won't go anywhere without first saying where she's going.

Braden agrees to lock up sharp objects and medications in the house, to take Allie to counseling, to call Tom if he has any concerns. Phee agrees to cover for Braden so that someone is always awake and available to keep an eye out for Allie. All of them will abstain from alcohol or any recreational drugs.

"It's been lovely to meet you all," Tom says as he packs the paperwork back into his briefcase. "But I hope to never see any of you again."

"Amen to that," Phee mutters as the door closes behind him.

Allie leans back against the pillow and closes her eyes, looking exhausted and fragile.

"So when are they going to spring you?" Phee asks, thumping the bag down on Allie's bedside table and unpacking breakfast sandwiches and hash browns. "Figured you'd be hungry this morning. Hospital food sucks."

Allie rewards her with a faint smile. "Thank you. For everything."

"Hey, that's what family is for," Phee replies, laughing.

"I don't know if she's supposed to eat yet," Braden objects. "We should check with the nurse."

"Are you hungry?" Phee asks.

"Totally."

"Perfect. Then she's supposed to eat. It was an overdose, Braden. Not a burst appendix or cancer or something."

Allie is already eating, and Braden's mouth is watering. Greasy and salty turns out to be the perfect comfort food. When the nurse comes in a few minutes later, all three of them stare at her, guilty, crumbs and empty wrappers all that is left of the transgression.

She laughs. "I was about to ask if Allie would like some breakfast, but I see the answer to that. So, how about a shower?"

"Please," Allie says. "That would be amazing."

"Why don't you go home and get some rest?" the nurse asks Braden. "Doctor says she can probably go home this afternoon."

"I'll stay," Braden begins, but Allie cuts him off.

"Dad. I'm fine."

"You're no good to her if you get sick yourself," the nurse admonishes.

Phee takes his hand and tugs. "Come on, Braden. You need to rest. We'll come back for her when they're ready to let her go."

"You'll call if there's any problem?" Braden asks the nurse. "Even the tiniest setback—"

"Of course! I promise. Go on, now. Shoo. Let the girl shower in peace."

"What time do you think she'll be released?"

"Not before three or four, I wouldn't think. I'll call you if there's any change to that plan as well. All right?"

Braden stands by Allie's bed, dares to stroke her hair. He wants to hug her more than anything in the world but tells himself he won't corner her, trapped as she is in the hospital bed.

"I love you, little bird," he says, and then the miracle happens and she lifts her arms to him, like she used to do when she was a little girl.

He stoops and gathers her against him, her arms tight around his neck as they cling to each other for a long moment. She doesn't say she loves him, but he thinks, maybe, he feels it in the rapid beating of her heart.

Chapter Thirty-One
ALLIE

Allie's new reality is as fragile as a spiderweb. All of the things she knew about life used to make a solid tapestry; now she feels as if somebody has unraveled the whole thing, handed her the threads, and suggested she weave them back together without a pattern.

A gift, she realizes with surprise. Her life, to be shaped and re-created however she chooses. The emotional place she was in when she swallowed the pills belongs to another girl in another life.

She's not numb anymore. The encounter with death has flayed her wide open. Grief hits her in huge, swamping waves, but there's compensation. The sky outside her window is outrageously blue. Even the faded colors in her hospital gown are beautiful, and she gets caught up in tracing the patterns with her eyes.

Best of all, her anger toward her father is not just muted but gone, washed away by that one bright moment of comprehension just before the pills sucked her into unconsciousness. He loves her. Has always loved her. And maybe, just maybe, she'll be able to make music again someday.

After her shower, she's more than happy to climb back into bed, still weak from the overdose. All afternoon, she drifts in and out of sleep. Nothing to do, nothing to worry about, nowhere to be.

It's a relief to be away from Ethan. He's alive, and that's all she wants to know about him right now. She's glad to be away from the house, away from the cello, away from the guilt about Steph and school. There's nothing she can do about any of it here, so far away, and that makes a quiet place in her brain that hasn't been there since the accident.

A shadow, the scuff of a chair moving, alert her to someone in the room, and her eyes flicker open to see Steph sitting in the chair watching her. It takes her a minute, blinking and clearing her eyes of sleep, to see why her friend's face looks all wrong. No makeup. Not the tiniest trace of eyeliner or mascara. No pale foundation. Not even lipstick.

Allie pushes herself up in bed. "Are you okay?"

"How the fuck would I be okay?" Steph's eyes are red and puffy. She's even taken out her nose and eyebrow rings, and she looks younger and alarmingly normal.

"I'm sorry," Allie says.

"You didn't even say goodbye. All of these years we've been friends, and you didn't think about me at all?"

"I did!" Allie protests. "I thought about you plenty. I just couldn't . . . You'd have said something. You helped my dad find me."

"Well, forgive me for caring," Steph snarls, but Allie can see how close she is to tears, knows the anger is a shield.

"I really am sorry, Steph. I can't explain it, or I would."

Steph flings herself onto the bed and hugs her. "You idiot. I was so worried. Life without you would have been devastating."

"If I'd told you, I wouldn't have been able to do it," Allie admits, hugging her back.

"Promise me you won't ever do it again." Steph grabs her by the shoulders and shakes her.

Allie laughs, even as she's wiping tears from her eyes. It's amazing how her body keeps manufacturing tears, like there's an endless supply of them. "Cross my heart. I didn't really want to die, Steph. What's with the new look?"

"What? Oh." Steph touches her face as if she needs a reminder. "I kept crying so much I got tired of redoing my eyes. And then I just said fuck it and scrubbed it all off. And the nose ring sucks when you're blowing your nose every five minutes. And the eyebrows looked stupid without the rest of it. So."

"I'm sorry," Allie says again.

"Your dad's not so bad, either," Steph says. "Just so you know."

"Not going to pepper spray him anymore?"

"He told you that? I thought he'd gone and killed you. You've put me through hell, Allie. You owe me big-time."

Allie sighs, the weight of the world settling back down on her, only not quite so heavy as it was before. Her eyes catch on something sitting on the floor by the door.

"What's the duffel bag for?"

"Suicide watch," Steph says cheerfully. "Brought some things. Are you ready?"

"To go home? I guess." And she is, all at once. She wants her own bed, to get a snack from the fridge. It will be different now that she's speaking to her father again. Easier.

"You're not going—" Steph claps both hands over her mouth.

"What? I'm not going where?"

"Nothing. I went by the house and got you clothes. Figured your dad would bring you stuff you hate."

It's an evasion. Steph sucks at lying, but Allie doesn't have the emotional energy to dig out the truth. It will come out soon enough. Steph also sucks at keeping secrets.

"One thing I need to tell you." Steph drops her eyes and picks a hair off her leggings. "Don't be mad."

"I won't."

"Promise."

It's going to be big, to extract this kind of promise, but Allie says, "I owe you, remember?"

Steph glances up at her, and then away again. "Me and that lady, Phee, we cleaned up Trey's room today."

Allie feels everything inside her go still.

Steph rushes on. "We didn't, like, get rid of his clothes or his trophies or anything. Just—we turned off the TV and did his laundry and cleaned up some. Like what your mom used to make him do on Saturdays. It's still his room."

"It will always be his room."

"Are you mad?"

"Dad and I couldn't do it." It's the closest she can come to saying thank-you.

"Go get dressed. They'll be here in a minute." Steph sits up on the bed and bounces. "This mattress sucks."

"It's not supposed to be a Hilton." Allie takes the bundle of clothes Steph hands her, stopping dead in her tracks on the way to the bathroom.

"They who?"

Steph's eyes go wide in a feigned innocence that Allie knows way too well. "Your dad. And Phee. Hurry up already."

Allie slams the door and locks it instead of leaving it cracked, penalty for the lie she knows her friend is telling her. She just can't figure out what Steph is on about. Her face in the mirror looks washed out and old, she thinks. Even her eyes look faded. It doesn't matter. She tries to comb through the tangles in her hair with her fingers. "Hey, did you bring me a comb?"

It's too late. She hears her father's voice, and Phee's.

She doesn't know how to relate to her father without the defensive anger, and she feels shy and naked. But Phee has brought Celestine, and that makes everything easy.

"Is he allowed?" Allie asks, bending over to hug the dog while he tries to lick her face.

"No, he's not," her father says. "Phee snuck him in by way of the back stairs. I suggest we make a break for it before they catch him."

"I think you're supposed to sign me out first. The nurse said."

"How about if I go to the desk and do that?" Braden says.

The dog, having thoroughly slobbered all over Allie's face, turns to sniffing every interesting inch of the room. His tail connects with the water jug on the lowered bedside table, sending it careening onto the floor, then he turns around and starts lapping up the puddle.

"Celestine, settle down," Phee says, but she's distracted by something on her phone, tapping rapidly with both thumbs.

Allie just wants to go. The minute her father reappears, she asks, "Are we good? Can we go now?"

"They want you to go in a wheelchair," he begins, but Allie is already walking.

"No way."

She runs into a nurse at the door, who looks from her to the dog to Braden and Phee, frowning. "Dogs aren't allowed. And it's policy—"

"We don't believe in policies," Steph says with exaggerated dignity. "We are rebels." She grabs Allie's hand and yanks her past the nurse. Celestine follows, his paws scrabbling on the slippery linoleum.

They take the elevator, not the stairs. Most people's faces light up at the sight of the big dog.

"Okay, little bird?" her father asks.

Her knees feel weak, her head a little light, but she nods at him. He puts an arm around her, as if he can see what she's not saying, and she lets herself lean against him the rest of the way out into the parking lot.

"Maybe we should wait here while you bring the car around," her father says to Phee.

"Actually, our ride is already waiting." Phee waves at a black SUV parked at the curb. An old man, white haired but agile, gets out of the driver's seat and walks over to meet them.

"You must be Allie," he says, taking her hand. His eyes are very blue, both kind and perceptive.

"Hey, Len," her father says. "What are you doing here?"

"Phee's car didn't exactly accommodate the whole crew."

"What crew?"

One of the doors opens from the inside, and Allie sees that several of the seats are already occupied by a man, a woman, and a girl with facial jewelry pretty much anywhere it will fit and all of the makeup Steph isn't wearing.

"Your chariot awaits," Len says, leading her toward the vehicle. "Let me help you up."

Allie finds herself sitting between Steph and the girl with the piercings. "Cool," Steph is already saying. "I want ink, but my mom would have a fit. She already had an aneurysm over my nose ring. Your tattoos are totally awesome."

"This is Katie," Len says. "Back there we have Jean and Dennis. Everybody, meet Allie and Steph."

"Nice to meet you," the man says. He has a quiet voice and a smile that says maybe he understands how Allie feels. "Welcome aboard the adventure bus."

The woman, Jean, huddled up inside her coat as if she's trying to disappear, just smiles and nods.

"I don't understand," Allie hears her father saying outside the vehicle.

"This is your intervention," Phee's voice replies. "Get in."

Chapter Thirty-Two

BRADEN

Braden shakes his head to clear it. "This is not a good time, Phee, for whatever this is. I thought you said next week."

"We prioritized you, because of Allie. It's a perfect time. We're all going to help you watch her. You'll see. Come on, Celestine."

The dog bounds behind her around to the back of the SUV, stopping to snuffle at the back tires.

"Oscar couldn't come," Phee says as she loads up the dog. "He couldn't get anybody to watch the shop on such short notice, and you can't leave fish and birds alone even for a couple of days. But everybody else is here. We've bumped Dennis's thing to later."

Braden reminds himself to breathe. "Where are we going? I'm sure Allie would be much more comfortable at home." He glances at his daughter for confirmation, surprised to see that her face looks animated, a spark of interest in her eyes.

"She doesn't want to go home," Steph says. "Too many memories and shit. Right, Al?"

He waits for Allie to protest, but she just shrugs, her eyes conveying some sort of message he can't decipher.

"I packed some things for you," Phee is saying. "And Steph packed for Allie. So no need to go back to the house at all." She faces him head-on, looks into his eyes.

He ought to trust her by now. She's been there for him and for Allie, and he feels guilty at his besetting doubts, but her face wears a wide-eyed, innocent expression, at odds with her usual directness. Cello music resonates in the air around them, and he has a presentiment that if he goes and looks in the cargo compartment, he's going to find the cello buried under luggage and one very large dog.

He wants to run both of his hands through Phee's wonderful hair and kiss her, right here and now, in front of God and everybody.

He wants to put his hands on her shoulders and shake sense into her.

"I feel like a hostage," he says, mostly to prevent himself from acting on either impulse.

She grins at him, as mischievous as a child. "It's an adventure! We're not going to duct-tape you and shove you in a closet. We want to make sure you stay sober and that Allie doesn't hurt herself. That's better done away from all temptation, don't you think?"

"Can't argue with that logic," Len says.

"Come on, Braden," Katie calls. "Let's get this show on the road."

Phee gives him a little shove, and despite all of his misgivings, Braden climbs into the available back seat, next to Jean. Celestine, in the cargo space right behind him, pokes a cold nose into his neck, leaving a string of slobber behind. Anxiety flutters in his belly as the door slams, closing him in.

Jean's thin hand rests on his arm, cool, gentle. "All will be well," she murmurs. "Don't fight what you cannot change."

The idea of letting go, of letting the thinking be done for him for a while, of having a group share the responsibility, of not having to go back to the house that shouts of Lilian and Trey and all of his failures, is surprisingly seductive.

"Am I allowed to ask where we're going?"

"You can always ask." Len shifts into gear. "As it happens, none of us know. Phee is the keeper of secrets on this one, and I only know enough to point us in the right direction."

"Wouldn't want to spoil the surprise," Phee says. "First destination point, Easton. Already checked the road conditions. Traffic normal. Snoqualmie Pass, clear and dry. No snow. Make it so, Captain."

"Aye, aye," Len says.

Allie cranes her neck around to look at Braden, eyebrows lifted in a question.

"I assume I'm allowed to share AA information with Allie and Steph, seeing as you've brought them into this?" he asks the group at large.

"They must be sworn to secrecy," Katie answers dramatically. "Raise your hands in the air and repeat after me." She raises her own right hand, and Steph and Allie mirror her. "I do solemnly swear that I will keep the secrets of the Adventure Angels. What happens on this adventure stays on this adventure."

Steph breaks up in a fit of giggles. Allie elbows her. Both of them recite the words with due solemnity.

"Do you go around kidnapping people on a regular basis?" Allie asks.

"Adventures are usually voluntary," Dennis answers. "Desperate times, desperate measures."

"This is our version of AA," Phee fills in. "Sobriety through adventure and creating fun for other people."

"Cool," Steph says. "Can I be one?"

"Maybe an honorary member. For God's sake, don't become an alcoholic just so you can join."

Braden listens to the chatter, small conversations here and there among the group, but his mind keeps drifting. His fatigue, born of a string of mostly sleepless nights and ongoing worry, catches up with him, and he drifts in and out of wakefulness.

When he jolts sharply awake out of a dream of falling, at first he has no idea where he is. It comes back to him in pieces. Allie's suicide attempt. The intervention. Jean beside him, the dog behind him. Also the cello. He can feel its presence, wants to turn around and reach for it. He also wants to touch Allie there in the seat in front of him, to reassure himself that she's okay. She's talking to Katie and Steph about some rock band they all listen to, and he contents himself with a visual check.

His gaze goes to the road outside, trying to gauge their location and how long he's been asleep.

"We're on the pass," Jean says, in answer to his unasked question. "Stopping in Easton for dinner."

"And after that?"

"Infinity and beyond," Dennis supplies. "Hey, this is a full-scale adventure planned and plotted by Phee. Likely to be epic."

Braden has his suspicions. Phee couldn't be farther away from him if she'd planned the seating arrangement. Which, of course, she has, he realizes with a little jolt of adrenaline. When they all bail out of the vehicle in Easton, she manages to be always somewhere he isn't. Walking the dog, sitting as far away as she can get in the café.

When she shifts places with Len and takes over the driver's seat, it's all plausible and reasonable. Len is tired, changing drivers makes perfect sense. Braden tries to guess where they're going, to calm the anxiety at his center. Until they reach the town of Ellensburg, there are still options that make sense to him. A cabin at a resort or a campground. An out-of-the-way bed-and-breakfast, maybe, or a resort. But when she turns north off the I-90 onto Highway 283, his suspicions and his anxiety both ratchet up to a whole new level.

Even Phee has to stop sometime. The rig is a gas guzzler. Steph and Katie have been clamoring for a rest stop for miles, and when Jean adds her quiet voice to their demands, Phee pulls into a service station in the little town of Soap Lake.

Braden is out of the vehicle before she has the keys out of the ignition, and he confronts her as she opens her door. "Where are we going, Phee?"

"Don't ask me to spoil the surprise."

"You're up to something."

"Of course I am! This is your intervention adventure." She laughs, but her eyes evade his. She hands him Celestine's leash.

"Can you walk him, please? I need to pee in the worst way."

Braden watches her retreating back with increasing misgiving. "Do you know?" he asks the dog.

Celestine just wags his tail, and Braden takes him to a narrow strip of winter-dead grass and lets him do his business. When Phee comes out, she gets directly into the driver's seat, leaving Braden to load up the dog. As he suspected, the cello is there, and he has a terrible presentiment of what Phee is planning.

His eyes seek out hers, which are watching him in the rearview, but she quickly glances away, ducking her head to adjust a to-go cup of coffee in the cup holder.

Braden scrambles for an escape. He could refuse to get back in. Pull Allie out of the SUV, supposing she'd be willing to go with him. And then what? He might be able to get a hotel for the night, but there's no bus station or car rental in this town. He hates to disappoint the rest of the Angels. For what seems an eternity, he stands there, the hatch still open, catching his breath. Phee's eyes meet his again in the rearview.

Trust me.

He doesn't. He can't. Not because she'd ever hurt him on purpose but because she doesn't know what she's doing.

His feet carry him back to his seat, but he feels now like a man going to his own execution. He leans forward. "Phee."

She ignores him.

"I know what you're doing," Braden says to the back of her head. "I believe you think this is a good idea. You have to listen to me, Phee. This is the worst idea ever."

"It's time," she says, eyes straight ahead, shifting the SUV into gear. "Don't you think that's my decision?"

"You've had eleven years. And now there's Allie to consider."

There's always been Allie, Braden thinks, with the weary old guilt seeping in. *I've always failed her. And now you'll push me into doing it again.*

"Ophelia MacPhee," Len says, "please tell me this isn't that theoretical dynamite scenario. I told you—"

"You said dynamite should be left to the experts. So I brought along an expert."

"I am not getting sucked into this! It's not ethical."

"Well, you can be an innocent bystander if you want."

"Why don't you stop the vehicle and we'll discuss this rationally?" Len asks.

"No."

"Phee!"

"Not stopping until we get where we are going."

"I don't get it." Allie sounds bewildered, maybe frightened. "Where are we going?"

She looks back at Braden over her shoulder.

"We're going to my family's cabin. The one where my hands got hurt. Where your uncle Mitch . . ." His throat closes over the words and he coughs to clear it. "Don't do this, Phee."

She doesn't answer, just keeps driving.

"Wow," Steph says with enthusiasm. "I've never been kidnapped before."

"It's not a kidnapping, precisely," Katie says. "No ransom. More like a hijacking."

Dennis glances across at Braden, his face registering consternation. "Hey, man. I had no idea."

Jean pats his hand. "It's the right thing, honey. You'll see."

"You knew about this?"

"Oh no. Not at all. I have no idea where we're going or why we are going there. I just feel that it is the right thing."

Braden tries again. "Phee. Can we at least talk about this? It's going to be midnight when we get there. The roads could be bad; there's still snow up there this time of year. Let's at least stop somewhere for the night, discuss this in the morning."

In answer, she turns the radio on, volume loud enough to bar communication.

Unless he wants to open the door and jump out of a moving vehicle, Braden is trapped on a road that was once part of a regular pilgrimage. When he and Lilian were first married, they visited regularly, once or twice a year. Family is family, even when you've got nothing in common. Even Lilian agreed with that. She accompanied him, though she hated the cabin and engaged in a running commentary of criticism over his father's endless smoking, Jo's language, Mitch's evening drinking.

She hated the long days outside by, on, or in the water. The mosquitoes, the blackflies, the dirt, the rain. She'd hovered over Allie, half sick with anxiety.

"Germs, Braden. Have you ever heard of germs? Does your family ever wash their hands before they eat?"

"Of course."

"Rinsing in the lake water is not washing, for God's sake. Do you want her to get sick? And could you please ask your father to smoke outside?"

Braden's family wasn't any fonder of Lilian than she was of them. His mother doted on Allie and was excruciatingly polite to Lilian. Jo took her in stride. Her husband, Mitch, handled the conflict by spending long hours on the lake fishing or sitting in a quiet corner nursing a beer.

Braden's father was never one to just go along with anything. In his eyes, marriage did not equate with blood ties, and Lilian was an intrusion in his routine at best. He didn't like her and didn't feel compelled to try to keep that to himself.

"That woman doesn't bend," he told Braden the first time he brought Lilian home. "Hard frost and a bit of wind, and she'll go right over like a tree without roots."

His mother's complaints were different. "She doesn't understand your music. She won't help your career."

They'd both been right, but so was Lilian. He had to be honest about that.

Managing a toddler at the cabin wasn't easy. Allie was forever crawling around in the dirt or toddling out onto the dock. Braden's parents were endlessly practical about that, just as Jo and Mitch were with their son, Jimmy.

"Put a life jacket on her and let her be. If she falls in, she'll float."

By the time Trey was born, Lilian refused to visit at all. "There is no way I'm going to try to wrangle two kids in that nightmare," she said. They started taking separate vacations. Braden off to the cabin while she watched the kids, and then Lilian somewhere warm and relaxing while he took his turn.

Over time, his visits grew increasingly infrequent. It was easy to find excuses, but the truth was that, between his mother's awe of his musical talent and his father's complete disregard of it, even as an adult he'd felt like a bone at the mercy of two very determined dogs.

"Are you much of a fisherman?" Dennis asks, trying to make conversation despite the nearly deafening music.

"Never had much chance," Braden shouts back. "My sister did the hunting and fishing. My mother was always too worried about my hands."

An irony, that. His mother had fussed about them endlessly.

"His hands, Frank. You can't risk his hands."

"It's just a fishing trip, for God's sake. We're not rock climbing or learning how to skin a bear. Do you think a fish is going to eat his precious hands? They're trout, Min. Not piranhas."

"Fishing hooks, fires, falls. He has a concert this weekend. It's an important one. There will be a professor from the music conservatory there."

"He's ten!" Dad's voice booms louder now. "You've got him so wrapped in cotton wool, he'll think he's a girl."

"I'm not a girl," Braden says. *"I want to go fishing."*

Neither one of them hears him. They are squared off, aware of nothing outside of each other and this war they are fighting. Even at ten, he's dimly aware that it isn't really about him but about something deeper that is broken between them.

It doesn't matter, or change anything, any more than his questions about God and the universe change the color of the sky or the temperature outdoors.

"What does a professor of some music conservatory have to do with the kid?"

"He's gifted!" his mother says. "Maybe even a prodigy. This could open doors for him. Scholarships. Opportunities."

"I don't care if he's a prodigy or a potato. I just want to take my son on a fishing trip. One weekend out of the summer."

"Maybe next weekend, then, if you're so set on it."

"Summer's almost over. He'll be back to school in a couple of weeks. What's wrong with this weekend?"

"He's committed. You want to teach him it's okay to be irresponsible? That he doesn't have to honor commitments? Be my guest."

"How committed can he be? He's ten."

"A ten-year-old genius. How do you not keep hearing this? The music, Frank. How can you not understand how important the music is?"

"What about being a man? What about me? All I ask for is a son."

"You have a son."

"No, I have a fucking prodigy. Never mind. I'll take Jo fishing. Is that okay with you? She hasn't turned into a genius lately, has she?"

Braden feels sweat cold on the back of his neck. His mother is dead and buried, five years ago, maybe six. He'd been drinking hard at the time. Jo had managed to track him down, tried to reel him in for the funeral, but he'd been unable to face it. Or at least that's what he'd told himself. In truth, he'd do pretty much anything to avoid the memories that are waiting for him here.

Bits and pieces surface as Phee drives him inexorably toward the last place in the world he wants to be.

Most of the drive is through nowhere, intercepted by a series of small towns. Darkness falls. Most of the occupants of the car drift into sleep. Allie's head leans on Steph's shoulder. Braden marks the landmarks, each town bringing him closer to his fate. They pass through Colville, and then onto Williams Lake Road. The headlights offer glimpses of dirty snowbanks and evergreen trees.

Not the cabin, then, or at least not yet. Dread crowds the car, an unwelcome passenger, and all the while the cello plays in his head.

Chapter Thirty-Three

PHEE

It has to be done, it has to be done, it has to be done.

Phee runs the words over and over in her head, her new mantra. Sometime during the long hours of the drive, they've meshed themselves with the haunting music and become a never-ending melody: The Song That Never Ends, arranged for cello, with variations.

All the same, her heart misgives her.

She feels like there's an invisible wire connecting her and Braden, and every shock of emotion that hits him travels directly from his heart to hers. Bringing him here, ambushing him, really, is something he's never going to forgive her for.

If it helps, if it heals him and heals Allie and brings both of them back to the music, then she can live with that. But what if she makes things worse by meddling? Bringing Braden out here to face his past in front of witnesses might be the stupidest thing she has ever done. What seemed like a brilliant idea earlier in the day has begun to feel like insanity.

Still.

It has to be done.

The directions Jo gave her are clear and concise, and she turns off what seems to her an already isolated road and onto a narrow driveway, closely lined by evergreens, packed and rutted with snow. As they emerge into a cleared space in front of a low, cozy-looking house, Phee is relieved to see lights on in the windows.

Almost midnight. The timing really couldn't be worse. It was Jo who insisted on her stopping here first, Phee reminds herself. Before she's even switched off the engine, a porch light comes on, illuminating a wide circle that includes the SUV.

The door opens and a woman steps out, striding across the yard and yanking Phee's door open.

"Phee? I can't believe you pulled this off."

"Got him," Phee says.

Jo looks past her into the back seat. "Braden. You're actually here."

"I was shanghaied." His voice is wound so tight, it sounds ready to snap.

"I wish . . . ," Jo says, then clears her throat. "Where is that Allie girl?"

"Here," Allie says.

"Don't suppose you remember me. I'm your aunt Jo."

"Hey," Allie says.

"Well, come on in, all of you. Dad will want to see you." She says it like she means everybody, but she's looking at Braden.

"It's so late," Phee says. "We don't want to intrude—"

"We've been expecting you. Dad waited up, and there's a pot of soup on the stove. I sure hope you are all hungry, because there's no way Dad and I are going to eat it all." As she talks, everybody unloads from the SUV and Jo leads them up to the house. "Mute that TV, would you, Dad? They're here."

The noise from the television shuts off sharply in response to her command.

Braden reaches for Allie's hand. "Come on, little bird. Nobody's going to eat you."

"Are you sure?"

"Reasonably." He tries to smile, but it looks more like a grimace. "If anybody gets eaten alive, it will be me."

The inside of the house is spotlessly clean. Heat emanates from a woodstove at the center of a room that holds a comfortable-looking couch and a couple of armchairs. An elderly man lays back in a recliner, a TV remote resting on a rounded belly. Tubing snakes from his nostrils down to an oxygen canister at his side, and his breathing is the loudest thing in the room.

He has the same face shape as Allie and Braden, the same cleft in his chin. As they enter the room, he slams his feet down to the floor and stands.

"Well, well, well. Look what the cat drug in. Come here and give me a hug, boy."

Braden crosses the room, stiff as a robot, and allows himself to be hugged. The old man is already looking past him to Allie.

"And this must be Alexandra. My God. Last time I saw you, you was just this little bit of a thing, all eyes and hair. Guess that hasn't changed much. Clear to see where you fit in the family tree, anyway. Well, are you just going to stand there?"

Allie gives him a hug that is fractionally less stiff than Braden's.

"So," the old man says, looking from Allie to Braden and back again. "What's new?"

"Dad!" Jo warns. "Behave yourself. We have company."

"Well, maybe you tell me what we're supposed to talk about," he retorts. "The weather? Can't talk about the last time you were here, orders from Jo. Can't talk about anything that matters. Don't know shit-all about your life over the last few years. Tell me about the funeral, then, since I wasn't invited."

"It wasn't exactly an invitation-type event." Braden stands frozen in the middle of the room, as if something will break if he dares to move.

"Maybe we could talk about your mother's funeral, then. How you weren't here. Or how she cried her eyes out over you after—"

"Dad!" Jo interrupts. She turns toward the little troop still standing just inside the door. "The bathroom is down the hall there, if any of you need it. Just jiggle the handle if it sticks. Food is in the kitchen, right through that door. I'll just put the pot of soup out on the counter. We're not fancy here; you can serve yourselves. Not enough chairs at the table, but you're welcome to have a seat in the living room. Don't be shy, now."

"I totally have to pee," Steph says, heading for the bathroom.

Katie follows. "Right behind you. Better hurry."

"Lovely house you have here." Dennis lowers himself onto the couch. "Did you build it yourself, Mr. Healey?"

"Can I help with anything?" Phee asks Jo, the word "dynamite" beginning to take on a whole new meaning. The relationship between Braden and his dad is full of land mines she could not have anticipated.

"Hey, you got my brother across the threshold," Jo says. "The least I can do is feed you. Allie, child, you look dead on your feet. Come in the kitchen, let's get you fed."

The girl does look like a pallid ghost. Phee drops an arm around her shoulder and guides her into the kitchen, and then into a chair, feeling even more misgivings about her plan. Allie could definitely have benefited from another day or two of rest.

"Don't mind those two," Jo says. "They never did get on, from the time Braden was a baby. Dad wanted him to follow the good-old-boy tradition—hunting and fishing and drinking beer with the guys on weekends. Mom was always encouraging his sensitive side, and the music, and bemoaning my total lack of either. It's like Braden and I got swapped, somehow, and both of our folks were disappointed."

"My mom was disappointed, too," Allie says, very low.

"Seems maybe that's the way with parents and kids," Jo replies, still matter-of-fact. "Expectations. And then some big surprise when kids are their own selves, as if we don't see that coming."

"It's that way with my parents," Phee agrees. "My mother definitely disapproves of me. Especially right this minute. She's going to hand me my ass on a silver platter the next time she sees me, on account of this escapade."

"Well, tell her I said thanks," Jo says. "Eleven years since I've seen my brother. Hard to believe it's been so long. Hard to believe it isn't longer."

"What happened to him? And to Uncle Mitch?" Allie asks. "Mom wouldn't talk about it."

"An accident happened." Jo lifts an enormous pot of soup off the stove and onto a trivet on the counter. "Bowls are in that cupboard right behind you, Phee, if you'd like to get them out. Braden thinks it's all his fault, what happened to Mitch. Been beating himself up over that for years."

"Was it?" Allie asks. "Dad's fault, I mean?"

"Of course not. But he won't hear that."

"Hey," Steph says, coming into the room and sniffing loudly. "That smells fantastic."

"Didn't I see a dog in the rig?" Jo asks. "I can scrounge up some scraps."

"He's in the car. He's fine out—" Phee is interrupted by raised voices in the living room.

"Enough with the bullshit excuses! It's about time you told us—"

"I can't tell you what I don't know!"

"Oh, for heaven's sake." Jo marches back into the living room. "Can't I leave the two of you alone for five minutes? Stop this at once."

Len and Dennis sit on the couch, their faces registering their discomfort. Jean and Katie are nowhere to be seen. Braden and his father are squared off in the middle of the room.

"Back off, Jo," the old man says. "It's time we had it out, man to man."

"We have *company*," Jo says, her voice a warning.

"If he doesn't want them to hear this, then he should have come here without them years ago." His dark eyes shift to Allie, who has followed, right behind Phee. "Aren't you tired of being in the dark? I sure as hell am."

"Dad. Don't," Jo pleads.

"Two men go out to the cabin. Only one comes home. He never talks about it, never says what happened. I think we deserve some goddamn answers. That's what I think."

Phee holds her breath, puts a steadying hand on Allie's shoulder.

"You sound like a politician," Braden's father says. "'*I'm sorry, I just don't recall.*' Be a man for once in your life."

"Let it go, already," Jo says. "The details won't bring Mitch back."

"What really matters to Dad," Braden answers, "is that I'm not Mitch. He was the son you never had and always wanted. He's dead, and I'm still here. That's the problem. What you really want to know is why it wasn't the other way around."

"Enough!" Jo snaps. "This is my house, and I won't hear one more word of this. Not now. Soup and bread in the kitchen. Come on." She begins herding people out of the living room and toward the kitchen.

Braden breaks away, out into the cold dark, slamming the door. Phee slips out behind him.

He's standing in the middle of the yard, his face turned up to the sky. Phee, born and raised in the city, has never seen so many stars all at once. She feels her way through the dark to the SUV and lets Celestine out. He rewards her with the swipe of a tongue across her hand before beginning an investigation of all the new smells.

"Amazing, isn't it?" Braden asks. "The stars make all of this mess seem small and petty."

"Hard to believe they are all suns," she says, taking his words as an invitation to stand beside him. "They look so cold and tiny."

"When I was a kid, I thought they were heavenly watchers who didn't give a damn what happens to us down here."

"And now?"

"Same as when I was a kid."

They are silent, staring up at the stars. Phee becomes aware of a silence as vast as the heavens above them, broken only by Celestine's snuffling and their own breathing. She's trying to think how to frame an explanation for what she's done, but Braden speaks first, the last words she was expecting to hear from him.

"Maybe you were right."

Phee sucks in a breath of surprise and chokes on her own saliva, her coughing shattering the silence and the mood.

"Are you okay?"

She nods to indicate yes, an edge of suppressed laughter making the paroxysm worse. When she can finally speak, she croaks, "Trust me to plunge us from a sublime contemplation of the heavens to the stupidity of trying to breathe my own spit." She wipes tears from her eyes, the moisture cold on fingers already starting to turn numb, and then shoves her hands into the pockets of her inadequate jacket.

"What's this about me being right?"

"My life. What's happened to my family. I spent the last eleven years being a victim. Poor Braden. Can't play the cello anymore. Can't see his kids. Please pass the bottle. Typical alcoholic wallowing. The truth is, all along I had choices. Could have fought for the kids. Could have found another outlet for my music. I did this, Phee. There is a curse, and I'm it."

"Hard on yourself much? Not being able to play is huge, and we both know alcohol is a—"

He interrupts her with an impatient brush of his hand. "Before it all went completely south. Before Mitch died and my hands were damaged and all of it, I made a choice then, too, Phee. I chose to stop playing the cello."

Cold shivers chase themselves up Phee's spine, butterflies flutter in her belly.

"See?" her grandfather's voice says in her head. *"I told you."*

"Why?" she asks, turning to face Braden. "How?"

He keeps his head tipped back, eyes on the stars.

"You were brilliant," Phee goes on. "Any orchestra in the world must have been open to you."

"Lil gave me an ultimatum. Her and the kids or the cello. Either or."

"But that's ridiculous, Braden. It's who you are."

"She had a point, maybe. We'd been fighting over the cello for years. I'd tried playing less, but music wanted all of me, and it left her out. When I was working on a song, it owned me for days. I'd drag myself away to spend time with her, with the kids, but it was just the surface of me. It wasn't fair to her."

Or maybe she was just a jealous bitch who didn't get music. Phee clamps her lips to keep the thought locked up.

"I remember this one time we were playing a game with some friends, one of those conversation-starter card games, you know? And this question came up. 'If there was a fire and you could only save one thing, what would it be?' My friend answered, 'My wife.' No hesitation, no consideration, just blurted it out almost before the question had been read. And then it was my turn to answer."

"And you said cello?"

"Not out loud. But I hesitated. In my mind I was like, 'Can't I manage both?' Or, 'surely I'll grab the cello and Lil can take care of herself.' I mean, if there really were a fire, I wouldn't ever have left her to burn, but I'd for sure be trying to save both of them. Lilian answered for me. 'He'd rescue the cello.'

"Our friends laughed. They thought it was a joke. But between the two of us, we knew there was a kernel of truth there. We didn't talk about it then. Maybe we should have, but there would have been no point. I couldn't alter who I was, and she wanted—needed—more from me. I shouldn't have ever married. Should have known better."

"Maybe you just married the wrong woman." The stars and the darkness give Phee the courage to say the words.

He shrugs. "What might have been. No sadder words, right? I can't go back. Can't change anything in the past. I thought I'd made the right decision, giving up the cello. Same as if there were a fire, right? Save my family first."

"And now?"

"Now? Just thinking about Allie not playing anymore makes me furious. How dare Lilian try to separate her from that? As a child, she was all music. She could sing on key almost as soon as she could talk. I taught her the names of the notes, and she'd go around the house telling us what note the vacuum cleaner was humming, or the dishwasher. She had color connections for every note in the scale. She'd stand between my legs, tucked between me and the cello for an hour at a time, just soaking up the vibrations."

"She blames the music for the accident," Phee murmurs.

"She told me. In the hospital, after . . . God, Phee. No wonder she tried to kill herself. If there's fault anywhere, it's her mother's for making her feel she had to sneak around to an audition."

"And maybe, just maybe, the same grace extends to you? Your wife was asking you to be something you're not, to give up your soul. How is that possibly okay?"

"Knowing that, maybe even believing it, changes nothing. I gave up the cello—not that my intended sacrifice mattered because I couldn't play anymore even if I'd chosén to. And she kicked me to the curb, anyway. She blamed the alcohol, but that was an excuse. It was already over between us that weekend I came up here to the cabin. And now, here I am, back at the scene of the crime."

"Do you hate me for dragging you here?"

The silence is long enough to be an answer in itself. "This is good for Allie," he says when he finally speaks. "I see that. And for my sister. It was selfish of me to stay away, unforgivable to keep Allie from her. So I ought to thank you for that."

Phee looks up at the stars, wondering which ones got crossed to put her at odds with the one man in the world who has ever held her heart. If he doesn't hate her, at the very least he must resent her intrusion and meddling.

"What will you do now?" she asks.

He shrugs. "We're all here now. Might as well press on."

"I thought it might help you remember."

"Maybe there's a reason for not remembering, did you think of that? Generally when people block out memories, they aren't happy ones."

"If it heals your hands—"

"It won't! You need to let that hope go, Phee. It's too late."

"Well, maybe you could at least let go of some guilt. Jo says you blame yourself for her husband's death, but he had a heart attack. That can't be your fault."

"I hit him." Braden turns to face her. "I keep having this flashback. The two of us are outside by the lake. He's sitting by a fire in the firepit, and out of nowhere, I punch him in the jaw. I keep seeing that one moment on repeat, like one of those obnoxious internet GIF things. Over and over and over. And every time, I feel so sick I want to puke."

"It's not like you were beating up on a woman or a child—"

"I've never been in a fight, Phee. Not before or since, on account of my hands. I'd never thrown a punch in my life. It doesn't take much of a detective to put together the evidence. Me, pissed off enough to punch him. And then, mysteriously, he winds up dead. Whatever memory you're dragging me back to isn't going to make Allie's life better. Or mine, or Jo's."

"But you're coming to the cabin, anyway?"

He answers with another question. "You know what Allie said? She said she changed her mind about dying and tried to call for help because she didn't want her death to be a lie. I guess I don't want the rest of my life to be a lie. And if there's the tiniest chance that there is some impossible curse, and that remembering will give me back my hands and that will help my daughter, then that's what I need to do."

"You're a good man, Braden."

"And you're a manipulative wench, you and your Angels."

"None of them know. The plan was to take you and Allie to a cabin in the woods somewhere. They all thought it would be a pleasant escape. I didn't tell them which cabin, or why. So don't blame them, whatever you do."

The door of the house opens, and Jo emerges onto the porch. Celestine bounds over to sniff her, tail wagging up a windstorm. "Am I interrupting?"

"Not at all," Braden says, the relief in his voice a knife thrust in Phee's heart.

Jo crosses the yard to join them. "The old man loves you, you know."

"Clearly," Braden says.

"He's worse since Mom died."

"I'm sorry I wasn't here for that. And grateful that you take care of him."

"We're all each other has, with Jimmy gone off to college."

"God," he says. "I'm so sorry, Jo. About Mitch—"

"Maybe if you'd let that go, I wouldn't have to lose you both."

"I didn't mean—"

"I know, honey," she says. She crosses to him and puts her arms around him. Phee goes back to the house and starts organizing everybody for the next stage of the journey.

Chapter Thirty-Four

BRADEN

Exhausted as he is, there is no sleep for Braden. A sense of heavy dread keeps his eyes open while his brain churns endlessly through the disconnected pieces of his memory. He lies on the lumpy foldout couch in the common area of the cabin, trying not to disturb the girls in the loft above with his restlessness. Phee and Jean share one of the bedrooms, Len and Dennis the other. Jo has promised—or threatened, he's not entirely sure which—to come out in the morning.

Despite the uncomfortable couch, Braden is relieved to be alone. Besides, here at the foot of the ladder that leads to the loft, he's closer to Allie. His ears are tuned for signs of restlessness. Twice already, he's climbed the ladder to check on the girls, Allie sandwiched between Steph and Katie, their version of suicide watch.

All three of them are sound asleep. He keeps hoping he'll drift into the solace of sleep, but the longer he lies here, the further away it seems. If he gets up and turns on a light, he fears it will wake Allie, who needs her rest, so there's nothing he can do to distract himself from his thinking.

The cello isn't helping. She's right here in the room with him, still in the case, invisible in the dark but vivid in his mind. He can call up in exquisite detail the sensation of her weight resting against him, the strings pressing into the pads of his fingers, the easy glide of the bow, how the music seemed as natural and necessary as breathing.

"Remember?" she whispers, and the lines of now and then blur as he drops into the memory of the last time the two of them made music, right here, in this room.

He's supposed to be practicing the Bach, but he can't focus. What's the point in mastering a piece if he's not going to play again? Letting his heart speak in the music, he moves through a series of laments and nameless melodies born from the union of his soul with the cello's.

"It's not that I don't love you," he whispers. "I have to do what's right. This one is goodbye."

He begins to play the lullaby he wrote for Allie . . .

In the present, in the now, something gives way inside him, a dam bursting under the pressure of a memory that refuses to be contained. He's lying on the lumpy mattress, his lower back aching, and he's also playing the lullaby, playing it for the very last time.

He's immersed in his thoughts and the music when he sees the head-lights, an unexpected flare in the dark window.

Hope leaps in his heart. Maybe it's Lilian come to tell him they'll figure something out. She's had time to think, to understand how the music is everything he is, that he'll be only half a man without it. He stops playing, watches the door as if it is his only hope of salvation.

But instead of Lilian, it's Mitch.

"No," the Braden lying on the lumpy mattress whispers, pushing back against the memory. "No, no, no." But it's too late; he can't stop it now.

Mitch, a cooler in his hands, stamps his feet on the doormat to shake off the snow. His eyes home in on Braden. "Good God, man, you look like hell warmed over."

Braden, stricken by the dashing of his last desperate hope, says nothing. Mitch clomps across the room in his boots, leaving a trail of precisely patterned prints behind him. He drops the cooler on the kitchen counter with a thud. "Want a beer?"

"Thank you, no."

"Suit yourself." Mitch pulls a six-pack out of the cooler, frees a can from the plastic and pops the top, takes a long drink. "That's what the doctor ordered. Jo sent food. She wasn't sure if you brought anything, said you might forget to eat. That's never going to be a problem for me."

Mitch drains half of his beer, opens a bag of chips. "We need to talk. That's why I came out here." His gaze slides away from Braden's. He crushes the can, already empty, and tosses it into the trash. Opens another.

"Might go easier with a beer. Sure you don't want one?"

Braden can't imagine what Mitch wants, why he's here. They're not close, have never had anything in common.

"What's going on? Jo okay?"

"For the moment. Look, this isn't easy to say. Seriously. Can you put that cello away for just a minute? Have a drink. Or two. It'll take the edge off."

Braden sits up in bed, breathing far too fast.

Don't tell me, don't tell me, don't tell me.

Getting up as quietly as possible, he grabs the box of matches from the shelf where they've been kept as far back as he can remember, pulls on his jacket and shoes, and eases out the back door.

It's not quite pitch-dark, the snow-covered lake and trees creating what he's always thought of as snow light, and he's able to make out dim shapes. The barbecue. The deck table and chairs. He takes care with his footing. The stairs that lead down from the deck are steep and can be icy and slick this time of year. Using the railing, taking his time, he works his way down to the firepit.

Firewood is neatly stacked and covered to keep it dry. The kindling box is full and also contains old newspapers wrapped in plastic. He pictures Jo out here replenishing the wood supply. Making kindling. Skills she was always better at than he was. His mother hadn't let him use the axe at all until he was old enough to defy her. He didn't do Boy

Scouts, he went to summer music camp. Everything in his world was music until suddenly it wasn't.

Back then it was Jo, not his father, who taught him how to make a fire. Who spirited him off from his mother's hovering and taught him how to fish and shoot a gun. It was Jo who took him hiking in the woods on the long summer days. And look how he has rewarded her.

Braden crumples a couple of sheets of newspaper and sets them in the center of the firepit. He adds kindling and tops it all off with two bigger pieces of wood. Then he strikes a match and holds it to the paper, the small flame quickly transferring itself to the edge of the paper, blossoming into light, licking at the kindling.

Now he can clearly see the chairs around the firepit, lightly dusted with snow. Mitch sat right there, across from where Braden is standing now, his back to the dark expanse of snow-covered lake.

The memory flash hits him again.

Snow drifting down.

Rage and grief and loss flooding his body.

Mitch's face, alternately shadowed and illuminated by the crackling fire.

The two loose ends of the flashback flail, loose in the breeze, connected to nothing. Braden watches the firelight, ironically amused at himself. On the trip here he'd fought a giant inner battle about whether to allow himself to remember, as if his psyche is a take-out window where he can order at will.

One memory to go, please, supersize the fries.

And now, nothing.

"Talk to me, Mitch," he murmurs out loud.

"Mitch is not the talkative type."

Braden startles at Jean's voice. He's been so lost in his own thoughts, he didn't hear her descending the stairs and coming toward him.

"Mind if I join you?" She sits before he can answer, across the fire in the place where Mitch sat so very long ago.

"Allie's fine," she says before he can ask. "I checked the loft before I came out. All three girls, sound asleep."

"What brings you out?" he asks, at a loss for what to say to this woman he barely knows.

"Same as you, I imagine. Couldn't sleep. Too much emotional processing. I heard you moving around, thought I'd see what you were up to."

"Just sitting here. Thinking. Not remembering." He gets up and adds wood to the fire, sending crackling sparks up into the darkness.

"This is not the typical intervention adventure," Jean says, her voice so quiet Braden needs to strain his ears to hear her. "Usually it's more celebration and party. Phee didn't tell us we'd be dragging you through the dirt."

"Have you had an intervention?"

She shakes her head. "It's rare with the Angels. Phee, once, not long after we started. Katie, a couple of times. You know about Dennis. And now you."

Braden thinks about Phee relapsing, replays the story she told him about the violinist and the old man, that she blames herself for what happened to both of them.

"You've remembered something," she says, scrutinizing his face.

"Written in flaming letters on my forehead?"

"Not like that. More like . . . you seem more solid. Like a piece of you came back."

"It's not a good piece," he says, poking at the fire with a stick. "My memories are going to hurt people."

"Whatever happened already happened," she says. "So the harm is already done."

"And if what I remember hurts them more? Things they don't need to know, for example."

"I think you need to trust that people are strong enough to carry the truth."

"Seems like maybe it would be better to keep my mouth shut."

"As your own private punishment? In which case, sooner or later, you'll go back to drinking. I'm a bit psychic." She glances up at him, measuring the impact of her words, then returns her gaze to the fire. "It left me wide open to people's emotions when I was younger. I didn't know how to shield myself. I didn't believe what I'm telling you now, that people have to carry their own burdens, that they're responsible for their own emotional journeys. I sank under the weight of it all. And so I started drinking."

"But you joined the Angels, and now you give people adventures and everything is hunky-dory." He regrets the bitterness in his voice, knowing she's only trying to help.

"Not quite so easy as all that. I drank because of other people's pain, or at least that was my excuse. And then I drove drunk and crashed my car and somebody died."

Braden, even though he's warm in the circle of the fire, shivers with the impact of what she's telling him. Her eyes meet his now, and she holds him with her gaze. "I did prison time. But being locked up wasn't justice for taking a life. So a month after I was incarcerated, I tried to kill myself. I failed. When I woke up in the hospital, I realized that wasn't justice, either. It didn't bring the woman back to her family. No possible form of punishing myself was going to make the world better for anybody.

"I came to believe that the only true recompense is to give to the world whatever I have to give. To live every minute enough for the two of us, myself and the woman whose life I stole. This is how I choose to repay her."

Braden takes this in but says nothing.

"This thing you've blocked out of your memory—maybe you're not the one who gets to say whether it will heal or hurt."

"Doesn't appear I have any control over it, want to or not," he says.

For a while both of them just sit, staring into the fire, then Jean stretches and gets to her feet. "I'm too old for all-nighters. I'm going to try for a couple of hours of sleep. Go easy on yourself."

He watches her walk away, turns back to the fire, and continues to ask himself the question he still can't answer.

Do I really want to remember?

He hadn't wanted to hear whatever Mitch had to tell him, all the way back then. Doesn't want to hear it now, but he takes a breath, pokes at the fire, hears his memory self, seated behind the cello in the long-ago cabin, say to Mitch:

"Whatever it is, spit it out."

And Mitch squares his shoulders and turns to face him. "Suit yourself. It's about Lilian. I'd suggest you sit down, but you already are. So. Here goes. Lil and I . . . we're having an affair."

The words make no sense. Not Lilian. Not this.

"Look, man, I know it's gotta be hard to hear. But I'm sick of sneaking around behind everybody's backs. I told her we needed to have it out—"

"Do you mean had an affair?" Braden interrupts. "Past tense." He can't work out the logistics. It's been years since all of them have been together; Lilian never comes out to Colville if she can avoid it.

Mitch shakes his head. "We Skype almost every day. Meet for a week together twice a year."

Braden's fingers tighten around the neck of the cello as the words sink in. The separate vacations. The continued education trainings Lil goes to for her nursing license, always somewhere out of town.

Still, he can't believe it. He pictures her kneeling by their bed every night to pray. Reading her Bible, going to church.

"She wouldn't." But even as he says it, he feels the cold certainty of the truth.

"I asked her to marry me," Mitch says. "Last week. Told her I'm sick to death of this. 'Let's both just get divorced and get it over with,' I said. She wanted to wait until the kids are older, but I want . . . I don't want to

wait. She'll be mad that I told you, but I figured you'd want to do the right thing and let her go."

Braden doesn't want to hear this, not any of it. He starts playing again, his hands finding their own music. Allie's lullaby, transposed this time into a minor key.

"How long?" he asks, but he knows, wants to stop what's coming, but it's already too late.

"Since before Trey was born." Mitch's gaze focuses on him directly, and Braden sees it now, sees what he didn't notice before because he was so damn trusting and never looked for it. Trey looks exactly like Mitch and Jo's son, Jimmy. Jimmy looks exactly like Mitch.

Mitch raises his voice to be heard above the music. "Trey is my son. Maybe you already guessed that."

Braden stops in the middle of a phrase, an unresolved chord hanging in the air between them. It seems to him that he and Mitch are in the eye of a storm, in an eerie and deceptive calm with destruction swirling all around them.

"And I suppose you want to get to know your son, now that we've got him past night feedings and diapers."

"Time to have this out in the open. Better for everybody."

"Really? I don't see how this can possibly be good for anybody."

"What I don't understand," Mitch says, "is how you never saw it. The boys could be brothers."

"I wasn't looking for it. It never occurred to me that I couldn't trust my wife, especially with my sister's husband. What the hell, Mitch?"

Mitch opens yet another beer. "Look, I'm not proud of any of this. But I will say this much. Lilian is dead right about you."

"In what way, exactly?"

"You don't see her. You don't notice anything that's not connected to that cello. She's a hell of a woman, and you don't deserve her."

Braden's body has become a sounding board for accusations and self-recriminations, all of it escalating toward rage.

"You've been fucking my wife and you're blaming me for it? Are you going to blame Jo, too?"

"Jo is an admirable woman, but she's so goddamn self-sufficient. Lilian, now, Lilian needs me."

Lilian is all need, Braden thinks. Needs he hasn't ever been able to meet. He can see, now, with terrible clarity, how she and Mitch would fit together. A strong man who wants to take care of a woman, a woman who wants to be taken care of. A fleeting sympathy for both of them, a tortured understanding, collides with an awareness of collateral damage.

Jo will be devastated. All of the kids will be marked by this. Jimmy. Allie. Trey.

"I've been trying to get her to marry me since Trey was born," Mitch says. "We made a point of not being seen together or letting the boys be in the same place at the same time. I told myself it was for the best, but I still love her, Braden. I'm tired of a long-distance relationship, and yes, I want to get to know my son."

"Are you asking for my blessing? Some old-school transaction where I, what, give her to you? She's my wife, Mitch. And Trey is my son in every way that counts. You don't even know him! And Lilian's not on board with your plan. She told me if I give up the cello, we stay together. So that's what I'm going to do. Lilian and I—and you—all of us will do the right thing. You stop the thing with Lil. Jo and the kids never need to know any of this."

"So we just go on and pretend it never happened?" Mitch laughs harshly and without humor. "How anybody can look at that boy and not know he's mine, I can never understand. It's going to all come out sooner or later. God. What a mess. You sure you don't want a beer?"

He's flushed and slurring, shifting from apologetic to belligerent. "This isn't over, but I've said what I came to say. I'll go home and let you think about it."

"You're drunk. It's snowing. You can't drive back tonight."

"I'm fine." He heads for the door, his footsteps weaving . . .

And there the memory ends.

Braden sits by the fire, attuning himself to Lilian's betrayal, the knowing that Trey, his golden-haired, sunny boy, wasn't really his. The memory doesn't feel new; rather, he has an odd sensation that it's always been right there, just outside the focus of his attention.

But it won't be that way for Jo, for Allie.

Does he say something? The only other two people on the planet who knew this secret are dead. Nothing would be served by Allie knowing that Trey was only her half brother, by Jo knowing that her beloved deceased husband was unfaithful for years.

Unless, as Jean says, he should trust them to be strong enough to hold the truth.

Allie's words come back to him.

"I didn't want my death to be a lie."

Chapter Thirty-Five

PHEE

Phee wakes to the smell of coffee. Dog drool is cooling on her arm, a sound of panting loud in her ear.

"Leave me alone," she grumbles, and then her eyes fly open as she remembers where she is, the audacity of what she has done.

Jean is still asleep beside her, turned on her side, a pillow half over her head. Celestine's tail wags dangerously, and Phee knows from long experience that there will be no sliding back into sleep once the big dog has ideas of outside and breakfast in his head. Not that she could sleep in, anyway. Not today.

She doesn't wear a watch, has no idea what time it is. Dim light could mean either very early morning or just an overcast winter day. Rolling out from under the covers as quietly as possible, she slips into her jeans, smooths the T-shirt she slept in, and attempts to run her fingers through her hair. It's hopelessly tangled, and she settles for weaving it into a messy braid. One hand on Celestine's collar, she tiptoes toward the bedroom door. Celestine is anything but stealthy, but Jean doesn't wake.

Out in the living area, Braden's pullout couch is empty, the blankets and sheets tangled and tossed aside. Katie is in the kitchen, clattering mugs out of a cupboard, a coffeepot on the counter generating the rich aroma of fresh coffee. Low voices and rustling in the loft signal that Steph and Allie are also awake.

Phee feels like she's been drugged with a tranquilizer, her movements all slow and clumsy, her thoughts heavy and lumbering.

"Where's Braden?" she manages. "And can I have a mug of that, like now?"

"He's outside. Coffee in about two minutes."

Which is time enough to go to the bathroom, to splash cold water over her face, to second-guess this trip about thirty-seven times.

Back in the kitchen, Katie hands her two mugs. "One for you, and one for him."

Phee accepts the mugs, taking a scalding sip of her own, letting the promise of caffeine nudge her brain cells into waking.

"How do you know he's outside?"

"You can see everything from the loft. Window on the world. I'll get the door. Also, hey, he's got a fire out there. Can we roast hot dogs for breakfast?"

"Those were meant to be dinner."

"So, we eat whatever was supposed to be breakfast for dinner. Come on, it will be fun. Whatever weird shit you're pulling with this intervention, Phee, we still get to have some fun."

"Fine, all right. I'll be back in—"

"I got it. The girls will help me. Right?" she calls up to the loft. "You two lazybones want to roast hot dogs on the fire for breakfast?"

Two heads appear over the railing of the loft a minute later, disheveled and sleepy eyed. "Yes! I've never roasted a hot dog," Steph says. "We're getting dressed."

Muffled voices in the room the men are sharing mean that Len and Dennis are now awake as well.

Katie opens the back door, and Phee steps out into wonderland. The sun, just emerging from behind a mountain, lights the tops of the evergreen trees across the lake and turns the snow pink. The sky is a shade of blue she's not sure she's ever seen before.

Celestine takes off running, or tries to, his feet scrabbling on the frosty deck. He slows, taking his time with the stairs, and Phee follows, placing each foot carefully, conscious both of the slippery surface and the two brimming mugs of hot coffee. Braden meets her halfway and relieves her of one mug.

"You need to hang on to the railing so you don't take a ride down on your ass."

Celestine sniffs around the campfire, then heads toward the open, flat expanse of snow.

"Hey, get back here!" Braden shouts, and the dog pauses, looking back over his shoulder.

"Cold today, but it's been warm," he explains to Phee. "Looks solid, but there are soft spots."

"Celestine!" Phee calls, and he heads back in the direction of the campfire, stopping to cock his leg on a nearby bush.

Braden sinks back down onto one of the camp chairs with an exhalation that is part sigh, part groan. He looks exhausted. Dark circles under his eyes, the lines of his face etched deeper.

"Did you sleep at all?" she asks.

"Spent most of the night out here. Thinking. You?"

"Slept like the dead," she says. "Sorry. That was not the best analogy."

He shrugs, drinks coffee. "Thank you for this."

"You've Katie to thank for the coffee."

He is closed and silent, avoiding eye contact.

A door slams above them, followed by a giggle. "Look out. Nearly fell on my butt."

"You girls be careful up there," Phee calls.

They come down off the deck in a procession. Katie has the hot dogs and buns, Steph a tray full of condiments, Allie a basket of paper plates and plastic cutlery. "Aunt Jo's here. She said to just bring stuff down here since it's so slippery and we don't want people going up and down. The guys are getting a folding table."

"What exactly are we doing?" Braden asks. He gets up and takes the basket from Allie. She gives him a look that says she loves him, even though she doesn't hug him or say so, and Phee feels a whisper of ease, that maybe her meddling has helped bring them together.

"Hot dog and marshmallow roast!" Steph crows. "Yes, we know this is not breakfast food. This is an adventure and rules do not apply."

"Is that so?" Braden says, raising his eyebrows at Phee. "Any other rule breaking I should know about?"

"Anything is fair during an intervention," Dennis says from up on the deck. He's got one end of a folding table, Len comes behind holding the other.

"I'm too old for this," Len says, but he looks more energetic than any of the rest of them.

"Really, there are no rules," Katie says. "Except for the coffee rules. Those always apply."

Celestine has forgotten all about the lake, for now. He's under everybody's feet, sniffing at the hot dogs and buns, asking to be petted.

"Can I give him one?" Allie begs. "He looks so sad. And starving."

"He is neither," Phee objects, shaking her head at the dog, who sits looking up into Allie's eyes as if his very last breath depends upon her giving him a handout. "He's too big to start feeding him table food. Little dogs are cute when they beg. A dog this size turns into a terrorist. If you really want to feed him, come with me. You can give him his breakfast."

"All right," Allie says, stroking the dog's head. "Come on, Celestine. Why'd you name him that, anyway? Since he's a boy dog."

"A whole bunch of popes were called Celestine, so it can be a boy's name. Plus, he was already named that when I got him. Enough things in his world were already different, I figured at least he could keep his name."

Jo is waiting at the top of the stairs, a bundle of blackened metal rods under one arm, a bag of marshmallows in her hand. "Roasting sticks. Haven't used them in years, but they were in the closet waiting. Everybody sleep okay?"

"Some did, some didn't," Phee says. "We'll be right down."

Once inside the cabin, she unpacks the box that holds the container full of Celestine's kibble, as well as his bowl and treats. "One scoop," she says to Allie. "Set it over by the door where we put his water bowl last night."

While the girl is feeding the dog, Phee proceeds with her real motive for getting Allie away from the crowd. She crosses to the cello case, unlatches it, and lifts out the cello.

Allie comes to stand beside her.

"You know you want to play. You're like your dad that way. Music is your soul."

"Even if I hurt people?"

"And people hurt you by trying to keep you from it. Listen, Allie." Phee turns to look directly into her eyes. "You'd be helping your dad out, if you play. It might help him remember. I think at the least it would comfort him to know that the cello is being played."

Allie floats her palm across the strings.

Jean emerges from the bedroom, looking from one to the other. "Could have sworn I heard something about breakfast."

"You did!" Allie says, taking a step back. "Down by the firepit. Oh, and Katie made coffee."

Jean is the most perceptive and sensitive woman Phee has ever met. The timing of this interruption isn't by accident. Jean doesn't give her an opportunity to ask, slipping out the door ahead of Allie.

Phee leaves Celestine inside, to keep him out of trouble and out of everybody's plates. She feels like she'll need her full attention for whatever is going to happen. Fifteen minutes later, she thinks maybe she's been wrong and that nothing is going to happen at all.

The mood has taken on the tone of a classic adventure. People laughing, burning hot dogs and their fingers. Dennis spills his coffee, and Katie fetches him a refill. Once, Allie actually laughs. Braden is the only one quiet, reserved, his face more like a man on the rack than a man on an adventure. Jean is watchful and anxious, but that's normal behavior for her.

When the last hot dog has been roasted, the last marshmallow burned, a silence falls, all of them sitting around the warmth of the fire. And that's when Jean says, very quietly, "Jo, Allie, Braden has something to tell you."

His eyes widen; he jerks upright in the chair. Phee feels the way his breath snags on something sharp in his throat. Feels the mood of the group shift to watchful, uncertain. Len glances at her, a small warning, but she shrugs her shoulders at him. This isn't her doing, at least not directly.

"It's better this way, Braden," Jean says. "Trust me. Trust them. Get it over with. Spit it out."

He pales visibly at those words.

"What?" Jo asks. She looks shaken, glancing from face to face around the circle as if she'll read an answer written somewhere.

"You sure about this, Jean?"

"I'm sure," she says.

Braden swallows, visibly. "I . . . remembered something last night."

Jo's hands dart to her face, and he shakes his head. "Not that, Jo. Not how he died. Something else. It's going to hurt you, both you and Allie."

He takes another breath. "When Mitch came out here to talk to me, that night, he wanted to tell me something. He had a confession."

Jo stares at him, lips parted, eyes dark. "Trey." A statement, not a question.

"How did you know?"

"I didn't, until now. Just always wondered. It's the only thing I could think of that would bring him out here."

"What about Trey?" Allie asks.

"Your mom and your uncle Mitch were . . . Trey is, was, your half-brother, Allie."

She stares at her father with her mouth gaping open, then closes it with a sharp snap. "Mom? You're kidding, right? I mean, Mom wouldn't even tell a fib. How could she ever . . ." Allie's eyes travel from Braden to Jo and back again, and her words fade into confusion.

"For real?"

"I'm so sorry," Braden says.

"What are you sorry for?" Jo snaps. "You're not the one who was having an affair."

"It happened because of the cello—"

"An excuse," Jo says. "If it wasn't that, she'd have found something else. I remember the way those two looked at each other. Let me guess—when he went off on his fishing trips, he didn't go alone."

"Seriously?" Allie asks again. "I kinda thought Mom was, like, perfect. Always right."

"The last thing I want to do is tarnish her memory—"

"It helps," Allie says, "that she wasn't perfect."

"See?" Jean says. "They're stronger than you think."

"I'm not done yet," he says grimly. "I sat out here all night, in the place that it happened, hoping it would all come back. It didn't. But reason doesn't take me to a good place." He pauses. "Mitch came up here to ask me to divorce Lilian so they could be together."

"Bastard," Jo says, then adds, "God rest his soul."

"So I put that together with this other tiny little flash. I keep seeing him sitting out here by the fire, right where Dennis is sitting now. And I punched him."

"Sounds like he deserved it," Dennis says. Len looks thoughtful, listening.

"You're not putting the pieces together." Braden raises his voice for emphasis. "Mitch comes out here to tell me he's been with my wife, that he's the father of my son. He was a threat to my family and my music. I hated him, in that moment. Enough to kill him." He waits, letting his words sink in.

"Whatever happened out here was so horrific, my own brain has protected me from remembering. Phee here thinks it was so intense that my brain has also protected me by taking away the use of my hands. Do the math. Two men alone, one of them in a murderous rage, and the other one ends up dead. What do you all think happened?"

"You couldn't," Allie breathes. "You wouldn't."

"We know I hit him. And then he drowned."

"He had a heart attack," Jo protests. "That's what the autopsy showed. It was a time bomb waiting to happen, they said."

"And maybe that bomb wouldn't have gone off if he hadn't fallen through the ice into shockingly cold water. How do you think that happened, Jo? An outdoorsman like Mitch? He knew better than to walk on the ice this time of year."

She's weeping now, softly. "He was drunk."

"Not that drunk, Jo. I think we all need to face the truth. I killed Mitch."

Chapter Thirty-Six

PHEE

Phee stares at Braden, stricken. This is not at all what she had in mind when she planned this intervention. She'd fully believed, curse or no curse, that there would at least be healing here. A new connection between Braden and Allie. Forgiveness. Hope.

Braden's eyes meet hers, and his lips twist in a half smile. "Sorry, Phee. There's no magic fairy-tale ending. No reversible curse. Everything that has happened to me happened because I deserved it."

He shifts his attention to his daughter, who is weeping silently. "Allie, honey, I would give anything to undo all of this . . ."

She makes an inarticulate sound, then gets up and climbs the stairs, head bent, not looking back.

"I'll watch her," Steph says, following.

Braden drops his head into his hands.

All of them sit in a shocked, awkward silence. Phee can't stand to watch Braden's suffering, her eyes wandering out over the expanse of the lake.

"This story isn't over," her grandfather's voice says.

Phee takes a breath. "There are flaws in your logic," she says. "He died here, that's clear. But when the ambulance came, he was up at the cabin."

"You had severe hypothermia," Jo adds. "You were cut and bruised. Frostbite to your hands and feet. How did that happen?"

"I don't remember."

Phee hears music. The cello has been blessedly silent since they arrived, but now a melody drifts into her ears. Braden hears it, too. His head comes up. And then she realizes it's not in her head, not this time. Every head turns toward the cabin.

"What is it?" Dennis asks.

Braden closes his eyes. "The last song I ever played."

Katie, uncharacteristically silent, gets up and climbs the stairs toward the cabin. By unspoken agreement, the rest of the Angels follow. Then Jo. Braden stays where he is, and Phee holds out a hand to him.

"Come on."

"I don't want—"

"I'm not leaving you here alone."

He laughs, short and harsh. "You think I'll, what, kill myself? Add that to Allie's burden?"

"She's playing for you," Phee says. "You need to let her know you hear her." Her hand remains outstretched. Finally, he accepts what she is offering, lets her tug him up to standing. Together they climb the stairs, side by side.

Allie, playing the cello, looks whole for the first time since Phee has met her. Her eyes focus immediately on her father, who drops Phee's hand and stands immobile, as if he's been flash frozen, an ice sculpture of a once living man.

"Phee said it might help you to remember," Allie says, her bow arm slowing, then coming to rest.

"Phee has said a lot of things." Braden takes one step forward. "There's no magic key, little bird. But I'm so glad to hear you play."

"I want you to remember." Her voice breaks. "I don't believe you killed him."

"Suppose I remember and I did kill him?"

"Well, then we'd know. Please," she says.

Braden shrugs, helplessly. "I can't. Even here. Even with that music. There's nothing beyond what I told you."

"We could try hypnosis," Phee says, lighting the fuse on the dynamite.

All eyes focus on her. Stunned silence.

"No," Len says. "This whole harebrained scheme of yours is unethical. I don't even have a license to practice anymore."

"Well, then, you have no risk of losing it."

"That may be the most outrageous thing to ever come out of your mouth. That's saying something."

"Would it help?" Braden interrupts. "Would that unlock my memory?"

"It can," Len says reluctantly. "Hypnosis bypasses the logical mind and the defense mechanisms. But—"

"Can we do it here? Now?"

"Hypnosis is not an exact science. It's helpful for many things, but memory recovery is controversial. It's not like the movies."

"But it might work."

"What good will it do?"

"I'll know," Braden says. "If it works. On some level, I've always believed that I was responsible for Mitch's death, but I still don't know. Not for sure. You can't face up to something you don't know. It's always lurking, always insinuating."

"Look," Len says, his voice falling into professional, soothing tones. "Why don't I set you up with a psychologist I know when we get back? He's also skilled with hypnotherapy and—"

"No. If anybody's going to do this, it will be you."

"Please," Allie says.

"Come on, Len," Phee says. "What are the risks?"

"The risk is that he remembers killing Mitch because he thinks that's what he's going to remember. Even if he didn't."

"In which case, we're no worse off than we are already," Braden says.

"Not like any of this is admissible in court," Dennis adds. "There's no evidence. A good lawyer could get him off easy. So it's not like you'd be sending him to prison."

Allie starts playing again, very softly, the music swirling around all of them, creating a mood of mystery and possibility.

"Let's take a vote," Phee says. "How many people are in favor of Len hypnotizing Braden?"

All hands go up except for Len's.

Braden is pale, but his face is set in lines of determination. "What do I do? Lie down?"

"Oh hell," Len says. "You're going to pay big-time for this, Phee."

"Don't I know it," she answers. She's already paying, she'll be paying for a lifetime. But it's worth it, on the off chance that this will work.

"Maybe everybody should go do something else," Len says. "Or we could go into one of the rooms."

"Right here, with witnesses. That way, they can tell me later if you ask leading questions or implant suspicious hypnotic suggestions." He flops down on the pullout and adjusts his pillow beneath his head. "This is convenient."

"You don't have to do this," Jo says. "It doesn't matter. What happened, happened."

"So remembering it won't change anything, to quote a very wise woman." He nods at Jean, and she smiles at him gently.

"Do you need a pendulum or something?" Phee asks.

"Everything we need is in Braden's head already." Len pulls up a chair, calm and businesslike now that he's made up his mind. "Keep playing, if you don't mind, Allie. Music can be helpful. The rest of you, please be very quiet. Do not speak to him or engage with him. Understood?" He looks around the circle of faces, making eye contact with everybody, one at a time. "Phee, can you get control of that dog?"

"Celestine, come," Phee commands, and he bounds over to lick her hands. "Lie down," she says, and then sits on the floor beside him to keep him there.

Katie and Steph cram themselves into an armchair together. Jo perches on the other. Jean and Dennis take up positions standing on the far side of the bed. Allie and the cello sit roughly at the foot.

"A circle of Angels," Braden says. "What could go wrong?"

The process of hypnosis isn't mysterious or complicated at all. Len takes Braden through some breathing, counts him down ten levels of an imaginary staircase. He goes through several safety exercises, establishing a safe place where Braden can return at any time if his memories become too painful.

"Now," Len says, "You are fully in a world of trance. Trust that your mind will take you where you need to go. Let it carry you back to a memory of this cabin, another night, when you played this music. Are you there?"

"Yes," Braden answers. His voice sounds distant, different.

"Are you alone?"

"No, Mitch is here. He's . . . leaving. I want him gone, but he's drunk. It's dark and snowing and I tell him to give me his keys."

"And does he?"

"No. He says, 'So I crash. Problem solved for you.'"

"What do you say to him?"

"'Give me your fucking car keys, Mitch.'"

"You're smiling," Len says.

"He doesn't give me the keys. I shove him. It feels good to shove him. A release. But then he says, 'What the hell, man? Out of my way.'

"I tell him I'm looking out for my sister.

"He says, 'What are you gonna do, fight me? I'd drop you and your precious hands like a fly meeting a fly swatter.'"

Jo squeezes her own hands into fists. There's a lump in Phee's throat that feels like a golf ball. Celestine whines and thumps his tail.

"My hands don't matter anymore," Braden says. "I'm giving up the cello. I've got nothing to lose. I want to hit him. Only, he gives in. Drops the key ring on the counter."

"And then what happens?" Len asks.

Phee holds her breath. This is the telling moment. Whether Braden will remember beyond what he's already told them or not.

"He takes the beer outside," Braden says. "Makes a fire in the pit. And I . . . I put the cello in her case and close it. I tell her this is goodbye. I can still hear the music, even though she's locked in the case, and I think maybe I need to bury her or burn her to make it stop."

Again, he goes silent, and Len prompts him.

"But you don't."

"No, I . . . start thinking about Mitch again. Blaming him. It's all his fault. He did this. He pushed Lilian into the affair, and it's all his fault that I have to give up music. I need to go talk to him, tell him to stay away from Lil and the kids. Make him swear he'll keep this whole thing a secret. I tell myself I just want to talk to him, but really I want to hit him.

"I'm furious, desperate. As soon as I step outside, the wind hits me, cuts right through my shirt, but I don't go back for a jacket. It's snowing like crazy, wind blowing, drifts above the tops of my tennis shoes, but I don't feel it.

"Mitch is sitting in a camp chair beside the fire, still drinking. When he sees me, he . . . asks me to talk about it. Offers me a drink."

"What do you do?" Len asks.

"I sit down. I start drinking. And we just sit there. I'm thinking a little more clearly, tell myself I just need to make him agree to keeping his mouth shut and then I'll go."

Braden stops talking again. Phee looks around the circle, all of the faces watchful, waiting. Allie still plays, tears flowing down her cheeks.

"So you drink for a while," Len prompts. "And then what happens?"

"And then I just tell him, 'I'm going home to her. You need to keep your mouth shut.' He doesn't answer. I tell him I want him to promise to break it off with Lilian, that nobody else needs to get hurt. We won't tell Jo, or the kids. This stays between us."

"What does he say?" Len asks.

"'Who says you get to decide?' That's what he says.

"'My wife. My kids,' I tell him.

"'Trey's not,' he says. He starts laughing, like the whole thing is a joke. 'We could fight for her,' he says."

Braden stops talking. He just lies there, breathing rapidly.

"What are you feeling?" Len prompts.

"Everything is black around the edges, I'm so mad. I punch him in the jaw. He's drunk, he's not ready, the chair tips over backward. He stays right there in the snow, legs in the air. Still got the can clutched in his hand. My hand hurts, but it hurts good.

"'That the best you can do?' he says. He sets the can in the snow and rolls over onto his hands and knees, staggers up onto his feet. He spreads his arms out wide. 'I'm a sporting man. Let's make it fair. You get one more hit free before I flatten you.'

"I . . . I lunge at him, head butt him in the chest. We go down together, me on top. He says, 'Missed your chance, music boy. Should have taken what I offered.'

"I . . . I punch him in the nose. Blood splatters on my face. Mitch, he's stronger, heavier. He flips me somehow. I'm on my back, can't breathe. Snow down my back, down inside my jeans. He's gonna hit me, any second, only he doesn't, he's . . . he's crying. Blood dripping down on my face from his nose, tears and blood all over his face.

"'You and that fucking cello,' he says. 'You made this mess, and now I'm the bad guy.' He says it broken, not mad anymore. I feel desperate, sick, I don't want to puke while I'm lying on my back. He's drunk, crying. I tip him off, get up.

"Mitch gets up, too. He . . . doesn't look good. He's breathing too hard, through his mouth because of his nose. His hand is pressed against his chest. I think maybe I've broken his ribs.

"He lunges at me, and I just . . . step aside. And he, he trips on something. His arms are flailing. He goes down on his hands and knees. And then he's just, he's not there. Like, he disappeared.

"I think he must have fallen into a snowdrift, I wait for him to sit up. But there's nothing."

There's sweat on Braden's forehead. He pauses, breathing hard. Phee wants to wipe it away, to touch him, reassure him. She scoots over beside the pullout couch, her hand hovers. Len warns her off with a vigorous shake of his head.

"What are you doing, Braden? Talk to me."

"I'm looking for Mitch. Can't find him anywhere. Oh God. No."

"What is it?"

"I'm on the lake. The ice keeps giving beneath my feet. There's water on the surface, it's soaking my shoes. Mitch was standing here. He must have fallen through."

He gasps. "Cold. Oh my God, that's cold. In up to my knees. Can't feel my feet."

Braden begins to shiver, his breathing rasping in his throat.

Dynamite, Len said. Unpredictable. But Phee didn't think it would be like this. It's not like she was expecting performance art, or a parlor trick of "Oh, now I remember, my hands are cured, let me play a song for you." But she wasn't prepared for this. She feels sick with fear. Allie stops playing. Jo goes to her, and Allie buries her face in her chest. Steph and Katie hold hands, their faces stricken.

"What's happening, Braden?" Len's face and voice are still calm, placid, even.

"I'm trying to find him. There's a hole in the ice. I'm feeling around, but there's just water and ice. My hands are numb, it's so cold, can't see, it's so dark and the snow won't stop.

307

"I feel something. Maybe a sleeve. Can't get a grip on it. Keeps slipping away. Got his hand, but he's too heavy. I can't get him out. My hands keep slipping. 'Mitch! Goddamn it, help me out.'"

"He's not moving. Oh God."

"What's happening, Braden?" Len's voice again, so calm. An anchor for all of them.

"Fell in. Cut my face on something. Whole body getting numb. I've got to get him out now. Last chance." Braden's voice has begun to slur, his breath coming in gasps as though he's been running. Another moment of silence, and then: "Off the lake. So tired. Must keep moving. God, he's so heavy. He won't wake up. Is he breathing? Can't tell. Can't feel a pulse.

"Gotta get him warm somehow. Dragging him. Up the steps. Legs won't work now. Too hard to get up. On my ass, one step at a time. Dragging him. Top of the stairs, across the deck. The door. Can't turn the knob. Can't break down the door. Can't stop here, so close."

"What's happening, Braden?"

"So tired. Got the door. We're in the cabin. He's not breathing. Nobody's face should be this color. He's dead, I let him die."

Phee's throat, her chest, burn with his anguish, tears blurring her vision. Again, she wants to go to Braden; again, Len warns her off.

"Braden, listen to me now. Do you hear me?"

"I hear you."

"It was an accident. You tried to save Mitch, but he was not able to be saved. Do you know why that is?"

"His heart."

"Yes. He had a massive heart attack. There was nothing you could have done. What happened was not your fault. Repeat these words, now. It was not my fault."

"Not my fault," Braden says.

"Your body is warming from the inside. Do you feel it?"

A moment, then a nod.

"The warmth is traveling outward, through your muscles, into your skin. Sensation is returning."

Braden's breathing slows, his shivering subsides.

"You can feel your toes, your feet, your legs. No pain, just a sensation of pleasant warmth, all through your extremities. You can move your fingers, they are flexible. There is no pain. Sensation returns, little by little, softly. Your hands, your fingers, are waking from a long sleep, refreshed. Ready to work for you."

Braden opens and closes both hands. Moves each finger in turn.

"And now, I'm going to bring you back," Len's smooth voice says. "I will count backward from three, and when I get to one, you will wake up. You will feel warm and comfortable. You will remember that an accident happened and that you made a heroic effort to save a man who had wronged you. And you will have full sensation restored to your hands and your fingers. I'm going to count now. Three, beginning to come back to this room and the people who love you. Two, whole in mind, body, and spirit. One, with your full memory restored."

His voice falls silent. Braden's eyes flicker open, glazed at first, then sharpening into intelligent awareness.

Allie runs to him and throws her arms around his neck. Moving slowly, as if he's a little dazed, Braden strokes her hair and pats her back.

"I'm okay," he says.

"Heart attack. I told you." Jo's face is wet with tears. "He did it to himself."

"I hit him," Braden argues.

"He provoked you. You can share the blame if you want, but you can't have all of it. Stupid menfolk, fighting over a woman." Jo laughs a little, scrubbing the tears from her face.

"What happened then?" Allie asks, sitting cross-legged beside him. Her eyes are dark and intent on his. "Between you and Mom. If you chose our family, and Uncle Mitch was dead, why did you leave us?"

"It was just . . . over between us. After I came home, your mom couldn't bear to look at me. I didn't remember about her and Mitch; the memory was already gone when I woke up in the hospital. We never talked about it. When I told her I didn't remember what happened, how he died, she cried about that for days. It must have torn her apart. I think . . . she blamed me. I started drinking."

"She shouldn't have tried to take away your music," Allie says fiercely.

"Or yours," he answers. "You're going to keep playing, yes?"

Allie nods. "I couldn't bear to stop a second time."

"God, I feel tired," Braden says.

"I'm sure," Len says. "Take it easy for a bit, let this settle in. You'll maybe have bits of memory coming in for days now that the floodgates are open."

Jean goes to the kitchen and comes back with a glass of water. "Drink up."

"How did you know I'm desert dry?"

"Just had a feeling."

He says nothing about his hands. Nobody asks. Allie sits tucked under his arm, and all of his focus is on her. At last, he looks up, reads the question in Phee's eyes.

He lifts his hands, bends his fingers, then shakes his head. "I'm sorry, Phee," he says. "Miracles only go so far."

Chapter Thirty-Seven

PHEE

Phee carefully tunes the violin, tucks it under her chin, and plays a few measures. The action is good, everything feels right, but the tone isn't quite what she would like it to be. Not surprising. The wood needs to season and settle before she'll know if her new creation is mediocre, good, or great.

Still, a glow of accomplishment floods through her, as it does every time she completes a new instrument. And, as also always happens when she completes a new instrument, she thinks about the unopened letter in her trunk upstairs, wonders what it might teach her. Maybe someday she'll read it, learn her grandfather's darkest secrets, but she will never, ever, add a brand-new MacPhee instrument to the specials on her list.

She's had enough of meddling with dynamite to last her for a good long time.

Since her return from the cabin five months ago, she's had one letter from Braden, handwritten and sent through the post office to the shop.

April 2, 2018

Colville, WA

Phee,

(Not "dear Phee," she notes, certainly not "dearest," or "darling," but she should be grateful he's communicating with her at all.)

I know you will worry, so I'm writing to update you on our status.

Thank you for the offer you made when the Angels all headed back to Seattle, but we won't be requiring a ride back home anytime soon. Allie and I have agreed to stay on at the cabin through the summer. It's good for her to spend time with Jo, and good for me, too, I admit.

We've hired a service to keep an eye on the house and tend to the yard.

It's peaceful here, a good place to think and to heal. Allie plans to retake her last semester of high school classes in the fall.

The cello is well and I believe happy. Allie plays every day, for hours, and I've been acting as her teacher. Hopefully this will be enough to keep your curse at bay.

I can't quite believe I'm saying this, but thank you for dragging us out here. I am coming to terms with my life and going through the grieving process. Yes, I am sober. I suppose being here with Allie is one ongoing adventure.

Tell the Angels thank you for me. I'll be back to meetings in the fall.

Be well,

Braden

Phee hasn't written back. Any letter containing anything of importance would have to include words to tell him that she lies awake at night thinking about him. That even when she's absorbed in crafting and repairing instruments, there's an emptiness in her chest that sometimes makes it hard to breathe. She has some pride, she tells herself. She's not going to throw herself at any man, not even Braden Healey.

All through the summer, she's waited for the sensation to ease, but if anything, it's grown stronger. She's spent longer and longer hours in the shop, breaking off only to take Celestine for walks or to engage in Adventure Angels activities, or to make music of her own. Twice, she's made herself visit Ethan, first in the hospital and then after his release from a psychiatric unit.

She doesn't like him, but she feels responsible, as if maybe he's yet another casualty of Braden's broken bond with the cello. The boy's parents, she has to admit, are self-absorbed and neglectful, and he's been shaped by their behaviors into who he is. Still, she's overwhelmingly grateful to Dennis, who has taken an interest in the boy and spirited him off on a series of adventures.

The instruments on her list are all currently well-loved and quiet.

All in all, things are going well, but she feels empty and restless; even the satisfaction of completing a new violin is transitory and small. Maybe she'll take Celestine for a vacation before the last of the summer weather is gone. A ferry to Canada, maybe. Camping on Vancouver Island. Or a road trip.

When the bell over the shop door signals a customer, she looks at the clock. Three minutes to five. She should have locked the shop door early. People who come in just before closing always seem to need an hour of her time.

Celestine, on the other hand, woofs a greeting as he explodes upward from his bed and runs out of the room. Somebody known, then. A regular.

Phee blinks as she emerges from the perfectly lit workroom into the dimmer lights of the storefront.

A tall man stands on the other side of the counter, a familiar cello case beside him.

"I need some repairs," he says.

Phee's entire world narrows down to that face, those eyes, the slim-fingered hands resting on her counter. Slowly, as if she's swimming underwater, she crosses the space between them. She's so close, she can see those green flecks in his eyes. She could reach out and trace the scar on his cheek, touch his hands.

But there's more than just a service counter between them. "What seems to be the problem?" she asks.

"Allie says the bridge needs adjusting. I think the cello misses you." There's music in his voice, something that was there when she knew him years ago, and then vanished.

"You look good," Phee says. He's tanned, his eyes are clear. There's a new vigor to the lines of his body that speaks of outdoor hikes, a healthy diet, the absence of alcohol. His hands on the counter are steady, and they look so normal they might just break her heart.

"You, too," he says, always polite. Phee owns a mirror. She knows she looks pale and tired. She fumbles under the counter for a service ticket. Braden bends down to pay attention to Celestine. Her fingers are trembling and it's hard to write, but she manages it, slides his half across the counter. As if a ticket is needed. As if she doesn't know both man and cello by heart.

His fingers graze hers as he accepts the small square of cardboard. Both of them freeze, and then he lifts one hand and lays it over hers. Their eyes lock, and she sees something there that draws the words out of her, willy-nilly, as if a spell has been cast and she's helpless beneath it.

"Something happened to me the day you met the cello," she says.

"I know." His fingers tighten around hers.

Phee's heart flutters, her knees feel weak. She's lost in his eyes, the sound of his breathing.

"I was only ten," she says. "I didn't understand. I still don't. But I feel . . . part of you. Part of the cello. Complete only when the three of us are together."

"Is that your grandfather's work?" he asks.

She shakes her head. "No. I just . . . it's impossible for a child that age to fall in love. But I did. With her. With you. Every time you brought her into the shop, I felt whole, alive, in a way I can't explain."

His free hand lifts, the index finger brushing her lips. "Hush, Phee. Maybe there are things that can't be explained. Or that don't need to be. I do have one question I need to ask."

"Anything," Phee says.

"Do you just love me for my cello? Take your time. It's an important question."

But Phee doesn't need to think. "Everything you are," she says. "The man, the musician, the amnesiac, the idiot. With or without the cello."

"I don't suppose you'd consider coming out from behind that counter."

"Why?"

"Some things don't require a why."

He keeps pace with her as she moves along the counter, never letting go of her hand. They meet at the far end, and before she has time to draw another breath, she's in his arms and his lips are on hers. Music swirls around them both, and Phee lets go of all of her control, surrendering herself without further question.

"I have a surprise for you," Braden says, a very long time later, after they've locked the store and climbed the stairs to Phee's apartment. After they've made love once, and then again, and are lying entwined and momentarily sated on her bed.

Their bodies fit together as perfectly as their souls, his arm draped over her shoulder, her leg curled between his thighs, and Phee is reluctant to move, to break this moment, as if maybe the spell will end and she'll find herself alone again.

"Does it require moving?" she murmurs, tracing the lines of his face over and over with her finger.

He catches her hand in his and kisses each finger separately, slowly, all the while looking into her eyes.

"It does," he says. "But I think it's worth it." He gets up, pulls on his jeans. "I'll be right back."

She stays where she is, listening to his feet on the stairs going away from her. He's left his shirt, she tells herself. And his shoes. He has to come back.

And sure enough, there is the sound of feet again on the stairs, heavier, slower. When he reemerges, he's carrying the cello case. Phee sits up, her heart in her throat, as he opens the case and lifts out the cello.

"It took time," he says as he sets the cello on her stand. "A gradual thing. I'd be combing my hair and notice that the comb felt hard and smooth. Or I'd give Allie a hug, touch her hair, and notice it felt like silk."

Phee covers her mouth with her hands. Tears fill her eyes, stream down her cheeks. She blinks hard and dashes them away, not wanting either man or cello to be blurred for even an instant.

He moves a chair away from her table. Tightens the bow, draws it across the strings.

"I'm not the musician I was; only time will tell if I recover that. But it doesn't matter. I have this. I have Allie. You gave them both back to me."

He begins to play a haunting melody, his eyes focused on hers all the while. "Allie's going to need a new cello—the two of us are close to fighting over this one. I'm afraid I'm as obsessed as I ever was."

Phee follows the music, hears the beating of his heart in it, the mystery of his soul.

"I can't imagine any woman being able to cope with that." His eyes ask the question he leaves unspoken.

Will you—can you—follow me into the music, Phee?

In answer, she crosses the room and lifts her violin from the stand. A moment to tune it, then she tucks it under her chin, lifts the bow, and twines her own music around his, joining him in the place that goes deeper than words.

For half an instant, she catches a glimpse of her grandfather standing in the doorway, translucent as mist. He bows formally.

"Well done," she hears him say. He blows her a kiss, then melts into the music and is gone.

ACKNOWLEDGMENTS

Every book is born out of an idea. This one, the concept of a cello with a life of its own, was particularly fragile and might never have come into being were it not for the encouragement of my agent and my editor, both of whom gave me the green light to go ahead.

Deidre, thank you for your support, encouragement, and wise guidance. And Jodi, your willingness to brainstorm, discuss, and work out book ideas is an incredible blessing.

Thank you so much to Heather Webb for the almost overnight read born of a way-too-tight deadline, and to my Viking for asking all of the important continuity questions.

To Marcella, my early-morning writing companion—thank you for your friendship and support, for holding me accountable, and for the virtual tour of the Ballard area.

Huge thanks to Jenna Free, my developmental editor, for not only agreeing to act as my guide for a hands-on tour of Ballard, but for driving out of the way to find me when I managed to get lost despite a perfectly good GPS system. Also, thank you for pushing me to go deeper with this story.

Celeste, thank you so much for being my invaluable cello consultant.

Megan and Linda, thank you for giving me the names Jo and Mitch—they turned out to be perfect and helped to shape the characters.

To all of my readers, thank you so much for sharing the magic of story with me. Without you, there would be no point to any of what I do.

Last of all, my thanks to all of the people who have brought music into my life, both music teachers and musicians, because I agree with Friedrich Nietzsche. Without music, what would be the point?

ABOUT THE AUTHOR

Photo © 2019 Diane Maehl

Kerry Anne King is the author of the international bestselling novels *Closer Home*, *I Wish You Happy*, and *Whisper Me This*. Licensed as both an RN and a mental-health counselor, she draws on her experience working in the medical and mental-health fields to explore themes of loss, grief, and transformation—but always with a dose of hope and humor. Kerry lives in a little house in the big woods of the Inland Northwest with her Viking, three cats, a dog, and a yard full of wild turkeys and deer. She also writes fantasy and mystery novels as Kerry Schafer. Visit Kerry at www.kerryanneking.com.